THE FIRST JEW
The Resurrection of Avraham

Nicholas Shane Jagdeo

ISBN-13: 978-1548113681

ISBN-10: 1548113689

Printed in the United States of America.

Edited by Laura Wilkinson.

For more information and for permission requests and contact details, visit the author's website:
http://www.nicholasjagdeo.com

For my grandparents:
Cheefee, Dorothy and Darling.
I did it.

"When we speak about Abraham, we must always remember that the Bible is not only a book narrating events that transpired so many millennia ago. It speaks of events that are still taking place before our eyes. Actually, it is a book not only of Abraham but also of the destiny of our people. We are an eternal people, and our destiny is eternal..."
— Rabbi Joseph B. Soloveitchik, *Abraham's Journey: Reflections on the Life of the Founding Patriarch*

"Abraham, Isaac and Jacob are not principles to be comprehended but lives to be continued. The life of him who joins the covenant of Abraham continues the life of Abraham. For the present is not apart from the past. 'Abraham is still standing before God' (Genesis 18:22). Abraham endures for ever. We are Abraham..."
— Rabbi Abraham Joshua Heschel, *God in Search of Man: A philosophy of Judaism*

PROLOGUE

*"Assuredly, the evil man will not escape,
But the offspring of the righteous will be safe."*
—Proverbs 11:21

<u>May 22, 1960: Tel Aviv, Israel</u>

He sat at the table—hands outstretched, fingers strumming the dull laminate, eyes darting. He twitched sporadically—an effect of the drugs they'd doped him with for the trip across the thousands of miles of oceans and continents. But the drugs were quickly detoxifying out of his system: he almost felt like himself again.

Alert.

Mindful.

Anxious.

He was not bound, but he was not free. They had trapped him in an interrogation room—possibly at their National Security headquarters, or maybe in one of their jails. Definitely a high security area; a place reserved for someone like him—someone they feared, someone they loathed, someone they thought needed to be brought to justice. He had been through a series of highly unfortunate events in the past few weeks: they'd found him, drugged and kidnapped him, and now they brought him here—into the epicenter of their population.

To be judged.

As if this worthless race could ever truly judge me.

According to them, he was a criminal of the highest order. According to them, he had perpetrated crimes against humanity. According to them, he deserved judgment at their hands and their hands only. Well, only according to *them*. Everyone knew they were

5

a verminous, substandard race. They knew nothing. He would be judged differently by history: *they* could brand him 'criminal', 'murderer', 'evil' today, but when *they* were all gone—when the solution was finally achieved—*he* would be remembered in perpetuity as a hero: one of the greatest men who had ever lived.

He looked around the room. It was a grey box with no real distinguishing features. The table was unremarkable, as were the generic folding-chairs scattered about. A shiny metal door hung to his left, a ventilation grill above the door. A one-way mirrored glass plastered the wall opposite him, and a surveillance camera was positioned in the upper right-hand corner of the room, aimed at his face.

They were looking at him right now—watching him, observing him, recording him. They reveled in his capture. He could sense their triumph. He couldn't see them, but he knew they were there. He wasn't certain of much, but one thing he'd figured out with absolute certainty: he would die in their country. There could be no escaping that.

He was scared.

The door opened and three men walked in.

The first man was unexceptional in every way: clearly some sort of administrative clerk. The papers he carried in his hands, and the diffident identification badge on the lapel of his jacket—"Avner", it read—were indicative of his clearly base position. Avner blundered into the room and sat demurely in the corner, concentrating squarely on the papers in his lap. It was obvious: Avner had no desire to look at him. Though he was scared, Avner was even more afraid than he was.

That's right, filthy grosse nase—*big nose. Be afraid of me. Don't look at me. Don't look at the monster.*

The other two men were entirely distinctive altogether. One wore a frumpy black suit, a black hat completing his look. Carefully arranged curly side-locks fell from either side of his face; relatively young—judging from the scraggly beard which struggled to spring from his chin—a bit chubby, but exuding an arrogance far beyond his years. Yes, the unmistakable religious regalia of an ultra-Orthodox Jew. The ultra-Orthodox Jew took a seat, and ogled him unabashedly.

Not afraid of der teufel—*the devil,* Juden? *Think your God will protect you when I come to strangle you in the night?*

The third man, dressed simply in a shirt and trousers, had an aura of power and authority. This third man emitted no such fear of him as Avner, no such interest in him as the religious Jew. Yes, he would evoke no such fear in this third man; no curiosity—only loathing. He could see it in the man's eyes: the contempt, the disgust, gleaming out of the man's eyes and directed at him.

He knew this man. This man had issued the orders for his capture. This man had overseen his kidnapping and forcible removal to this country. This man was Isser Harel, the director of the Israeli Mossad.

"*Guten tag,* Isser," he said quietly.

Harel sat across from him and dropped a sheaf of papers onto the table.

He smiled at Harel, disregarding the papers. "You are not going to return the salutations to me? What is it you Jews say? *Shalom*?"

7

Harel bypassed the subtle taunt, but answered in German. "What are these, Eichmann?" he responded, gesturing to the papers.

"You have come to question me? The great head of the Israeli intelligence unit himself has come to question this worthless Nazi in person? Am I that great?"

"It isn't you I've come to ask after. It's these papers. Let's make a long story short: what are they?"

Eichmann facetiously shook his head and placed his hands over his heart. "My esteem has been shot."

Harel ignored him again. "What are these, Eichmann?"

Eichmann scanned the papers frivolously. "How should I know? I've never seen these papers before."

"We know these papers were top secret Nazi plans. We found them in the course of our investigations – and we know you are connected to them."

"I've never seen these papers before," Eichmann repeated obstinately, but his voice trembled.

Harel leaned forward. "We've already partially figured out what secrets these papers contain: the codes are not unbreakable. It's some sort of biochemical weapon you Nazis were developing with a specific target in mind."

Eichmann shrugged. "Why do you need me to admit to it if you think you've already figured it out?"

"Is that what these are? Blueprints for some sort of weapon?"

"It's whatever you say it is, Isser."

Harel sighed. "Make this easy on all of us. Just cooperate."

"How can I cooperate if I don't know what it is you're talking about?"

Harel regarded Eichmann. "You are stubborn."

"And you are a Jew. We are what we are."

Harel stood and walked to the one-way mirrored window. "Ben Gurion will announce your capture tomorrow. The world will know we've found you. You know you will be tried here—in Israel?"

Eichmann gulped, trying to swallow his fear, refusing to show any chinks in his armor.

Harel studied Eichmann through the reflection on the mirror. "You are afraid."

"I fear nothing," Eichmann spat.

"You fear death. Even in your reflection, I can see it in your eyes."

Eichmann looked at his fingers, which trembled slightly. He quickly folded them around his chest.

"Why do we carry on this charade?" Harel asked quietly, his eyes steady on Eichmann's reflection. "The Nazis are gone, faded away, defeated. You've lost, Adolf. You tried to destroy us, but we won. We're still here, while all of you are gone. We'll probably take a year or two, or maybe even ten to determine what it is you were building, but we'll figure it out, and in the meantime, you will die, just like all of your Nazi cohorts. So, save us the time; just tell me what it is."

Eichmann spasmed, but forced himself to stay steady. "*Viel Glück*, Isser. Good luck with finding it out."

The plump, religiously-garbed man cleared his throat. Harel turned and looked at him. "This isn't the time."

"I'm here for a reason, Isser. As you very well know."

Harel threw his hands up. "You might as well. I'm not getting anywhere."

"My name is Rabbi Eliezer Goldenberg," the religious man introduced himself to Eichmann in fluent German.

"You speak the father tongue like a native. I sent many Jews who infested *Vaterland* to the concentration camps; many rabbis to their deaths. I saw them all die as their God ignored their cries for help," Eichmann responded, with a wry smile.

"And I'm sure you enjoyed murdering them all."

"Why did they send you? Surely my presence here is not a religious matter. Or do you plan to convert me? Do you want to save my soul, rabbi?" He laughed throatily.

"Your presence here is a national issue; one which impacts the entire Jewish nation, not just the State of Israel," said Goldenberg pompously. "Had it been you alone the Mossad had found, then, it would have simply been a security issue—a justice issue. But as it stands, these papers came with you and what they represent has far more dire consequences than we thought possible."

Eichmann didn't answer.

"These papers, they are a blueprint for a weapon, not so?"

"As I said before, I don't know what these papers are."

"You lie, evil Nazi," Goldenberg said forcefully. "We know what these papers hold. They are the blueprint for a weapon of some kind that you were developing to target Jews. You did nothing to hide that in naming it: *Judenmaschine*—Jew machine. This is the name you gave this weapon."

"Fine. That's what it is. A Jew machine."

"But what is that? Is it some sort of machine to solely kill Jews?"

10

Eichmann shrugged.

Goldenberg was annoyed. "Is that what it is?" he persisted. "Is this some sort of machine designed to attack only Jews?"

Eichmann smiled benignly.

"But how?" Goldenberg asked, genuinely confused. "You cannot make a weapon to target a race. All the racial theories have been disproven."

"Perhaps race is deeper than we understand."

"What do you mean?"

"'The Jew has always been a race with definite racial characteristics and never a religion'."

"You quote from the head barbarian himself," Goldenberg said, dryly. "But he was wrong. Jews are a race; just as we are a religion. We encompass these two definitive aspects and so much more. We are a peoplehood."

"Semantics."

Harel pounded the table, wary of the theological curve the conversation had taken. "So, you admit that this," he interjected, gesturing to the papers, "is the blueprint for some sort of machine to target Jews?"

Eichmann laughed. "You don't even know what it is you're looking at. You don't even know what you are." He glared at them all. "Dirty vermin. All of you."

Goldenberg and Harel looked at each other, their worst suspicions ostensibly confirmed.

Suddenly, Avner, who had been sitting quietly in the corner—seemingly oblivious to the exchanges going on, yelped and jumped from the chair. Eichmann had initially pegged him as a clerk, which was a most incorrect assumption. Avner was, in fact, a prized member of the Mossad: an engineer with the deepest, most analytical mind and a profound ability to solve

11

puzzles. He had been brought into the room for precisely this reason: to sit quietly and unthreateningly in the corner, and thus discreetly pick up on whatever hints could be gleaned from the interrogation.

"What is it, Avner?" Harel and Goldenberg asked anxiously, in unison.

"I know what it is!" Avner responded vigorously, shaking his hands at the sheaf of papers on the table, but carefully avoiding Eichmann's curious gaze. "It's not a weapon!"

"What is it then?" Harel asked, excitedly.

"The technology is beyond anything we can imagine today; decades, possibly centuries beyond its time," Avner said, awed. "The Nazis were even more cunning and terrible than we could have imagined."

"Ok, ok. But *what is it*?"

"We've been working under the assumption it's a weapon. Only, it's not. It's an identifier." Shaul gulped. "It measures who's Jewish and who's not."

Harel shook his head. "I don't understand."

Avner finally looked across at Eichmann, into the eyes which had seen the life spark of millions extinguished, into the eyes of evil which had gloried in those deaths. Avner spoke, his voice quiet, scared. "It's a machine which identifies the *neshama*. It goes beyond the physical: beyond genetics, beyond blood, beyond race. It tells who is Jewish and who isn't, but not on a corporeal level, not even through beliefs or thoughts." He turned to look at Harel and Goldenberg. "It tells who is a Jew based on his or her very soul."

Eichmann smiled wanly. "*Ja*. Judenmaschine. Who is a Jew?"

CHAPTER 1

"The LORD said to Abram, 'Go forth from your native land and from your father's house to the land that I will show you.'"
—Genesis 12:1

He bolted upright and hit his head on something hard.

Ouch.

Someone had awoken him.

He rubbed his eyes and looked around. He was in a room—or was it was a cave?—he wasn't quite sure. Wherever he was, it was a naturally dark space, yet, as he blinked his eyes, he realized that he could see quite well, as some sort of otherworldly light seemed to emanate from the walls. Coarse dirt covered the floor and he could feel grains of sand stuck to his body. There was no mistaking it, he was definitely in a cave. He could make out the rocky ceiling above and he most certainly felt the unhewn floor beneath his posterior. He rubbed his head. It hurt from where he had hit it.

He lay down again, but a voice called out to him. "It's time to wake up."

"Leave me alone, dammit! I want to sleep!"

"Arise, Avraham," the voice said, regally.

Avraham's annoyance evaporated at once. He recognized the voice. It was no ordinary voice.

It was *The* Voice.

"Oh, it's You," he said contritely, hanging his head in shame. "Speak, for Your servant hears."

"I trust you've slept well?" The Voice sounded slightly amused.

"It's a *mitzvah* to not wake someone from sleep, You know."

The Voice chuckled. "I think you've slept enough, don't you?"

Avraham pulled himself up from the ground, but his legs were unsteady, as if they had been lying dormant for quite some time. He put out his hands to balance himself.

"Where am I?"

"You are in the Cave of Machpelah," The Voice answered (not to be confused with Tessanne Chin, the earth-bound winner of the popular NBC show, rather, The Voice in question was The Original Primordial Voice, popularly known since before the creation of the universe as the Great Omniscient Dunastes—G.O.D).

Machpelah? The word was painfully familiar, but Avraham couldn't place it. "Oh," he said in response. If God didn't care to elaborate, then who was Avraham to twist God's figurative Arm?

Avraham took a tentative step, and was surprised to find that he could, as, for some reason, he didn't think he would have been able to. But apparently, walking—like riding a camel, circumcising oneself, or battling Sodomites—was something you simply did not forget how to do.

He walked towards the nearest wall of the cave, curious to find the source of light that illuminated the space so subtly, when suddenly, he realized there was a host of seven-foot tall, glowing angels, lined up uniformly along the walls. He pulled back, startled at the sight of them all: their celestial forms wrapped in three pairs of large, translucent wings; wings which fluttered like ripples of incandescent water and cloaked them mysteriously, making their true figures difficult to decipher. Avraham spotted the archangel Michael beaming down at him from inside the throng of angels.

14

Wait a second. Michael never *beamed*; at least he'd not beamed at Avraham for the past nearly forty centuries that they'd been co-citizens of the celestial plane. Sure, angels were pretty decent to souls when souls were firmly ensconced in bodies. Angels were actually quite protective of and endearing towards those bodily-clad souls: shielding them from harm, guiding them, soothing them, and just generally being their guardian angels and all that the job entails—but once a soul entered into the next world, with its mortal shell of a body cast aside, then all decency was out the heavenly door and it was fair game for all.

Immortal angel versus immortal soul, round one of billions.

They were a puerile, raucous bunch—those angels—prone to playing tricks and easily amused. Angels and the formerly alive never quite managed to see eye to eye on anything. Whatever human souls agreed on, angels could be counted upon to disagree with. Heaven was quite noisy due to the indelible squabbling between these two opposing groups. They argued over the meaning of life, they debated the true nature of God, they quarreled over the unification of gravitation using quantum chromodynamics theory, and, most noisily of all, they bickered over control of the divine television remote control (dearly departed human souls tended to stick to good, old family-values, PG-type programming like *The Cosby Show* and *Once Upon A Time*; angels couldn't get enough of *American Horror Story* and *Honey Boo Boo*).

Yes, there was no way in hell that Michael would be beaming at Avraham, as he had been dead for just about four millennia, and had been the butt of Michael's pranks for a large portion of that time. No way, Jehoshaphat. Michael wasn't beaming; none of the angels were beaming. Those Tilda Swinton archetypes were snickering gleefully as they looked directly at him.

"What's so funny?"

Michael pointed low. "Thought it would be bigger. I mean, you *are* Avraham, the great progenitor of Israel, after all." He burst out laughing and the rest of the heavenly throng followed suit. "No wonder it took you so long to knock Sarah up!"

Avraham looked down and realized he was naked. Blushing, he quickly put his hand over his private region. "It's cold in here!"

The angels laughed louder, their wings fluttering in time with their laughing.

Avraham glowered and continued to cover himself with his right hand. "Clearly, we need to cancel our subscription to HBO!" he yelled.

He was about to give them the finger when, suddenly, it hit him: he shouldn't be naked; he shouldn't have a *body* to be naked with in the first place! He'd been dead for almost four thousand years! He shouldn't have a middle finger with which to extend vulgarly; he shouldn't have legs with which to walk; hell, he shouldn't have a penis with which to—well, pretty much just hide for the moment.

"God?"

"Yes, Avraham?"

"What's going on here? Am I alive?"

"Yes."

"Alive, alive? Like breathing with a pulse and needing food and so on and so forth?"

"That's the general gist of being alive, yes."

Avraham breathed in deeply and closed his eyes tightly. True, he had been through some pretty weird stuff in his time—but this definitely took the cake.

The last thing he remembered, he'd been sitting in heaven (well, not exactly sitting, per se, as souls can't sit. He was relaxing as well as a soul could. But for the sake of simplicity, let's just say he was sitting) with Moses and the Buddha, debating where Guiliana Ransic's forehead ended and her hairline began (heaven has E! on its local cable line-up), when boom! there was a flash of bright light, and suddenly he was walking down a long tunnel, away from that bright light and towards a darkness in the distance.

That was the last thing he remembered, and now, here he was. *Alive.*

"Alive. Wow. I'm alive."

Avraham wasn't sure what this meant. Sure, reincarnation happened on a pretty regular basis in the cosmos, but this was not reincarnation in the traditional sense. Reincarnation involved babies and the cutting of umbilical cords and lots of crying and forgetting from whence one came. This scenario encompassed none of these things.

As if reading Avraham's thoughts (He was the Great Omniscient Dunastes, after all; He pretty much knew everything that was going on), God said to him, "You have not been reincarnated in the conventional manner, Avraham. Your soul has returned to your previous body and mind, intact and whole. I have regenerated your body and mind for My purpose."

Avraham's eyes widened. "Bloody Gehinnom, God, You didn't even consult me on this! You just took it upon Yourself to bring me back! What if I didn't want to come back? What if I don't want to be here? I was having fun in heaven. Why in Your Name would You bring me back?"

The angels fluttered their wings brusquely and shook their heads. Humans were always so demanding of God. It was the Free Will thing. Existence got way too existentially complicated when you were in control of your own existence.

God answered Avraham evenly. "Avraham, I have resurrected you because I have a mission for you."

The mention of the word "mission" sobered Avraham's anger. The last time he'd been alive and God had asked him to complete a mission, it had involved an altar, his only son, and a knife. He wasn't entirely ready for something like that again.

"What do You need to me to do?" he asked, tentatively.

"The era of mashiach is here. I need you to make known to mashiach that I have called and it is time to answer."

"Why do you need me to do that? Wasn't it prophesied that was a job for Elijah and Moses?" (Avraham did *not* want to cross Elijah. Of all the dead Hebrew prophets, Elijah was the most easily riled. If he ever got wind of Avraham usurping his job—well, let's just say the angels didn't call Elijah 'Chariots of Fire' because of his choice of transportation).

"No, Avraham. Elijah's and Moses' mission, as prophesied, is to herald the coming of mashiach to the entire world. Your job, on the other hand, is a mission which concerns only mashiach. I need you to make known to mashiach that I have called and it is time to answer. The era of mashiach is here."

"But why me, Lord? Why not Jeremiah or Amos or one of the more expendable Minor League Prophets?"

18

Avraham lit up as he was struck with a brilliant thought. "Or why not Balaam? He's won the least favorite prophet award every year for the past two millennia."

"Avraham, you are special in My eyes. Of all the men and women who lived upon this earth, you were the only one who actively sought Me when you had no one to direct you, no previous knowledge of Me upon which to build. You were the first to look for Me, and you were the first to find Me. In that vein, you are the only one who will be able to look for mashiach. Find mashiach, and let mashiach know that I have called and it is time to answer. You have a strength like none other, My friend; You chose Me insomuch as I chose you and it is for this reason that this mission can only be fulfilled by you. You are the only one who can return to earth to do this for Me."

Avraham gulped. In the time he'd been gone, the earthly population had exploded and had just crossed the seven billion mark. To find the mashiach among that bunch would take Avraham quite a while.

"Can You give me a description of the mashiach, God? Or maybe the mashiach's Facebook profile? I know You like humans to work things out on our own, but surely this is a case of 'been there done that'! I don't need to go through all of that again. I don't need to be tested again, do I?"

"I have not brought you back to be tested, for you have proven yourself beyond the shadow of a doubt previously. I will not make the mission of finding mashiach difficult for you. Hearken unto My words: the neshama you encounter upon exiting this cave will be mashiach; you will know you have found mashiach and mashiach will answer you."

Avraham narrowed his eyes. "What's the catch, Buddy?"

"No catch. That's your mission; that's the high and low of it. Nothing else. Elijah and Moses will take care of the rest when they return. Will you accept this mission?"

Avraham thought for a bit and then shrugged. True, God did have a very dry, subtle sense of humor and He had a tendency to do things which would be considered a bit—well—"different" by normal standards, but Avraham could discern no fine lines in this mission contract. Simple, easy, piece of manna: find the mashiach, tell the mashiach that God was looking for him, then it was back up to heaven for Avraham, and Elijah and Moses would take care of the rest. Mission accomplished.

"I do," Avraham answered humbly.

"Like you had a choice," Michael snickered under his breath.

Avraham stuck out his tongue at Michael, ready to retort, but God cut him off.

"Avraham does have a choice, Michael," God said firmly, His Voice as calm and soft as ever. "Avraham is human again, in all ways. Earthly laws apply to him—including Free Will." God turned His attention back onto Avraham. "This is why I did not inform you of this mission in Heaven, Avraham. I had to bring you back into this regenerated body, in this realm where Free Will reigns, to present you with the facts and allow you the choice to accept this mission, or to deny it. I am glad that you have opted to accept it. Do you have any questions, My friend?"

Avraham considered. It was more difficult thinking, now that he was dependent on the synapses and neurons in his brain to facilitate the cognitive process. The magnitude of heavenly knowledge was simply too much for the limited human mind to comprehend, and Avraham felt constrained by his bounded rationality.

"I do have a few questions."

"And I am more than happy to answer them."

"Where are we exactly? What sort of body am I in?"

"We are on the outskirts of the town of Hebron in what you know to be the land of Canaan, in the true Cave of Machpelah—the cave you purchased in your previous incarnation to serve as your family tomb and in which your body had been interred. I have shrouded the actual location of this cave from all people since the time of the burial of your great-grandson, Joseph, son of Jacob. The body you inhabited when alive, I have supernaturally brought back to life. You are as you were when you were twenty years of age—in the prime of life."

"What will I remember of heaven? It's already difficult for me to remember—and I'm remembering less with each passing second."

"The World to Come is not a concern of souls which populate the physical world, and as such, its secrets shall not be made known to any who reside in this mortal world. This law cannot be broken, and I apologize, My friend, but by the time you leave this cave, you will remember nothing of the dimension from whence you came. You will know you have returned from life after death, but as to the details of that life after death, you shall remember nothing. However, I will bestow upon you the privilege of remembering your life as you lived in your previous incarnation."

"Thanks, I guess." Avraham shrugged. "Although I don't see why it would matter, but thanks all the same."

The angels bristled. "Rudeness!" they cried. "Insubordination!"

"I'm not being rude!" Avraham said indignantly. "I just don't see the point of that!"

God intervened. "Angels, remember he is once again a twenty-year-old boy. You know how they are at that age."

The angels nodded and looked pityingly at Avraham, which annoyed him.

"Ok, God. I think it's time for me to go. The quicker I get my mission done, the quicker I can get back to heaven and win my debate against the angels on the Copenhagen Interpretation."

"Final points before you leave: firstly, I have made it possible for you to speak and understand all the modern languages. The ancient Ivrit, Sumerian and Shemite you spoke in your time are no longer spoken.

"Secondly, I have granted you the boon of increasing your learning capabilities. It will be imperative to your journey that you are able to understand the world around you. While it is natural for a child to learn slowly and with patience, you have returned to the physical sphere as a fully-grown man, and as such, time is of the essence to your learning process. I have fashioned your new mind to absorb facts, theories, statistics, philosophies and stories quickly. Your memory has been expanded to accommodate this ability, as well as to house the memories of your previous life, which, I assure you, despite your skepticism, will serve you well.

"Thirdly, I have allowed that all you choose to reveal your true identity to will know that you are indeed

Avraham of ancient times, returned to life to do My bidding. The human mind slips easily into a state of skepticism, but I will allow for all who meet you to spiritually recognize the power of your soul and to know you for who you really are, after you make it known to them. None will discount your testimony of who you are.

"Finally, Michael will accompany you on this mission. Be mindful of his presence. He is there to protect and guide you. Heed his counsel and trust in him. You are entering a world which has advanced much from the time of your first transmigration—yet, in many ways, the world is still very much the same. You will need Michael near for support and for guidance, and he will be there. And, as you know, I, too, am always with you. You need only call out to Me and I will answer." God paused. "I suppose you'd want some clothing before you embark on your mission?"

Avraham blushed and covered his privates again. He had forgotten he was naked and had taken his hands off in all his discussions with God. The angels had been unabashedly making notes and drawing rude pictures of his body. "Yes, please, some clothes would be nice."

"You will find appropriate clothing laid out for you upon exiting the cave." God paused. "Go now, My friend. Go forth from this cave which has kept your body safe and go from My Presence, to the land I have given to you and your wife, Sarah, and to the chosen offspring of that union for all time. Go with My blessing. And thank you for doing this for Me."

Avraham bowed low to the ground. "Thank you for trusting me, Lord."

Michael flew up, out of the crowd of angels and went towards the end of the cave. He tapped the stone and a massive boulder rolled away, exposing the brilliant sun outside. Michael beckoned to Avraham and flew out into the light. Avraham cautiously walked towards the exit, feeling his supernal knowledge of the afterlife draining away quickly. When he reached the opening in the cave wall, however, one memory of heaven lingered in his mind: angels were bitches. He turned around, smiled widely, stuck up his middle finger at them and followed Michael into the world outside.

CHAPTER 2

"I turn my eyes to the mountains; from where will my help come? My help comes from the LORD, Maker of heaven and earth."
—Psalms 121:1-2

Israel: Present Day

Tzippy lay stretched out comfortably on a towel, her elbows propping her up as the stream rippled merrily in front of her. There was a large tree under which she could have sheltered, but she preferred the spot she'd chosen: on the bank of the stream, where the sun could pour unfettered on her skin and make her feel warm and happy. Her trusty cooler, brimming with ice and deliciously cold beers was strategically placed right next to her.

Tzippy wore a decorous, one-piece bathing suit she'd bought specifically for this occasion; not at all the type of bath suit she would generally wear to frolic on an excursion such as this, but out of deference to her cousin's new-found religiousness, she capitulated and opted for this unobtrusive outfit. Unfortunately, despite this act of consideration on Tzippy's part, any bathing suit which exposed delicate female flesh would offend her cousin, Max, who had recently donned the lifestyle of a black-hat, ultra-Orthodox Jew. Max pursed his lips and shook his head disapprovingly when Tzippy revealed her conservative bath suit. Tzippy ignored him. She had been considerate of his recently acquired faith, and had worn this sorrowful, granny-type bathing suit in order to not offend the newly religious Max. Furthermore, Tzippy could remember a little over a year ago when her cousin had hypocritically first come to

Israel and had gone bat-shit, girl-crazy at the sight of all the sexy Israeli *frekhot*. Just because he'd become afflicted with Jerusalem Syndrome some six months after he'd arrived in Israel and thought he'd found God, it gave him no right to cast aspersions on her secular lifestyle. Tzippy adjusted the straps of her one-piece, perched her Ray Bans on her nose, stretched herself out in the sun, and blissfully ignored the censorious looks her cousin threw her way.

It was well past four in the afternoon, but they had only arrived at the stream half an hour earlier— Tzippy, Max, and Max's friend, Natan. Their day had been encumbered with Natan and Tzippy driving from Tel Aviv to Jerusalem to collect Max, who was on a week's break from his *yeshiva*, and then out into the Judean desert. The traffic to the capital city had been horrendous, and Max's religious distaste for cell phones further sullied them, for it had proven difficult to manually locate him in the large yeshiva complex. But they were determined to stick to their original plan, and as late as it was, they continued the trek away from civilization. The sun had cooled significantly by the time they'd reached this tranquil spot in the Judean desert, but they didn't want to waste the day. They unloaded their portable barbeque grill and coolers of food and drinks, quickly changed into their bath suits, and equally as quickly, shelved the memory of the stressful day. Natan, who was the antithesis of Max's religiousness in every way, had gone straight for the cooling waters of the stream, decked out in a tiny speedo—the kind that only Mediterranean men can look apposite in. After some deliberation on his part, Max surrendered and followed Natan into the water, fully-clothed.

This is the life, Tzippy thought to herself. *No cares, no responsibilities, no worries; just beer, food, friends, and fun.*

It was such an idyllically Israeli pastime: to be out in the wilderness on *tiyul*, connecting with the land and enjoying nature. Sure, it would've been nice to have the entire day to lie out in the open air and relax, but even a couple hours would suffice. Besides, she could always head down to Gordon Beach the next day to continue her tanning progress. Nothing was a problem for Tzippy. She hummed Matthew Wilder's *Break My Stride* quietly to herself.

Two years of national service in the Israeli army was done and over with; a backpacking trip to South America was coming up in two months; she had a fully-stocked cooler of beers sitting right beside her and burgers to look forward to—what more could Tzippy possibly want from life? And yes, while Max had indeed become a tad bit annoying recently, Tzippy was happy to be here with her cousin. They were actually quite close and she had not been able to spend much time with him in the past few months, what with her army service and his enrollment in the religious school in Jerusalem. Though she hadn't known Natan for very long, she felt comfortable around him and was happy for his no-nonsense, logical, yet easy-going presence. She had no idea how Natan and Max had met, but this was part of the magic of Israel: firm friendships were established within days and best friends were discovered in minutes. Worldly, tanned, lithe Natan and pale, dour, religious Max had become fast friends, and Tzippy was only too happy to have Natan along for the ride, since he countered Max's religiousness nicely.

Yes, this is definitely *the life.* Tzippy sighed contentedly and threw her head back, allowing the sun to fully bathe her face.

Tzippy was a looker and she knew it. Her father, Alex, was a tall, blond-haired man—the curious type of American Ashkenazi Jew who, no matter how long he sat out in the sun, never managed to tan, rather, he went from pale, to pink, to blotchy red in a very short space of time. Her mother was part of the Beta Israel community—one of the first who had managed to flee to safety in Israel from persecution in Ethiopia in the late-80's. Tiny, brown, and slim, with the most delicate of facial features, Tzippy's exotic mother, Adina, had caught the eye of the rich American student who was studying at the Hebrew University. They spent hours, days, and months together, and quickly fell in love: she, who spoke little but Amharic and Tigrinya, and he, an Upper East Side boy who was headed directly for a life in investment banking with no stops at "Go" and no pause to collect two hundred dollars, since there were millions waiting to be pocketed on Wall Street. As Alex's year in Israel ground to a close, he realized that what he had with Adina had been no casual fling and he knew exactly what needed to be done. Like a modern, Israeli-Cinderella story, Alex gathered up the bewitching Ethiopian Jewess up unto himself and flew her back to America, where he obstinately argued to his father how in love he was. Alex's father yielded, and, just to be sure of Adina's Jewishness, Tzippy's mother was rabbinically converted, learnt English, married Alex, and finally became pregnant with Tzippy (or so Adina always told Tzippy, though Tzippy highly doubted it had happened as neatly and chastely as her mother outlined). Theirs was a union destined to result in issue which would be

28

beautiful, as ethnically diverse children often are. Average height though she was, it was the only average thing about Tzippy. Her slender frame indicated one of those feminine bodies which would always stay petite and never experience the rigors of weight fluctuations. A slim, straight nose at the center of her face—which was a telltale sign of her Ethiopian ancestry—allowed for her wide, dark brown eyes and full, pouty lips to shine forth. Long, dark tresses of hair cascaded down her back. A light honey color bathed her skin, so that even in the most sunless of winters, she glowed. She combined the best that both her parents had to offer physically, and magnified those attributes, leading to a most beautiful example of race mixing, which was at once admired and desired.

After she had completed high school, when all her Hebraic girlfriends were excited about heading off to their various Ivy League colleges, Tzippy had opted to go to Israel. Tales of dark, mysterious, beautiful Israeli men had reached her ears, and the allure of a vacation romance appealed to her. She had never been particularly religious or Zionist or attached Jewishly— and indeed, had indulged in the occasional romp with the sporadic gentile and the foreskin that inevitably came attached—but like most East Coast Jewish girls, she wanted to marry a nice Jewish boy. But not the pasty type that New York had to offer. No sir-ee. Tzippy wanted the Jewish boy that was, at the same time, a real man: an Israeli soldier. She fantasized about the stereotypical rough and tough, manly, tanned Israeli soldier, and so, she booked her ticket for Israel. But the moment she arrived, an immediate love sprung up within her for the land of her forefathers, a mystical love so strong that all thoughts of romance and marriage flew

29

straight out of her fickle mind. She immersed herself in the culture and, within three months, she had arranged her papers and officially became an Israeli citizen. She was quickly drafted into the army, and the irony that she'd now become the very soldier she'd come to look for was not lost on her. Life, Tzippy comprehended, was more than boys and the ultimate goal of marriage; she enjoyed being single and though she occasionally gave in to her hormones and frolicked with the random, odd passerby, ultimately, Tzippy had changed. She was in her ancestral homeland, she was amongst her people, she was contributing in a tangible way to the betterment of the State, and she was content and happy.

By the time Max and Natan had come out from the water, Tzippy had lit the coals for the barbeque. Still clad in his speedo trunks, and not seeing the need for clothes, Natan took over from Tzippy and grilled the beef patties in quick succession with Max—who had had to be coaxed out of the water—as his grudging assistant. The boys assured Tzippy that they needed no help, and she spread a blanket underneath the tree and put the cooler of drinks in the shade as well. While she waited on the food to be cooked, she nursed a fresh Tuborg and sifted through her iPhone. Natan soon announced that the food was ready, and Tzippy jumped up with an empty plastic plate to collect her ration. She placed the beef patty she'd been given carefully on a lightly toasted bun, and smothered it in mustard, hot sauce, and pickles. She plopped down on the blanket she had spread under the tree and waited for the boys to join her. The three of them, on the blanket with their respective plates in front of them, toasted *l'chaim* with their beers and proceeded to tackle their food.

Tzippy was hungry. Sunbathing tended to have that effect on her. She finished eating first, noisily burped and grinned all around. It was at that moment she noticed—up on the hill above her—a lonely figure standing against the backdrop of the sun, looking down at them.

✡

If Natan hadn't insisted that Max assist with grilling the burger patties, he doubted Max would have gotten out of the water. After much pleading, begging and eventual threatening on Natan's part, Max finally relented and stepped out of the water, only to panic when he realized his yarmulke had dislodged itself from his head and disappeared somewhere in the stream.

"I don't know where my *yarmulke* is!" Max yelled, terrified.

"*Ein baya*. It's ok. You don't need a *kipa*. Just use your hat to cover your head," Natan suggested, ever the practical Israeli.

Natan chalked up Max's current religiousness to a phase. He had seen this happen with many a visiting Anglo-Jew. They'd come to Israel, fresh out of university; get lost in the hedonism available to them in Tel Aviv; journey to Jerusalem, miraculously find God, suddenly start wearing full length black suits, and become ferociously Charedi; then, after some months, go back to their comfortable, easy lives in their home country and revert to a life of two-times-a-year synagogue and pork.

Like most irreligious Israeli Jews, religious Jews mystified Natan. But unlike most secular Israeli Jews, Natan had grown up with a front seat view into the inner workings of Jewish Orthodoxy. Natan's *Saba*—

grandfather—was a distinguished rabbi who came from a long line of Sephardi *tzaddikim*. Unfortunately for Natan's Saba, his son—Natan's Aba—rebelled and had become a staunchly secular atheist. The moment he was discharged from the army, Aba moved from Jerusalem to Tel Aviv, where he chopped off his *peyot*, declared himself an atheist, successfully established a chain of supermarkets, married Natan's mother, had four children by her, divorced her, and shacked up with a blond Croatian beauty who was clearly *goyish* through and through. Despite the differences of lifestyle and religious opinion that Natan's Saba and Aba had, they respected each other and maintained a healthy relationship, inextricably linked because of their strong Zionist beliefs. Saba, an ardent follower of the great Zionist rabbis of the early twentieth century, Rabbi Avraham Kook and Rabbi Chaim David Halevy, believed that spiritual redemption for *Am Yisrael*—the people of Israel—would come about only with the ingathering of Jews to their ancestral homeland, and so, in demonstration of his faith, he had put his *semicha* on hold and volunteered for the army in the War of Independence in 1948. Aba, on the other hand, was a devotee of the great Israeli generals, Moshe Dayan and Ariel Sharon, and he believed that having a strong, national homeland to serve as place of refuge for Jews and to reawaken the warrior spirit of the Jews was the only way to stamp out antisemitism. He had served in the army for the 1967 Six Day War, and then again in the 1973 Yom Kippur War as part of a reserve battalion. Both men—each a thorough Zionist, though holding vastly different reasons for having this viewpoint: one religious, and one nationalist—had performed well on the battlefield, and had each come out of the army sporting heavy decorations.

Due to the good rapport that existed between grandfather and father, Natan was close to his Saba, and as such, was well-acquainted with Judaism at its most Orthodox, having spent many a vacation at his grandparent's home in Jerusalem. He had gone to the *beit knesset* with his Saba every day; he had learnt his Torah portion for his bar mitzvah from his Saba directly; he had helped prepare his Saba's home for *Pesach* ever since he could remember; he knew how to lay *tefillin* and how to keep *kashrut*; he could read the weekly *parasha* and *haftarah*; and he knew how to make himself and his home ready to usher in the Shabbat. Saba had done his job and had passed the Jewish knowledge directly on to Natan: unfiltered, undiluted, and uncensored.

But despite all the learning Natan had received each summer and on all the *Yamim Tovim* from his Saba, he always returned home to Tel Aviv—and the weeks of Jewish instruction would quickly fade away as the electric lights of the fun White City shone brightly and eclipsed the holiness of the City of Gold. And, as a now grown man, Natan had fully embraced the Tel Aviv in his upbringing. The religiousness his grandfather had so earnestly tried to impress upon him seemed archaic and quaint to Natan. The mumbling prayers, the numerous rituals, the inane traditions: none of it made sense to him. Not that he had any problems with anyone who chose a life of *derech haTorah*, but it just was not for him. As far as he was concerned, religion should be a purely personal matter—to be conducted between a person and his, or her, God. *If* they believed in a God, that is. For him, that path of religion was much too murky, much too political, much too hypocritical, and, oftentimes, much too nonsensical; instead, Natan chose the path of least resistance, the path of secularism.

Saba says I should follow in the faith of my forefathers. Well, I am. It's just I'm following in the faith of my most direct forefather, my Aba.

Natan wasn't as sure as his Saba that there was a God, nor was he as sure as his Aba that there wasn't. His life thus far had given ammunition to both sides of the argument, and for the time being, Natan chose to formulate no opinion.

Natan was somewhat older than Max, who was twenty-three, and considerably older than Tzippy, who was twenty. At twenty-nine, Natan had already served a distinguished four years in the army, received his undergraduate degree on an accelerated path from the Wharton School of Business, and had returned home to Israel and founded a computer software start-up company which was raking in shekels in the six-figure range. But he had never had a chance to just breathe, and when he randomly met Max one day in the Carmel *shuk* (before Max had become smitten with religiousness) and spent the day conversing with him, Natan realized that he was inspired by Max's story. There was Max: an adventurer in a country far away from home, taking time off from life to just be. And there was Natan: on the fast track to success, but never having had the luxury of a time-out to figure out who he was and if this was what he really wanted. The day spent with Max had signaled a turning point for Natan.

Should success be judged by advancements in the business world, or by achievements on the battleground, or by position in the religious world? None of it seemed tangible to Natan, and he was determined to find out what life was really about. He had three weeks ahead of him before he left for India, where he hoped, in the ashrams of holy Hindu Sadhus, to find an answer.

In the meantime, there were burgers to be grilled, which Natan did to perfection. He drank two Malcha beers while he worked. When he was done, he served Tzippy and Max their burgers, then put some *pitot* onto the grill to toast. He pulled on a pair of shorts and a t-shirt, fixed a burger for himself, grabbed a couple of the toasted pitot and joined the cousins on a blanket Tzippy had spread under a tree for shade. He dipped his hand into the cooler and pulled out a large container of hummus. Grinning broadly, he said l'chaim and clinked bottles with the other two. Very politely, he offered the hummus and pitot around, but Tzippy was already tucking deeply into her burger, and Max, being the ever-faithful Charedi that he so suddenly was, had already gone off to do *al n'tilat yadayim*. Natan shrugged and tucked into his appetizer of pita and hummus. He had just finished his starter, and was ready to move on to the main course when Tzippy let out a decadent burp. She grinned around at them, and Max laughed jovially, but Natan frowned, for he had spotted—up on the hill above him—a lonely figure standing against the backdrop of the sun, looking down at them.

✡

Max, the Newly-Religious, wrestled within himself—with an issue not entirely as lofty as the one his very distant forefather, Jacob, had struggled with all those centuries before. Max was not completely sure what the *halachically* right thing to do was. The Unreligious Max (who was still very much alive inside of him) badly wanted to escape the heat and splash about in the water like Natan, but at the same time, he wasn't sure if it was appropriate for him to do so while his basically nude and highly inappropriate female cousin looked on. True, Tzippy had seen him bareback on previous trips to beaches and pools, but Max was now a *baal teshuvah*: a prodigal Jewish son who had come home to Charedi Judaism after a life of secular wantonness; and as such, the issue of *tznius*—modesty—was at the forefront of his mind.

What should I do?

Luckily, Max's conversion to *yeshiva bocher* was much too recent for it to have totally eradicated his abilities to think for himself without having to consult the Shulchan Aruch, so after mentally torturing himself whilst sitting next to his indecently exposed cousin, he decided it would be more in keeping with tznius for him to get into the water with Natan where Tzippy's nubile body wouldn't be in his direct line of vision. After all, it was all about protecting his own tznius, since Tzippy seemed to glaringly have none. Quickly ripping off his black hat and securing his yarmulke with two extra bobby pins before he could change his mind, Max yelped elatedly and rushed to the water, fully clothed. The stream cooled him off immediately, and he sighed contentedly, happy that he had made the decision to go into the water. Unfortunately, his clothes quickly soaked up the water and weighed him down, making the splashing not as enjoyable as he would have hoped. Max was no prissy yeshiva boy—he had spent a considerable amount of his youth in the gym and had developed a nicely toned body. However, he had not been frequenting the gym in the past six months he'd been religious, and, that—coupled with the heavily fatty,

Eastern European-Jewish foods he received thrice daily from the yeshiva kitchen—had transformed Max into a somewhat doughy fellow. After ten minutes of flopping around in the water with drenched clothes, Max threw all thoughts of tznius to the wind and shed his white shirt, *tzitzis* and black trousers, flinging them unceremoniously onto the sandy bank with a loud thud.

Beneath Max's fussy, ultra-Orthodox exterior, there was, concealed, a pair of lime-green board shorts.

Max loved this freedom to be out in the open and not having to be stuck in the *beis midrash*, but a large part of him felt guilty for enjoying himself so much. The past few months of study had taken a lot of getting used to, and he wasn't sure he had become completely accustomed to the new Charedi lifestyle he'd adopted. He sometimes felt the urge to flick the timed light switches on and off on *Shabbos*; he sometimes, when the Talmudic tractate he was studying was especially long, wished that there wasn't so much commentary to wade through; and sometimes, he wished that *shacharis* didn't have to happen as early as it did, or take as long as it did. He knew that his choice to be a yeshiva bocher wasn't going to immediately lead to him being *kadosh* and a tzaddik all at once, and the Rosh Yeshiva had directed him with some sage counsel: "You need to allow yourself a transition period. Righteousness does not happen all at once", and that was what he was doing. He was one-hundred-and-fifty percent sure that he wanted to be Charedi: he was absorbing page after page of Gemara at an alarming rate; he was extremely punctual and altogether sincere for *davening*, three times a day, every day; he was loud and compellingly argumentative with his *chavrusah*; he stayed up late at nights, going over what he had learnt from the preceding day, and still managed to read ahead. The rabbis at the yeshiva were proud of him. They had seen many a *hiloni* come into their yeshiva and leave within weeks because the stark adjustment had been too much for them to bear, but Max was a most brilliant exception. Not only had he kept up with those boys who were born Charedi, but he was actually surpassing them in many ways and then some. He had an eye for transgression, and many of his fellow *talmidim* were as wary of him as they were of their teachers. He had quickly garnered a reputation as being belligerent for *mitzvos*.

The rabbis who taught him were particularly pleased with his penchant for arguing vociferously in favor of stringent, stricter viewpoints, and they liked to joke that Max was Rabbi Shammai, of Antiquity, come back to life. Indeed, Max took a tough stance on every viewpoint, from divisive topics like homosexuality, conversion, and the role of women, down to less controversial mitzvos like *tzedakah* and singing songs at the Shabbat table.

"Rabbi Hillel the Elder, *zikhrono livrakha*," Max had argued passionately only the week before, "lived at a time when it was possible to be lenient and take the less severe view. Our opponents argue that we must advance Torah according to the times. Well, I agree. Times have changed: the time for softness is over. While I admire and respect Rabbi Hillel for giving us a period of grace and clemency, it is now time for *Am Yisroel* to adopt the harsher stance and truly accept the yoke of the covenant—for if it were easy, it would not be called a 'yoke', would it? We are facing existential threats of an unprecedented number, and it is our softness for the past two thousand years which have now led to these problems: we have to deal with non-halachic conversions—from those farcical people who pretend to be Jews, but have formed their own religions which have nothing to do with true Judaism, those reformists, those conservatives, and those posing as Orthodox but who cut off their *peis* and term themselves 'modern'; our land is flooded with all sorts of non-Jews, including those Russians, Arabs and Ethiopians who pretend to be part of us, but are bringing in pork and marking themselves with crosses and altogether degrading *Eretz Yisroel*; the secular government of this state, which challenges our holy obligation to *midrashim* full-time, and the hilonim, who call us 'leeches'. Do they not see that it is through the merit of our mitzvos, our midrashim, our *tefillos* that *Medinas Yisroel* has been re-born, and, thus, sustained? Do they—the hilonim, the watered-down Jews, the unhalachically converted *gerim* and every person in between—do they not see that it is their wishy-washy attitude toward Torah which facilitated our expulsion and consequent dispersion for the past two thousand years? Yes, distinguished *rabbanim* and fellow talmidim, it is time for a new era in Judaism, an era where the strength of the Torah will reign supreme in this land, and we shall be returned to our former glory. No more secularism, no more Zionism, no more democracy, which are all, singularly and combined, inferior to the *emet* of our *kadosh* Torah. Let us weed out the unworthy, for they will only sully us as a people; let us do right by *HaShem* and follow His mitzvos; let us coax *moshiach* to make himself known—let us show him, though he may tarry, that we are preparing the way for his coming." The rabbis nodded their head in assent and beamed at the prodigy before them.

However, the truth was, Max was no fundamentalist. Most of what he said, he had no true convictions about, and he'd said them just to sound impressive before his contemporaries and his instructors. He recognized the many similarities which existed between the exclusivity of ultra-Orthodox Judaism and the extremism of Christian evangelicalism. Though, as a liberal American Jew, he had always internally and externally battled against the intolerance of the Christian right, now, as a Charedi man, he was finding himself using the tenets of evangelical Christianity to serve a basis for his own outward ultra-Orthodox arguments. In fact, he had ironically modeled his own speech as a Jewish equivalent of things Jerry Falwell, the fundamentalist evangelical Christian preacher, had said in the past. Deep inside, Max felt that some of the things he was learning were simply not in sync with who he was as a person, and he knew it was unbearably sardonic that the version of Judaism to which he was now attached had more in common with the Christian right than the more mainstream humanist Judaism he had just left behind. But he was convinced of the legitimacy of Charedi Judaism, and wherever a contradiction arose, he joined the side of the yeshiva. He would rather err as a sincere tzaddik than let the hiloni in him do what his mind dictated.

Now that he was on this trip with Tzippy and Natan, he could not bring himself to mouth his yeshiva opinions to them. Yes, he had been quite ostentatious with his davening and Charedi outfits and whatnot in front of Tzippy and Natan, but that was to be expected of a Charedi baal teshuva. To sample even the slightest excerpts of his speech to them would lead to strife. Not only would it upset the sensibilities of his two travel companions, it would also offend them both on an emotional level and destroy the relationships he had with them individually. He had referred to the Ethiopian Jewish community derogatorily, claiming that they were part and parcel of the problem facing Judaism as a whole. Clearly this was something which would not bode well with Tzippy. In actuality, however, Max was quite fond of his aunt Adina, and indeed, had no doubts as to her Jewishness at all. In fact, Max had a peculiar fascination with all the stories of lost Jewish tribes being discovered around the world and gathered into Israel, as had been predicted all those centuries ago. *Kibbutz galuyos* was happening right before his eyes and he knew he was privileged to be a part of it. As for Natan, Max's disparaging remarks about the Israeli hilonim would be sure to set off sparks, as Natan was most undoubtedly a hiloni and was sure to be offended that Max had dared question his Jewishness. So, in order to keep peace, Max decided resolutely: *what happens in the yeshiva stays in the yeshiva.*

In a way, Max felt as if there were two sides to himself. He had not been in any real contact with any secular people since he had started attending classes at the Charedi yeshiva in Jerusalem. This was his first encounter in nearly six months with people who lived the way he once lived, and he viewed this trip as a test. If he could withstand the temptations that this trip was sure to present to him, he knew it would be easy going back to the yeshiva. Thus far, with the notable exception of the throwing off of his clothes when he was in the water, he had done well and he was proud of himself.

When Natan had served Max his burgers, Max immediately filled his washer with water and went to the stream to say the *bracha* for washing hands. He poured water over his hands, then held them up to the sky and said the devotion quietly to himself. After drying his hands carefully, he returned to the blanket where Tzippy, who was woefully unaware of Orthodox etiquette, asked him if he wanted mustard. Unable to answer, for he had yet to say the blessing over bread, Max said loudly, much to Tzippy's alarm, "*Baruch attah HaShem Elokeinu melech ha oylam, ha motzi lechem min ha aretz*", and broke off a piece of the bread bun and munched it. Tzippy looked daggers at him for demonstrating his faith so unexpectedly and so openly, but she said nothing and tucked into her meal. Max, who liked to savor his food, had only had a few bites when Tzippy let out a raucous burp. Unable to control the old Max hidden inside of himself, he laughed until he realized that his friends had fallen quiet and were staring up at the hill behind him. Whipping his head around, Max saw what had caught the attention of the other two: up on the hill above him, a lonely figure stood against the backdrop of the sun, looking down at them.

CHAPTER 3

"Looking up, he saw three men standing near him. As soon as he saw them, he ran from the entrance of the tent to greet them and, bowing to the ground, he said, 'My lords, if it please you, do not go on past your servant. Let a little water be brought; bathe your feet and recline under the tree. And let me fetch a morsel of bread that you may refresh yourselves."
—Genesis 18:2-5

"So, why exactly did God need me to be here?" Avraham asked.

It had been three days since Avraham stepped out of the cave, and just as God had warned, Avraham had forgotten every blessed thing about the hereafter, including what had transpired in the cave. When he had followed Michael out of the cave, Avraham had found, waiting for him right outside of the cave (which had miraculously re-sealed itself and was now indistinguishable from the mountain which contained it), an uninhabited tent, inside of which held a clean change of clothes, just as God had promised. Also inside of the tent was everything one could conceive of to comfortably camp outdoors. Inside, Avraham had found—among other things—an ample supply of fresh water, canned foods, an electric griddle, a sleeping bag, a Voltaic solar-powered battery, an iPad, an iPod full of cheesy 80's love songs, a portable electric fan, and, perhaps, most important of all, a big can of bug repellent.

"I could live here forever!" Avraham had exclaimed, as he happily sprayed bug repellent at a sizeable mosquito which zinged around his leg. Naturally, as all he had to compare the tent and its

43

amenities to was the ancient life he had once lived and the accompanying camel dung that such ancient life suggests, it was inevitable that he would be impressed and awed by what had been provided for him.

As the oscillating fan blew cool breeze over his face, Avraham allowed Michael to instruct him on how to power up and use the iPad. Quickly, he mastered the use of the machine and in no time, he had powered through thousands of internet pages which detailed history, economics, engineering, politics, art and science; downloaded and read the Tanakh, the Christian Bible, the Koran, the Bhagvad Gita, the Book of Mormon, the seven books of the *Harry Potter* series, and the *Hunger Games* trilogy; waded through the complete online Talmudic tractates and sifted through tons of pages worth of Jewish commentary; laughed through all of the Jenna Marbles videos on YouTube; watched the entire *'Allo 'Allo* and *Keeping up Appearances* series' online; set up Facebook and Twitter accounts for himself; conquered *Mario Brothers 1, 2, 3, Ms. Pacman* and *Yoshi's World*; and did a cursory Google search on himself (he was slightly put out that there was no mention of the *Chaldean Girls Love Avram* group in any of the historical accounts about his life). God had not been joking when He said He'd given Avraham greater mental prowess.

However, mental prowess is no substitute for supernatural abilities, and in his mortal body, Avraham could no longer see Michael, his angelic companion. He could vaguely ascertain a particular shimmer emanating next to him, and, most importantly, he could hear Michael as clearly as he could hear the wind sweeping the dust of the desert all around him.

Three days had passed since the peculiar duo had been placed on earth, and they had spent that time in the comforts of the tent, where Michael had recounted God's words in the cave, and where the break-neck study session facilitated by the iPad occurred, but it was now time for them to truly embark on their mission. As far as Avraham could ascertain, from what Michael had said, the mission was clear-cut: the first soul Avraham would encounter after exiting the cave would be the mashiach. Avraham was to inform the mashiach of who he was, and then high-tail it back to heaven (wherever that may be, he was not quite sure). Since he had encountered no one in the three days he'd been sojourning in the tent, Avraham realized that he needed to hit the road in order to find the mashiach. *God helps those who help themselves*, he thought wryly to himself. *Some things never change.*

He packed some essentials—water, rope, knife, some cans of food, a lighter and the fully-charged iPod—into a knapsack, and with Michael floating somewhere to his left, he started on his way. Avraham had initially been conflicted about using the resources of the tent, but Michael assured him that God had placed the tent and its contents there specifically for Avraham's use and, therefore, there was no need to feel guilty.

"So, He just conjured it up out of thin air?"

"No. He caused it to be there. It's not important how it came to be there. It was put there for your use," Michael had answered cryptically.

"Then all of this belongs to someone?"

Michael made an awkward sound. "In a manner, yes."

"And I am using it like it was God's special miracle gift to me? God is turning me into a thief?"

45

Michael shimmered hotly, but answered evenly. "All things serve His purpose."

"Even blatant thievery?"

"All things serve His purpose, but nothing He would sanction would ever involve thievery."

Avraham clamped his mouth shut.

As they journeyed, Michael tutored Avraham on the topics his internet crash course had not covered. They talked about the theory of global warming, modern systems of government, Zionist history, Jewish history, religious philosophy, and Miley Cyrus' penchant for sticking her tongue out, until eventually, the issue of the mashiach arose—the ultimate reason for both of them being on earth.

"So, why exactly did God need me to be here?" Avraham asked. "Why couldn't He just use Elijah and Moses to announce the mashiach? Why bring me back into this whole debacle?"

"It does seem somewhat superfluous to make you part of this episode of human history, but God did impress upon us in the cave that this mission—to find the mashiach and inform the mashiach that he is the mashiach—was something that could only be done by you. You were the first man to find God at a time when God was more hidden from the world than He ever was before. Your success in finding Him then is the main criteria, it seems, in making you the most viable candidate to locate the mashiach now. God is not only the Creator, He is the Savior; similarly, the mashiach will be a savior for the Jewish people and the world at large. Besides, your return was foretold."

Avraham stopped in his tracks and did a double-take. "Foretold! By whom?"

"The prophet Ezekiel," Michael answered simply.

"What did Ezekiel foretell?"

"As it is written: 'Thus said the Lord God to these bones: 'I will cause breath to enter you and you shall live again. I will lay sinews upon you, and cover you with flesh, and form skin over you. And I will put breath into you, and you shall live again. And you shall know that I am the Lord'.'"

"But that was a prophecy concerning the people of Israel!" Avraham exclaimed. "I thought that was to do with the rebuilding of Israel as a nation?"

"And so it is," Michael answered simply.

"So how do I pertain to that, Michael?"

"Seventy-two faces of Torah, Avraham."

"I don't understand."

"Each letter, each space, each word, each sentence, each paragraph, each chapter, each scroll— the entire Tanakh, from Torah to *Ketuvim*; it was all chosen, placed and preserved for a reason higher than you or I can comprehend. There is depth to the Scriptures; such depth that one can dive deeper and deeper into it and still find a level waiting to be excavated below. Just as there are seventy-two letters in God's Name, so, too, are there seventy-two faces to every letter, every space, every word, every sentence, every paragraph, every chapter, every scroll of Tanakh. Multiply the seventy-two meanings of each letter by the seventy-two meanings of each space by the seventy-two meanings of each word, and so on, and what you are left with is a number of meanings that boggle even my supernal mind."

"So, the prophecy had nothing to do with Israel?"

"It has *everything* to do with Israel—that's the point of every prophecy in Tanakh. That's the whole point of Tanakh: Israel. Israel is the reason it was written and the reason it was given. You are the first of all of Israel. Without you, there will be no reason to rebuild Israel, and without Israel, you will be no one's father. The Torah was given to Israel because of you."

"It's all interrelated."

"Yes. The Torah has ambiguous meanings, which many seek to uncover, but it also carries its literal meaning, which, sometimes, is even more shrouded than the deeper meanings though it is in plain sight for all to see. *Ain mikreh yotzai meday pshuto*—a verse can never be divorced from its literal meaning. Ezekiel foretold the resurrection of Avraham insomuch as he foresaw the rebuilding of Israel within the same vision: both the literal and figurative contained in one. The two events are intertwined.

"The Torah is a mystery, my earthly companion. It is a mystery that you, as a human of this era, are privileged to unravel."

Avraham had first encountered the Hebrew Bible a mere seventy-two odd hours ago, and it had drawn him in completely and left him utterly mesmerized. He wished he'd had more time to study it properly, but as he'd had many more subjects to catch up on, he had only been able to go through it twice. He was determined to sit down and read it through again— once he'd finished with this business of finding the mashiach and informing him that he was mashiach.

He walked quicker.

✡

Avraham felt great pride in learning about the accomplishments of his offspring, these modern Jews. Against all odds, they had survived and had made great strides in contributing to humanity's story. True, they had never flourished numerically, but what they lacked in numbers, they more than made up for in quality. As he trekked through the desert, he couldn't help but feel overwhelmed at the thought that the familiar land he was treading on, every inch of it, had been given to his progeny just as God had promised him and his wife, Sarah. What he and Sarah had started all those years before had culminated in a most profound and marvelous way. He felt humbled. It had turned out even more amazingly and miraculously than he could ever have hoped for.

To be honest, he did feel slightly put off that his descendants were identified by his grandson, Jacob, instead of him—after all, they, individually, collectively, and as a nation and state were termed 'Israel', the name that God Himself had given to Jacob. But Avraham could see the merit of the name. It specifically identified which branch of Avraham's family were the true spiritual heirs of his and Sarah's legacy. Additionally, the name 'Israel' itself was as mysterious and powerful as the Name of God; a fitting term for these descendants of his.

Much had changed with the movement he had started. In the time he had been gone, his descendants had gone through a radical, mystical change in which they had collectively been privileged to receive the Torah and be its inheritors for all time. And ever since then, they were subject to a hatred which, though it changed its name every few decades, remained constant and determined to destroy them. But, Avraham was back. He was here to start the mashiach on his journey, and if the prophecies were right (and they most definitely would be right, given that they emanated from the most infallible Source possible), then all that hatred would soon be put to rest once and for all, God's will would reign supreme, and life on earth would be just honky dory.

After Avraham and Michael had journeyed for about two hours, they came to a gently sloping but relatively high range of hills. Logically, it would have been better if Avraham avoided the hills altogether— after all, he was in the desert and he could get dehydrated easily—but he had a strange, powerful conviction to climb the hill directly in front of him. As he neared the summit, Avraham stopped in his tracks. He felt another compulsion, even stronger than the first.

"Wait."

"What is it?" Michael asked.

"I feel like I need to pray here."

Avraham had not prayed properly since they had stepped out of the cave. "So now you remember God. I was wondering when you'd remember Him," Michael responded, sardonically.

"Don't start," Avraham replied tersely, and Michael shimmered off to the side.

The sun was on the verge of setting, but Avraham would have preferred if it was morning, for he had always found morning to be the most propitious time for prayer. Interestingly, he had read an online commentary which said that he had instituted the morning prayer service in Judaism, all those many thousands of years ago, and he was pleased to know that the prayer time he had favored most had become enshrined in the spiritual fabric of his descendants. However, regardless of the time at present, the push

Avraham was feeling to commune with his God was something he could not ignore and needed to address immediately.

Although, through his recent studies, he was aware of the modern ways in which prayer had evolved, he still was—at heart—a boy of 1,900BCE. He cleared the area in which he'd felt the compulsion to pray, found a sizeable rock and placed it there to serve as an altar, washed himself, slipped his hiking boots off, covered his head with a small towel he'd packed into the knapsack, and knelt before the rock. He had not prayed in over three millennia, but he effortlessly fell into a state of prayer.

"Blessed are You, O Lord my God," he whispered quietly, "Creator of all things, and by Whose grace I was resurrected to complete the mission of locating the mashiach. I kneel before you in reverence and in thanks, O gracious and compassionate Father, and I thank You for this life that You have once again bestowed upon me. I had forgotten the wonders of being alive: the rush of my heart beating, the warmth of my breath, the feel of the wind against my skin, the smells of the desert, and the soothing effect of the blue of the sky on my eyes. I thank You for once again allowing me the privilege of experiencing life, and I thank You for trusting me to fulfill this most important mission of locating the mashiach. Although I have been back on earth for only a few days, I suspect that my mission is almost complete. I know You have led me up this hill for a reason, and I strongly feel that the reason is because, on the other side of this hill, the mashiach awaits. I ask that You guide these final steps of mine, and bestow Your blessings upon me and the mashiach as I complete this mission. May the thoughts of my heart and the expressions of my

51

mouth find favor before You, O God, my Rock and my Redeemer."

He stood up and walked backward, away from the rock, and then uncovered his head and squatted on the ground to put on his boots. The laces were tricky.

"What now?" Michael asked.

Avraham stood up. "I think the mashiach is on the other side of this hill."

"This is it, then?"

"This is it."

It was now or never. Time to get this mission accomplished. Within ten strides, Avraham was at the top of the hill. He closed his eyes and took a deep breath and then looked down upon the valley below him. It was similar to the other side of the hill from where he had just come, but with a few minor and not so minor differences. On this side of the hill, there were more trees, a rippling brook, and the most marked difference: there, in the valley below him, three figures sat comradely in the shade, enjoying a meal.

✡

"Which one is the mashiach?" Avraham asked Michael urgently.

"I don't know."

This was completely unexpected, and yet, at the same time, somehow expected. Avraham knew that if God could find a way to throw a spoke into his wheel, then He would. It's just the way He operated.

"Tell me again what He said to me in the cave? *Exactly* what He said."

"Thus, says the Lord God," Michael began.

"Skip the histrionics. Just say what He said."

"He said it in three ways: first, 'The era of mashiach is here. I need you to make known to mashiach that I have called and it is time to answer', second, 'You are to make known to mashiach that I have called and it is time to answer. The era of mashiach is here', and finally, the third way, 'You are the only one who will be able to look for mashiach, find mashiach, and let mashiach know that I have called and it is time to answer'."

"But those three ways are each saying the same thing, that I have to find the mashiach and tell him that he's mashiach." Avraham paused. "Right? Or is there some 'seventy-two faces of Torah' law at work here? Is there a deeper meaning to what He said? Come clean, Michael."

"Not that I can discern. And I am not holding anything back from you. You know what I know."

"How did He say I was to identify the mashiach?"

"He said, 'Hearken unto My words: the neshama you encounter upon exiting this cave will be mashiach; you will know you have found mashiach and mashiach will answer you.'"

"But there are three souls down there, Michael! Three! And I don't know which one of them it is I've found!"

"I can see that plainly."

"So, which one of them is it?" Avraham asked hysterically.

"Calm down. Let's be logical," Michael answered evenly. "Which is the first one you saw?"

"I don't know!"

"You must have seen one of them first. Which one was it?"

"I saw them all first!"

"You couldn't possibly have seen them all first."

"Well, I did. They are so far away that they all came into my line of vision at the same time." Avraham moaned. "Why, oh why, is He doing this to me!"

"He's not doing anything to you," Michael retorted. "You just don't remember which one of them you saw first."

"I am telling you, I saw them all first!" Avraham hissed. "If you had to choose, which one of them would you say looks most like the mashiach?"

"Avraham!" Michael exclaimed, shocked. "That is not the way God intended you to do it!"

"You don't know which way He intended me to do it, so just hurry up and help me choose!"

Michael answered in hushed tones. "What if it's all of them? After all, God didn't say specifically that the mashiach would be the *first* soul you'd encounter upon exiting the cave. He said it would be the neshama you encountered."

"Soul, Michael. *Soul*. Singular. He didn't say 'souls'. There is only one mashiach, and it's one of them sitting there under that tree. Now hurry up and tell me which one it is. Hurry!"

"This is an enormous decision. Must you be so rushed?"

"Yes, I have to be rushed because they've seen me, and if I don't go down and identify myself right now, they're probably going to shoot me dead while you flutter away on the breeze."

Avraham waved his hand at the group below and began walking down the hill to meet them.

"Quickly," he whispered out of the side of his mouth at Michael, all the while trying to keep a friendly smile plastered on his face at the people looking up at him, "which one?"

"That's your call."

Avraham groaned and continued walking down the hill. He could see the group consisted of a female and two males. "We can rule out the girl. And before you say anything, it has nothing to do with me being sexist. The commentaries all say the mashiach will be male."

Michael didn't answer.

"Right?"

"Whatever you say. This is your mission. I'm just the sidekick."

Avraham groaned again. "You are not helping!" He was nearing the group now and could make out their features more clearly. Flanking the girl, who was actually quite beautiful, were the two boys. One was very dour and pale-faced, dressed entirely in black, and the other was tall and dark and quite striking-looking. Immediately, Avraham was drawn to the taller, better-looking male. Besides being good-looking, he emanated calmness and self-assuredness, and seemed to be, at least physically, everything one would expect the mashiach to be.

"It's the tall boy," Avraham whispered to Michael. "It has to be."

Michael said nothing.

"Right? It's him—he's the mashiach. Right, Michael?"

Michael finally answered. "Whatever you say. It's your mission. I'm just the sidekick."

✡

In all her years of life, Tzippy had never felt any sort of compulsion to be religious. She was born Jewish and that was that. But she knew there was something deeper to being a Jew than just religion, ethnicity or culture. The one time she was actually paying attention in Torah Studies as a child, the teacher had mentioned the 'neshama'— the Jewish soul—and the idea had captured her imagination and remained with her all her life. The teacher had explained that Jews, while not better or superior to anyone else, did have something 'different' about them—something which sometimes inspired hate from other people, yet made Jews identifiable to each other. This something 'different', the teacher explained, was the neshama. Although the concept had fascinated her, never in her life had Tzippy been able to know unreservedly that someone was Jewish. Of course, she could always tell when there were blatantly identifiable markers, such as the Charedim with their black suits, or people with very stereotypically Jewish faces, or noisy Birthright kids with their hoodies proclaiming 'Taglit 2014!', but when it came to her neshama recognizing the neshama of another Jew—that had never happened.

Not until this day.

She didn't know what it was about the man who was quickly cascading down the hill towards them, but something deep inside of her instantly recognized that he was one of her own. In a land where it was oftentimes racially difficult to differentiate who was who, Tzippy was able to—without a shadow of a doubt—ascertain that the man possessed a powerful neshama. There was nothing about his outward appearance that readily signaled the man's Jewishness but something about him screamed to her that he was Jewish.

"He's Jewish," she said quietly, not really for the benefit of Natan or Max, but they heard nonetheless.

"How do you know that?" Max asked, curiously.

"I'm not sure," she answered thoughtfully. "I just do."

When they had first spotted the strange silhouette on the hill, an immediate fear had shot through them, after all, it was not unheard of for terrorists to sneak into the country and randomly shoot at innocent Israeli civilians. The soldier in both Natan and Tzippy had awoken and they sprung to their feet, when suddenly, the person on the hill waved maniacally and began to shimmy down to them. As he drew closer, they could see that he was slim, almost on the point of skinny, with jet black wavy hair, and dark features. His skin was smooth, almost like a baby's, and his face was remarkably attractive. A slight stubble played on his chin and upper lip, but there was no apparent hair anywhere else on his face. He was a boy. He couldn't be older than twenty. He wore droopy khaki cargo shorts, a white cotton shirt two sizes too large, and ill-fitting black hiking boots. An army-green knapsack was affixed to his back. Tzippy, who had pegged the character as Jewish, was fairly certain that he was either of Yemenite-Jewish or Iraqi-Jewish origin.

Although the boy seemed to pose no threat, both Natan and Tzippy were on their guard. Max, too, was wary of the approaching figure, but as he'd had no military training, he kept quiet and allowed the other two to take charge of the situation.

The boy came up to them with a smile, both his hands in the air. "Shalom, *chaverim*!" Peace, friends. His Hebrew was curiously pronounced.

"Shalom," Natan answered cautiously. "How can we help you?"

The boy stopped right in front of Natan and put both his arms on Natan's shoulders and looked up at Natan, who towered over the boy. Natan was tempted to draw back, but held his ground.

"*Kol beseder?*" Everything alright? Natan asked the boy, tentatively.

The boy lit up. "*Nehedar*. I am wonderful. I have come looking for you and I've found you. So, what else can I be but wonderful?"

"You are looking for us because you need help?"

The boy shook his head vehemently. "I was looking for you *specifically*, my tall friend."

Natan frowned. "Why were you looking for me?"

"Because, *chaver*," the boy answered. "I have been sent by the one true God of Israel to tell you this: you are the mashiach." The boy beamed up at Natan.

Natan, Tzippy, and Max spontaneously burst into laughter. The relief of finding out that this boy was really no threat, rather, he was simply an addled soul, caused the tension they'd felt upon first seeing the boy to dissipate, and a rush of laughter filled the empty air.

Clearly, this was not the reaction the boy expected. He frowned and dropped his hands from Natan's shoulders, turned to the side and began talking to himself, as the threesome looked on amusedly at the pantomime playing out before them.

"I thought he would believe me?" There was a pause. "What did he say exactly? *Exactly*. No dramatic replays." Another pause. Longer this time. The boy threw his hands up in the air. "Well, if you'd told me that I needed to identify myself first, this could have gone much differently!"

The boy turned his attention to them again. "Greetings, my friends!" he exclaimed. "I am Avraham of old, resurrected by the grace of the one true God of Israel, here on earth once again to do His bidding."

The words fell on them like thunder and their laughter dried up. Something in them clicked, and they instinctively knew that the boy was telling the truth.

Tzippy's jaw dropped, Natan frowned, and Max dropped to his knees.

"*Avraham Aveinu*?" Abraham our father? Max asked reverently, his hands clasped tightly to his chest.

Avraham smiled weakly at Max. "I guess." He turned his attention back to Natan. "I made you laugh before, but now that you know who I am, can you believe me when I tell you that you are the mashiach?"

Natan frowned deeper. "Me?" he asked disbelievingly. "The mashiach?"

Avraham smiled widely. "Yes. You."

Natan brushed his hands through his hair. This was surreal to say the least. Tzippy and Max were staring at him with their mouths agape. "God sent you to tell me—me specifically—that I am the mashiach?"

Avraham stopped smiling and looked uncomfortable. "He sent me, yes."

Max jumped to his feet and interjected incredulously. "Natan is the moshiach? But he's not even religious!"

Avraham ignored Max's outburst. "Is that your name? Natan?"

Natan shook himself. "I am Natan Nasi, son of Yossi Nasi and Sonia Rahamin. These are my friends, Max Feldman, and his cousin, Tzipporah Feldman."

"An honor to make your acquaintance!" Avraham beamed.

Tzippy caught herself. "An honor to make yours. I suppose you're our very, very, very great grandfather."

Avraham blushed. "I suppose so, although it does seem odd to think of myself as anyone's very, very, very great grandfather."

"Odd is an understatement for what's going on here." Tzippy laughed totteringly. "I am sure that this is the first time under the sun that a very, very, very great grandfather has met his very, very, very great descendants."

Avraham grinned. "Never say never. Odder things have happened in this world. My wife was ninety when our son was born. I think that's just as odd as this—if not odder."

Tzippy giggled and relaxed. She liked Avraham's humor. She noticed the beads of perspiration dribbling down Avraham's forehead. "You must be hot." She ducked into the cooler and pulled out an icy bottle of water. "Would you like something to drink?"

Avraham gratefully took the water from Tzippy's outstretched hand. "Thank you. I have some water in my bag, but it has become hot." He fumbled with the cork, and Tzippy reached forward and unscrewed it for him. "Thank you," he said again. He drank deeply.

Max looked at all of this with bulging eyes.

Avraham lowered the bottle and caught Max ogling him. He smiled awkwardly at Max.

"Is everything ok?"

Max continued to stare bug-eyed. "This is surreal."

Tzippy punched him on the arm.

Max grimaced but continued to ogle. "Avraham Aveinu is resurrected, standing in front of us, naming our friend as moshiach, and drinking water. This is beyond surreal."

"I suppose it is, but as I'm very much real and standing here, it makes me feel a bit put out that you'd say I'm surreal."

Max shook himself and smiled weakly. "Sorry," he mumbled. He turned to Tzippy and punched her back belatedly. "Should we offer him food?" he whispered loudly. "He must be hungry. Why haven't we offered him food?"

Avraham cleared his throat. "I won't mind something to eat," he said shyly. "I've been walking all day."

Natan—who had been standing still and saying nothing, as he had been reeling from the pronouncement that he was the identified mashiach—immediately sprung to life. The hospitable Israeli in him was aghast that he had not offered his guest food sooner. He quickly packed a plate of pita, hummus, salad, and beef patties for Avraham and bade him to sit on the blanket. Avraham gratefully accepted the food and sat next to Natan, said a quiet prayer of thanks, and tucked in with vigor. After three days of only canned foods, the freshness of the meal, despite its simplicity, was a welcome taste to Avraham's taste buds and he ate with relish.

Tzippy comradely sat next to Avraham. "And what do we call you? Saba? Avraham?" She paused. "Avraham seems a little... severe. Can I call you Avi? You look like an Avi."

"Before I was known as Avraham, I was named Avram by my parents. Avi was the nickname they used to call me," he said, in between mouthfuls of food.

Max, who was still standing awkwardly, turned up his face. "We can't possibly call you Avi," he said imperiously. "You are Avraham Aveinu, for crying out loud."

"It's fine. I don't feel like an 'Avraham Aveinu'. Pretty weird that you're calling me 'our father' when I look and feel like a twenty-year-old."

"But it's who you are," Max insisted.

"I prefer Avi."

"But Avraham Aveinu—"

"Avi," Avi said firmly.

"It's too common."

"Avi," Avi said again, with forceful resolution

"But—"

"He said call him 'Avi', Max! Good Lord!" Tzippy interjected. She stared daggers at her cousin.

Max sighed and threw up his hands in surrender.

Avraham continued to eat.

"Are you enjoying the food?" Tzippy asked.

"Very much."

Max sat tentatively across from Avraham and smiled weakly.

Avraham returned the smile, but with less gusto than Max would've liked. He worried that he had offended the patriarch. Max cleared his throat. "Is it strange to be alive again?" he asked, trying to sound light.

Avraham shrugged. "I've been alive for three days now. I've pretty much acclimatized. It feels good to be alive—and young—again."

"Can you tell us anything about heaven? Or God?"

"I don't remember anything of the afterlife, to be honest."

"How come?"

Avi fell silent for a moment and craned his neck upwards. Tzippy had the fleeting impression that Avi was listening to someone, but she dismissed the thought as quickly as it entered her mind. It was too silly to even think.

"I quote, verbatim: 'The World to Come is not a concern of souls which populate the physical world, and as such, its secrets shall not be made known to any who reside in this mortal world'."

"Who said that?" Max asked.

"God," Avi said, matter-of-factly, and he took another bite of the beef.

Max's eyes grew wide. "God? Is God talking to you right now? I mean, do you hear His voice? Is He directing you right now?"

"He returned me to this world with a guardian angel. My guardian angel speaks to me. He knows what God sent me to do and he informs me of it, and, I suppose, any other updates from the Big Guy. That's what angels are there for."

"Do I have a guardian angel?" Tzippy asked timidly.

Avi touched her gently. "We all have our own angels. We're born with a guardian angel and there are always angels around us at all moments."

"How come I can't see mine?"

"I can't see mine either—but I can hear my angel." Avi considered. "Our angels are like that little voice of conscience inside of us that tells us what's wrong and what's right. Our angels are those little pangs of premonition that warn us: 'Don't go to the supermarket today', and we don't, then we realize that if we had gone, we could've gotten into an accident because the brakes weren't working properly in our car. Our angels are always whispering to us, but sometimes we don't hear them. It takes time to deepen our spiritual selves to hear our angels properly as more than just a whispering conscience." Avi smiled around at the group. "It's strange, but you three remind me of some angels I met when I was previously alive."

Tzippy chuckled. "Max and I are definitely no angels. We fight too much." She looked warmly at Natan. "Maybe Natan is an angel. He's super nice."

"Well, he is the moshiach," Max said. "The moshiach has to be nice."

Avraham nodded in assent and took the final bite of his food. Max sprung up and fetched a wet-wipe for Avraham. "You've watered me, fed me, and cleaned me." Avi beamed. "You are all angels, despite your protestations. Thank you."

Natan, who had politely been waiting for Avi to finish eating, finally spoke. "*Ani lo mevin.*" I don't understand. "How is it you came to be here?"

"I walked," Avraham said evenly. He wiped his fingers clean with the wet-wipe and then accepted a second wet-wipe, which he used to soothe his dusty face.

Natan shook his head. "How is it you are back here on earth?"

"God resurrected me."

"Yes, you said that. But how?"

Avraham scratched his head. "I'm not entirely sure." He stood and went to the side and began talking to himself. After a minute, he faced Natan. "I am sorry, but I honestly don't know. He resurrected me in the cave I'd been buried in. That's all I know." He looked daggers at the empty space next to him.

"So, there is a God?" Natan asked quietly.

Avraham chuckled. "How else do we explain my being here?"

"I'm not sure," Natan responded, pensively.

Avi looked anxious. "But you believe me?"

Tzippy and Max nodded enthusiastically, but Natan answered slowly. "I believe you are Avraham our forefather, yes."

Avi relaxed.

"So, you just reappeared here?" Natan continued. "How did you get out of Hevron? Weren't there soldiers at the entrance to Machpelah? Did you just walk out of your tomb and straight past the soldiers?"

"Soldiers? Why would there be soldiers?"

As Natan explained that there was a mosque and synagogue built cohesively yet conflictingly over the site of Machpelah, the cave in which Avraham's body had been interred for the past few thousand years, Avraham's eyes glazed over. Before Natan could finish expounding on the detailed security patrolling *Me'arat ha-Machpelah* due to the religiously sensitive nature of the site itself and its competitive importance to Judaism, Christianity and Islam correspondingly, Avraham giggled.

"I am sorry," Avraham apologized, quickly stifling his laughter. "But you seem to be mistaken. That site is not the real Machpelah. The real Machpelah was sealed and concealed by God in order for the prophecy of my return to be fulfilled. All the hullaballoo over that place people think I'm buried at—well, it's highly unnecessary."

"What prophecies of your return?" Max asked.

Avraham repeated the biblical verse Michael had quoted to him.

"But that's not about you," Max said quickly.

Avraham narrowed his eyes at Max. "I assure you, it is also about me."

"None of the commentaries say that."

"Do you presume to tell me that the commentators know more than the Author?"

"No, but I'm sure at least one of the commentators would have divined that there was a prophecy which pertained to the resurrection of our founding patriarch."

"What if that was never meant to be public knowledge? What if the prophecy was supposed to be known by me and the mashiach only?" Avi retorted.

"Well, maybe, but I still think that a Torah scholar would've discerned it."

Tzippy groaned. "Are you kidding me, Max? What more evidence do you want? There was a prophecy concerning Avi's return—and he's standing right in front of you! What else do you want?"

"I don't want anything! I believe Avraham Aveinu! I know he's in front of me! I'm just saying that maybe it wasn't prophesied that he'd come back!" Max yelled shrilly.

"He just told you it was!" Tzippy snapped.

"Thank you, Tzippy for trying to make your cousin understand that the world is bigger than simply his perceptions." Avi turned to face Max. "I suggest you open up your mind a bit more. You strike me as someone who doesn't think much for himself," he said severely.

Max reddened.

Natan called them all to attention. "*Slicha.*" Excuse me. "It's getting dark. I think we should pack up and head back."

"Can't we stay just a bit longer?" Tzippy pleaded. "I mean it's not every day you get to meet your distant ancestor."

Natan shook his head. "This desert is harsh to those who approach it without reverence. Last week when I came to camp, it started raining without warning, causing a huge flash flood that separated me from my camping site. It was all I could do to get to my jeep and get out of danger, but I was forced to leave all my camping equipment behind. If I still had my camping things, we could have stayed here and talked all night long, but as it stands, we have made no preparations to stay overnight. We need to make a move."

Avraham's eyes grew wide at Natan's speech. "Wait a second. You left camping equipment behind. Do you know where?"

"I am not sure exactly."

"What was it exactly that you left behind?" Avraham asked Natan. "Was it a fully-equipped tent with a laptop, a solar-charged battery, two sleeping bags, an oscillating fan, and an iPod full of cheesy 80's love songs?"

Natan blushed. "The iPod belongs to my friend who went camping with me actually, but yes, it sounds like that was my tent."

"The tent was yours!" Avraham exclaimed. "Then the clothes I found in it must be yours as well. Look at my outfit. Does it look familiar?"

Natan glanced at Avraham uncomfortably. "No."

"The clothes you're wearing can't be Natan's," Tzippy said. "Yes, they are large on you, Avi, but they are much too small for Natan."

Natan coughed and looked away. Tzippy's curiosity was piqued, but before she could pursue the issue, Avraham, who refused to be deterred, pulled the iPod from the knapsack and handed it to Natan. "Does this belong to your friend?"

Natan studied the iPod carefully. "Yes." Natan turned it around. "See? His name is on the back."

Tzippy peered at the iPod in Natan's hand, but said nothing.

Avraham clapped excitedly. "I knew it! I knew it! You are the mashiach! You have to be. God sent me directly to your tent after I left the cave! Is this knapsack your friends' or even yours?"

Natan looked at the bag. "It's mine."

"You are the mashiach! You are! *Baruch HaMakom!*"

"It seems like you needed some validation to be sure that I was the mashiach. I would have thought God sending you would have been enough."

Avraham gulped. "Oh yes. Yes. It's enough. I— it's just that I wanted to be sure. The fact that the tent you left behind was where I found shelter after my reemergence on earth—well, that is sort of the clincher on this whole thing, don't you think?" He turned to the side. "So, He didn't make me into a thief!" Pause. "I never said that." Pause. "Whatever." Avraham focused his attention back to Natan and clasped Natan's hands. "I knew it. I knew you were the mashiach."

"Avi," Natan interjected, "do you know where you found the tent? Maybe we can go back and collect my stuff."

Avraham nodded. "I can lead you there. Shall we go now?"

"No. We shouldn't go messing around in the dark. We can return during the day. Ok, guys, we really need to go. Avi, what's the next step?"

"I suppose the prophets Elijah and Moses will arrive soon to instruct you further and announce you to the world as the mashiach."

Natan laughed uneasily. "I'm not sure if I'm ready to meet any new resurrected historical figures just yet. I meant what's the next step for you? Are you coming with us? Are you staying here? What are you doing?"

Avraham scratched his head. "I don't rightly know. My mission was to find you and tell you you're the mashiach, and now that I've done that, I suppose I'll be heading back to heaven now."

Natan looked amused. "And how are you getting there?"

"God will provide. He always does."

Natan laughed. "Maybe you should come with us back to Tel Aviv? When God is ready for you, He will find you. I don't feel right leaving you out here in the desert."

Avraham hmm-ed for a bit, then excused himself and scuttled off to the side, where he held a whispered discussion with his invisible companion. Finally, he straightened up and returned to the group with a big smile. "I suppose I could come back with you to your city. It would be nice to see what's going on in the world. And maybe when Elijah comes to announce you

69

to the world, he will come on his chariot of fire and I can use that to shuttle back to heaven." He winked at Tzippy. "After all, it isn't every day that one gets to meet one's very, very, very great descendants."

CHAPTER 4

"Then the LORD said to Abraham, 'Why did Sarah laugh saying, 'Shall I in truth bear a child, old as I am?' Is anything too wondrous for the LORD? I will return to you at the time next year, and Sarah shall have a son.'"
—Genesis 18:13-14

The coming of Avi and his declaration that Natan was the mashiach overwhelmed Natan. He didn't understand why, but without any hesitation, Natan—who was always a most skeptical chap when it came to matters of religion—had readily accepted and unreservedly believed Avi's claim that he was Avraham of old, come back to life. This raised disturbing theological and philosophical questions in Natan's head that could not be ignored. Since he believed wholeheartedly that Avi was the resurrected Avraham, was he now supposed to believe God existed? The implication of Avi's arrival had resonating effects on everything Natan had put aside and hoped to ignore through his agnostic status. Avi had said God had sent him; Avi had talked unabashedly to an invisible guardian angel; Avi had spoken of heaven as if it were the most routine destination one could travel to, using Expedia to get the best prices. And Natan, who had recently decided to embark on a journey to India to explore the plaguing question of his agnosticism, was left unsettled with the arrival of his most ancient ancestor. The issue of him being named the mashiach, well, that was the least of his philosophical problems at the moment.

What does it all mean?

Mere months before, he had sat in this very jeep and had struggled with finding meaning in his life. Now, here he was, the supposed mashiach designate, chauffeuring Avraham of old.

Mashiach designate. He laughed inwardly at his own joke. He didn't feel like the mashiach. He felt much too confused about himself to be the human who would set in motion the chain of events which would facilitate the redemption of Israel and the world at large. His mind was reeling, and he kept quiet for most of the ride.

Max, meanwhile, was also troubled and was equally silent in the front passenger seat. As a true believer, he had no existential qualms believing Avi was Avraham Aveinu, nor did he have any problem with Natan being named the mashiach. True, Natan as the mashiach had initially surprised him, but the more he thought about it, Max realized that it was a pragmatic move on God's part to choose Natan. Although not religious, Natan was the descendant of rabbis, and, as such, was well-acquainted with Judaism on the religious level. Also, as a hiloni, Natan—who would clearly become more religious as a result of his mashiach-hood—would be amply poised to draw the secular masses into a more religious lifestyle. Yes, Max was completely fine with all of that.

The big problem for Max was Avi's dislike toward him. From the moment they'd met, Max had managed to insert his foot deeper and deeper into his mouth causing Avi to go from initial annoyance and frustration to outright dislike and disgust. Max had hoped to remedy this by tempering his out-of-timing comments, so he tried pursuing the topic of the afterlife again when they'd first sat in the jeep, but Avi had cut him off brusquely: "I told you already, I cannot remember it, and that is how God intends it to be. The afterlife is not for you, me, or anyone else alive to know. Focus on this life you're living here, not there."

Max replayed the first hour of meeting Avi in his mind, and he blushed profusely to himself as he recalled his rude outbursts. Yes, he had been a little (*what was the word Tzippy had called him when she and Natan had picked him up from yeshiva earlier that day? Oh, yes,*) priggish. What made it worse was that he was the only one in the group who'd been sufficiently reverent toward Avi; the others had been so disrespectfully chummy. He wished he could have a do over. Maybe he shouldn't have questioned the patriarch? Maybe he should have been more reverential? It didn't matter. He had royally messed everything up and now Avraham Aveinu hated him. Max mulled over his thoughts quietly in the passenger seat.

While things were quieter and more pensive in the front of the jeep, in the backseat, there was a much lighter, friendlier vibe. Avi and Tzippy had an instant connection, and it was deepening with each passing moment. Partially it was because they were closest in age (both being twenty, give or take a few millennia), but mainly it was because they recognized, in each other, a kindred spirit. Avi had no idea of the particulars of Tzippy's background, but he could infer that they shared similar traits. As they traveled in Natan's jeep, the two further solidified their bond with friendly banter and easy conversation.

Tzippy was at once fascinated by and proud of Avi. She also ascertained that there were striking similarities between them. In many ways, she felt as if she had met a long-lost brother, and wondered privately whether on a genetic level they shared almost exactly the same genes. Despite the disparity of the time periods that shaped them and the scant resemblance between them, their behavioral and attitudinal similarities ran too deep to be discounted as anything but familial. They even made the same gestures when speaking and were quickly formulating their own private jokes. Tzippy enjoyed Avi's company tremendously, and was delightfully surprised to find that the man she had always perceived to be the stern, humorless, God-obsessed Avraham of the Torah was actually an easy-going, refreshingly open-minded, charming, and magnificently witty personality.

Tzippy pointed out modern parts of the landscape as they went whizzing by, with infrequent contributions from Natan and Max. She pointed out the power lines and electric lights, the airplanes in the sky and cars on the well-paved roads, the gas stations and towns lit up in the distance. Tzippy was the tour guide who introduced Avi to the updates that the twenty-first century had wrought upon the world, and he was grateful to her for explaining everything to him and being patient with his questions. He was undoubtedly happy that he'd made the decision to come with them to Tel Aviv instead of staying in the desert. This new world was fantastic. Avi was impressed at how far mankind had come, and was curious about everything. Although he had perused some of the accomplishments humanity had made on the Internet, and had been coached by Michael, seeing the tangible product was an entirely different and much more breathtaking way to become acquainted with the modern world.

Within an hour of leaving the desert, they arrived in Tel Aviv and dropped Tzippy off at her apartment in Neve Tzedek. Tzippy hugged them all goodbye, grabbed her carrier, promised Avi she'd come visit him the next day, and went up to the apartment she shared with an American friend who had come to Israel for the summer. The boys drove to Rechov HaYarkon, where Natan's penthouse apartment was located. Tastefully and carefully decorated in minimalist, masculine tones, with three bedrooms, a gourmet kitchen, two large balconies and a rooftop terrace which looked out over the Mediterranean Sea to the west, Natan was proud of his home. He had bought it and renovated it with the money he had made from his company, and relished in the fact that at only twenty-nine, he had procured such sumptuous living quarters.

Avi was awed by the sheer modernity of the apartment, and, like a child, delighted in everything from the silent coolness emitted by the central air, to the plush touch of the cashmere throw on the couch. Natan chuckled at Avi and took over Tzippy's role as chief explainer of all things modern. Max, who was still smarting from Avi's coolness towards him, withdrew to the kitchen and sipped a bottle of water.

Natan's apartment had three bedrooms: a well-appointed master bedroom, and two smaller bedrooms which shared a Jack-and-Jill bathroom. Max had left his small carrier at the front door and Natan picked it up and placed it in the larger of the two guest rooms and then ushered Avi into the other room. Avi frolicked into the room and then stopped dead in his tracks when his eyes beheld the bed. For a second, Natan panicked that the bed had scared Avi, but just as quickly as Avi had been stumped, he recovered, and with reckless abandon, he rushed over to the bed and threw himself on it happily. Natan laughed. Avi's enchantment with the modern world was infectious, and though he was, technically, Natan's senior by a few thousand years, Natan couldn't

75

help but feel a cousinly protectiveness over his new acquaintance.

"You like?"

"Oh, yes. I do!" Avi exclaimed, his cheeks brushing the silky cool sheets. "This is luxury! It is so deliciously soft. I will enjoy sleeping on this!"

Natan laughed.

"Thank you for this wonderful hospitality!"

"*Al lo dvar.*" No problem.

Avi sat up and then crinkled his nose. He sniffed at his underarms and then looked at Natan sheepishly. "Do you mind if I wash myself? I haven't touched water properly for three days. I don't smell my best. If Elijah and Moses show up, I want to make a good impression."

✡

It was only after Natan had lent Avi a change of clothing and instructed him on how to work the modern bathroom, that Natan noticed Max's morose disappearance. He walked into the kitchen and found Max sitting quietly at the breakfast bar.

"Kol beseder?"

Max looked up at him with the most sorrowful look Natan had ever seen on an adult man's face. "Avi hates me," he whispered mournfully.

Natan cleared his throat and thought through his answer. "He hasn't taken to you." No sense in beating around the bush. "But perhaps as he gets to know you better, things will be different. Besides, personalities clash—you know that. I doubt this is the first time someone hasn't liked you."

"But this is not just any 'someone'. This is Avraham Aveinu."

"I think that's the problem, this 'Avraham Aveinu' stuff. You have to stop that. He asked us to call him Avi. Don't you see what that means? He doesn't want to feel different, he wants to feel part of the crowd. You have to treat him as you would anyone else," Natan advised.

"You think so?"

"I definitely think so. Don't shower him with reverence. Be his friend." Natan smiled kindly.

"You're right. Maybe I should start treating you with reverence instead, huh, Mr. Moshiach."

Natan blushed. "Don't."

Max threw his hands in the air. "Come on buddy—you're moshiach! You're going to do great things. You've got to get used to people fawning over you. I could almost see it now, you walking down the street and the girls running after you with autograph books yelling, 'Moshiach Natan!'"

"*Dai, bevakasha.*" Enough, please. "I don't feel very mashiach-like. I can't help but wonder if Avi made a mistake. Didn't he seem to falter when I asked him if he was sure I was the mashiach?" Natan stroked his chin thoughtfully. "You'd make a better mashiach than I would, any day."

"What?" Max exclaimed. "You're out of your mind. You are the best choice for the moshiach. Yes, I did notice Avi's initial hesitance about assuring you that you were the moshiach, and even though Avi, as a human, is fallible, God isn't, and God sent Avi to tell you that you were the moshiach, ergo, you are the moshiach."

"It's going to take some getting used to—this mashiach business. In the meantime, let's just not refer to me as that. Let's stick with Natan, the Confused and Conflicted."

Max shrugged. "Ok, it's your call. You're the moshiach—confused and conflicted, though you may be." He laughed and then spoke cautiously. "It's interesting though, isn't it?"

"That I got named the mashiach by a twenty-year-old kid?"

Max shook his head. "It's interesting that we believe that twenty-year-old kid is Avraham of biblical fame. Don't you find that strange?"

"Do you believe him?"

Max nodded. "Without the slightest doubt. And it's obvious Tzippy does as well." He paused. "Do you believe him?"

Natan nodded.

"Why?" Max asked.

"I don't know. I just know he's telling the truth. Why do you believe him?"

"Same reason as you. I just do." Natan sighed. "The implications of us believing Avi is Avraham are well, sort of, mind boggling. Is it proof?"

"Proof of what?"

"Proof that God exists? We both believe—and, assumedly Tzippy, too—that Avi is our distant forefather, Avraham. No, it's more than belief. We all know that Avi is Avraham. They're the same person. So, does it mean that God resurrected Avi to life? I know Avi is Avraham, but I don't know if God brought him back. I still don't know if there is a God, at least not in the way religion envisages Him—or Her—to be."

"How else would Avi have returned to life?" Max enquired. "How else can we explain our knowing that he is Avraham?"

"There are things science has yet to discover. Miracles happen every day and people chalk it up to religion and to some mythical being we think of as God, but what if, someday—a hundred years from now—we discover that a certain amount of ultraviolet rays, coupled with desert heat and some other variable can cause the resurrection of the body? What if there is some easily explainable reason for physical miracles?"

"But how does that negate the existence of God?" Max asked evenly. "God works in mysterious ways. Personally, I think every miracle that He performs—be it on an individual level, the communal level, the national level, or even the global level—occurs within the confines of the physical laws which He made to govern this universe. I don't think He's going to break those laws of physics just to prove He's God. I think He's sublimely subtler than that. So, if someday science can recreate the necessary factors needed to instigate physical resurrection, or the parting of the Red Sea, or the supernatural crumbling of the walls of Jericho, well, at least to me, it doesn't change my belief in Him, because I can discern God in it all."

Natan sighed. "You have faith where I don't. I just don't know if He exists or not. I have no reason to believe in Him, or disbelieve."

"I think God exists whether we believe in Him or not. But I'm no skeptic; I'm a believer. Always have been, even before this—" he gestured to his outfit. "I never felt conflicted about the existence of God. I always felt as if He was somewhere out there and at the same time, right next to me. However, to be really honest with you—and I'll deny this if you tell any of my rabbis I said it: I don't think He cares if we believe in Him or not."

"Huh?"

"I think God is more than we can comprehend. We've compartmentalized Him with human attributes in order for us and our limited human minds to understand Him, but He's so much more than that, you know? Our belief in His existence has no bearing on anything whatsoever. He exists because He exists; outside of our understanding and above anything we can comprehend—and at the end of the day, my friend, individual belief or disbelief in Him does not negate His existence. He's there. He just is. That's what I think."

"*Ayer asher ayeh.*" I will be what I will be.

"Precisely, my Israeli friend. You really are a closet Torah scholar, aren't you?" Max observed smilingly.

At that moment, Avi walked into the room. "Am I intruding?" Avi asked hesitantly. He was showered and clean, and looked slightly clownish in Natan's much-larger clothes.

"Of course not," Natan replied. "Come join us, bevakasha."

Avi perched himself on a barstool. They opened a bottle of red wine and Natan continued to question Avi about his life in ancient times. Max, meanwhile, who had taken Natan's advice to heart, listened attentively to Avi's recollecting, and, where appropriate, tried inserting tasteful, non-priggish jokes. Although Max still felt awed by Avi's presence, he put aside his reverence and tried to interact with Avi as if they were long-lost fraternity brothers. Unfortunately, Avi didn't seem to be impressed by Max's new approach, despite the wine which plied his system, but he did soften towards Max and was noticeably less caustic. Natan discreetly observed the pointed—yet polite—exchanges between the two boys, but didn't comment. He could see it would take some work on Max's part, but he was sure Max would eventually win Avi over.

When the bottle of wine was emptied of its last drop, Natan suggested it was time for dinner and fetched vegetarian lasagna, bread, and salad from the refrigerator, heated it up and he and Avi heartily dug in. Max, meanwhile, unwrapped a sandwich he had brought with him from Jerusalem. As an ultra-Orthodox man, Max would not eat food cooked in Natan's house since Natan did not keep kosher, Natan explained to Avi. Avi was intrigued, and while the three of them ate, he interrogated Max about the laws of kashrut. Pathetically pleased with Avi's interest, Max eagerly answered Avi's questions. "It's about being holy," Max summed up earnestly, "just as God is holy, so too must we be holy in every aspect of our lives. We must watch what comes out of our mouths as ferociously as we watch what we put in it. Insomuch as He is holy, we most also strive to follow His precepts and emulate His holiness."

Avi nodded contemplatively and fell quiet until his plate was empty of food. He looked up with a bright smile and asked Natan if there was any *metukah* to top the meal off with. Natan chuckled and retrieved an ice cream cake from the freezer and dished out equal servings for himself and Avi. Max pulled a pre-packaged *parve* chocolate pudding out of the fridge, and together, the three of them enjoyed their individual desserts. Avi moaned ecstatically throughout the duration of the ice cream cake eating. He declared rapturously that the entire meal was delicious, but the ice cream cake had truly captured his heart. "I've always had a sweet tooth," he explained. "And my wife, Sarah, was always hiding the honey pot from me. She was positive that too much sweet was never good. Said it caused worms."

When the meal was over, they advanced onto the rooftop terrace, with its sweeping views of modern Tel Aviv. Natan switched on his stereo and while the soulful sound of Ran Danker's album *Shavim* played diffidently in the background, he pulled out another bottle of wine, and then another, and the night continued on, with the conversation flowing, until they all sauntered off to their respective bedrooms at four in the morning and drifted off to sleep.

✡

While the boys had been wiling the night away with wine, Tzippy's evening had followed a more subdued and entirely more educational tone. She'd slipped her glasses on and spent her time Googling Avi's life as Avraham. She had never truly paid attention in Hebrew day school to the stories of the lives of the first Hebrews—for they had all seemed quite stoic and humorless—but Avi's endearing personality had propelled her curiosity. As she read up on him, she found it difficult to reconcile in her mind the character presented in the written accounts with the boy she had met earlier that day; there was a marked difference in personality between the two, and she inferred that much had been omitted from the account of the patriarch's life. She read that there was no proof for his existence, and many scholars debated whether he'd truly existed, or, whether he was simply a mythological figure created by the ancient Israelites to solidify, unite, and give purpose to their own nationality and religion. *I wonder what the scholars would say if they'd had the day I'd had?* She chuckled and kept on reading.

The biblical narrative of Avi's life ran thus: he'd been born Avram ben Terah, anywhere between 1976BCE and 1637BCE in a city known generically as Ur, but specified by Jewish sources as Cutha, which was somewhere in the vicinity of present-day Iraq. He had initially discovered the existence of his God when he was still living in his father's house; a discovery which would only deepen as the years went by, with a series of tests, prophecies and revelations, culminating in Avraham being given the honorific title of "Friend of God", the only person in all of biblical history to have been referred to by this magnanimous term. He had challenged the establishment of Ur about their pagan beliefs, and, Tzippy thought ruefully, Avraham seemed to channel Max and had priggishly broken all the idols in his father's statue shop in order to demonstrate that idols were not God. This act of faith caused a big hullaballoo in Ur. He was thus thrown into a pit of fire by the evil King Nimrod, but an angel (perhaps the very guardian angel he'd been conversing with earlier that day) stopped him from getting singed in the flames. The King was forced to let him go, and after the death of his mother, Avi left Ur with his father, his wife/half-sister/cousin, Sarah (the text was quite ambiguous about what Sarah's genetic connection to Avraham actually was—but altogether, Tzippy found the idea of marrying one's sister/cousin unwholesome), and nephew, Lot, to Padan-Aram, which was an area in modern Syria. Upon the death of his father, Avraham was called by God to journey to a distant land which was to be given to him and his descendants for perpetuity, the site of the State of Israel today, and he ultimately settled in Beersheva.

Having no issue to carry on the family name, Avraham was compelled by Sarah, who was supposedly barren as she had long passed that period in a woman's life of hot flushes and mood swings, to bed her handmaiden—a union which resulted in the birth of Ishmael, the supposed progenitor of modern Arabs. Thirteen years later, at the age of 99, Avraham was commanded by God to circumcise himself, and it was at this point that his name was changed from Avram to Avraham. Concurrently at this time, when Sarah was well into her senior years, she and Avraham miraculously conceived, and upon the birth of their son, Isaac, Sarah was stricken with jealousy over Ishmael and entreated Avraham to send Ishmael and his mother away forthwith. Avraham reluctantly agreed and obliged. The years passed by with various machinations and intrigues, and when Isaac was around thirty years old, God commanded Avraham to sacrifice Isaac in order to prove his faith. Avraham dutifully acquiesced, and he took Isaac up to the future site of the Jewish Temple, bound Isaac and placed him on an altar. Before Avraham could descend the knife into the flesh of his son, an angel appeared and halted him, explaining that God never intended a human sacrifice, since He abhorred such gestures; rather He'd just been testing Avraham. And so, in lieu of Isaac, Avraham joyously sacrificed a ram goat which had unfortunately stumbled onto the scene. This episode, known as the *Akeida*—'The Binding'—was the last of a series of tests and was the crucial pivotal point in the entire Avraham storyline, for it confirmed his role as the covenantal partner of God, whose offspring would merit the spiritual inheritance he would leave behind. Avraham died at the age of 175, and his body was interred in the Cave of Machpelah.

84

Well, interred until now.

✡

The next day, after making a pit stop to collect Tzippy from her apartment, the little group headed to Pizza Fino, a kosher restaurant on Ben Yehuda, for lunch. Max was hesitant about dining there. Though the place was officially kosher, he wasn't sure it was up to his strict, *kosher mehadrin* standards. But rather than risk a fight with Tzippy, who would invariably accuse him of being overly zealous in his Charedi pursuits, he chose to focus on the *hechsher* which hung in the restaurant's window and just eat what was put in front of him.

Avi, who had quite enjoyed the cheesy vegetarian lasagna the night before, fell head over heels in love with the pizza they'd ordered and managed to devour a large one all on his own. Tomato—and the subsequent tomato paste—had not been discovered in his time, and he was mesmerized by the taste and the way it complemented the cheese. The others took great delight in his appetite, and after Tzippy was informed of his sweet-tooth, she insisted they take him to the Max Brenner store at the Namal for a delicious ice cream dessert to top off the lunch. Avi licked at the ice cream (they had gotten him a double scoop waffle cone) happily as they strolled through the Namal on this sunny day.

Natan, who had been appraising Avi properly all through lunch, whispered to Tzippy and Max that he thought it would be fun to get Avi a stylish new haircut. The cousins gleefully agreed (although Max's initial suggestion that they tell the hairdresser not to cut Avi's sideburns had been shot down by the other two with

85

harrowing looks of disgust). Avi, blissfully unaware of the schemes to modernize his look, went into the salon and sat on the hairdresser's chair and serenely allowed her to chop, cut, wash, style, and blow-dry his hair to her heart's content. She remarked on the soft smoothness of his hair and enquired about the products he used to treat it. Tzippy yelled out, "Paul Mitchell!", Natan cried out, "ReVive!", and Max screamed, "Pantene!", before Avi could say anything. Avi ignored them all and looked at the hairdresser. "Garnier," he answered evenly (he did not lie. It was the very shampoo he had found and used in Natan's guest bathroom the night before). The new haircut suited him perfectly. He looked cool and young, but the swimmingly large clothes he wore detracted from his overall appearance. So, it was immediately and unanimously decided that an entire new collection of clothes was necessary. Max parted ways with them, and headed to purchase as much candy as he could from the Trinidad Chocolate store on Ibn Gavriol to give to Avi as a surprise gift. Natan and Tzippy stayed with Avi to act as his stylists and financiers. Avi was overwhelmed by the generosity of his new friends. He insisted that only one t-shirt, one pair of shorts and underwear was sufficient, but Tzippy shot him down immediately. "You need more than that, Avi," she said pointedly, counting on her fingers. "You'd need clothes for clubbing, for going to the beach, for going to the mall, for going to shul—because I suppose Max will want to take you there—and for God knows what else!" They zipped him in and out of Castro Men, Renuar Men—and within two hours, with one of Natan's credits cards maxed out and Tzippy's wallet emptied of cash, Avi had a complete set of clothes for every conceivable occasion, including clothing for just lounging around the house, a black leather wallet, a fedora and other various hats, two new watches and a black leather motorcycle jacket "because it's super cute," Tzippy had said. Then, before he could say no, Natan and Tzippy took him to get a pair of designer sunglasses. When Max returned and presented Avi with a big hamper of chocolates, Avi looked out at them all from behind his new Ray Ban silver aviator sunglasses and immediately burst into tears.

His three companions, caught unaware at this unexpected outburst, quickly ushered him outside.

"What's wrong?"

Avi, who had subsided into downcast sniffling at this point, pulled the sunglasses off of his eyes and looked at his new friends. "You have all been so kind to me when you didn't have to be. You've taken me in and befriended me and clothed me and sheltered me and fed me and have given me the most sumptuous gifts, and have been so terribly kind, although you know I have nothing to offer in return for your generosity." He turned his attention to Max. "And you. You who I've not treated kindly, you have gone out of your way and presented me with this delicious basket of metukah—chocolate, you call it?—you've managed to take my breath away by surprising me with such an unexpected, thoughtful gift. How could you, all of you, be so kind to me? These gifts," he gestured to the clothes he was wearing and the many, many, many bags which lined Tzippy's and Natan's arms, "what can I say? How can I possibly show you how grateful I am for this? You are both so munificent to delve into your pockets and lavish me with such considerate gifts. You were both so patient and kind to answer my questions and explain everything to me and to introduce me to wonders of this modern world. When I was previously alive, it was my highest ideal to be hospitable and to perform acts of *chesed*—loving-kindness—particularly towards strangers, and now, I see my descendants exhibiting this mitzvah in such a forceful and beautiful way. Taking me, a virtual stranger, and showering me with loving-kindness and hospitality in such copious doses. It touches my heart to know that my heritage of hospitality and loving-kindness—those two virtues which are of supreme importance—has been passed down through the generations and is something you all possess in such bounteous quantities. Thank you. Thank you, all of you."

They were all taken aback by this little speech and didn't know what to say. Spontaneously, Max rushed out and hugged Avi around his neck, which brought about a fresh wave of sobbing. "Thank you, Avi," Max said, his voice thick with emotion, "for passing on this trait of hospitality and chesed."

Natan cleared his throat. "You are our ancestor, Avi. Whatever we give to you, we give you in thanks for what you've given to us: a peoplehood that's lasted for thousands of years. Please, there is no need to thank us. We need to thank you." He reached out and squeezed Avi's hand.

"And I thank you for giving me the opportunity to be generous," Tzippy cried. "I am not always this generous—I don't always give tzedakah and I sometimes turn a blind eye to those in need. I know I should give more often, and with more graciousness. You've reminded me that there is much joy in giving, and the goodness that comes from giving is worth much more than saving up for the new iPad mini. Thank you, Avi, for re-instilling this in me."

Avi smiled a watery smile. "All this emotion." He sniffed, and then reached into the basket of chocolates. "I really need some metukah."

CHAPTER 5

*"Terah took his son Abram, his grandson Lot the son of
Haran, and his daughter-in-law Sarai, the wife of his son
Abram, and they set out together from Ur of the
Chaldeans for the land of Canaan."*
—Genesis 11:31

In his incarnation as Avraham, Avi had been
born in a city, but circumstances, fate, and his quest for
God had led him away from the ease and luxury of city
life, and out into the grasslands of the Fertile Crescent to
live the contemplative, modest and arduous life of a tent-
dweller; a man without a physical house, but one whose
home was built upon his family, his enduring faith, and
his God. There is a certain security and mental stability
which comes with city dwelling, a specific comfort
which cannot be experienced if one dons the cap of a
wandering shepherd.

City life entails mass manufacturing,
specialization, cottage industry, economies of scale and
all the benefits that these suggest. With this comes an
ease in lifestyle, a particular sense of wellbeing in
knowing that residing in the midst of a community will
inevitably facilitate easy living: the baker will bake
bread, the public transport will jettison one from point A
to point B, babysitters can easily be found to watch over
the children, neighbors can receive the mail if one goes
abroad, the bartender will hand over a fizzy mug of beer,
the streets will be cleaned, the city council will ensure
law and order, and every need and want can and will be
met through the conduit of the communal forces of
demand and supply. The harsh, lonely, singular life of
the desert-dweller encompasses none of these things, as
it is him and him alone against the world. Food must be

sourced—tilled, reared, milled, and kneaded—by one's own hands; the sword remains poised in the ever-present promise of danger—wild animals, marauding brigands, or the threat of a heated argument within the family; the tent flaps are never secure, always ready to flap away with the strong billowing of a desert storm. The life of a wanderer enjoys none of the luxuries of having a steady home; none of the security and anonymity, which is part and parcel of city-living. For the first time since he had left Ur, those many thousands of years before, Avi experienced the peculiar and comfortable sensation of feeling secure, of feeling as if he had roots, as if he had a permanent family which didn't have to be uprooted in order to pursue food, water, and resources, or to flee persecution and strife.

Tel Aviv was a beautiful, glistening, new city—a modern metropolis, and the financial, economic and cultural center of the Zionist dream. The first entirely Hebrew-speaking city of modern times, the city was full of inhabitants who carried Avraham's genes within themselves. With a Jewish demographic of over ninety percent, it amazed Avi that all around him were people who were his descendants. Spiritual descendants, genetic descendants, religious descendants—they were his family. The city itself delighted him, as it was nothing compared to any city he had seen in the past—its beautiful Bauhaus buildings, wide tree-lined avenues, glistening windows, side-walk cafes, and the salty breeze of the beach which blew all around him, but it was the bustle of the Tel Aviv citizenry which truly awed him— the bicycling hipsters, the genteel shoppers, the busy entrepreneurs, the gamboling children, the lazy beach-goers, the cell-phone users, the heavy-footed bus drivers, the hormonal teenagers, the older pedestrians, the art-lovers, the dog-walkers, the newspaper agents, the skateboarders, and the strumming musicians: every one of them a descendant of his; every one of them, a child of Avraham. Every face he passed reminded him of his wife Sarah, or his son Isaac, or his daughter-in-law Rebecca, or one of his grandsons, Esau and Jacob—every gesture, every facial expression, every laugh was hereditarily connected. Each face that passed him by was a testament to the enduring covenant God had made with him; every smile signaled God's continued providence; every laugh was a fulfillment of prophecy and hope. The Jewish neshama shone forth brightly from them all, and Avi felt his heart soar.

The three friends had intended to continue introducing their new-found ancestor to the joys of modern living after the fast-paced shopping spree, but a shrill ring of Natan's cell phone and the surreptitious, whispered conversation he held upon answering it, unfortunately put a spoke into the wheel of this plan. Natan apologized profusely, but he had to leave them to attend to some pressing matters. Tzippy looked at him queerly, but Natan, who suddenly seemed out of sorts, didn't notice her quizzical mien. He assured them he would be back later and handing Max a spare key, he insisted they continue to tour the city and return to the apartment whenever they wanted to. "*Habayit sheli, zeh habayit shelach.*" My home is your home. He bade them a polite goodbye and left Avi in the care of the Feldman cousins.

As they were all still quite full from their heavy lunch, Tzippy suggested they visit the beach and continue along the Tel Aviv Tayelet to Natan's apartment. Both boys were amenable to this suggestion and so the little group carried on.

92

The beach was alive at this time of day. People were busily enjoying their free time, playing *matkot*, splashing in the water, lounging around on beach chairs. Avi had always loved the seaside and he was happy to see the Mediterranean was as blue as it had always been. He was excited to jump into the water, but all the new clothes they'd bought that day had been stashed in the back of Natan's jeep and with Natan gone, there was no way of finding Avi a second outfit to change into. Luckily, Tzippy's large handbag held two beach towels and a bottle of sunscreen lotion, so although Avi couldn't go into the water, at least they could spend the rest of the daylight hours enjoying the sun. They stopped at Metztzim beach, spread the towels, and anointed their skin with copious amounts of the sunscreen. Avi still had his new sunglasses with him, so he put them on and enjoyed the antiglare resolution of the lenses, which allowed him to fully take in the scene without having to squint. Max, who wasn't wearing his full Charedi costume that day, but just a plain white shirt and black trousers, pulled up his trousers to his calves, peeled off his shoes and black socks and happily sunk his toes into the warm, grainy sand. Tzippy knotted her curly hair into a bun, lay on one of the towels, and promptly dropped asleep, leaving the two boys to their own devices.

The surprise basket of chocolates that Max gifted to Avi had cast Max in an entirely new light in Avi's eyes. He looked deeper than the rigidly religious exterior Max had initially presented and Avi saw there was something endearing about him. There was a kindness and concern for other people that had not been obvious from the start. Avi could tell that Max's attempt at being religious was entirely sincere—convoluted and extreme though it was. There was a definite spiritual authenticity

93

to him and a genuine desire to become spiritually stronger. He had a true love for God and while Avi had not recognized that at first, he found that as he dug deeper into Max's personality, he was finding intrinsic layers of holiness. However, Avi intuited that Max was a person who had not come into his own and had yet to truly understand who he really was. Avi suspected that Max's religiousness was a façade; but instead of using this façade to deviously mask who he really was, Avi felt that Max used his religiousness as a front because he simply had not discovered his own personality as yet. As such, Max tended to mouth the opinions of others, not because he was brainwashed—far from it—rather, because he had yet to sort life out in his mind and decide which bits were really Max and which bits could be trashed.

Now that Avi could see beyond the surface of Max's personality, he was much more comfortable with his new friend. They sat together on the second towel, each keenly aware that it was their first one-on-one interaction. They warmed to each other nicely and chatted easily and openly. Max told Avi about the time when he was young and his baby brother had been born (a jealous three-year-old Max had climbed into his mother's arms while she was nursing, only to be told, "Give me a few minutes, darling, and when I am done with your brother, you and I will have a little game, ok?" This move to seemingly put the baby first infuriated the young Max, who immediately began a year-long crusade which entailed ignoring his mother in every regard. Max blushed as he told his tale, but laughed at the silliness of his puerile days. "My mom and I laugh about it now, how I'd walk out of any room she came into, and not speak to her or look at her." Max blushed again. "I was such a punk."). Avi told Max the fantastic story of his first date with his wife, Sarah (they'd gone to a Young Mesopotamians Mixer, and when it was over and time to drop Sarah to her house, Avi's donkey had refused to pull the cart back from the city hall to their house, so they'd spent the rest of the evening pushing the cart home themselves while the donkey followed, gleefully trotting after them and heehawing at their predicament, causing the neighborhood kids to look out their windows and point and laugh. Avi had not expected a second date—but Sarah had proven to be charmed by the eccentricity of their date and graciously accepted the invitation to a second one. The rest, as they say, is Before Common Era History). They traded stories, enthralled by each other's lives, when a loud crash from the pavement behind them caused them to whip their heads around. A small boy had blown his bicycle tire and was now lying on the ground, crying. Max sprung to action and rushed to the boy's aid. Avi was concerned about the child, but didn't want to leave the very soundly sleeping Tzippy to the whims and fancies of the conscious public around her, so he stayed where he was, but observed Max handling the scene from a distance. Max helped the boy wash his grazed knee and then ran back to tell Avi that the boy was lost and he was going to assist him in finding a police-officer. Avi nodded in understanding and spent the next forty-five minutes enjoying the beach scene on his own, until his idle mind began to creep with troublesome thoughts. When Max returned, he noticed Avi's subdued mood. Given the rocky start to their relationship, Max was instantly anxious that his disappearance had caused the patriarch to turn glum.

"Is everything alright?" he asked tentatively.

Avi cleared his throat and forced a smile, giving a half nod.

Max felt more worried. "Are you sure? I shouldn't have left you on your own, should I? It's just that the boy—"

Avi cut him off. "Don't be silly—of course you had to help him. That was more important than leaving me to babysit Sleeping Beauty over here." He jerked his thumb at Tzippy, and the two boys laughed. "It's just that—" Avi hesitated. "You know, Max, I was thinking."

"What about?"

"Jews."

"Ok," Max said slowly.

"I mean, Jews are my descendants, right?"

"Yes. Why?"

"Why aren't Jews called Hebrews, then?"

Max considered. "We may not be called it as often as we were in the past, but we're still Hebrews. I think 'Hebrew' is just a more archaic way of saying 'Jew'."

"So 'Hebrew' and 'Jew' are one and the same?"

"Yes—I suppose. In a manner."

Avi raised an eyebrow. "Explain?"

"Well, yes and no. It's the same, but it's not. Jews are a subset of Hebrew. You can't be Jewish without being Hebrew, but you can be Hebrew without being Jewish."

"How do you mean?"

Max flushed, keenly aware that he was being asked to elucidate history to Avraham Aveinu, but he kept his composure and spoke evenly. "Jews are descendants of the tribe of Judah. Way back when, there used to be twelve tribes, descendants of the twelve sons of Jacob, your grandson, who was later named Israel.

96

Then—to make a long story short—ten of the tribes were exiled and subsequently lost or assimilated through the passage of time. The large tribe of Judah, the smaller one of Benjamin and the non-tribe of Levi were all that were left. Because Judah was the more numerous of the remaining tribes, the remaining Hebrews came to be identified by the tribal nomenclature of Jews. That's not to say that they stopped being Hebrews, it's just that being of the tribe of Judah—being Jews—became the more common way to refer to our people by outsiders and Jews themselves."

"I see."

"Let me put it this way, being Hebrew is my overall nationality, but being Jewish is comparable to what constituency I'm from, you know?"

"Hebrew first, Jew second?"

"No—both, equally pertinent and equally descriptive, although, admittedly, the word 'Jewish' does get bandied about more. But it doesn't mean anything."

"But what about lost tribes that are found today which aren't descendants of Judah—they aren't Jewish?"

"No," Max answered. "I mean, generally, we call them—and, more importantly, they call themselves—'lost tribes of Israel', or 'House of Israel' or 'House of Whichever-Tribe-They-Claim-Descent-From', so I suppose they identify with Israel and their particular tribe rather than being Jewish or Hebrew for that matter. But that's also the same thing: Hebrew and Israel—also interchangeable. At the end of the day, our country is called Israel: the most all-encompassing name for our people."

"Is it?"

"Yes. Jacob-Israel had twelve sons, and those twelve sons headed the twelve tribes, and despite the clearly demarcated lines between those tribes, their common denominator and most powerful linkage was through Jacob-Israel."

"So it's sort of a non-issue, then, whether one is called Hebrew or Jew or Israel; in modern terminology, they're all basically the same."

"Exactly." Max beamed. "It's a non-issue which word is used."

"But what about me, Max?" Avi said quietly, his eyes peering hotly through the darkened lenses of his sunglasses. "I'm not a Jew—"

"You're the first Jew," Max interjected before Avi had finished.

"—and I'm not one of the tribes so I'm not Israel either."

Max didn't answer.

"I'm the first Hebrew."

"The words are interchangeable," Max answered, falteringly.

"Judah was my great-grandson. How would you feel if your grandson's name suddenly became the surname of your descendants?"

Max didn't know what to say. Avi definitely had a point there.

"I'm not disputing the validity of the name 'Jew', I'm just saying if the tribes don't exist in actuality today, if the lines between Judah and Benjamin have been blurred, and if the lost tribes that are found are finding problems with being referred to as 'Jewish', then why not revert to the more universal term of 'Hebrew'?"

"But we do use the word Hebrew," Max protested. "Lots of synagogues and Jewish organizations identify with the word 'Hebrew'; there are tons of organizations with the word 'Hebrew' in their names.

There's the 'United Hebrew Congregations' and 'Hebrew Immigrant Aid Society', and there's 'Hebrew Union College'. The word Hebrew is still integral to who we are. Our language is still Hebrew. We're in the Hebrew land."

"We're in the *Jewish* land: the *Jewish* state."

"Honestly, I think they all mean the same thing. It doesn't matter anymore."

"If they're the same thing, then tell me what's represented and who is represented by those interchangeable words: Jew and Hebrew."

Max considered. "Well, what is represented is the Mosaic religion, and who is represented is the nation of Israel."

Avi smiled weakly. "There ya go."

"What?"

"Mosaic, Israel; Avraham pre-dates Jacob-Israel and Moses."

"Yes, he does, I mean, *you* do pre-date all of us as you were the first—but the Mosaic religion is the continuation and deepening of the Avrahamic religion." Max paused. "I don't mean to be presumptuous, but you know about the second covenant, right? The one God made with Moses on behalf of Israel after, well, long after you'd... you know... died?"

"What second covenant?"

"Well, the covenant you made with God was the first covenant—where He promised you the Land of Israel—Canaan—for your descendants, if they promise to circumcise their sons."

"That's basically the gist of it, yes."

Max was intrigued. "Was there more?"

"Sort of. Ethical interaction with one's fellow-man and living right in the eyes of God entailed a lot of

99

it. It wasn't very detailed, but it went unsaid as the fine-print of the covenant God made with Sarah and me."

"That was the point of the second covenant: to detail those issues that went unsaid in the covenant with you, and to present the contract to your descendants as a whole, so that they could affirm the original covenant you had made centuries before.

"It was the second step in a legal, binding process. You signed the first contract when you made your covenant with God, and later on, that contract had to be reaffirmed in greater detail by your offspring—hence the Mosaic covenant at Mt Sinai when the Torah and all the *mitzvos*—laws—were given to the Israelites. The covenant made at Mt. Sinai doesn't cancel you; it deepens and expands you."

"I understand all of that. That's no problem with me. You don't understand." Avi shook his head. "I have no petty hang-ups over Moses or Jacob or Israel or my children being called Jews."

"Then what's the problem?"

Avi sighed. "The problem is... I don't know where or how *I* fit in."

"You're the first patriarch."

"Yes, Avraham was the first patriarch. Call him Jewish, call him Israelite, call him Hebrew; slap a skirt on him and call him Isabelle, it didn't matter. He's no longer alive, but Avi is, and Avi doesn't know who he is."

Max fell into a troubled silence.

Avi spoke again. "I'm not saying that Jews should change their designation as Jews. I understand that Jewish history is a four-thousand-year long story that's still moseying along and it's not the Avi/Avraham show—many people have contributed: Moses, Jacob-

Israel, Jabotinsky, Herzl and all the rest. It's just that I don't know where I fit in to everything today. I understand my previous role, but who am I in the context of this unraveling story today? Am I anyone at all? Or am I just a blip since all I was resurrected for was to name the mashiach? Is that the sum total of my purpose here now, and thus, are my troubled questions of 'Where do I belong' a non-issue like the issue of 'Jew' or 'Hebrew'?"

"Hmm. Does the label really matter?

"Does it matter for you?"

Max nodded immediately. "I understand."

Avi shrugged. "Look, I'm not going to be here much longer anyway. I've done my part. I told Natan he was the mashiach."

"What do you mean?"

Avi chuckled bitterly. "Well, I've fulfilled what I came here to do, haven't I? God sent me to tell Natan he was the mashiach. I've done my part. Now it's time for Elijah and Moses to step in and take over. They are both post-Sinai, so they're both Jews or Israel or Hebrew or what have you—they'll fit in well."

Max hesitated, but touched Avi lightly on the shoulder. "I understand your conflict—who are you in the context of Israel today. Are you Jewish? Maybe not. Are you Hebrew? Perhaps that's the better term to describe you. But outside of all these words—which, you must remember are simply that: just words—there's one thing that is unquestionable. The neshama which resides in you is the same as the neshama which resides in any one of yours and Sarah's descendants: Jewish, Hebrew, or Israel."

Avi brightened. "You know, Max, I didn't think of that."

Max nodded sagely. "I'm very wise."

The both laughed in comradely humor. Their combined laughter roused the sleeping Tzippy, who suddenly turned and pulled herself up with a yawn. "Hey guys," she said with a smile. "Sorry I fell asleep."

"That's ok," Avi replied. "Had a good nap?"

Tzippy stretched and nodded.

"What did I miss?"

The boys looked at each other. "Not much."

Tzippy shrugged and stretched lazily.

Max rolled his eyes at her. "You could sleep anywhere," he said, teasingly. "You are such a bum."

"Mmm. Yes," Tzippy said, unphased. "And you are such an idiot to be sitting in the sun in a long-sleeved shirt and black trousers." She pulled out her compact-case and began touching up her make-up.

Avi giggled. He liked the way they bantered. They were clearly fond of each other and he felt they'd really accepted him. He turned his eyes to the blue sea and realized, suddenly, that he was thirsty. All the philosophizing in the hot sun had made him parched "Is there anywhere we can have a drink of water?" he asked.

Max pointed to the man selling drinks from a cart on the pavement. "Let's go. I can get us all bottles of water."

Avi hesitated. "Is it ok to leave you alone, Tzippy?"

Max laughed and jumped up. "She's a big girl. And we'll only be ten feet away. Come on, Heeb." He tugged at Avi.

"Heeb?" Avi asked, curiously.

"Short for Hebrew. If we've determined anything from our discussion, it's that you are, conclusively—if not a Jew and if not part of Israel—at least, most definitely, a Hebrew." He tugged more urgently.

Avi allowed himself to be pulled up with a grin. "Ok, Jew."

Tzippy looked up from her compact-case and snapped it shut. "You guys are weird," she observed. She turned away from them and began to brush her hair.

The boys laughed and went for their drinks.

✡

When they arrived at Natan's apartment an hour later, he wasn't there. Tzippy tried calling him from her cell phone, but there was no answer. The sun had already begun to set, and as they were all feeling hungry, they decided to head back out. They walked up HaYarkon and cut through Gordon Street, then continued northwards on Rechov Ben Yehuda.

Avi was excited to be out at dusk. The electric lights of the city were blazing and people ambled by casually. After the dismal thoughts which had hit him earlier on the beach, he felt happier and balanced once again. Max's sage counsel that the labels were irrelevant—rather, it was the neshama which Avi and his descendants possessed that was important—had steadied Avi and returned him to feelings of normalcy and inclusion. He felt lighter, which allowed him to enjoy the giddiness of the Tel Aviv night scene.

They stopped at a kosher mehadrin coffee shop for dinner. Tzippy ordered a salad and hot chocolate, Max opted for a sandwich and juice, and Avi requested a sandwich and an iced tea. After they'd eaten, Tzippy tried calling Natan again, but reaped the same result. Both boys commented on Natan's marked desertion, but, as both assumed Natan's disappearance had to do with Natan's business, they sympathized with their missing friend and hoped he wouldn't be too tired out from a day at the office when he did eventually return to them. Tzippy said nothing, but thoughtfully sipped her hot chocolate. Max ordered a sandwich to take back for Natan, paid the bill, and they left for the apartment once again, stopping at a *makholet* on the way to purchase some snacks and two bottles of white wine.

The waiting apartment was still empty upon their return. The boys took turns showering in their shared bathroom. Tzippy withdrew to Natan's en suite bathroom, then donned one of Natan's t-shirts and pulled on a pair of her boy-shorts she'd found in her bulging bag which, Avi remarked in amazement, seemed to contain everything under the sun.

They retreated to the rooftop terrace and opened the bags of potato chips they'd bought and pulled the corks out from the bottles of wine and sat back to enjoy a leisurely evening of friendship. Avi—who wasn't used to continuous drinking, having had wine the night before—declined the offer of wine, but ate the potato chips; the salty, vinegary crispness delighting his taste buds. Natan finally texted Tzippy's cell phone. He apologized for leaving them earlier and was running late, but said to feel free to spend the night at the apartment with the boys. Tzippy promptly texted back sassily that she was already planning to spend the night there and would be sleeping on Natan's bed; the couch was available for him, but if he'd like, he was welcome to share the bed with Tzippy. "A couch was not made for a girl to sleep on. Boys should always give girls their beds," she ended her message in a flourish. Natan responded with a clinical "LOL".

By ten o'clock, the snacks were finished and the wine fully consumed by the cousins, and Avi was yawning without stopping. It had been a long day for them all. They tidied up the strewn about plastic bags and bottles, gathered up the wine glasses and headed downstairs into the main living area. Tzippy emptied the trash, while Max washed the few glasses they'd used and Avi put them away into cupboards. With a sleepy goodnight to each other, the three retired to their separate sleeping areas. Despite her earlier bravado, Tzippy made up a bed for herself on the living room couch.

Avi lay on his bed, skimming through a battered old copy of the Tanakh he had found on the bookshelf in his bedroom. He struggled to read, for he badly wanted to and had not gotten any time since he left the desert to do so, but his eyes were closing of their own accord, so he shut the book securely, memorizing the page reached, and tucked it under his pillow. He lay still in the dark for a few minutes, in which he sleepily managed to thank God for delivering him to such wonderful friends, who were not only kind and generous, but remarkably wise. He prayed for their well-being and happiness, and that Natan would reach home soon and get some rest. He gave thanks for the day and earnestly prayed for as a good a day tomorrow as he'd experienced today. And finally, he thanked God for maintaining the covenant with his descendants. With a final 'amen', he adjusted himself into a comfortable sleeping position. Thoughts of his day lingered on his mind as he slowly shifted into unconsciousness. Before he was fully asleep, however, a few thoughts slipped serenely through his mind: *Why am I still here? Why haven't Elijah and Moses come yet? Did they get lost?*

The thoughts passed as quickly through his mind as they'd entered it, and without giving them a second notice, Avi drifted off into dream world.

Around two in the morning, Tzippy awoke when she heard the front door close with a soft thud. She opened her eyes and looked up to see a figure tiptoeing through living room. She lay still. It was Natan. She heard him whispering on his cellphone as he passed her by, but she was unable to catch what was being said. A second later, she heard his bedroom door creak open and then close with a deft click.

CHAPTER 6

"'I beg you, my friends, do not commit such a wrong.'"
—Genesis 19:7

The next day, they jumped into Natan's jeep and with Avi sitting in the front passenger seat directing the way, they managed to find the site of Natan's lost camping equipment. The foursome chatted excitedly and Avi answered Max's eager questions about the real Cave of Machpelah.

When they'd gotten to the site, which nestled cozily on a little ledge right above a valley between a range of hills, and after Natan had confirmed that the tent and the items contained therein were indeed his, they packed everything into the jeep and decided it would be nice to lull about for the day. The sun was high in the sky and while Tzippy dozed and sunbathed on a towel (which Avi was quickly realizing was Tzippy's favorite thing to do) and Natan conducted business by cellphone in the air-conditioned coolness of his jeep, Max and Avi scoured the area, trying to locate the entrance to the real Cave of Machpelah—but search high, search low, they could not find it. They looked at the bottom of hills, at the tops of hills, behind trees, under boulders, but sadly, nowhere they looked exposed the entrance of the cave. And no matter how hard Avi tried, he simply could not remember where the entrance was. After an hour of excessive searching, they concluded that the elusive Cave was divinely meant to remain hidden. Max excused himself and under a tree, with his *siddur* in hand, began *shokeling* and saying prayers, leaving Avi free to entertain himself.

With his friends sufficiently occupied, Avi decided to climb a particularly high hill in order to get a better view of the land, and after ten minutes of huffing and puffing, he reached the summit. With his new Ray Ban sunglasses on, he surveyed everything. Below him, he could plainly make out his companions, and on the other side of the hill, was, unexpectedly, a group of about thirty Asian tourists and three Israeli men. The Asians were sitting, lotus-style on the desert ground, their attention focused on one of their own who stood at their helm. The three Israelis were lounging near the tour bus, each with his own cellphone out, busy texting and not paying attention to the tourists. An Uzi hung off the shoulder of one of the Israelis. Natan had told Avi about the enormous moral support Israel received from evangelical Christians, and had explained that a large proportion of that support came from the huge, growing evangelical Christian population in Asia. Avi was sure that the Asian group represented those Christians Natan had spoken about, and that the Israelis were their tour guide, bus driver, and security dispatch respectively. He strained his ear to hear what was going on below. But being so high up, he couldn't exactly hear what was being said, although he could just make out the vague sound of singing. As he focused his eyes more intently on the group sitting peacefully on the ground, he noticed their hands were up, waving around like tree branches in a soft wind. Their leader brandished a black Bible in her hands while she, too, had her hands extended up in the air. Yes, they were most definitely Christians.

Pleased that he'd correctly ascertained the identity of the group below, Avi turned his back on them and looked to the horizon which stretched out to the north. The crisp air gave a clear view of the clean desert.

He breathed in deeply, and the sharp, sandy smell entered his nose and took him back to his life in ancient times. He closed his eyes and spent a few minutes reminiscing, then shook himself out of his stupor and brought himself back to the present. He continued to take in the view, and in the distance, he could just make out a sparkling white town on the horizon. He wondered aloud if it was the modern town of Hevron, the site of the bogus Cave of Machpelah.

Michael's voice cut into his thoughts. "You're right. That's Hevron."

Avi grinned. Since he'd joined the group of friends, Michael had kept quiet. Avi had felt Michael's presence with him constantly, but there had been no communication between them. "So, you're talking to me again?" Avi asked teasingly.

"I was giving you time to integrate into the group. It would have distracted the establishment of your friendships with these people had I been relentlessly whispering in your ear. My policy is to stay quiet and only speak when spoken to whenever you're in the company of other living people."

"I suppose that makes sense." Avi grinned again. "*Baruch HaShem*! Michael, I am so happy to be alive! The world is so beautiful and full of beautiful things and beautiful people!"

"It really is a wonderful world, is it not?"

Avi sighed and looked out at the wide expanse of pristine land which lay spread out like a blanket before him. "It is—it most definitely is. It's changed so much from when I was last alive. And yet, it's still familiar. People have come so far. I'm so proud of what they've accomplished." He smiled and then looked towards the vague shimmer which emanated next to him. "I don't understand what's going on with my mission, though, Michael."

"What do you mean?"

"I thought after I'd found the mashiach that it would be the end of my mission and God would transport us back to heaven at once. But we're still here, and the longer I stay here, the more I want to stay here. I don't remember heaven. I know it must've been infinitely wonderful to have been there, but now that I'm here, I'm not looking forward to the moment God sends for me. I don't want to die, Michael." He breathed in deeply. "I want to eat pizza. I want to discover all the advancements society has made. I want to listen to music and sing along to Hadag Nachash in concert. I want to run and feel my heart beat fast. I want to drink wine and feel the giddiness of being tipsy. I want to eat that delicious metukah—chocolate—every minute of every hour of every day. I want to live, Michael."

"You are human again, Avi. Your mind, body and soul are naturally biased towards life and living. Death and the afterlife are not innate focuses of the living soul. Man—in his natural, balanced state—wants to live; to experience; to breathe; to love; to be. It is the unstable human—whose mind, body, soul and heart are out of sync—it is he who ignores bounty the Creator has bestowed upon him with this life, and it is he who unnaturally craves death. No matter how you return to the afterlife, death will be involved, and, as a human, you naturally abhor the process of death, for it will end this period of learning and experience, so do not be surprised that you cling to life and do not wish to give up that life." Michael paused. "It is natural for you to want to stay here. As a mortal man with an intact mind, body and soul, this is the place where you belong. When the
110

Holy One, blessed be He, is ready for you, He will take you. In the meantime, He leaves you here for a purpose. Give thanks for the blessing that He has bestowed upon you."

"What is that purpose, Michael? I've done what He's asked of me. I've found the mashiach, just as He asked. So why am I still here?"

"I don't know. That is only something you can discover."

Avi felt anxious. "And when I discover the reason for me still being here, would I have to die again?"

"All who are born, die. It is the intrinsic order of this realm."

"I had the notion that He would take me up, the way He did with Elijah and Enoch."

"They, too, died, Avi. All die. It is an unbreakable law. He personally plucked Elijah and Enoch from this life, yes, but their bodies died and were left behind. They, too, experienced the process of dying and death. One cannot access the afterlife otherwise."

"I don't remember dying the first time around."

"I've never died myself," Michael said with a chuckle, "but I remember how you passed away."

"Was I in a lot of pain?"

"I don't think so. You closed your eyes and your face suddenly slackened and a peace came over your features. I then saw your spirit shed your body and ascend. It was a powerful moment."

Avi sighed. "When is He going to take me from this world, Michael?"

"That, I suspect, will happen only when you determine why you're still here considering that you've fulfilled the mission He sent you here to oblige. As for the precise time of His calling you home, I cannot tell you, for I do not know the answer."

"You don't know why I'm still here; you don't know my purpose; you don't know when I'm going to die. What's your purpose for being here, Michael?" His eyes twinkled.

Michael laughed. "To serve, to guide, and to protect you. You're a pain, but it's a job I happily perform."

Avi rolled his eyes. "You sound like a slogan for a police force."

"Michael the angelic policeman," Michael said thoughtfully. "Sounds like a great pitch for a television show."

Avi laughed. "It sure does." He paused. "Can I at least enjoy myself while I'm here, Michael? There are so many delicious things I want to indulge in."

"Of course you can enjoy yourself!" Michael exclaimed. "The earth is the Lord's and the fullness thereof. Enjoy the wonderful world your God has created. Enjoy the marvels his people have envisaged and made realities. Your previous incarnation offered you fewer options for enjoyment. You deserve a bit of happiness in this life. But be mindful of indulging too much—anything consumed in moderation is good, overindulgence is never good."

Suddenly, from the side of the hill where Avi had spotted the Asian tourists, he heard voices calling up to him. He whipped his head around and down below, the Israelis were calling out to him. The one he'd pinpointed as the security was alert and his hands were no longer busy texting on his cellphone; rather, they were securely placed on his Uzi. The entire scenario was eerily reminiscent of the moment he'd met Natan, Tzippy, and Max.

Avi smiled widely and waved his hands at the people below him.

"Don't go down there," Michael said urgently. "Go to your friends and leave this place."

Avi looked incredulously at the shimmer that was Michael. "Are you crazy? That one there has a machine gun. Do you know what such a gun could do to me? I just told you I don't want to die. I'm going there to talk to them."

"I think if you go down there, you're going to have to do a lot of lying, and I don't think lying is exactly the reason why the Creator has left you here."

Avi humphed. "Who said anything about lying? I'm not going to lie about anything. That's not my style." He looked at the people below him and waved again. "I'm going down there."

"No, Avi, don't," Michael began, but Avi was already shimmying down the side of the hill. Michael sighed and glided after Avi.

Avi had already reached the group of people by the time Michael caught up with him. The tourists had fled for the relative safety of the bus, and they peered out at the scene through the unopened windows. The three Israelis stood firm, and with the black Uzi shining menacingly in the sun, they looked at Avi coldly.

"Why were you up there on the hill?" the one with the Uzi asked pointedly in English. Avi had originally thought the guy was simply a security guard, but now that he was up close, he realized that the man with the gun was too alert to be simple security. He was clearly a plain-clothed soldier.

Avi threw his arms up unthreateningly. "I mean no harm. I was simply admiring the view. I am spending the day with my friends on the other side of these hills."

Michael whispered in his ear. "Good. Keep it simple. Cut this short and get back to your friends."

The soldier did not buy Avi's reason. "Why were you looking in the direction you were?"

Avi shrugged. "I was just admiring Hebron."

"Why?"

"Because I was looking north, and Hebron is in that general direction, so naturally I had to look at it. If that offends you, then I'm sorry."

The soldier raised an eyebrow. "Are you giving me flack?"

"Don't antagonize him, just excuse yourself and leave," Michael said.

Avi smiled wanly at the soldier. "I don't know what you mean."

The soldier looked at Avi suspiciously. "You were talking to someone. We all saw you."

From the corner of his eye, Avi could make out the tourists nodding in assent with the soldier. They'd left the bus door open and could clearly hear everything taking place outside.

"Well?" the soldier prompted.

Avi smiled benignly. "Well, what? You didn't ask me anything. You made a statement."

The soldier was persistent. "Who were you talking to?"

"Avi, don't say it," Michael warned.

"My guardian angel," Avi answered matter-of-factly, disregarding Michael's sage counsel.

Michael groaned. "Now you're in for it."

Avi's answer disturbed the Israelis. They were unsure if he was a harmless mind addled by the effects of Jerusalem Syndrome, or whether something more sinister was at play. While the soldier kept his Uzi leveled at Avi, the two other Israelis hastily spoke in whispers behind him.

"Where are you from?" the soldier asked.

Avi racked his brain. What was the name of that new country which contained his ancient city of Ur? Ah yes. "Iraq."

Michael yelped. "Are you insane? Iraq is an enemy state of Israel! They're going to think you're a spy, or worse, a terrorist! You're just digging yourself deeper and deeper into a hole!"

The tension was immediate. "How did you come to be here?" the soldier asked, his voice hardening. "Do you have any identification?"

"Identification?"

"Passport, I.D. card, driver's license."

Avi laughed. "I have none of those things."

The one Avi had identified as the tour guide brushed the soldier aside and spoke in an authoritative tone. "*Yelid*, these are dangerous times in which we live. This is not the time to mess around. Identify yourself. Who are you?"

"Is that what this is all about? All this talk of passports and driver's licenses? You just want to know who I am?" Avi straightened up and looked at the man squarely in the eyes. "Allow me to introduce myself—"

"No! Avi, don't!" Michael cried.

"—I am Avraham of old, resurrected by the grace of the one true God of Israel, here on earth once again to do His bidding."

115

Everything stood still for a moment, then the soldier fainted, and Avi was momentarily stupefied as the brilliant lights of the tourists' cameras went off from inside the bus.

CHAPTER 7

"When Abram heard that his kinsmen had been taken captive, he mustered his retainers, born into his household, numbering three hundred and eighteen, and went in pursuit as far as Dan."
—Genesis 14:14

The wind whipped strongly outside of Natan's apartment. At that moment, Avi was standing outside on the mirpeset, his hair belting around his head in the thickness of the gale. He was seemingly arguing with himself, but Natan, Tzippy, and Max knew better. Avi was arguing—most heatedly—with his guardian angel.

The drive back to Tel Aviv from the desert had been most uncomfortable. Avi had suddenly appeared out of nowhere, presumably from the other side of the hill, and had run straight for the jeep in which Natan had been sleeping soundly. Shaking him vigorously, Avi had pulled Natan out of his nap. Tzippy and Max were startled at Avi's obvious frantic state and they followed him to the jeep where they heard the vestiges of Avi's breathlessly urgent story. "We have to go," Avi said to Natan, summing up his tale. "We have to go *now*."

Natan took one look at the desperate exigency in Avi's eyes and within minutes, the four friends were bundled into the jeep and roaring out of the valley. It was not a minute too late, for as they exited the valley, in the rearview mirror, Natan saw a ragtag group of Asian tourists and three Israeli men rush into the valley on foot, their faces twisted with desperation.

No one said anything for the entire drive back. Avi had kept his eyes closed and his lips pursed, and from time to time, he grimaced in his conscious closed-eye state. When they'd arrived in Tel Aviv and had entered Natan's apartment, Avi had fled for the mirpeset and had slammed the sliding glass door behind him. The three friends looked on, staggered, as a pantomime of arguing began. They couldn't hear what Avi was saying—for Natan had securely sound proofed his apartment—but with the gesticulations and facial expressions they could plainly see, it was clear that a raging argument was taking place. After a few minutes of ogling at the spectacle playing out before them, Tzippy suggested that they move into the kitchen. The boys reluctantly agreed and they served themselves individual meals and ate silently, contemplating the fight taking place on the mirpeset.

Sometime later, as the last remnants of food disappeared from their plates, they heard the sliding glass door slam again and they heard the stomp of approaching footsteps. Avi entered the kitchen, and with a groan, collapsed onto the chair next to Natan.

They all looked at him quizzically.

"My guardian angel is mad at me," Avi said eventually.

Tzippy formulated her question carefully. "Why?"

"He thinks it was reckless of me to expose myself. He thinks I shouldn't have done it."

"So, you told those people on purpose who you were?" Max asked quietly.

Avi nodded and sighed.

"How exactly did you 'out' yourself?" Natan asked.

"They asked who I was, and I told them," Avi answered simply.

"And they believed you?"

Avi sighed. "If I identify myself as I truly am, then people will believe me. Just like you guys did."

Natan frowned. "Why is it when you identify yourself as who you truly are that people believe you?"

Avi shrugged. "That's the way God wanted it to be, I guess."

"But doesn't that contradict the rule of Free Will? Or is there no such thing as Free Will?"

Avi thought for a while and then responded. "There is Free Will. But there is also divine intervention, and, I suppose, this is a case where God has intervened to make people believe me when I tell them who I really am."

"So, He abrogated the law of Free Will?" Natan persisted.

Avi shook his head. "Free Will means you have the right to choose between right and wrong. The issue of believing me, in believing that I am Avraham of ancient times, blah blah blah, that does not infringe upon a person's Free Will."

"Yes, it does!" Natan said, heatedly. "Free Will also suggests that one has a right to believe what one wants to believe."

"Yes, that's true," Avi responded. "But the fact of the matter is, believing I am Avraham does not compromise your Free Will since it doesn't stop you from your beliefs."

"Yes, it does!" Natan repeated.

"How?"

"Because I should have the choice to believe your claim or reject it!" Natan exploded. "I should not be forced to believe you are who you say you are!"

Avi paused. "I understand what you're saying," he said slowly. "Perhaps I phrased this all wrong.

Consider this: what keeps us anchored to the ground and keeps us from flying into outer space?"

"Gravity?"

"Exactly. We all know gravity exists. It's a fact of life. Likewise, I am Avraham of old, come back to life. That, too, is a fact of life. Hence, God has seen it fit to make you believe me when I tell you who I am."

Natan guffawed. "Well, in that case, He should just make it fit to make belief in His existence a fact of life and intrinsic to the human condition, just like gravity is and belief in your existence apparently also is."

"Should He?"

"He might as well."

Avi sighed. "Natan, you believe I am Avraham because you've met me. You believe gravity exists because you experience it on a constant basis. You don't believe God exists because you haven't opened up yourself to the possibility of His existence."

Max interjected. "So, you're saying we believe in gravity—and we believe in you—because we've experienced both first-hand?"

Avi beamed. "Precisely! Your Free Will is not compromised in either of these instances. As for belief in God, if you've not experienced Him, you can't be expected to automatically believe in Him. *That* would be infringing on your right to Free Will."

Natan groaned. "Nothing you're saying makes sense."

Avi felt a schism of annoyance rip through him. "Well, I don't know how else to explain it," he snapped. "I've just had a huge fight with my guardian angel, and now you're goading me to have one with you? Fine! Don't believe I am Avraham! I don't care! Don't believe in God; I double don't care!" He shoved himself off of the kitchen chair and stormed off to the guest bedroom.

They sat quietly for a few seconds and Tzippy opened her mouth to comment, but before any words could escape her lips, Natan stood up angrily. "Save it, Tzippy," he said. "I don't want to hear your opinion on this."

Tzippy threw up her hands in surrender. "Fine," she said. "I won't say anything."

"*Tov*." Natan grabbed his keys and left the apartment.

The cousins looked at each other. "And then there were two," Max said.

Tzippy rolled her eyes. "I'm glad to know your time in the yeshiva hasn't impaired your ability to subtract." She stood up. "Come on. Let's go check on Avi."

They walked down the corridor to Avi's bedroom. Tzippy knocked lightly on the door. "Avi?"

"Come in," he answered.

He was sitting on the bed. The anger on his face was completely gone. He smiled sadly. "When it rains, it pours, huh?"

Tzippy eased herself next to him.

Max stood awkwardly and adjusted his kipa.

"What exactly happened with those tourists?" Tzippy asked.

"I told them who I was and their reaction was immediate," Avi replied. "They all believed me without question. The Christian tourists rushed out of their tour bus and began crying and praising God and kneeling in front of me and asking me to bless them. The Israelis thought that since I was their literal ancestor, their primary mission shifted from protecting the tourists to protecting me. The two groups began arguing, and in the pandemonium, I turned and ran back to you guys."

"Ok," Tzippy said slowly. "And why is your guardian angel mad at you?"

Avi sighed. "He is upset that I let other people know who I am. He says it is counterproductive to my mission. I told him that my mission was simply to inform the mashiach who he was, and since I've located and informed the mashiach that he is mashiach, I don't think I'm bound by any rules regarding the mission. The mission is completed."

Tzippy put a protective arm around her ancestor. "Was there any stipulation in the mission which said you can't reveal yourself to people?"

Avi shook his head vigorously. "No. God never said I had to hide who I was. My guardian angel is just being difficult."

Tzippy squeezed him tighter in her embrace and said nothing. Max, however, nervously piped up. "But was it necessary to tell those people who you were? I mean, wasn't that a little... vain?" He blushed deeply.

Avi looked up at him oddly. "What do you mean?"

Max coughed. "It just seems—given what you told us about what happened with the tourists—that telling them you were Avraham was a little unnecessary. And there seemed to be a little pompousness on your part in telling them. You could have just said you were out camping with your friends and then left. I know you said the security guard had a gun and everything, but you could have talked your way out of it without giving yourself way. I think you wanted to tell them." Max squinted his eyes and braced himself, expecting Avi to yell the way he'd done with Natan.

Avi surprisingly remained calm. After a moment's pause, he lowered his gaze. "It's true. I was being vain. I wanted them to know who I was. My guardian angel was right and you are right. I was being a vain, egotistical idiot."

"You're not a vain, egotistical idiot!" Tzippy quickly retorted.

"He *was* being a vain, egotistical idiot," Max said firmly, feeling confident. Then, to Avi. "Why?"

Avi continued to look down. "I don't know. It's just the human condition, I guess, to want acceptance and veneration. I knew it was stupid when I did it. I knew it, but I wanted them to know; I just wanted some recognition. In this world, I'm nobody. I've nothing behind my name. Yeah, yeah, Avraham of ancient times did a hell of a lot, but Avi of this life? He's nobody."

Tzippy patted him on the back. "That's ok, Avi. It's ok to be human."

Max rolled his eyes at Tzippy. *Suck up*, he mouthed at her.

Tzippy pursed her lips.

Max continued on with Avi. "What's going to happen now that those people know who you are?"

Avi shrugged. "I don't know. That's what has my guardian angel so worked up. He has no control over what the repercussions of my foolishness will be, and he said that this was not something he'd been prepared for." Avi looked around miserably. "He's not even here anymore. He's gone."

"He's abandoned you?" Tzippy asked, surprised. "Can a guardian angel do that?"

Avi sniffed. "I don't know. I guess? Mine has done it."

Max ignored the piteous track the conversation had taken and redirected it to the issues at hand. "So, what about you and Natan?"

"Is he very angry with me? I didn't mean to yell at him and storm out the way I did."

Max folded his arms. "I don't think he was angry with you. I think he was angry because what you said violated his fundamental beliefs. I agree with what you said and I understood the tack you were taking. But I don't think Natan was able to understand your argument, and so, he felt threatened. And whenever someone's beliefs are being injected with doubt—well, they tend to lash out. I don't think it had anything to do with you."

Avi shook himself. "I messed up. I messed up big time. My selfish desire for recognition led to my guardian angel being angry with me, and now, the mashiach as well. See what happens with acting upon one little flaw? Who'd think that being vain would cause so many problems?" He stood. "Well, there's only one person who can fix all of this: me. Where's Natan? I want to apologize to him."

✡

They found Natan right outside the building, sitting in his jeep and smoking one of his L&M cigarettes. Avi shyly apologized for blowing up and explained that he wasn't sure how the belief that he was Avraham and Free Will concurred with each other—"I had just been hypothesizing"—but he was pretty certain that there was no contradiction between the two, although there was the enormous possibility that he could be wrong and that Free Will didn't exist at all. Natan did not comment, but he accepted Avi's apology quietly. Avi smiled unsurely, and Natan flicked his cigarette and they all walked uneasily back into the building and up the elevator into Natan's apartment.

Once inside, and relieved that everyone was, if not best buddies again, at least on speaking terms, Tzippy suggested they go out that night. They didn't have anything planned for the next morning, so they could sleep in late. "Besides," Tzippy said, "it's Thursday night. What are Thursday nights in Israel for if not for going out? And Avi has all those new clothes to wear. It will be a waste if he never gets to see the Tel Aviv night scene." Max, who was still very much Charedi, was reluctant to go out, but when he saw how excited Avi was at the thought of going dancing, he submitted and agreed to go. Natan, too, was hesitant about going out that night given the tumultuous events of the day, but he did not voice his disinclination and went to his room to get ready. By nine, the boys were ready and they cabbed to Tzippy's apartment, where she quickly slipped into a simple black dress, and then they made their way to Allenby and Rothschild, where they grabbed a quick bite, before walking down to the Billy Jean dance bar. It was an odd group. Natan, who was still subdued, ambled pensively; Max, who was still dressed in his familiar Charedi get up of white shirt, black suit, and wide brimmed hat, felt ill at ease with the thought of going clubbing, and was mostly quiet; Avi, who was looking forward to the night but was well-aware that things between him and Natan were not fully restored, chatted exuberantly with everyone, hoping to cut the tension he felt with Natan, and also wishing to infect Max with excitement; Tzippy, who also picked up on Natan's sullen mood and Max's discomfort, giggled

125

nervously at Avi and wondered if she'd made a mistake in insisting they go clubbing that night.

It was an undeniably unhappy group which stood in front of the ultra-exclusive Abraxsas club a half hour later.

Natan knew the bouncer who stood at the front, and a quick meander through the crowd positioned them at the front of the line. Pleasantries were exchanged, and after Natan assured the bouncer that Max was indeed part of his entourage (the bouncer looked Max up and down sneeringly in his ultra-Orthodox ensemble, causing Max to turn beet red and almost volunteer to leave so that the others could get in), they were inside.

The bar was surprisingly well-populated. It was only eleven thirty, and in Israel, clubs never really got going until well past midnight, but there was a concert in progress. A Trinidadian singer named Hillary Sargeant, crooning sultry soul lyrics with her band behind her, stood on stage, and this, no doubt was the reason for the full colonization of the club. Avi, enthralled by the fast beats of the live band, hypnotically found himself directly in front of the stage where he swayed to the music and mesmerizing performance of the lead singer. Max followed Avi and stood awkwardly next to him, while Natan and Tzippy went to the bar.

While they waited for the drinks to arrive, Tzippy timidly touched Natan on his arm. He looked down at her and she pulled him close.

"Are you still mad at Avi?" she asked in his ear, above the loudness of the music.

Natan shook his head and bent towards her ear. "No," he said. "I am not mad at him. But our little spat has made things weird."

Tzippy nodded. "I know. The whole group dynamic is off because of that fight. Please try to not be weird with him. He feels awful about everything."

The bartender placed their drinks before them. Natan gestured to the beverages. "There's nothing like alcohol to make everyone get along, *nachon*?" Right? He winked.

Tzippy smiled widely, hopeful that everything would soon be back to normal. She gathered up her drink and Max's, while Natan held his and Avi's drinks, and together they traversed the crowd to reach their companions. Natan grinned at Avi and handed him his drink, which caused a ripple of warmth to spread through the latter.

Tzippy held up her drink. "To the best night ever!" she toasted. The three boys grinned and they all drank deeply.

Hillary Sargeant wrapped her show up within ten minutes. Since the friends had arrived late, they'd missed the bulk of it and Avi was sorry to see the enigmatic singer leave the stage. But by then, they'd all finished their drinks, and so, they headed back to the bar to refresh themselves. In his life as Avraham, alcoholic choices had been limited to wine and beer. The well-stocked bar which stood before Avi presented a whole new world of possibilities and Avi was raring to try something new. He deliberated, and then settled on Tzippy's suggestion and ordered a vodka and cranberry juice. Tzippy decided to surprise them, and in addition to buying the cocktails, she ordered them shots of arak. With a quick l'chaim, they downed their shots. Avi loved the shot, and Max, who had originally come into the club with every intention of staying sober, was quick to buy them another round of the licorice-sweet shots. Avi wiped his mouth and pulled his new friends into a group hug and loudly thanked them for being so good to him and entreated them to promise that they would never fight again.

The music, which had been subdued following the exit of Hillary Sargeant, now began to pick up in intensity as the DJ began spinning faster tracks. Avi brightened, and with the alcohol coursing through his system, he took his glass from and shuffled backwards to dance. Tzippy and Natan went to the outdoor area to have a smoke, and when they returned, they found an exuberant Avi and equally jovial Max surrounded by a group of young, twenty-something year olds, chatting and dancing away. Tzippy clapped her hands happily. She'd wanted Avi to enjoy himself and here he was, most definitely doing so in copious amounts.

Avi was indeed having a ball of a time. He'd never experienced anything like this in either of his incarnations. The darkened lights, the fast tempo of the music, the rush of the heat-inducing drinks, the laughter and movements that the music brought out in his body: it was singularly the most exhilarating experience of his reincarnated life. He moved rhythmically, impressing his co-clubbers. One particular group of girls was so enchanted by him, they pulled him away from his friends and bought him a shot. He protested, "I am poor! I can't return the favor," which the girls thought was hilarious and they assured him it was perfectly fine, and for the rest of the night, whenever they procured themselves shots, Avi was at their side, downing the drinks like a pro.

Avi was particularly enjoying the anonymity which came with being Avi. True, earlier that day he had been keen to expose his true persona, but as simply Avi, he was not treated any differently from the average Tomer, Gilad, or Harry who stood all around him. He danced madly, letting the pulsating music move him. Nicki Minaj's *Pound the alarm* blasted out of the speakers, and Avi lost himself completely in the music. He threw his hands up into the air in rapturous abandon. He quickly picked up the words of the song and was singing along in no time. With his eyes closed tightly, and the music washing over him, Avi thought happily to himself, *I don't ever want this night to end.*

Unfortunately, all good things must come to an end, and this night was no exception. Just as Avi had had his joyful thought, he felt someone tugging on his arm. He stopped dancing and opened his eyes, sweat trickling down his face, to see an obviously drunk Natan with a group of people behind him, looking at Avi expectantly.

"This is my famous friend!" Natan bellowed.

Caught unaware, Avi looked at Natan dumbfounded.

Natan grinned drunkenly at Avi. "I've told these people you're someone famous. They think you are an actor, or a singer, or probably even a porn star," Natan slurred with a giggle. "Imagine the looks on their faces when they realize who you are!"

Avi, unable to speak, just stared at the crowd stupidly.

"Come on, tell them who you are. Who you really are," Natan prodded.

Avi pursed his lips.

"Please?" Natan entreated. Avi didn't answer. Natan pressed himself close to Avi's ear. "If you don't tell them, I'm going to look like a fool." Natan looked pained. "Please?" he slurred.

Avi scanned the people who'd followed Natan to hear Avi identify himself. He spotted the girls he'd been doing shots with all night among them. They were snickering, ready to burst out laughing, both at Avi and at Natan. Avi didn't know what to do. Tzippy and Max were nowhere around, and Nicki Minaj was still pounding the alarm over the loudspeakers. He felt like a freak show, being put on stage to entertain the masses, but then he looked at Natan, whose face was silently imploring Avi to out himself. Remembering all Natan had done for him since they'd met, the least Avi could do to return all kindnesses Natan had bestowed upon him was to confirm his story. Plus, given the fight they'd had earlier, Avi didn't want to cross Natan again. So, with an audible sigh, Avi looked out at the crowd and said: "I am Avraham of old, resurrected by the grace of the one true God of Israel, here on earth once again to do His bidding."

CHAPTER 8

*"And He said, 'Take your son, your favored one,
Isaac, whom you love, and go to the land of Moriah..."*
—Genesis 22:2

Rabbi Eliezer Goldenberg, former Ashkenazi Chief Rabbi of Israel, sat quietly in his office in Har Nof, Jerusalem, and sipped his tea slowly. He drummed his fingers on the desk and cast his eyes once again over the file which lay spread out before him. The file in question was the student profile of a particularly captivating yeshiva bocher who learnt at *haMerkaz shel Emet*—The Center of Truth—Rabbi Eliezer's alma mater. He had initially been studying the profiles of four principal talmidim, but the week before, he'd listened in on a speech given by another student (one who hadn't been on his original list) and he'd been blown away. The original four files were returned in exchange for this one specific student, and since then, he'd studied and re-studied the particulars of the boy and realized that this boy could perhaps be the one he'd been seeking for the past ten years.

It was only nine in the morning, but Rabbi Eliezer had already showered, gone to *shul,* and wrapped tefillin and prayed, studied from the Shulchan Aruch, Pirkei Avot and Talmud, logged in a chapter of the new book he was writing which addressed the issue of separation of the sexes—both inside the synagogue and in general life, and now retired to his office where he filled out the paperwork which sat in the inbox tray on his desk. Indeed, he was a man who'd absorbed the concept of time management (though he'd never heard of it before) and applied it liberally in his own life.

At ninety years of age, Rabbi Eliezer had lived a full and exciting life. He'd been born in Germany into a well-respected Charedi family. With the rapid rise of Hitler and the conversion of his home country into a bastion of the deepest anti-Semitic hatred, he'd fled with his parents and siblings to Palestine. A prodigy from his earliest years, Rabbi Eliezer was debating Torah with the greatest minds in the Orthodox Jewish world in Jerusalem at the ripe age of twelve. He followed in his father's footsteps and received his semicha when he was fifteen, a month before the outbreak of World War 2. Although he'd escaped the Holocaust itself, the effects of it reached across the sea and pierced his heart. He wept when the news of what was happening in Germany reached his ears, and, though he was only eighteen, as part of a delegation of rabbis, he had journeyed to New York to raise funds from Diaspora Jewry to bring refugees fleeing Nazism to their ancestral homeland. Although he had never officially joined any of the competing underground Jewish liberation movements which were in operation at the time, Rabbi Eliezer had contacts inside of them all, and with the money he collected, he assisted those groups in their efforts to rescue thousands of persecuted Jews. Six years later, on May 14, 1948, Rabbi Eliezer listened to the powerful address of David Ben Gurion to the national council on the radio: "By virtue of the national and historical right of the Jewish people and of the Resolution of the General Assembly of the United Nations, we hereby proclaim the establishment of the Jewish State in Palestine to be called, Israel". Immediately, Rabbi Eliezer ingrained himself into the politics of the new country, and at the age of thirty, he succeeded his father as *Rosh* of the yeshiva his father had founded. Young, energetic, knowledgeable, and wildly popular, Rabbi Eliezer was viewed as the changing face of Jewish Orthodoxy. He seemingly continued the work of the great compassionate Zionist Ashkenazi rabbi, Rav Avraham Kook, and he pushed for enormous reforms in the Charedi population. By 1959, he had risen to the position of Chief Rabbi of Tel Aviv, the youngest rabbi to ever achieve this post, before or since. He was profiled in numerous Jewish periodicals and hailed for his progressive, tolerant and Zionist views. However, Zionist though he may have appeared to the public, Rabbi Eliezer could never truly support a secular state. Ben Gurion's original proclamation of the "national and historical right of the Jewish people" to a state of their own had irked Rabbi Eliezer, since it made no mention of the *religious* right of the Jewish people to their historic homeland. He privately yearned for a time when a religious theocracy could be established in Israel. With the ascension of Golda Meir as prime minister of the country, Rabbi Eliezer issued a scathing press release, announcing that it was religiously incompatible for a woman to lead, and thus exposed his true intentions and ruined his reputation as a defender of progressive, tolerant values. The public outcry was at once instant and thunderous, and the disgraced rabbi capitulated to the pressure and resigned from his post. Defeated but undeterred, he returned home to Jerusalem where he vowed to never again mask his true feelings, and instead, to be upfront about his beliefs, regardless of the repercussions which may result. He resumed his position as Rosh of the yeshiva, and by the time he was sixty, despite his established intolerant views, he had risen through the ranks again and was confirmed as the new Chief Ashkenazi Rabbi of Israel, a position which wielded enormous power and a position which he changed indelibly to ensure that only equally intolerant rabbis would successively hold it. His ascent to power was due largely to the exploding Charedi population—he was highly respected by them, and, at the same time, was abhorred by the much larger secular segment of Israeli society. In the quiet war between Charedim and hilonim, Rabbi Eliezer was the general of the religious camp. He won many a political and judicial battle against formidable opponents who sought to oust him from power, and in so doing, he further consolidated his position and robustly imposed his worldview onto mainstream Israeli society, and Judaism as a whole. When he left the post of Chief Rabbi, he became the spiritual adviser to a powerful religious political party, a position which carried no official title, but held all the real power of the party.

Rabbi Eliezer, who still fervently prayed every day for the coming of the mashiach and hoped dearly for the development of a religious theocracy, realized that he did not have much time left: he was getting old. Since the mashiach tarried, he realized he needed to formulate a plan to ensure his beliefs were carried forward undiluted. True, he'd pushed for legislation in the Knesset which legalized some of his archaic beliefs, and true, he had an army of rabbis which emulated him and shared many of his opinions, but he wanted more than that. He wanted a protégé whom he could mold and pass his legacy on to; someone to rule after he was gone. He wanted an heir.

He'd always remained heavily involved in haMerkaz shel Emet which had offered him sanctuary after his expulsion from Tel Aviv's religious circuit, and, during his tenure as Rosh Yeshiva, he'd restructured the curriculum to reflect the Judaic worldview he held. The boys who enrolled were inculcated with Rabbi Eliezer's dogmatic thinking, and were turned out into the world thinking that the beliefs they so passionately believed in were their own. For the past decade, Rabbi Eliezer had been patiently scanning the boys, eagerly looking for a suitable candidate he could adopt to carry on his fight for the advancement of true Judaism. Thus far, none had managed to capture his attention. His own children had been sore disappointments. His two sons were mediocre rabbis. One served as a chaplain in the IDF and the other as an assistant rabbi in a small shul in Bnei Brak; both showing a real compunction towards power. Rabbi Eliezer's three daughters were women, and therefore, unable to halachically contribute to the fabric of Judaism, but he knew he could use them to gain a possible successor to his legacy. After careful and selective scheming, Rabbi Eliezer had ensured that all of his daughters had married into prominent rabbinic families, but thus far, each of his sons-in-law were equally as middling as his sons, and, as such, unworthy of being taken under his wing. So, Rabbi Eliezer shifted his search to encompass an area much larger than his woefully disappointing family: he would find the one to carry on his legacy from among the student body at haMerkaz shel Emet. But ten years had passed by, and though in that time he had occasionally felt his interest pique in a particular talmid, he was inevitably always forced to give up on the boy for many varied reasons. But finally—*finally*—Rabbi Eliezer found a boy who seemed to fulfill all the traits he desperately sought in a potential candidate. Presently, the yeshiva was in the midst of a thorough fumigation, and, as such, the talmidim were enjoying an unexpected break, but they

135

were scheduled to return by the end of the week. The moment the boy was back, Rabbi Eliezer had issued a command to be immediately notified so he could travel to the yeshiva to interview the boy and confirm in his mind the possibility of anointing the boy as his protégé.

He cast his eyes once again on the boy's file and read the name emblazoned on the front: Max Feldman.

✡

Jerusalem was nothing like Tel Aviv. Avi had thoroughly enjoyed the heady, secular brilliance of Tel Aviv, but he absolutely adored the tranquil, old world feel of the ancient city. True, he had yet to meet Mea Shearim or Givat Shaul—two of the city's less beautiful neighborhoods—but the little he'd seen of Jerusalem that day had truly made him fall madly in love with the ancient capital.

The little group had arrived in Jerusalem late that Friday morning, and though Max hyperventilated about the incoming Shabbat, they had stopped on the picturesque Emek Rafaim. Max bought some *challot* and a bottle of wine, Tzippy went into a plant shop and bought a big bouquet of flowers, and Natan entered the quaint supermarket, Super Mosheva, and came out with ten bags full of groceries.

Avi loved the tree-lined, European feel of Emek Rafaim, with its little boutique shops and bohemian art stores and English-speaking residents. He'd been alive for five days already, and in that time, he'd not heard as much English spoken as he did in the fifteen minutes he'd been strolling this street. While Max, Tzippy, and Natan did their personal shopping, Avi sat on a little bench, licked at a double scoop chocolate ice-cream cone and happily observed the passersby bustle to get their shopping done before the Shabbat began. They ducked into stores, and held on to their full, bursting shopping bags, and from time to time, stopped to chat with other pedestrians they knew before they bade each other farewell with a merry "Shabbat shalom!" and carried on with their business. He could somewhat ascertain who was religious and who was not, simply by the way they dressed, and more so by the level of haste with which they walked. But religious and non-religious alike, they all hurried by him and paid no attention to THE young man sitting on the bench, licking an ice-cream cone.

Within half an hour, Avi's friends were all assembled next to him, and together they walked up the street. They stopped at Caffit, a sandwich and coffee shop, and sat at a table on the pavement and had their lunch there. They then walked back to the jeep, which Natan had parked on Rechov Cremieux, and bundling themselves and their purchases in, they headed out to Derech Beit Lechem, and then across the busy Derech Hevron, and into Arnona, where Natan's Saba had recently moved into a high-rise apartment. It was the first time the cousins and Avi would be meeting the rabbi-grandfather, and Saba proved to be equally as kind, gracious, and amiable as his grandson. He greeted them all warmly, and hugged Natan tightly to himself. Natan hugged back, then pulled away, and started packing away the groceries he'd bought on Emek Rafaim. Saba smiled widely and said to no one in particular, "See how my wonderful grandson takes care of me? He is too kind." Max passed the challot and wine to the old man, and was thanked profusely. Tzippy handed Saba the bouquet of flowers, being careful not to touch him, for

137

she was sure he was *shomer negiah*. Saba, without any regard for Orthodox Jewish laws of propriety, clasped Tzippy's hand and shook it warmly. "When my wife was alive, my home was filled with flowers for Shabbat. Now that she's gone, and I can hardly make it to my bathroom from my bedroom, much less to the shops, flowers are something which don't appear in my home very often. I thank you for this, dear child." Faint tears appeared around his eyes, but the old man blinked them back and, with his walking stick in hand, showed the guests around his small, but well-furnished apartment. He then led them out to the balcony which faced north and gave sweeping views of the new city of West Jerusalem to the west, the Old City to the north and the rolling Judean desert to the east. Bidding them to sit, he brought out a large teapot of nana tea and handed cups around and poured for them all. Max enquired about Shabbat preparations and volunteered his assistance to set up for the holy day, but Saba shook his head and assured them that everything had already been arranged thanks to the live-in nurse who looked after him. "Please," Saba implored, "just relax and enjoy yourselves. Shabbat will be here soon. Let us decompress from the rigors of the week and grace our minds with joyful thoughts for when Shabbat arrives." They all sat on the balcony and chatted, enjoying the views which the high altitude of the apartment offered them. Avi felt content and happy, and as he sipped the nana tea, he almost felt as if the previous night had not happened.

Almost, but not quite.

✡

As had happened when he'd first met Natan, Tzippy, and Max—and then, subsequently, with the Christian-Asian tourists and their Israeli chaperones—when Avi announced who he was to the club at large, the collective belief was immediate and intense. Despite the pounding noise of the music, his voice had travelled and no less than thirty persons had heard him. They all generally knew Avraham of biblical fame—his life, his exploits, his story. After all, Avraham was the reason they existed: he was the first Hebrew, the first Jew and their direct spiritual and genetic ancestor. Recognizing Avraham in Avi took no time for them to adjust to. Unlike the Christians, the Israelis in the club were not religious, and they were all intoxicated to varying degrees, and, as such, their reactions to his news didn't carry the same level of reverence. That's not to say they took the revelation negatively; on the contrary, they embraced him, but in a more affable, familial manner. And so, the Avi who had been the belle of the ball a few moments earlier was suddenly catapulted even further into a higher popularity. He was an instant companionable celebrity. Soon, the original thirty persons who had heard Avi reveal his true identity had grown to include the entire club, even though Avi had not repeated the revealing statement to any others besides the original thirty who had heard him. Baffled by this, Avi called upon Michael to explain the phenomena, but there was no answer. Michael was still gone.

Everyone wanted to shake Avi's hand; buy him a drink; take pictures with him; hug him; know him. He felt the crowd press onto him adoringly, and he felt nauseous. The adulation was too much. He wanted desperately to leave, but his guardian angel had seemingly abandoned him. He felt closed in by the crowd and his head was reeling from the effects of the alcohol, which, by now, was no longer a pleasant feeling. He knew he had really had far too much to drink. His last thought before he heaved all over the floor (and onto some of his new fans who stood directly in front of him) was, *Michael said I should enjoy everything in moderation. Why didn't I listen to him?*

As he expelled the contents of his whirring stomach, those nearest to him instinctively backed away. It was at that moment, with vomit still spilling out of his mouth, he felt someone grab him and pull him through the crowd and out onto the pavement. He looked around, dazed, and realized it was Natan.

"Run!" Natan commanded, and though Avi desperately wanted to do so, he felt too woozy to control his legs in any coherent manner. Natan lifted him and sped down the street, where a cab was waiting for them at the curb. Max was sitting in the front passenger seat next to the cab driver, and Tzippy in the backseat. Natan yanked open the back door, flung Avi inside, jumped in, and yelled "Go!" to the driver. Without bothering for an explanation, the cab driver slammed his foot onto the accelerator and the car lurched forward and screeched down the street. When they arrived at Natan's apartment, Tzippy flung some shekel notes at the driver and with Natan and Max supporting Avi, they half-carried, half-dragged him up the stairs. Avi managed to make it to the bathroom where over the toilet bowl, he threw up twice in the space of twenty minutes. Feeling less intoxicated, but still physically distraught, Avi rinsed out his mouth, crawled into bed, and sunk into an immediate sleep.

The next morning, Avi, though suffering from a most painful hangover, remembered the events of the previous evening with stark clarity. He pulled himself out of bed and made his way to the kitchen. Tzippy, who had not drunk a lot, was busy making breakfast. He sat at the table and buried his head in his hands.

"I feel like I am on the verge of death," he whispered.

Tzippy set a glass of milk in front of him. "You're just hung over. Drink this. You'll feel better."

Avi gulped the milk down and then Tzippy handed him a plate of scrambled eggs, bread, and a fresh salad of cherry tomatoes. Avi suddenly found himself hungry and quickly cleared the plate, which was followed by a course of water and two Advil's.

"It's going to take about twenty minutes before the Advil starts to really make you feel better," Tzippy said, and she sat across from him. "But you will feel better."

Avi nodded. "I am never drinking ever again."

Tzippy laughed. "I've made that vow countless times. The trick is to figure out what your limit is and don't go over it." She paused. "We should've been taking better care of you. We just let you go wild last night."

"I should've known not to overdo it. I'm a big boy. I take responsibility for my own stupidity. Plus, my guardian angel had cautioned me to enjoy the world in moderation. I ignored that advice last night."

Tzippy patted his hand from across the table. "You live, you learn. That's what life is about."

Natan and Max entered the room, both also hung over, but not nearly as far gone as Avi. Immediately, Natan strode over to Avi and pled for forgiveness. "I don't know what the hell I was thinking," he said, summarizing. "I really don't."

Max snorted from behind. "You outted Avi, but funny, you didn't out yourself."

Natan whipped around. "What's that supposed to mean?" he asked quickly, his voice terse.

"You told everyone Avi was Avraham, but you forgot to say that you were the moshiach. Convenient, much?"

Natan visibly relaxed. "I didn't tell people I'm the supposed mashiach because I don't feel like the mashiach."

Tzippy, who had said nothing since the two boys had come into the room, interjected, "Fine, but why out Avi?"

"I don't know," Natan replied miserably. "I was being stupid, and I guess, deep down, I was still angry with Avi."

"So, telling an entire club that Avi is Avraham was your way of getting back at him?" Tzippy retorted angrily.

"I didn't tell them he was Avraham. I merely said he was someone famous. And I certainly didn't tell the whole club! I just told a few people!"

Tzippy sucked her teeth. "Yes, but you forced Avi to say he was Avraham, knowing full well what the result of that would be."

"And I'm sorry for that—"

Tzippy cut him off. She stood up and glared at Natan. "Sorry isn't going to cut it, Natan! His guardian angel was pissed that he told the tourists in the desert yesterday, and not ten hours later, you force him to repeat that mistake!" She flung her hand out and pointed to Avi. "He is the one who is going to suffer for this. His guardian angel clearly wants him to reveal himself on a need-to-know basis and the only people who need to know are standing in this room." She paused. "And I don't even know if Max and I are two too many. Avi came for you, Natan. And you have royally screwed him over."

Avi put his hand up. "Stop, Tzippy. Stop," he said hoarsely. "Look, there's no sense in us fighting or trying to make sense of last night. It was pure, unadulterated stupidity on all our parts to have had so much to drink that we didn't know what the hell we were doing." He turned to Natan. "I don't hold anything against you, chaver. We are fine, ok?"

Natan smiled weakly and nodded. "Beseder."

Avi looked around at the group as a whole. "There's something else which is bothering me."

They looked back at him expectantly.

"Last night, when Natan asked me to say I am Avraham, the people who heard me say it could not have been more than thirty—forty. What confuses is me is how the entire club came to know—and much more than know, *believe*—that I am Avraham. Isn't that odd?"

Tzippy looked confused. "Why is that odd?"

"Because," Avi replied, "only the people I tell—those who hear it directly from me—are supposed to believe me."

"Are you sure about that?" a voice whispered in Avi's ear.

Avi sprang up from the table, his hangover briefly suspended as the adrenaline of excitement coursed through his body. "You're back!"

Tzippy, Natan, and Max were momentarily alarmed at this unexpected outburst, but quickly regained themselves when they realized that Avi must have been addressing his guardian angel. They were unsure about whether to give the two privacy, or

143

whether to stay. Avi seemed so engrossed in his guardian angel. They didn't want to eavesdrop, but, at the same time, they didn't want to interrupt the reunion by excusing themselves. Feeling horrendously uncomfortable, they all stayed where they were and tried to look inconspicuous.

"I have returned, yes," Michael answered grimly.

"Can you ever forgive me?"

Michael sighed. "You did a foolish thing yesterday, Avraham. And you refused to admit it."

"I admit it," Avi said, quickly. "I was stupid, I was wrong, I was vain."

"It is good that you have come to realize that."

"I am sorry, Michael."

"You are forgiven. But recollect, Avraham. You are not simply Avi of this time period. You must remember, you are also Avraham of ancient times. You are the product of two lifetimes and two sets of experiences; one life has been lived already and lessons have already been learnt. You are not Avi. You are not Avraham. You are both of these personalities. The Avi of today needs not relearn the problems which inevitably accompany the issue of being prideful, for the Avraham of old has already overcome his ego. Draw upon what you already know to be true. Be the fullest you that you are."

Avi nodded. He was not a twenty-year-old boy—he was a unique combination of a twenty-year-old boy and a one-hundred-and-twenty-seven-year-old man resurrected to life. It was a surreal position to be in, but he needed to remember who he really was and not simply get lost in the here and now.

Michael spoke again: "Tell me what transpired last night."

Avi spoke at length, describing every detail of the previous evening. Tzippy, Max, and Natan found themselves drawn in to the tale, for Avi's abilities at story-telling were quite good. Michael said nothing and it was only when Avi had exhausted his story that he spoke.

"It seems that you started to have a domino effect, Avraham. When you reveal your true personality to an individual, you unwittingly also convey your authority upon that person and, as a result, if that person tells another person about you, the second person will believe you are Avraham, even though they did not hear it directly from your mouth." Michael paused. "And, it seems, to go even further, that if the second person tells another, belief in you as Avraham will also be carried on. If the original source of information was you, then, presumably, the possibilities are endless."

Avi blanched.

"I suspected that this would happen, which is why I counseled you to keep quiet about who you truly are. If the club goers from last night, or the tourists from yesterday, begin to tell others about you, and then those others tell more, then—suffice it to say—in a relatively short space of time, everyone will know Avraham has returned."

Avi's mind was boggled. He quickly relayed the information to his friends.

Natan, who felt responsible for the situation, suggested they go to Jerusalem. "We can spend Shabbat with my Saba," he said. "That way, we can lay low for a while. If we stay in Tel Aviv, we might run into any number of the people who were at the club last night, and Avi could be recognized, and that may cause a mob scene again."

Max, who had intended to return to Jerusalem anyway for the Shabbat, readily agreed. Tzippy was apprehensive. She knew Natan's Saba was an Orthodox rabbi, and she wasn't keen on staying over at a rabbi's house for a night. But she knew Natan's logic made sense, and so she agreed to accompany them. They were in this together; it was one for all and all for one.

✡

Natan's Saba had provided a vast spread for the Shabbat evening meal, and after Natan, Max, and Avi had returned from Shabbat service at the Sephardi shul on Rechov Shimzon in Baka (Saba was too frail to make the ten minute trek to shul, and instead, had stayed at home with Tzippy and kindly instructed her on candle lighting—a unique custom which Jewish women were privileged to practice. Tzippy had never lighted Shabbat candles before and she found the ritual comforting and strangely familiar. She imagined her female ancestors indulging in the practice and it made her feel more connected to her Jewishness), they made *kiddush*, said the blessing over the *challah*, washed, and tucked into the meal. Max had been surviving on a particularly bland diet at his Ashkenazi yeshiva, and he welcomed the spiciness of the Middle Eastern cuisine which Saba had provided. They ate and laughed, and altogether, enjoyed the Shabbat evening, which proved to be a beautiful distraction from the problems which they'd left behind in Tel Aviv.

Saba was particularly happy to have Natan visiting, and he was equally as pleased to have his home full of young people. He joined in on the easy teasing and gentle banter and was quickly absorbed into the group. By nine o' clock, the Shabbat timers around the apartment began to do their job, and lights automatically went off, while air conditioning units in the three bedrooms magically turned on. Saba had prepared the two spare bedrooms for his guests: in the second bedroom, which also served as his study, he had laid out three foldable cots for the boys; Tzippy was given the third, smaller bedroom for her own use. Saba bade them goodnight, and with his live-in nurse attending to him, ambled off. Given the excitable night they'd experienced the day before, the four friends did not mind the early bedtime which had been thrust upon them, and after a quick wash, Natan, Max, and Tzippy fell asleep soundly.

CHAPTER 9

*"And King Melchizedek of Salem brought out
bread and wine; he was a priest of God Most High. He
blessed him, saying, 'Blessed be Abram of God Most
High, Creator of heaven and earth. And blessed be God
Most High, Who has delivered your foes into your
hand."*
—Genesis 14:18-20

Avi—who'd been drunker than any of his friends
the night before—should have been equally, if not more,
sleepy, but try as he may, he could not fall asleep. His
mind kept whirring with various thoughts. The thought of
his fight with Natan; the thought of his fight with
Michael; the thought of the mess he'd made of
everything with the tourists, and then the people in the
club—all in the short space of one day. It all sprung from
one core issue: the fact that he was still on earth. He had
accomplished his mission; he had found the mashiach.
Why was he still alive? Shouldn't he have been
catapulted back to heaven by now? Where were Elijah
and Moses? Why hadn't they come yet?

Avi was troubled.

Had he misidentified the mashiach? In the time
he had gotten to know his three new friends, Avi was
even surer now that he'd made the right choice. Max
had not come into his own as a person; Tzippy was
much too young and limited in her development; so
Natan was, comparatively speaking, the best choice for
the mashiach. He *had* to be the mashiach. So why was
Avi still on earth? Added to this turmoil in Avi's mind
was his confusion about the concept of the mashiach as
a whole. There had been no hint of a coming mashiach
when he'd last traversed the earth, so the concept was
148

entirely new to him. His only understanding of it had come from his crash course on Natan's laptop, and his understanding of the concept was hazy at best.

Why is the mashiach so important?

He fleetingly thought of discussing his troubled thoughts with Michael, but he felt that Michael would not be amenable to conversing about the mashiach given the process Avi went through which had chosen Natan for the job. Avi sighed and closed his eyes, but to no avail. He tossed and turned for an hour. He tried to pray, but he simply couldn't settle his mind. He continued to mull over his worrying thoughts, until finally, exasperated at his inability to fall asleep, he tiptoed out of the room and went into the kitchen to have a glass of water.

The kitchen was dark, save for the faint light of the blinking timer on the microwave. He'd read up on the laws of Shabbat following his exit from the cave, and he did not wish to violate the laws, one of which expressly forbid the manipulation of electricity on the holy day itself. So, grasping around like a blind man, he searched the cupboards quietly until his hand affixed itself around something which felt reasonably vessel-like: it was a mug. Satisfied with his discovery, he took it across to the sink and filled it with water from the tap. He downed the refreshing water and then re-filled the mug and proceeded to tiptoe back to the bedroom. As he passed by the darkened living room, he realized the glass doors which led to the balcony were open. He went over to the door, intending to close it, when he heard a voice call out to him from outside. "Can't sleep, Avi?"

Avi poked his head outside. Saba was sitting on the chaise-lounge, snuggled under a thick blanket, with two big pillows propping up his head. "Saba!" Avi exclaimed. "Why are you out here by yourself?"

Saba chuckled. "You'd think my life would be easier now that I am old, but no. Insomnia has found its way into my life."

"Are you ok?" Avi asked, concerned.

"Baruch HaShem. It is a blessing to be awake. Some people my age can't do anything but sleep." Saba points heavenward. "He keeps me awake, and it is a blessing, for it gives me the opportunity to commune with Him. The nights are especially good for prayer. The world is silent, and all that exists is a man and His God." Saba patted his siddur which was tucked securely next to him. "When I can sleep, I sleep, when I can't, I pray. It is good to pray. It is good to talk to God." He looked up at Avi, his watery eyes large in the luminescence of the reflected lights of the city.

Avi thought back to his own old age. He remembered that he had also suffered from acute insomnia. He smiled softly at Saba. "Would you like company?"

"I would love company, *todah rabah*." Thank you. "Sit a spell."

Avi ventured out onto the balcony and sat on a chair next to Saba.

"You are enjoying the Shabbat?"

Avi nodded. "I am, very much. Thank you. Thank you for having us."

"It has been my pleasure. I love when my grandson visits; he so rarely does now that he has his own business. And it is such a delight to meet his friends."

Avi smiled. He gestured to the many books which lay scattered on the table.

"Do you read much?"

"Oh, yes!"

"Only Jewish religious books?"

"Good grief, no! I read widely. Nothing is too taboo for me to read. I particularly enjoyed *Running of the bride* by Rachel Eddy." Saba chuckled. "That was a particularly funny read."

Avi was taken aback. "Aren't you Orthodox?"

"Yes."

"But aren't you supposed to only read religious Jewish texts?"

Saba waved his hand dismissively. "Only a fool will limit himself in such a way. I am indeed Orthodox, but sadly, there are a growing number of religious Jews who believe such nonsense, particularly among the Charedim. Ironically, the Vilna Gaon, who many of the Charedim revere, argued forcibly that Judaism needs to be supplemented by a broad, secular education. I am Sephardi, as you can plainly see, and I follow the writings of the great medieval Sephardi rabbi, Moshe ben Maimon, and he also spoke of this. In fact, he was a physician, in addition to being the foremost authority on all things Jewish. Judaism, in its truest form, is not a limiting religion. It promotes open-mindedness; it actively encourages the exploration of the secular world."

"So, true Judaism is not exclusive to the Charedim? The way Max speaks, it seems as if the black hats hold the franchise on authentic Judaism."

"Dear me, not at all! Judaism is not a dogmatic religion, and anyone who tries to make it that will be lost in the pages of time. Judaism is dynamic and changing." Saba paused. "How familiar are you with Judaism?"

Avi considered. "I suppose you can say I am theoretically acquainted with modern Judaism. I know there are different streams: Orthodox or Charedi, Conservative and Reform."

"You are right, but theory is never the same as reality. Those are the main headings, but inside of each type of Judaism, there are even more subheadings. Take Orthodox Judaism for instance, there are the Charedim, like Max, who wear black suits and rush about to deny everyone else the possibilities of thinking outside of the box and instead attempt to infringe their beliefs on others. And the black suits they wear—ha! They would tell you that Moshe Rabbeinu stood on top of Mount Sinai and received the Torah wearing such an outfit. Can you believe it? The Charedim are but a small section of Judaism. In fact, Orthodox Judaism, as a whole, is the minority in the Jewish world. I, myself, am Orthodox. The correct term for my stream of Orthodoxy in Israel would be *dati leumi*—religiously nationalist, or *kipot serugot*, which refers to the knitted kipah," he pointed to his head, "which I wear to identify myself as dati leumi. But in a broader sense, my stream of Judaic thinking is referred to as modern Orthodoxy in the Western World. We believe that the Torah given to us is unchanging and authored exclusively by God Himself—hence, Orthodox—but at the same time, we believe that Judaism should embrace the secular world and promote good for everyone, not just Jews alone, while not compromising our Orthodox beliefs—hence, modern. We do not shut ourselves away in ghettoes of our own making. We embrace the world as far as we can without violating Torah mitzvoth. And so, this is who I am: a modern Orthodox Jew. But at the same time, modern Orthodox Jews are also staunchly Zionist and we support

152

the State of Israel as it is, because we believe in democratic values and principles. Hence, the nationalist aspect of modern Orthodoxy. Further, I am Sephardi; that is to say, my Jewish culture came from Spain. My ancestors were interred during the past two thousand years of Jewish dispersal and Diaspora Spain and then, in the lands of the Middle East, and, as such, my culture and the *minhag*, tradition, I adhere to is dissimilar to the larger Ashkenazi, or Jewish-European culture which dominates Judaism today.

"Then there are the streams of Conservative and Reform Judaism; and these two, separately, and combined, form the bulk of world Jewry today. To deny them or ignore them—as the Charedim do—causes deep schisms in the Jewish world. I believe that every Jew, as free men, is privileged to choose the Judaism we believe in. To me, a Reform Jew is equally a Jew as much as an atheist Jew is a Jew, and as much I am, or Max is a Jew. Judaism is not a totalitarian religion, and like I said before, it is not dogmatic. Everyone contributes to the fabric of the religion—everyone has his or her role to play. We are all parts of a composite whole. The great Rabbi Avraham haKook, *zikhrono livrakha*, was Orthodox, and when the Conservative movement wished to come into Israel, he welcomed them with open arms. 'Who I cannot reach, you can,' is what he said to them. Jewishness can be expressed in numerous different ways, and Jews must be aware of embracing each other. Diversity is the spice of life, is it not?

"At the same time, it is impossible to know who a person is or what he believes simply by knowing which stream of Judaism he identifies with. For instance, as an Orthodox rabbi, modern Orthodox though I may be, it is not acceptable for interaction between the sexes.

Yet, I see no problem with shaking a woman's hand or even hugging her. The point I'm trying to make is this: you may think you know who someone is based on a stereotype, but that's hardly ever the case."

Avi nodded. "You are right. It is easy to misjudge a person based on how he dresses, or by the company he keeps, or by the groups he is affiliated with, but we are hardly ever right in our assumptions. Even with historical figures, I'm sure that we have misconceptions of them."

Saba looked at Avi intently. "Indeed."

Avi looked out at the view from the balcony, to the lights of the Old City which shined in the close distance. "Saba?"

"Yes?"

"There is an issue which troubles me, and, in fact, it is this issue which keeps me from sleeping tonight, for it weighs on my mind. But I haven't been able to talk to anyone about it because I don't think any of the people I've met are knowledgeable enough to explain it to me, that is, until I met you."

"I am not the smartest man in the world, Avi, but if it's a topic that I have some knowledge about, I'll be happy to share that knowledge with you. Feel free to talk to me about anything," Saba laughed, "although, I have been talking non-stop for the past half hour."

Avi smiled and patted the old man's hand. He recognized the loneliness that plagued the old man's life. "You are much too modest, and I like listening to you expound Judaism." He paused. "What's all this fuss about the mashiach? I don't understand it. It seems to be such a momentous issue in terms of the Abrahamic religions, particularly Judaism. Why all the hullaballoo, and what is the mashiach supposed to be exactly?"

154

"You tread on a very mystical topic, Avi. In summary, the idea of the mashiach in the purely Judaic sense resonates for our people the idea of mankind's redemption, the completion of the Jewish mission and the ultimate fulfillment of God's promise to our forefathers, Avraham, Isaac, and Jacob. The concept of the mashiach contains at its very core the ideology of hope; hope not just for us, but hope for the entire world. At the same time, no other idea we have conceptualized has caused our people more suffering, heartache, and destruction than this concept of the mashiach. It is a topic that will take much time to elucidate upon."

Avi grinned and arranged himself comfortably in his chair. "The night is young and neither of us can sleep. Elucidate away, Saba."

"As you wish—but I warn you, my sermon will be lengthy as this topic needs much explanation to be fully understood."

"I am eager to understand. Please, proceed."

"The word mashiach itself simply means 'anointed' and it has been used to describe numerous things throughout the history of our people; everything from the *Beit haMikdash*—the Holy Temple, to objects used in the rituals of the Beit haMikdash cult, to people themselves. To be mashiach means to be anointed by God, not in the kingly sense that medieval monarchs used it, but rather, in the sense that that an object or a person—the Beit haMikdash or even the Jewish nation— was consecrated by God for His holy purpose. The Tanakh describes the whole of Israel as being mashiach. It depicts King David as being mashiach, and it describes the non-Jewish Persian king, Cyrus the Great, in a similar manner. Mashiach was not a term limited to Jews, nor was it considered in the messianic capacity that we regard it today.

"To understand how the modern concept of the mashiach as deliverer came about, one must be familiar with the wide scope of Jewish history to understand why and how this theory was formulated and why and how it evolved into what it is today, and one must also understand what the Jewish mission in this world is. To ignore either of these things will give one a limited and unbalanced understanding of the contemporary concept of the mashiach.

"Prior to the first exile, Judaism was a religion limited in its worldview and content to exist within its own limiting realities. When compared with other religious pathways which abounded at that time, Judaism was indeed morally and ethically superior, yet it was a mere shadow of the religion it is today. Judaism was first centered on the *Mishkan*—the Holy Tabernacle—and, later on, centered on the Beit haMikdash, which was built by King Solomon. The Beit haMikdash is famed for the sacrificial cult which existed within its walls, but what is less known is that the Beit haMikdash was not merely the building; it was a compound. Sitting on this compound, adjacent to the Beit haMikdash itself, was the seat of what can be considered in modern terms as the Jewish supreme court: the Sanhedrin, which had been established by Moshe Rabbeinu hundreds of years earlier as an assembly of seventy elders of the people of Israel to preside over all judicial matters. This body was independent from the priestly caste which ruled the Beit haMikdash, and analogously, it was autonomous from the political rulers of the country. The Sanhedrin served an even greater purpose than simply being a judicial court. It conferred official authority on the prophets, the priests, and the political rulers of the land. You see, Avi, the members of the Sanhedrin were not a capriciously collected group of random old men; no, they were the democratically nominated representatives of the people. And so, with a cohesive system of state, judiciary, and religion in place, Judaism—from a theocratic and religious standpoint—having seemingly achieved all that it had set out to achieve, remained constant and unchanging. There was a dominant view that Judaism could not be conquered. How could it, when it was seemingly so complete? How could it be usurped by anything else, given that the fulfillment of the promises at Sinai were now manifest? While there were challenges which the Jewish people faced from time to time, those challenges were readily defeated because, in the eyes of the people, God was on their side; after all, He had given them everything He'd promised them. He had anchored them in the land He had promised to their forefathers; He had established the Beit haMikdash for them; He had ordained them to be His chosen people; He had sent them prophets to keep them in check; He had helped them defeat their enemies. What else was needed? They had it all. And so, Judaism, unchallenged as it was, remained stagnant.

"But then, something remarkable happened, something no Jew believed possible: Israel was defeated, seemingly beyond repair. Ten tribes were taken away and lost, while the remaining tribes were ejected from the land of Israel and taken away into captivity to Babylon, the land which had conquered them. The seemingly eternal Beit haMikdash was destroyed; the Aron haBrit—the Ark of the Covenant—was lost in the pages of time, never to be recovered; and Jerusalem, the city where the God of Israel had promised to make His

157

great Name known to all the earth, was razed to the ground. All seemed lost. To the people who lived then, it was as if the covenant which had been made at Sinai had been nullified and the nation of Israel would cease to exist. It was as if God Himself had turned His back on His people. But, oftentimes we can only perceive the divine purpose of tragedy in hindsight; and it is only today that we can truly appreciate the wisdom that was behind the first exile. The covenant had not been nullified; rather, it was reaffirmed in exile. God did not turn His back on Israel; rather, Israel now reached out to Him with more desire than they'd ever done before. The exile acted as a catalyst for Judaism to change into the dynamic religion it is today, and correspondingly conceive and advance the mashiach concept of deliverance. Civilizations advance when there is tumult. People are forced to find hope when all they can see is despair—and thus, with the tragedy of the exile, our ancestors were forced to adapt, forced to expand their worldview, and forced to hope. Judaism matured in exile; it expanded from the constriction of the Beit haMikdash cult into the universalism of the synagogue era. Judaism became a world religion, and it was finally understood that our God was not limited to the land of Israel. He was the God of the entire world. That is not to say we lost our connection to the land. Not in the slightest, my friend. For whilst Judaism may be practiced anywhere in the world, Judaism can only be fully experienced in *Eretz Yisrael*—the land of Israel. And so, in exile, our ancestors always longed for their homeland, and it was this hope of a return to the Eretz Yisrael that facilitated the seeds for the concept of messianic deliverance to be planted.

"For seventy years, the exiles languished in Babylon, until the conquering Persian army, under King Cyrus the Great, took control. Through a mixture of Cyrus' own policy and the bargaining of the political maverick, Nehemiah, the Jews were allowed to return to Zion where the Beit haMikdash was rebuilt a second time, the Sanhedrin was restored, and Torah rule and study was strictly enforced under the guidance of Nehemiah and later, Ezra the Scribe. The returned community flourished. What you must understand is that Nehemiah and Ezra together brought about the return to Israel, the rebuilding of Jerusalem and the Beit haMikdash, and the observance of Torah law—three key concepts of redemption which later would become attached to the job description of the mashiach—and the combination of these two personalities were, in all likelihood, viewed by the Jews of the time as echoes of the Mosaic past: together, Nehemiah and Ezra were the present deliverers of the House of Israel; forerunners of the final mashiach.

"Although those who returned to the land lived somewhat independently under Cyrus' decree, free to live in accordance with Torah law and be Jewish, they were still beholden to a foreign empire: a satrap of a non-Jewish power. Eventually, their Persian rulers were replaced by Alexander the Great, who was, upon his death, succeeded by the Greek Seleucids. While persecution in the anti-Semitic sense was not really something they experienced under the Persians and Alexander the Great, it became a real problem with the ascension of the Seleucids as their overlords. They viewed our Jewish mitzvoth and *minhagim* as barbaric, and in order to promote their Hellenistic worldview, the Seleucids pillaged the Beit haMikdash and outlawed

159

circumcision, Shabbat observance, and the keeping of kashrut. The Jews of Israel at the time cried out for deliverance—much in the way they'd cried out to God for deliverance many times in their ancient past. They hoped once again for a man to rise up among them who would lead them to this deliverance, where Jews would be free to practice Judaism without interference from foreign powers—a man like the great Moshe Rabbeinu of olden days, or men like Nehemiah and Ezra of their recent past—to lead them out from spiritual and political captivity, and into freedom.

"It was thus that the concept of the mashiach as we know it today was being prepared. It was not exactly as precise a concept as it is understood today, but a rudimentary form of the theory was there, in that the Jews yearned for deliverance, and in yearning, yearned for a man to rise up and lead them to this longed-for deliverance. They'd experienced this throughout their history: periods of strife and persecution where the God of their forefathers lifted men up to lead *Clal Yisrael*—the Congregation of Israel—to freedom. First it was Moshe, followed by Joshua, then it was the various judges, then it was King David and all the prophets, and finally, Nehemiah and Ezra. Let's be clear, though, the deliverance they prayed for in this particular period was purely for religious freedom from tyrannical oppressors. Each period of Jewish history in which Jews experienced persecution called for a different sort of freedom: national freedom, religious freedom, spiritual freedom, political freedom, societal freedom, and so on. And in each period, there arose a man to free them from whatever specific problem it was that afflicted them. And, just as in the past, now when Jewish religious freedom was being threatened by the Seleucids, a man did arise to liberate Israel: Judah the Maccabee, a man of the tribe of Levi and a descendant of Moshe's brother Aaron. Together with his sons, Maccabee sparked a revolution which expelled the Seleucids from the land, and for the first time in hundreds of years, Israel was a free, self-governing land once again; free to be religiously Jewish.

"However, there were three key differences in this post-Seleucid period of deliverance from Jewish deliverance in pre-exilic times which directly contributed to the evolution of the mashiach concept.

"Firstly, world Jewry was no longer limited to the land of Israel, although Cyrus had allowed the Jews to return to their promised land, not all Jews did. Many Jews had stayed behind in Babylon and established communities there. Many other Jews travelled to other metropolises of that era and settled there. No longer was world Jewry concentrated in the land of Israel; Jews voluntarily chose to live outside of their promised land. The Diaspora Era had officially begun, and this era stretches out even unto our own times.

"The second difference was that, with advent of the Diaspora and the subsequent culture of synagogues which arose, Judaism became strongly entrenched in the mitzvah of education. *Yeshivot*—Jewish schools—were established everywhere in the Diaspora, and also throughout the length and breadth of the land of Israel. Jews everywhere had access to the Torah and the emerging Talmudic literature. For the first time in Jewish history, Jews were accessing their holy Scriptures and studying it in a way that had never been done before. They were critically analyzing Torah, and finding things they'd never seen before. The books of their prophets were being re-read and re-evaluated, and the message of

161

the prophets—that God sought the sincerity of a man's heart rather than empty sacrificial rituals—were finally being understood and applied. The power of the re-built Beit haMikdash cult began to wane as the synagogue started to emerge as the place where Judaism as a world religion could be best expressed and promoted.

"The final difference was that, upon freeing themselves from Seleucid oppression, for the first time since the pre-exilic period, there was a ruling family of Israel. The familial successors of Maccabee, the Hasmoneans, established a dynasty which combined both the kingly and priestly roles. This was a dangerous double violation of Torah dictates. Jewish law expressly forbids the combination of religious and political leadership; the King was in charge of economic, political, and defensive matters, and the high priest was in charge of religious affairs. Neither was greater than the other; both were equally accountable to the other and to the populace. Now, for the first time in Jewish history, despotism from a Jewish monarch had arrived. There was no separation of Beit haMikdash and state, and thus, corruption abounded. Secondly, although as descendants of Aaron the Hasmoneans did have legitimate claim to the position of high priests, they had absolutely no claim to the kingly role. That position had been, for perpetuity, given to David and his descendants, through his son, Solomon.

"These three factors: the establishment of the Diaspora, the implementation of universal education among Jews, and the illegitimate, un-halachic rule of the Hasmoneans, came together to advance the mashiach concept even further and it is here that the concept of the mashiach as we understand it today began to fully take shape.

"The Diaspora represented a voluntary rejection of living in the land of Israel. Although the Diaspora did, and still does, serve a great purpose—at the end of the day, Jews cannot be fully Jewish anywhere but in the land of Israel. It is only in a Jewish society that Jewishness can be fully expressed, and it is only in the land of Israel that Jews can 'plug' into their fullest potential as Jews. Jewish mystics have ascribed the end of the era of Jewish prophecy to one thing: the fact that, since the time of the first exile, the bulk of world Jewry has lived outside of the land of Israel. Even today, with the establishment of the State of Israel, the majority of the world's Jews are citizens of other countries. Regarding the mashiach concept, it was at this point that Jewish scholars began to hope for a return of all Jews to the land of Israel, as it had been prior to the first exile. Correspondingly, Jews have never forgotten the disappearance of the ten tribes: the famous 'lost tribes of Israel', and there existed an equal hope that these lost brothers would surface and return to Clal Yisrael someday. The emerging hope for the reconstitution of Israel—through the return of the lost tribes and the ingathering of the Diaspora—became entrenched in the mashiach concept, as it became seen as part of the final redemption of Israel.

"Universal education, as I mentioned before, meant that the Torah was being studied in a more in-depth way, and by the bulk of Jews. This resulted in the emergence of Jewish mysticism and a strong interest in the prophecies contained in the entire Tanakh. With the sojourn in the Diaspora, Jews were, for the first time, exposed to other religious and other spiritual ideas. The Persians were followers of the Zoroastrian religion, which placed a huge emphasis on apocalyptic, end-of-times teachings. Jews became interested in this subject, and began searching their own Scriptures for references to this time. It's said that when you look for something, you'll find it, and Jews found what they were looking for. The end-of-times cited in the Hebrew Scriptures spoke about a messianic age, which would be heralded in by a person who would be anointed by God: a final mashiach.

"The Hasmonean dynasty which illegitimately ruled Israel sat in the seat of power for one-hundred-and-three years until they were usurped by the infamous King Herod. Although the populace may not have loved the Hasmoneans, and were generally aware that their rule flew in the face of halacha, they were even less enthused about Herod. Herod's family was of Idumean and not of Jewish descent. Herod's family had been forcibly converted three generations earlier when religious fanaticism ran rampant in Israel right after the revolution of the Maccabees. This was the only time in Jewish history when, through the order of the Hasmoneans, Jews forcibly converted any group of people, and, the resulting irony is that the very people the Hasmoneans forcibly converted later usurped their position, ordered the killing of the entire Hasmonean family, and sat upon the throne of Israel. Whatever murmurings there were about the Hasmonean rule were now intensified with the rule of Herod. Yet, if they thought Herod was bad, things would later devolve even further. Eventually, the Herodian line itself was eradicated within two generations, and Rome had seized total power and now ruled Israel. The era of Jewish independence was officially over. The Sanhedrin which had survived the first destruction of the Beit haMikdash now lingered on for a few hundred years, but by 400CE, it ceased to exist.

164

The populace longed for a return to legitimate and halachically-appropriate rule; that is, rule by a descendant of David, through the line of David's son, Solomon. And this was to be a crucial element of who the longed-for mashiach would be. As the future ruler of Israel, he must have a legitimate claim to that role. He must be a descendant of David.

"And, thereupon we come to the final conclusion of the Judaic understanding of who the mashiach would be; we can now put together all the historic pieces of the puzzle. Overall, the mashiach will be a man responsible for the redemption of Israel; a man who will free Israel from the pressures which it faces, and, in so doing, he will facilitate the fulfillment of the promise that God had made to our patriarchs many, many moons ago.

"The redemption of Israel was now understood to have unambiguous components, and these components became attached to the mashiach criteria and his mission. Specifically, there are seven criteria which are associated with the mashiach. Should he fail in fulfilling any of these, he will invalidate his claim to being the mashiach. These criteria are not time-sensitive and can happen in any order.

"Firstly, the mashiach must be Jewish; because the mashiach in Judaic understanding will be primarily responsible for the redemption of the Jewish people, and, thus, can only do so if he, himself, were Jewish. Secondly, he must be descended from King David, through his son, King Solomon—the only legitimate lineage for Israel's throne. Thirdly, he will be personally responsible for the collective return of world Jewry to Israel. Fourth, he will locate and return the lost ten tribes to their rightful place among the Jews. These fourth and

165

fifth criterions would together reinstate the period of prophecy among the Jewish people, for it is only when the majority of Israel lives within the boundaries of Eretz Yisrael that prophecy among the Jewish people would begin anew. Fifth, he will re-establish Jewish independence in the land of Israel and be directly responsible for the rebuilding of Jerusalem. Sixth, as was established by Moshe, the mashiach will re-establish religious courts of justice in the land by reassembling the Sanhedrin, and thus, Jews would once again live under a halachically-appropriate model of governance. It should be noted that it is the Sanhedrin which would declare the authenticity of the mashiach. In a way, it is somewhat akin to the chicken and the egg. The mashiach will reconvene the Sanhedrin, but at the same time, only the Sanhedrin can confer official authority upon him.

"Now, to understand the seventh criterion set for the mashiach, one needs to dive once more into history to understand how this final factor became attached to the mashiach concept. Under Roman rule, Jewish aspirations for independence reached its zenith. Jews rebelled and the result was that the second Beit haMikdash was destroyed and Jerusalem was, once again, razed to the ground by a foreign power. Rome forbade the entrance of Jews into their holy city, and for a painful two thousand years, the repercussions of this act by the ancient Romans reverberated in the Jewish world. By the time the second Beit haMikdash was destroyed by the Romans, the concept of mashiach had roughly taken shape as we know it to be. However, the seventh and final criterion had yet to be established. It was only when the destruction of the Beit haMikdash and Jerusalem became the final lament of the Jewish people that they recognized that the mashiach, when he arrived, in addition to other criterion he would have to achieve, would also have to facilitate the rebuilding of Jerusalem and the Beit haMikdash. The mashiach could not come at a time when there was a Beit haMikdash, because he would have to be the builder of the Beit haMikdash, much in the same way King Solomon had been.

"And there we have it. All seven criteria set out and combined to give us the modern concept of whom, how, what, and why the mashiach will be.

"Now, Avi, you must understand, all these criteria were not disparately formulated. They were all rooted in Scripture, and they were all prophesied to happen in connection with the mashiach's role. However, you must concurrently realize that the understanding of the mashiach did not happen all at once. Each tragedy the Jewish people faced opened their eyes to a different understanding of the Scriptures and allowed them to see deeper into the prophecies God had made through their prophets about the promised mashiach. There were times in the Jewish past where God had sent heroes to free them of oppression and persecution and indignities, but the mashiach would bring about ultimate freedom, not just national freedom, or spiritual freedom, or religious freedom, or political freedom, or freedom from prejudice and hate; no, he would bring about freedom of all these things and so much more. He is the collective Jewish ideal of the ultimate hero: the mashiach would be Moshe and Joshua, Samuel and Deborah, King David and Sampson, Ezra and Nehemiah, Judah the Maccabee and Theodore Herzl all rolled into one, and at the same time, he would be so much more.

"However, you must also bear in mind that with every painful step over the centuries and millennia which led to our formulation of the mashiach concept, the remembrance of God was always strongly connected to this concept. The two are inextricably linked. The mashiach cannot be considered outside the context of God. Each of the seven criteria is rooted in God's plan for the Jewish people. The mashiach will be God's instrument to bring about the perfection of the Jewish people and the fulfillment of their purpose.

"Which brings us to the question: what is the Jewish purpose? I've explained to you the historical context of the mashiach, but I must now explain to you the theological and philosophical factors behind the mashiach concept, and to do so, I must clarify the Jewish mission in this life, for the mashiach's purpose runs parallel with the purpose of the Jewish people as a whole. The purpose of the mashiach is to bring the House of Israel together and help them complete their mission. I understand that we will now enter the waters of spirituality, mysticism and the divine—areas into which the modern, secular Jew would rather not wade— but to ignore this aspect of the concept would render it merely an anthropological and sociological theory, and I assure you, Avi, the mashiach is more than a means to trace the evolution of Jewish thought over the passage of time.

"To fully expound to you the ultimate purpose of the Jewish people, I must take you back to the very beginning: to Creation itself, as it was described in the Torah.

"The Hebrew Bible speaks about Creation in a very symbolic manner. The Creation story describes the universe and all that is contained therein being created by an all-powerful, omniscient Creator in six days. Then, on the seventh day, the Torah says, "He rested", that is, much more than simply resting, God stopped working. He stopped instigating the Creation process. He halted. Why did He do this? Why did He stop creating?

"Numbers play a significant role in Judaic teaching, and the number seven itself has a particularly divine connotation. The number seven speaks of completion, of perfection, yet, the Torah says God stopped the Creation process right before the seventh day. In fact, He completely pulls out of Creation when He created man.

"Shabbat is a weekly reminder of the Creation story. As God rested, so, too, did He command the Jewish people to observe the Shabbat. However, we are not told to simply rest; Shabbat is celebrated beyond that: it observed in *remembrance* of Creation. Why? Why would He want Jews—*specifically* Jews, because Shabbat is a Jew-specific commandment—to remember Creation on such a regular basis?

"And it is here we find the first of two clues which explain the Jewish mission and explain the Jewish story as a whole. The Creation story and the subsequent weekly reminder of the Creation story in the form of Shabbat direct us to what the Jewish mission is. But before we sift the lesson out of Creation and Shabbat, let us find the second clue. To do so, we must digress a little further in time to the covenant God made with the Jewish people at Mount Sinai.

"Like the Creation story, the recollection of the Sinaitic experience, as testified in the Torah, is replete with symbolic meaning. To summarize the story as simply as possible: at Mount Sinai, the God of the universe plucked these recently rescued, downtrodden descendants of Avraham, Isaac, and Jacob and offered to them the great gift of Torah. It was not demanded of them or forced upon them. He, the Holy One, extended His Hand to them and asked them, 'Will you accept My statutes?', and they responded, 'We hear and we obey.' It was not that He commanded them and they simply obeyed. It was that there was an offer, and the people accepted a contract. It is thus implied that there was a measure of partnership; and that is the key lesson that is derived from the Sinaitic narrative. God did not seek to enforce His rules or Himself upon the early Israelites. He offered Himself and His Torah to them and they accepted. It was a marriage of partners; partnership is the cornerstone of the relationship between God and the Jewish people, and it is the principle of partnership which colors the Jewish mission from the very start of the Jewish story, many thousands of years ago with Avraham Aveinu. As you trace Avraham's journey, you see that he was not involved with a distant God Who autocratically and indiscriminately leads him around on a wild goose chase with no end in sight. Numerous times, it is mentioned that Avraham debated with Him, argued with Him, disagreed with Him, and in fact, throughout Tanakh, God is involved in similar dialogues with many different people. The God of Avraham, the God of Israel, the God of the world is a God who involves Himself with Creation and pulls man from his lowly state into an elevated partnership with the Creator Himself.

"The God of the Jews is not an aloof Creator Who sits away from the world and demands worship. The God of the Jews seeks active partnership with mankind, and this has been the constant theme throughout the Jewish story. There was always dialogue; there was always the meeting of partners—and this is the miraculous thing about the Sinaitic covenant. God chose to enter into a partnership with man: a creature He created, a creature far below His awesome majesty and stature. He chose to meet us on our level.

"Have you figured out the first clue now, Avi? The clue from the Creation story? Throughout the history of mankind—this has been God's plan. *Partnership*. When He created man, He pulled out of the Creation process. He was the Builder, and when He ushered us into our new home, He stepped back—allowing us, the tenants, to choose how we wished to decorate it. He created Adam and Eve and then told them that they had dominion over the earth and over the animals of the land, and the fish of the sea, and the birds of the air. He stepped back and let the symbolic first two humans name the animals and plants He had created for their benefit and enjoyment. He intentionally delegated to them the power and authority to complete the work which He had started.

"The earth was meant for us to enjoy in fellowship and partnership with our Creator, Who most magnanimously—though we are but dust compared to His splendor—wants to be our Partner. It was never His intention to infringe Himself upon us. He created this universe, and then He created us, and with total faith and hope in mankind, He handed us the keys and gave us the choice. 'Color it how you will—with good, or with bad. The choice is yours.'

"In the story of Adam and Eve, He rejoiced in their happiness. The only thing He wanted was fellowship and collusion with them. Free Will has always been His plan for mankind. It was always our choice to do good or to do bad; to decorate our home the way we wished to. Since the moment God 'rested', we've been living the seventh day of the Creation story. The Creation process continues, with mankind at the helm of it.

"Do not misunderstand me, though, as I do not believe that God stepped away from the world after that symbolic day six of Creation and I do not believe that He is far away in some mythical heaven, passively observing us as if we are some controlled experiment. I am not a deist. Rather, I believe that, although He pulled away from directly controlling the process of creation, He has been there all along, guiding us, seeking us, loving us, trying to help us construct a world which will reach its fullest potential.

"Unfortunately, mankind has not been very kind to Him; we've not allowed Him the chance to guide us and help us with this part of the Creation process. We've shut Him out, time and time again. We have followed the limited wisdom of our very tiny brains and instead of helping the world to reach its fullest potential, we have made for ourselves a world of strife and hatred. Instead of choosing good, instead of letting Him be our Partner, we oftentimes choose the less opportune path. And this where the Jewish purpose comes into play; this is why the Jewish people were tasked with a particular mission that no other nation was privileged to.

"What is that mission? It is the quintessentially Jewish mission of *tikkun olam*: to assist in the perfection and completion of the world; to be God's partner in the process of Creation and to help the world reach its fullest potential. This is why He gave us the Torah, for it is a blueprint of how the great Architect meant the world to be. Within the pages of the Bible is found the precepts for life: the mitzvoth. He has told us the most direct and simplest way to perfect the world: the Torah.

"Yet, you must understand one crucial point. Judaism, its Torah and its mission are not the directives of mankind as a whole. The religion of Israel is confined to Israel. The Torah of Israel is confined to Israel. The mission of Israel is confined to Israel. This is why I told you before that Shabbat is a specifically Jewish mitzvah. Shabbat—and all the other mitzvoth—leaps out at us from this Torah which he gave specifically to the Jewish people. Judaism is a particular religion in that it is particular to the people of Israel. Other religions seek the path of universalism and try to apply a common standard to all of mankind, but this is not the Jewish path. Judaism, its scriptures, and its mission are particular to the Jewish people. Every nation has a separate path to follow and every nation has their particular mission, but ours is uniquely different from all other missions.

"Why is this so? It is because, in trying and trying with the world, God has been unable to make the whole of mankind see that He is calling to us all, as individuals, as societies, as nations, as the world at large, to enter into partnership with Him and complete this seventh day. What He chose to do was to make a nation for Himself—a nation that will be a light unto the world and lead the way to perfecting the world with God as our partner, until all nations and all people recognize Him as their partner and turn to Him for love, guidance, and assistance. The nation He chose, those many years ago, at the foot of Mount Sinai, was Clal Yisrael, and our primary mission, to perform tikkun olam, is rooted in the concept of a partnership-type covenant with God. Take our emblematic symbol, for instance, the Star of David. It consists of two triangles, inversely superimposed upon each other. What does the Star of David mean? Simply, the downward facing triangle represents God reaching

173

out to us, and the upward pointing triangle shows our reaching out to him. The classic symbol of our people, which flies proudly at the center of the flag of our State, is the purest reflection of our purpose: to be in partnership with God. Mind you, we are not better than any other people, we are simply chosen for a different purpose: to show mankind that we are all worthy of God's love and partnership, and that our problems are of our own making and the remedy for the ills of this world are within grasp if only we would meet God halfway. We are the example. We are the pioneers.

"Like I said, the Jewish people are not better than any other people, we are simply that: people. And, as such, we sometimes fall short of achieving our mission. And it is in this way that the mashiach concept comes into play. Because we were chosen for a specific purpose, we are judged by a different standard, so when we fail, our failures are magnified. Not as a means to embarrass or punish us, but it is done to show the world, in a most forceful way: 'Look! This could be you!' It is hard to be a Jew; it is hard to be different. And because we so very often fall short of achieving our mission, we cry out for help—we cry out for a deliverer.

"The mashiach is not just a graphical map of the build-up of historical Jewish hopes, he is the ultimate redemption of the Jewish people: for our redemption will lead to global redemption. When we do our part in being partners with God in the process of Creation, the world will follow our example. Jews have an innate passion for justice and charity; the plight of the unfortunate man plagues us and we feel that we must step in. This is why so many secular Jews are involved in charitable organizations, and this is why non-religious Jews are among the first to assist those in need and

174

protest injustice around the world. On the spiritual level, we crave the perfection of the world. It is part of our neshama; it is part of what makes us unique. It is what our forefather, Avraham started and it has never stopped. The mashiach will be the eventual conclusion of this process. He will help us achieve our national goal of tikkun olam. He will bring us redemption, and he will bring the world redemption."

The last word was said with finality. It was clear that the Saba's expounding of the mashiach concept was finished. Avi did not know what time it was exactly. He knew that hours had slipped by while Saba had lectured. The streets below them were silent, except for the occasional bark of a dog. Inside the apartment, all was still, as the others slept on. Saba sipped on a glass of water to refresh himself after his exhausting talk, and Avi mulled over his thoughts. He had said nothing throughout Saba's lengthy lecture. So much had been said, so much information had been conveyed, that even with Avi's superior brain, it was a lot to process.

"The last time I talked this much was when I lectured thirty years ago," Saba said, clearing his throat. "I hope I didn't overwhelm you. It is not often that I come across one so young who has such an earnest interest in religious concepts."

"You didn't overwhelm me—not at all. You explained everything so well, that the entire concept of the mashiach is mostly understandable to me now." Avi grinned. "And don't be surprised at my interest. I'm not as young as I look."

Saba looked at him. "Things are sometimes not what they seem, nachon?"

Avi smiled uncomfortably. "I suppose." He coughed. "Thank you, Saba, for this talk."

175

"Bevakasha. Was it understandable or did I overload you with information?"

"Well, it was a lot of information, yes, and it will take some time for me to process it all. But your explanation was brilliant. Besides, it is necessary for me to understand."

"Necessary? How so?"

Avi considered before answering. "Necessary for my own edification. I am new here. Your explanation helps me understand things a bit more."

"You are new here, you say. Interesting. I have spoken for a long time, and it is late, but would you mind if I kept you up for a tad bit more?"

Avi shrugged. "I don't mind. Do you have more to tell me about the mashiach?"

Saba smiled wryly. "Actually, I wanted to talk about you."

"Me?" Avi asked, surprised. "Why?"

"You intrigue me."

"There is nothing special about me," Avi said hastily.

"There is something special about everyone," Saba replied simply. "Do you mind if I asked you some questions? Just to get to know you better."

"I suppose," Avi answered, cautiously. "It is only fair after that informative speech you've just given to me."

"Where are you from, Avi?"

"A city far away from here."

"Who are your parents?"

"They died a long time ago."

"Who takes care of you?"

"Your grandson, Tzippy, and Max have been very kind to me, and—let's just say I have other friends who are there for me."

"Do you have a job?"

"No. I don't think I'm going to be here for much longer."

"Where are you leaving to go?"

"Somewhere far away."

"Why will you be going there?"

"Because it is not my purpose to be here for very long."

"Why not?"

"I've accomplished what I came to Israel to accomplish."

"So, you will be heading back home now that you've accomplished your goal?"

"Yes."

"How long have you been here on—in Israel?"

"Less than a week."

"That's a short time. Don't you want to stay?"

"Israel intrigues me, and yes I would like to stay very much. But I don't think that's in the cards for me."

"Why not? Is someone forcing you to leave?"

"Not really. I just don't think it's my destiny to be here for much longer."

"I see."

"It is what it is."

"Your answers are very vague."

Avi shrugged. "I can't help that."

"How old are you, Avi?"

"Twenty. Or thereabouts."

Saba laughed. "'Or thereabouts'? You don't know your age?"

"It's the age he tells me I am."

Saba raised an eyebrow. "Who is 'he'?"

Avi blushed. "Oh, just a friend. What is age anyway, right? We are as old or as young as we tell ourselves we are."

Saba seemed distracted. "Forgive me for being blunt, Avi, and you need not answer, but are you Jewish?"

Avi considered. "No, I am not Jewish."

"I see. You say that you're not Jewish, yet I perceive a strong Jewish aura emanating from you."

"The neshama," Avi answered quietly, thinking back to his discussion with Max a few days before.

"Yes," said Saba. "You have a strong neshama. And you do seem to have an understanding of Judaism, despite your protest of not being Jewish."

"Whatever snippets of knowledge I have gleaned about your faith is very imprecise, I can assure you. In fact, I won't call it knowledge, per se. It's more like information because I haven't processed it all as yet. To be honest, I've only learnt what I know about Judaism very recently."

"What did you know about before?"

"Different things," Avi said mysteriously.

"What does that mean?"

Avi shrugged.

Saba considered. "You say you've only recently become acquainted with Judaism, nachon?"

"That's right."

"In your recent introduction, did you have the chance to study Torah?"

"I've not studied formally in a yeshiva or anything—but I've waded through the Tanakh and Talmud a couple times."

"I'm impressed! You've 'waded' through the Talmud? That's quite an extensive body of Judaic religious literature. Yet, you say you've only just become acquainted with Judaism. Curious."

Avi shrugged. "I read quickly."

"Speed-reading course?"

Avi laughed. "Something like that."

"Did you read the Talmud in its original Aramaic?"

"I think so."

Saba looked surprised. "You read Aramaic?"

"I think so."

"You confuse me. What do you mean 'you think so'?"

"It's hard to explain. I have a gift—I suppose you can say—which makes it easy for me to understand languages. Sometimes I don't even realize I'm hearing or reading a different language. My brain just automatically understands."

"Do you care to elucidate?"

Avi shrugged. "If I could, I would. I don't know how I do it. I just do." Avi smiled ruefully. "It is how God made me this time around, I suppose."

"Well, He has greatly blessed you, for that is quite an ability."

"It makes me odd."

"It makes you gifted," Saba said firmly. "What did you think of your Torah and Talmud readings?"

"Like I said, it was a lot to process. I'm still sifting it all out in my mind."

"What I meant was, did you enjoy it?"

"It was quite interesting and deep—it gave me a lot to think about. I'm not sure if enjoyable is the right word to describe the experience."

179

"Honest answer."

Avi smiled. "I try to always be truthful."

"Do I look like an eighty-five-year-old man?"

Caught off-guard, Avi answered stutteringly. "No. Not exactly."

Saba laughed. "There you go—I've caught you out in a lie."

Avi grinned mischievously. "I was going to say you actually look ninety-five."

Saba spluttered with laughter. He leaned forward and looked at Avi. "Are you sure you're not Jewish?"

Avi shook his head. "No, I am not."

"What are you, then?"

"I don't like labels."

"Ah, the insufferable angst of youth: 'I cannot be classified."

Avi laughed. "It's not that at all. I just really can't say what I am."

"Try. If you had to describe yourself ethnically, spiritually, nationally, and religiously, what words would you choose?"

Avi considered. "Ethnically: Semitic. Spiritually: a friend of the Divine. Nationally: a man of no nation. Religiously: Hebrew."

"Hebrew is the same as Jewish."

"No," Avi insisted. "It's not. I am a Hebrew. I am *Ivri*. I am the 'other'."

Saba waved his hand dismissively. "You are playing semantics. The Hebrew of yesteryear is the same as the Israelite which he spawned, and the same as the Jew of today and the Israeli of tomorrow. We share the commonality of being the 'other'. The names which represent us may have evolved over the ages, but it's the same thing."

Avi shook his head forcefully. "There is a difference. A Jew is a descendant of Judah. How can I be a descendant of my—" Avi stopped.

"A descendant of your what?"

"Nothing. I'm not a Jew."

Saba smiled chastely. "Let's agree to disagree."

Avi nodded agreeably. "That is usually always the best approach to disagreements."

"You know, Avi, you remind me of someone."

"I do? Who?"

"You remind me of a man I've never met, but only read about. Your personality is how I imagine his would be."

Avi laughed. "Messed up, unsure of himself, contrary and odd?"

"No—inquisitive, intelligent, intriguing, patient, blessed with abundant gifts, open-minded, compassionate, strong, assertive, bright-eyed, and diligent in his quest for truth."

Avi laughed. "He doesn't sound like me—or anyone I know for that matter. He sounds like a fictional character."

"I suppose some would say he's that."

"You wouldn't?"

Saba smiled and put his hand to his heart. "He's real to me. He's the reason I'm alive today."

"Who is this man?"

"Avraham Aveinu. The first Jew. The founder of my faith and my people."

Avi twisted uncomfortably in his seat.

Saba looked at Avi. "You have heard of him?"

Avi coughed. "Yes, of course. I've read about him."

"What have you read?"

Avi shrugged. "Nothing more than you've read, I'm sure."

"Somehow, I think you're much more authoritative on the subject of Avraham Aveinu than I am," Saba said softly. "I think you know more about him than anyone else alive today."

Avi stood awkwardly. "Saba, it's late. Perhaps it's time we go to bed."

"What is your full name, Avi?" Saba asked, ignoring Avi's suggestion.

Avi concentrated on the floor.

"Are you Avraham ben Terah?" Saba asked, quietly, intently.

Avi looked at the old man, shocked. "How did you know?"

Saba gestured to the shimmer that was Michael, who hovered next to Avi. "I, too, talk to angels." He clasped Avi's hand. "Please, tell me. Let me hear the words from your lips. I know it is you. My angel whispers to me in my ear that it is you. He has told me you would come. I have looked forward to your coming for a long time. But you must confirm it for me for I will only believe it when you say it. Please, Avi, tell me who you are."

Avi didn't know how to respond. He looked down at the old man's hands which were softly, desperately, pathetically holding on to his. He closed his eyes tightly and did not answer.

"Please, tell me."

Avi gently shook his hands free and walked over to the balcony, and muttered quietly. "Michael, are you there?"

"I am," came his guardian angel's prompt response.

"What should I do?"

"Follow your heart."

"You told me not to tell any more people who I was. Should I tell him?"

"Follow your heart."

"Give me more direction, my angelic friend."

"When you told people other than Natan, Tzippy, and Max, clearly it was not done for a higher purpose. In this instance, you must ask yourself, will my telling this man who I truly am serve the higher purpose?"

"Thank you, Michael." Avi turned his attention back to the old man and looked him squarely in his eyes. There was hope emanating from the aged eyes. "You hear your guardian angel?" Avi asked.

"I talk to him often. Did you just talk to your angel?"

Avi nodded.

"What did he tell you?"

"He told me to follow my heart and to ask myself whether telling you who I was would serve the higher purpose. It wasn't very palpable advice."

"Angels are not cryptic on purpose. They can advise us, but they cannot command us." Saba paused. "What does your heart tell you, Avi?"

"It tells me that you are an enlightened soul and that you deserve to know who I am—that it will bring you peace. But I am afraid to say it."

"Why?"

"Because I made the mistake of telling who I am to people before and it was not good."

"Why was that so?"

"I only told them out of vanity, and then, because a friend asked me to, although I did not want to. It did not serve the higher purpose."

"If you tell me who you are, would it be out of vanity? Or would you feel pressured? I would not want you to do anything you do not want to do, but at the same time, I am eager to hear you say it."

Avi considered and then smiled. "It is not vanity and there is no pressure. I will tell you who I am because you deserve an honest answer from me. Not because you talk to angels, and not because deep down you already know, and not because you are most clearly a man of God. I will tell you because I am going to follow my heart, although I am not sure if it serves a higher purpose or not. I will tell you because you have shown me true hospitality and that is the greatest gift any person can bestow upon another. You've taken me into your home and have expounded to me your knowledge without expectation of reciprocation. I will tell you who I am, Saba." Avi breathed in deeply and then exhaled. "I am Avraham of old, resurrected by the grace of the one true God of Israel, here on earth once again to do His bidding."

"Baruch HaShem." Saba closed his eyes tightly, then opened them and jumped from his seat excitedly and held Avi's hands again. "Baruch HaShem!" He did a sort of jig and then sat back heavily in his chair. "You are alive again! And you are in my home! And I have met you!" Saba grinned widely. Excitement poured out from every pore in him.

Avi giggled. "I'm the same person I was two minutes ago, Saba."

Saba nodded. "Yes, but now I know who you really are. Avraham Aveinu! On my balcony! And he asked me to teach him Torah concepts. Oysh!" Saba grinned again. "I feel like a teenage girl. I'm almost tempted to ask you for your autograph."

Avi laughed. "Please, don't. I am simply Avi. Don't treat me any differently."

Saba hung his head. "I am sorry. I have made you uncomfortable. You are the great champion of hospitality and here I am, not being hospitable."

"Not at all!" Avi exclaimed. "You are a marvelous host. Just treat me as you would anyone else."

Saba nodded. "Your request is granted." He grinned again, unable to contain himself. "A million questions are zooming around my head. I want to know everything about your life back then. I want to know about Sarah and hear about your marriage to her. I want to know how Isaac was as a child. I want to know about your childhood and when was the first time you kissed a girl. I want to know how it was growing up in Ur. I want to know how you discovered God. I want to know why you decided to look for Him. I want to know if you knew about the mitzvoth and Torah. I want to know what you did in the mornings and what you ate and what sort of clothes you wore. But there is one thing I want to know more than anything else."

"What's that?"

"Why did God bring you back?"

Avi was surprised. "Didn't your angel tell you?"

"No, all he knew was that you would come. Angels, like us, are not all-knowing; you don't have to tell me if you can't."

"I was resurrected to find the mashiach and inform him he was the mashiach."

Saba's eyes bulged. "The mashiach? You mean to tell me the mashiach is alive right now?"

"He is alive. Very much so."

"Did you find him?"

Avi nodded.

Saba threw his hands up in the air in excitement. "The mashiach is alive?" he exclaimed. "Baruch HaShem! Avraham has been resurrected and the mashiach has been identified? Oh, what joy to be alive in these times! I am blessed. The Lord has blessed me richly. No wonder you wanted to know about the mashiach!" Saba beamed.

"Do you want to know who the mashiach is?" Avi asked quietly.

"Do I know him?"

"He's asleep inside your apartment. The mashiach is Natan."

Saba inhaled deeply and visibly trembled. "My grandson is the mashiach? Oh, bless the Lord. Bless His Holy Name that He has honored my family in this way." Saba smiled. "My life is complete. I have waited for you, for so long, Avi. And I have prayed every day that the mashiach would come. And to have met you and been told that my grandson is the mashiach in the space of one evening? Oh, I am a happy, happy, happy man."

Avi gently touched the old man on his arm. "You are a good man. You deserve the merit of having the mashiach be your descendant."

"He is also your descendant. It is through your merit that Natan was chosen; it is through your merit that we are all here today." Saba lifted his thin arms in the air to the heavens. "It is a blessing, a true blessing beyond anything I could have hoped for. The Lord, He is good."

Avi nodded. "He is indeed."

"I must pray, Avi. I must give thanks to my God. He has given me so much on this night. I must ask that you excuse me."

"Of course. I completely understand. I will leave you to it."

"Before you leave, please, come to me."

Avi strode over to the old man, who stood shakily and placed his hands on Avi's shoulders. "May the Lord bless you and safeguard you; may the Lord cause His face to shine upon you and be gracious to you; may the Lord turn His face toward you and establish peace for you."

Avi was touched. "That's the *Birkat Kohanim*, not so?"

Saba smiled and sat back. "It is—I am not a Kohen, but it is traditional to recite it for one's children before the Shabbat meal. It is still Shabbat, and you may not be my child, but I am your child, Avi, and I ask that the Lord bless you, for everything you were and everything you are and everything you will be. May the Lord bless you."

"Thank you."

Saba smiled. Avi could see the tiredness in his face.

"I will leave you to your prayers."

"One thing?"

"Yes?"

"Tomorrow, promise me we can talk about your life as Avraham Aveinu. I am eager to hear all about it. But for right now, I must give thanks to God for the many blessings He has revealed to me through you on this night."

Avi smiled at the old man. "I promise I will answer all your questions. We will talk tomorrow. Pray well, Saba."

"Lila tov, Avi." Good night.

CHAPTER 10

"The men set out from there and looked down toward Sodom, Abraham walking with them to see them off."
— Genesis 18:16

The funeral for Rabbi Yehonatan Nasi was a small affair, attended by his children, grandchildren, and two great grandchildren. Rabbi Nasi had died peacefully in his sleep in the wee hours of that Saturday morning; sound asleep in his chair on the balcony, with his blanket tucked around him and his hands holding his siddur. The funeral took place that Sunday morning, immediately following the death. Avi, Max, and Tzippy were in attendance for the burial, and had journeyed back with Natan and his family to Saba's Arnona apartment, where the relevant family members sat *shiva*, and the rest of them bustled around entertaining well-wishers who had come to pay their respects. None of Rabbi Nasi's descendants were Orthodox as he had been, so Max took it upon himself to coach the family on the halacha behind the rituals of mourning. When the evening drew to a close, the relatives thanked Max for his teaching, hugged each other, wept over the death of their ancestor, and then returned to their respective lives. Natan stayed behind in his Saba's apartment and, although he was not one of the first seven-degree relatives, he decided to sit shiva for the allotted week of mourning since his Saba had been like a father to him.

Avi had not told anyone about the conversation he'd had with Natan's Saba on the night of his death. Avi was fairly certain that Natan's Saba had simply been waiting to meet him, and once the old man's long wait was over, Saba had given up the ghost and passed on.

Avi realized that Saba had been a powerfully spiritual man, and he was privileged to have had some of the old man's wisdom imparted to him. Saba had given him much to think about and Avi pondered the information carefully. Avi was particularly thankful that he'd been able to give Saba the exceptionally good news that his grandson was the prophesied mashiach the world had long been waiting on.

Max called his yeshiva and explained to them that he would be returning a week later than expected. Without even asking for a reason for his continued absence, they granted him the necessary leave. They asked for the address he would be staying at until he returned. "For security purposes," they'd said, "as you are a foreign student, it would be in everyone's best interest to know where you are." Max readily gave them the address and went back to attending to his grieving friend.

Tzippy and Avi had gallantly risen to the occasion and had taken over preparing meals and keeping the place clean. Every morning, Avi would arise early and go out onto the balcony to pray and then sit quietly in the living room as the others awoke one by one. Then, after breakfast, he and Tzippy would walk to the large supermarket on the corner of Daniel Yanovski and Beitar, and shop for things the pantry needed and for what they knew would be easy to prepare. As neither of them were expert cooks, the food they cooked was simple but nourishing. The four friends would eat the simply-prepared meals together, and then Avi, Tzippy, and Max would spend the afternoons tidying the apartment, while Natan sat out on the balcony and smoked cigarettes. Every evening, just before the sun set, Natan and Max would eat their supper and philosophize about God, death, life, the afterlife, and the universe, and Tzippy and Avi would quietly slip out of the apartment and wander around New Jerusalem. The boys had tried to cajole Avi and Tzippy into joining in their discussions, but Tzippy said bluntly that she had no interest in those discussions, and Avi had politely shied away. His mind was jam-packed with the philosophies he'd read online and the knowledge which had been imparted by Natan's Saba, and so, he much preferred the simplicity of Tzippy's company—away from the mourner and the resident Torah scholar. Together, he and Tzippy would explore different aspects of the city, and as they travelled, Avi would tell Tzippy about his previous life as Avraham. It was cathartic for him; he had truly looked forward to telling Saba how his previous life had unraveled, for he felt as if Saba had been the one person who'd been truly interested in hearing about it, but Saba's untimely death had left a gaping hole in that hope. But next to Tzippy, Avi felt comfortable enough to open up, and as they meandered the city together—both of them unfamiliar with the landscape before them—Avi quietly told her the things no one in the modern world knew about Avraham Aveinu. Tzippy listened with quiet fascination. She asked no questions, and they both preferred it that way. One evening, they strolled along the Tayelet and enjoyed the views of the Old City. Another night, they went to Rav Chen, the multi-theatre cinema in Talpiot and watched a movie. Another evening, they took the number 7 bus and got off on Rechov King George and dined at the Burger's Bar off of Yafo, and then walked to Rivlin where they sat at one of the rickety bars and had a beer and watched young people run around drunkenly. Another time, they walked to Rehavia and had dinner at a coffee shop. Another

191

evening, they bought roast beef and tahini sandwiches from a deli on Beit Lechem and then walked to the Old Train Station and sat on benches and ate and talked. And every night, they came back to the apartment and they would sit out on the balcony with Natan and Max and drink mugs of hot chocolate. Natan and Max would have exhausted their ability to speak philosophically by this point, and Avi, Tzippy, and Max would listen to Natan's subdued stories of his deceased grandfather.

It was a difficult time for Natan, for he had loved his Saba dearly, but Max's constant presence, counsel, and prayers made him feel better. And he was most grateful to Tzippy and Avi for doing all they did to help; knowing they were quietly in the background gave him comfort. Like most people, when faced with tragedy, the group quickly became accustomed to the routines of their days. They had no contact with the outside world, except for the occasional concerned person who called to extend sympathies to Natan. From time to time, callers would enquire about visiting the house of mourning, but Natan did not want visitors and Max would demurely turn them away. And while Tzippy and Avi did venture out to do the shopping and to take their routine evening strolls, they never stopped to chat with anyone, and always kept to themselves. It was in this way that the week of shiva passed by with the four friends contained in a little bubble of their own making.

A week later, it was time to return to regular life. Natan desperately had to return to Tel Aviv. His business affairs were in dire need of attention, and he wanted to cancel the trip to India he had booked and was supposed to embark on in a few weeks. Tzippy, too, needed to get back. Although she wasn't currently employed, she had bills to pay and errands to run. Max's authorized extended time of leave from his yeshiva had come to a close and he needed to return.

Everyone had lives to attend to.

Unfortunately, Avi had no life to return to, as his three friends had become everything to him since his resurrection. Natan and Tzippy offered him a place to stay in their respective apartments in Tel Aviv and Max suggested Avi enroll in yeshiva with him. Avi sat quietly for a few moments before offering up his own suggestion, that he could perhaps stay behind in Jerusalem at Natan's Saba's apartment for a while; the little he had seen of the city had made him want to continue exploring and become better-acquainted with it. The three friends were all quite taken by this proposal, and it was quickly agreed that, as a temporary measure, Avi could take up residence in Jerusalem for a while, after which they could discuss what long-term options there were for him. Avi, who'd thus far depended upon his friends for monetary support, was insistent on getting a job. He wanted to make his own money and did not want to feel like a charity-case. Unfortunately, as Avi had no papers or identification with which to acquire a legal job, fulfilling this wish proved difficult for his three friends. Eventually, however, Natan came across a friend whose parents owned a small makholet on Rechov Ein Gedi, and were looking for help in their shop. With a quick explanation that Avi was technically an illegal worker, and a promise that he would not be exploited, they secured a job for him in the makholet. The job itself was not particularly strenuous: a little packing, some cleaning, some re-organizing, and just generally being all that a shop assistant entails. Avi was tremendously excited to earn his own money, and he looked forward to starting the job the next week. Max was disturbed by this turn of events. Though he no longer thought of Avi in terms of his previous lofty accomplishments, he felt the menial tasks involved in the job were beneath someone of Avi's stature. Avi assured Max that he felt no compunction towards hard work, and indeed, reminded Max that hard work was part and parcel of the religious, Jewish ideal. "There is no shame in honest, physical labor," Avi said. "Just read the commentaries written by the Rambam. Study without work is the same as ritual without essence. Besides, I've been helping with cooking and washing up and cleaning all week here at the apartment. My job wouldn't be much different from that." Max pursed his lips, and he thought of his fellow talmidim back at his yeshiva who would inevitably be turned out into the world as perennial students, with no work skills or trade to support their families, rather, they would look to the State to support them with welfare while they raised large families which would be subject to lives of poverty. He recognized the merit in Avi's words and was left with troubled thoughts about the Charedi lifestyle he'd embraced.

With everything settled, Natan and Tzippy prepared to depart Jerusalem for Tel Aviv, and Max organized himself for the return to his yeshiva. All three of them would be leaving the next day. The four friends had a late lunch at an Israeli fast-food restaurant on Pierre Koenig and then returned to the apartment where they began to go through Natan's Saba's belongings. Natan nostalgically pointed out to Tzippy the keepsakes and mementos he wished to keep and Avi boxed the less important items, which would be donated to charity. Max stuffed the remaining odds and ends into big, black garbage bags and placed them next to the front door. Natan then moved into his Saba's bedroom and started

194

to clear out the more personal belongings his Saba had left behind. As he rummaged through the large chest of drawers, which was easily nearly as old as Natan's Saba had been, the ancient furniture piece collapsed. The others, who had stayed in the main living area of the apartment in order to give Natan privacy, rushed into the room upon hearing the noise. The mess caused by the collapsed chest of drawers was too much for the small-sized bedroom to contain, and with Avi's and Max's assistance, Natan heaved it out onto the tiny mirpeset which led out from his Saba's bedroom. Tzippy returned to the living room, where she began packing Natan's Saba's clothes into boxes to give to charity.

✡

Rabbi Eliezer Goldenberg had been supremely annoyed when he heard from the yeshiva administration that Max Feldman would not be returning to campus at the scheduled time. "Why will he not be returning?" Rabbi Eliezer had asked the man over the telephone. When the man was unable to provide an answer, Rabbi Eliezer spent fifteen minutes ranting at the man about his ineptness. The man protested that he had not been the one who had spoken to Max and asked if Rabbi Eliezer would kindly not kill the messenger. Rabbi Eliezer held the phone to his ear in silent rage for a total of ten seconds, then promptly hung up on the man. He then re-dialed the Rosh Yeshiva's direct number and informed the Rosh Yeshiva that he wanted the man fired. The Rosh Yeshiva quickly capitulated and after apologizing profusely to Rabbi Eliezer, was allowed to return to his more genteel duties. Placated, Rabbi Eliezer concentrated on the information the school had provided him concerning Max's extended leave of absence: there was an address, in Jerusalem itself—in the largely secular neighborhood of Arnona, to be exact—where Max was residing. Max had said he would return to the yeshiva the following Monday. Rabbi Eliezer pondered the situation carefully. He decided he would wait until Sunday and then drop by unannounced at the place Max was staying and catch him off-guard, in order to inspect the conditions under which Max lived when he was away from the glare of the religious establishment. What better way to ascertain properly whether Max Feldman was indeed the one Rabbi Eliezer hoped to groom as his protégé?

That Sunday evening, Rabbi Eliezer loaded his large frame into the backseat of his car, and took the scenic route from where he lived in Har Nof to the apartment building in Arnona where Max was staying. His driver pulled up alongside the building and jumped out and ran around to the back door to open it and let Rabbi Eliezer out. Rabbi Eliezer shook himself, curtly told his driver to wait there, and then walked over to the entrance of the building. It was a modern apartment complex, and, as such, he could not just walk in as the lobby of the building was electronically locked. He scanned the list of apartment numbers until he came to the one Max was reportedly staying at. The surname "Nasi" was scrawled in large, firm Hebrew next to the apartment number. Rabbi Eliezer frowned. *Sephardi?* Was his possible heir overnighting in the home of a Sephardi family? His heart plummeted, but he forced himself to keep the hope. There must be a reason for this. He put his finger to the buzzer and pressed firmly.

A female voice came to the intercom and spoke in American-accented Hebrew. "Shalom?"

Rabbi Eliezer straightened himself and spoke clearly. "Shalom. I am here to see Max Feldman. I was told he is staying at this address."

There was a pause and then the female voice responded. "Yes, he is here. Whom shall I say is calling, please?"

Rabbi Eliezer considered. He could announce himself, but that would possibly awe Max and make him less inclined to show his true self. Furthermore, saying it was Rabbi Eliezer Goldenberg would, no doubt, alarm the boy. On the other hand, Rabbi Eliezer knew he wouldn't be admitted unless he told the truth, or at least some semblance of it. "I am connected with his yeshiva," he responded, carefully.

"Oh, yes," came the girl's reply. "Please, come up."

The door clicked and Rabbi Eliezer strode into the lobby of the building and made his way up the elevator to the third floor where the Nasi apartment was located. He rang the bell and the door was immediately opened by a girl, presumably the same one who spoke to him through the intercom. Unable to determine her ethnicity, Rabbi Eliezer was immediately put off by her appearance. She wore short shorts and a white tank top. Her hair was pulled back in a high pony tail. Her face, though bare of make-up, was flushed. She was a clearly beautiful girl, but she was also clearly a hiloni. *Frekha*, Rabbi Eliezer thought disparagingly to himself. He clenched inside and hoped that Max was not engaging in anything immoral with this girl.

"Hi!" she said. "Please, come in."

"*Shalom aleykhem,*" Rabbi Eliezer muttered. He hesitated and then moved himself through the doorway carefully, so as to not make physical contact with the girl.

He looked around the room. There was a modern kitchen right next to the entryway, which opened out onto an airy living room. Boxes, books, papers, odd tchotchkes and other various items were strewn around the place. A heaping number of trash bags were piled in the foyer. Rabbi Eliezer hated chaos and disorder, and the sight of the messy room annoyed him.

The girl made to close the door. Rabbi Eliezer turned and looked in her direction, but did not focus his eyes on her. "Please leave the door open," he said quietly.

The girl looked confused. "Is someone else coming up?"

"Just leave it open. I will be more comfortable with it open." He intrinsically understood that explaining to the girl that it was not halachically appropriate for him to be in a room alone with an unrelated female would be wasted on someone like her.

The girl raised an eyebrow. "Ok," she said slowly. She left the door open and eased around Rabbi Eliezer. "Would you like something to drink?"

At that moment, a boy clad in Charedi clothes, followed by two other boys, not in Charedi attire, stepped into the living room from a hallway. The Charedi boy spoke, "I am sorry I kept you waiting. We were moving some things into the bedroom, as you can see—" The boy stopped speaking and his eyes bulged open. "R-Rabbi Goldenberg," he whispered, croakily.

Rabbi Eliezer strode over to the boy and firmly shook his hand. "Max Feldman, I presume?"

The boy nodded. "Yes. Tha-that's me. Please, please, sit." He guided Rabbi Eliezer to the only chair in
198

the living room not occupied by things. "Would you like something to drink?" Max asked, as he sat carefully on the armrest of the sofa directly across from Rabbi Eliezer.

Rabbi Eliezer drank in the particulars of Max and he beamed. Physically, at least, Max fit the picture of what a good Jewish boy should look like. His complexion was pale and he was slightly pudgy. A scraggly beard covered his face and he wore a large black velvet kipa on his head. His tzitzit hung askew from the sides of his shirt. Rabbi Eliezer had had a moment of worry when he'd first entered the apartment that Max had rushed to change his clothes when he'd heard that someone from his yeshiva had dropped by, but it was clear, given the streaks of sweat which ran down his face and onto his shirt, that he had been dressed appropriately the entire time. However, Rabbi Eliezer had seen many a talmid who physically fit the bill of what he wanted his heir to be; as pleased as he was at Max's appearance, he had yet to determine whether Max's personality was what he sought.

"The young lady has already offered me a drink. But no, thank you."

"We have bottled water," Max responded, knowing that Rabbi Eliezer would loathe drinking anything that did not carry a hechsher.

Rabbi Eliezer laughed. "I assure you, I am not thirsty."

Max smiled weakly. His friends were standing awkwardly. "Rabbi Goldenberg, please allow me to introduce everyone. These are my friends, Natan and Avi. And you've met my cousin, Tzipporah."

Rabbi Eliezer felt a tremble of relief. The frekha was Max's cousin. Thank God. There was no way Max would be involved with her. She must probably be

199

sleeping with one of the other two boys—Rabbi Eliezer was sure of it. The *frekhot* were harlots, all of them, and it was a shame that they had to be part of Am Yisroel. Rabbi Eliezer scanned the two boys. They both wore shorts and the taller boy was barefoot. The shorter boy looked more disheveled than his peers. His long hair was uncombed and there were cobwebs all over his t-shirt. Both boys were clearly Sephardi trash. *Arsim*, he thought ruefully. He inwardly praised himself for summing up the three characters. The only thing left to do was figure out why Max was associating with them. He smiled. "It is a pleasure to meet all of you."

The three young people muttered back niceties to him.

"I don't mean to be rude, Rabbi Eliezer," Max said slowly, "but why are you here?"

Rabbi Eliezer sat back into his seat, folded his hands on his lap and smiled widely. He was causing them all discomfort and he liked it. "I came to see you, Feldman."

Max looked confused. "But why?"

"You took an extra week off from yeshiva. I came to make sure you were fine."

"Baruch HaShem, thank you. Forgive me for asking, but surely this isn't part of your job description, to check up on yeshiva bocherim who aren't at yeshiva?"

Rabbi Eliezer smiled again. "I am concerned about the welfare of all the talmidim who attend haMerkaz shel Emet. To be concerned about the well-being of my charges is indeed part of my job description."

Max nodded. Rabbi Eliezer could tell his answer had impressed the impressionable boy. "Would you like to speak with me alone?" Max asked.

Rabbi Eliezer considered. He would have loved to speak to Max in an intimate setting, but at the same time, he dearly wanted to observe Max in his natural surroundings. For now, the company of the hilonim was somewhat appealing. "I don't mind speaking to you right here for now." He looked up at the others. "Please, sit."

The three non-Charedim pulled chairs from the dining table and sat awkwardly, as there was no space on the living room seats to sit upon.

Rabbi Eliezer smiled at them. His eyes narrowed in on the area around Tzippy, but still didn't focus on her directly. "Girl, how is it you know Max?"

Tzippy looked at Rabbi Eliezer coldly. "My name is Tzipporah. And as Max told you, not a minute ago, we are cousins. That is how we know each other."

"Indeed, indeed," Rabbi Eliezer replied. "You must forgive me—I am getting up there in age. Sometimes I forget." Tzippy looked sufficiently annoyed. Rabbi Eliezer felt satisfied. He turned his attention to Avi.

"And how do you know Max?" he asked lightly.

"I only met him last week, out in the desert."

Rabbi Eliezer looked over at Max and raised an eyebrow. "In the desert? That is no place for a talmid to be traipsing around. Your place is in the beis midrash." He turned back to Avi. "So, you went camping?"

"Not exactly."

"Well, what—exactly?"

Avi shrugged.

"Come, boy, you must answer when an elder speaks to you. It is a mitzvah."

Avi smiled ruefully.

"Is something funny?"

Avi shook his head but continued smiling.

"Then why are you smiling?"

"You wouldn't get it. Inside joke."

"Try me."

"Technically speaking, you're not my elder."

Rabbi Eliezer raised an eyebrow. "Am I not older than you are?"

"I suppose, conventionally speaking at least, one might assume that you are. But you aren't my elder." Avi smiled again.

"I am older than you, ergo, I am your elder."

"Perhaps."

"You think you are funny?"

"Not particularly."

"Then you just enjoy being difficult?"

"I am not being difficult. Not in the slightest. I am just saying that you aren't my elder. You may be Max's, but you're not mine."

"Why is that? Because Max and I are Charedi?"

"I suppose that's a small part of it. But despite that, you'd still not be my elder. I'm older than I look, you see."

Tzippy giggled. Avi looked over at her and grinned. For a fleeting moment, Max thought Avi was about to reveal himself and Natan as the mashiach to Rabbi Eliezer. But with his grin still plastered on his face, Avi glanced at Max and shook his head and then winked. The mischievousness of the gesture was not lost on Max; Avi had no intention of revealing anything to Rabbi Eliezer—he was simply teasing the cantankerous old man.

Rabbi Eliezer groaned with annoyance. "I have no time for childish riddles, boy."

"And I am not giving you any riddles. I told you, it is an inside joke. You won't understand, yet you persist."

202

Rabbi Eliezer held his gaze on Avi. There was something about Avi which he didn't like. He couldn't put his finger on it; it was something more than the boy's arrogance, something more than his beastly attitude. Rabbi Eliezer was not sure what it was, but he knew he did not like Avi. In fact, he disliked Avi the most of all of the three non-Charedim who sat across from him.

"Avi, is it?"

Avi nodded.

"I will remember you," Rabbi Eliezer said evenly and then turned his attention to Natan.

"And how do you know Max?"

"We met in the shuk some time ago."

"And you are good friends?"

"Yes, we are. Is that a problem?"

"Of course not," Rabbi Eliezer said with a light laugh. "So, tell me, what is it you do?"

"I recently sold my business. Right now, you can say I am deciding the course of my future."

"I see."

Natan shrugged.

"Rabbi Goldenberg," Max said, "Natan is the reason I did not return to yeshiva. His Saba, zichrono livracha, passed away last week, and I have been staying with him through the shiva period."

Rabbi Eliezer peered at Natan. "Do you not have family and relatives to give you emotional support? Why did you need Max to take time out of studies to attend to you?"

Max shook his head quickly. "Rabbi Goldenberg, I am sorry, but you have it all wrong. Natan didn't ask me to stay here for this week."

"Then why did you choose to stay?"

"His family is not religious, and his Saba was. He felt like someone needed to sit shiva for his Saba since none of his relatives would. I thought I would stay here and guide him through the mourning process."

Rabbi Eliezer frowned. "But a grandson is not one of the seven first-degree relatives. He can only sit shiva if his father is here sitting shiva as well. You should know that, Feldman."

"I do, Rabbi, but—" Max began.

Natan cut him off. "Well, I've done it. I've sat shiva for my Saba without my Aba being here."

"That's not right."

Natan looked daggers at Rabbi Eliezer. "I also plan to say *kaddish* for my Saba," he said obstinately.

"*Mein sohn*," Rabbi Eliezer said, "is your father alive? Or does he have brothers?"

"Yes, and yes."

"You've erred by sitting shiva, but I am here as a *posek* and I will set you on the right path. You cannot say kaddish for your Saba since your father and his brothers are alive. It is not appropriate that you recite it when your father is still alive."

Natan breathed in deeply. "Rabbi Goldenberg, my family is not religious. They are not going to say kaddish for my Saba. And even if they were religious, I'd still say kaddish for him. He was closer to me than my own father was."

Rabbi Eliezer shook his head. "You cannot do that. It will anger God."

"I don't care about what angers your mythical God. Kaddish will help me deal with the loss. I plan to do it regardless of what anyone says."

Rabbi Eliezer turned his attention to Max. "Feldman, did you not tell him that this flies in the face of halacha?"

Max looked sheepishly at the ground. "I don't think Natan cares about halacha very much, Rabbi Goldenberg."

Rabbi Eliezer pounded his lap. "You are a talmid, Feldman! You are part of the religious elite of our people. It is your duty and obligation and privilege to lead the lesser ones among us in derech Torah. Have you been keeping the mitzvos since you've been among these people?"

Avi interjected. "Excuse me for butting in, but I think it must be said Max has been very scrupulous in his observance since I've been acquainted with him. But you cannot expect him to enforce his views upon us 'lesser ones'."

"Was I speaking to you?"

"No, but—"

"If I was not directly addressing you, do not interrupt me. Were you dragged up or raised up? Who are your parents?"

"Who my parents are is not important, because I am fairly certain you've never met them. What's important is that your father was a wandering Aramean and I don't think he would be particularly pleased with your behavior."

Rabbi Eliezer exploded. "And you think you are qualified to tell me what Avraham Aveinu would think of me?"

Avi shrugged. "I think I am more qualified than you."

"My entire life has been spent in the pursuit and study of Torah, little boy. I think I know much more about the Patriarchs of our people than you do."

"Perhaps," Avi said, while Tzippy snorted, "but your behavior thus far has been quite unbecoming."

"My behavior has been unbecoming? You speak to your elder—yes, I am your elder, regardless of what you say—you sit there and speak to me with such insubordination and you say I have not behaved becomingly?"

"Yes, I am saying that," Avi responded simply. "You have been made aware of Natan's loss and you have made no attempt to offer him condolences or prayers or anything of the sort. Respect is a two-way street, and you've been nothing but disrespectful since you've been here."

"How dare you speak to me like that!"

"I am sorry if I offend you, but I am merely pointing out the obvious."

"I think you are quite out of place and need to know your place in the grand scheme of things!"

"And I think you are a vile, yet quite entertaining old man, with a chip on his shoulder and a bitter heart. And that's all I have to say. I am going to wash up. I feel dirty." He stood. "Mister Goldenberg, it was surreal meeting you. Grow a heart. *Lila tov.*" He looked at the others. "I'll come help finish sorting out this mess after our visitor has left." He strode leisurely to the bathroom and closed the door.

Rabbi Eliezer pursed his lips and said nothing.

The tension hung in the room.

Max spoke quickly, nervously. "Rabbi Goldenberg, please, I must apologize for my friend—"

"Never have I been more insulted in my life. Never."

"I am sorry."

"I have come into this house with only the best of intentions and I am treated in this way? No, I tell you, no, I will not stand for it." He looked self-piteous and continued to sit in his chair.

"Rabbi Goldenberg," Max entreated, "please do not take to heart what my friend said. It has been a trying week for all of us. Please, we are sorry."

Tzippy raised an eyebrow. "Speak for yourself," she muttered.

Rabbi Eliezer ignored her. "I accept your humble apology," he said, self-effacingly.

Natan spoke. "I didn't apologize, and Avi did have a valid point."

"And what exactly does that mean?"

"I think you've been a little caustic with us."

"Me? Caustic?" Rabbi Eliezer looked hurt. "My only concern in coming here was to see that Feldman was well. Then I ran into all of you fine people and I was merely trying to determine how you knew Feldman and to impart halacha to you. If that is what you call caustic, my dear boy, then I would much rather stay the way I am."

Tzippy, who had been sitting quietly the whole time, interjected. "You weren't trying to determine how we knew Max. You were interrogating us."

Rabbi Eliezer felt the anger grow within, but he breathed in deeply and stifled it, and forced himself to smile beatifically. "I was merely trying to establish the links between all of you and Feldman."

"Why? Because we are hilonim? Does it worry you that your precious talmid is associating with scum like us?" Tzippy asked forcefully.

Rabbi Eliezer gripped his side of the seat he was sitting on and forced himself with all his might to reel in his anger.

Max stood. "Tzippy," he started.

Tzippy stood and glared at her cousin.

"He is an arrogant old toad, Max!"

"He is Rabbi Eliezer Goldenberg, Tzippy!" Max yelled. "He is the former Chief Ashkenazi rabbi of the State and a renowned religious scholar!"

"I know who he is!" Tzippy yelled back. "He is a bigot and a sexist! Everyone knows that! And he's proven himself to be an insufferable snob by the way he's acted since he's been here!"

"Tzippy!" Max exclaimed, shocked. "How can you say such a thing?"

Rabbi Eliezer slackened his face and looked crestfallen. "Zeh beseder, Feldman. The world thinks the worst of me, and all I want to do is ensure the purity and continuation of our people." He looked at Tzippy for the first time. "I forgive you, girl."

"My name," Tzippy said, through gritted teeth, "is Tzipporah. And you forgive me for telling the truth?"

Rabbi Eliezer did not answer. Max bent over, quickly grabbed the old man's hand and excused them both to the balcony, leaving Tzippy seething and Natan almost as angry behind him in the living room. He pulled the glass door shut behind him. He was amazed at how quickly things had depreciated; he was amazed at the way his friends acted; and what he was most amazed at was that he somewhat agreed with them. Max shook himself and pushed the thoughts out of his head.

This was the great Rabbi Eliezer Goldenberg, for heaven's sake! If Rabbi Eliezer had been caustic, it was only because his friends had been caustic to start with. Yes, Max told himself, that was it. He ignored the nagging feeling inside of him and addressed Rabbi Eliezer.

"Rabbi Goldenberg, I am truly sorry for the way my friends behaved."

Rabbi Eliezer peered at him. "Why are they your friends?"

"They are good people."

"I am sure they are, but you are on a different level from them. I am not saying you shouldn't associate with them—dear me, no. They are Jews, but they are Jews of a different class. You should surround yourself with Jews who are of your ilk." Rabbi Eliezer paused. "I must tell you, Feldman, this visit has disappointed me."

"I don't understand."

"You gave a speech before your yeshiva went on break."

Max looked surprised. "You heard about my speech?"

"I heard it directly. I was there."

"I didn't see you, Rabbi Goldenberg."

Rabbi Eliezer looked amused. "I was not in the crowd, but I heard everything you said. It impressed me. I must admit to you, Feldman, your words touched me on a deep level. And, to be perfectly honest, it is the reason I came here tonight. You spoke like a true warrior for Torah."

Max blushed profusely. "Thank you."

"However, the boy I saw tonight is not a Torah warrior. You were surrounded by the very people you spoke out against; and what is more, you let them lambaste and humiliate one who stands high in the world of the living and eternal God, that is to say, me. I did not retaliate for I have spent many years battling against the hilonim and I have come to realize that argument with them, or even reasoning with them produces no fruit, for they are a stiff-necked and stubborn segment of Am Yisroel. You have disappointed me, Feldman."

Max looked chastened. "I am sorry, Rabbi Goldenberg."

Rabbi Eliezer nodded smugly. "I accept your apology, mein sohn. And although you have disappointed me, I still hold on to the hope that you can redeem yourself and show yourself to be the man who spoke so vociferously two weeks ago." He paused. "Tell me, Feldman, did you mean what you said when you gave your speech?"

Max nodded hesitantly.

"You don't seem sure," Rabbi Eliezer said anxiously.

Max cleared his throat. "Yes, I meant what I said."

Rabbi Eliezer relaxed. "Good. You will be returning to yeshiva tomorrow?"

"Yes, Rabbi Goldenberg. I am eager to return to my studies."

"Very well. I would like to meet with you tomorrow. I have things I wish to discuss with you further."

"I would be honored."

Rabbi Eliezer nodded and then patted Max on his hand. "Feldman, it is not easy—this life of derech haTorah. I understand you are baal teshuvah, and, as such, the road will be harder for you than for one who was born into Torah. You need to fortify yourself from the distractions and temptations that your previous life can bring to you. You must separate yourself from the people and things which will do nothing to help you achieve your goal of being the man I know you can be."

Max nodded.

"I will take my leave now."

"I'll walk you out.

CHAPTER 11

"'I thought,' said Abraham, 'surely there is no
fear of God in this place'."
—Genesis 20:11

Pastor Yuvie sat under the awning of a café in the Jewish Section of the Old City of Jerusalem and sipped his third Coke of the day. He had already consumed a cup of coffee, sitting where he was—waiting—but the Turkish coffee he had ordered had been stronger than he bargained for. He had switched to the more familiar Coke, which, much to his relief, was the same world over.

He fidgeted anxiously and swiveled his head and eyes around at the people who passed him by. The caffeine was running amok in his blood stream and making him jumpy. He knew he needed to calm down, but he desperately needed the caffeine to keep him awake as he had not slept a wink the night before—and it must be said, Pastor Yuvie was a man who always needed a full nine hours of sleep to be able to function with any semblance of productivity the next day. Given that he had registered a total of zero hours sleep the night before, it was abundantly clear why Pastor Yuvie needed and wanted as much caffeine as he did. He finished the last of his Coke and called the waiter over. "I'll have another Coke, please," he said, and then he added, "just keep them coming."

Pastor Yuvie had gone through his regular nighttime procedure the night before as usual: he had brushed his teeth, read his Bible, knelt on the floor and said his prayers, and then crawled into bed. Never the sort of man to toss and turn in bed, Pastor Yuvie had found himself doing just that. He shifted from the right to

212

the left, and then onto his back; he propped two pillows behind his head, and then went back to just one; he kicked the sheets off of himself, and then pulled them back on; he arched his back and then curled up in the fetal position. Nothing he was doing was allowing him to fall asleep. That had never happened before.

Confused about this abnormal, intrusive schism into his routine, he switched on the bedside lamp and went into the bathroom, filled a glass with water and drank it down. He returned to his bed, propped himself up against the headboard and picked up his Bible from where he had left it on the bedside table. He slipped his glasses onto his face and began to read, but he couldn't settle his mind. He tried reading for several minutes but he couldn't focus. The words simply weren't translating into thoughts. He closed the Bible and looked around the hotel room. The curtains were open and from his bed, he could just make out the view of Rechov Keren haYesod on the outside. He sighed.

It was his first time in the holy land. He had been there for only two days so far and the experience had been beyond anything he had imagined. He had dreamt about coming to Israel ever since he had first converted to Christianity, many decades before, and now, he was here, and for the first time in his life, he was unable to fall asleep. The next day, he would be joining the rest of his tour group and going to the town of Bethlehem to tour the church where Jesus had been born. The tour bus was scheduled to leave at eight in the morning. Pastor Yuvie looked at the blinking clock on the side table. It was two in the morning. He desperately needed sleep. He placed his Bible back on the bedside table, switched off the lamp, and snuggled down under the covers. But still, he could not fall asleep. Something was amiss. Then it hit him: the holy spirit must be near.

He quieted his thoughts, and almost instantly, he felt himself shift into the supernatural plane. Yes, the holy spirit was in the room with him and it wanted to commune with him. He felt the regular thrill and chill descend upon him, the sort of feeling he always felt whenever the holy spirit came close to him. He emptied his mind of all thoughts, and within minutes, the holy spirit had entered him, taking control of his body and causing his mouth to sputter with unintelligent mumblings which had no root in the human language.

He was slain in the spirit.

The powerful presence had entered him in its uniquely curious way. It had control of him, but he was, for all intents and purposes, still very much there, though no longer in control of his body.

The holy spirit had helped Pastor Yuvie accomplish many curious and miraculous things in his lifetime: it had helped him heal the sick, restore sight to the blind, make the lame walk, and, most importantly, it had made him privy to things that no one else knew. It took a lot of effort on Pastor Yuvie's part to cajole the holy spirit into assisting him with performing the miracles he wanted to demonstrate and to reveal the things he wanted to know. Sacrifice in the form of self-deprivation, and the abundantly constant, almost grating, playing of music were the two key elements which were needed to convince the holy spirit to come to Pastor Yuvie's aid. It was hard work, fasting for days on end from food and water, and then listening to the gregarious pounding of the drums, but it was what was needed to be done to have the holy spirit be drawn into the situation at hand and perform its awesome works. But it was work which Pastor Yuvie did not loathe to perform, for no matter what, it was being done with the most joyful of results and with the sincerest of intentions on Pastor Yuvie's part: it was being done so souls could be won for the kingdom of God. Every miraculous act Pastor Yuvie performed taxed his whole body, mind, and soul, but the rewards were so great; the glory of God was being proclaimed; the war against Satan was being won—and so Pastor Yuvie selflessly did what needed to be done. He afflicted himself and played the music, and like a moth to a flame, the holy spirit came and aided him in his ultimate objective of rescuing men from the pathway to hell.

However, never before this night did Pastor Yuvie ever experience the holy spirit descending upon him without it being first inveigled. He lay on his bed as the holy spirit possessed him, and in his semi-paralyzed state, he listened to the news the holy spirit proclaimed to him that night; news which was more miraculous than anything the holy spirit had ever said to Pastor Yuvie before. Within minutes, the holy spirit had exhausted itself of its information and it removed itself from Pastor Yuvie's body and had exited from the room, leaving Pastor Yuvie once again in control of his body with an excessively accelerated heart-beat due to the enormity of the news that had been revealed. Pastor Yuvie clutched his hands together. "Hallelujah," he whispered quietly to himself. Then, he threw his hands in the air and yelled out, "Blessed be the Lord of hosts! He is worthy to be praised and adored! Abraham has returned! Hallelujah!"

✡

When Avi awoke the next morning to say his prayers, he was surprised to find all of his roommates bustling around the living room. Usually, Avi would be the only one up and about at the crack of dawn, but today was a whole new beginning for all of them. Natan and Tzippy would be returning to Tel Aviv, and Max would be heading back to his yeshiva. The apartment was busy with the commotion of preparations. Knapsacks, duffel bags, and one pull-along luggage stood in the foyer, next to the bags of trash which had yet to be taken down to the dumpster. The smell of breakfast pervaded the entire apartment and the kitchen counters were cluttered with the dirty dishes that had been used to cook breakfast. The apartment's only bathroom was foggy with steam, as it received a constant, revolving cache of visitors.

Only Avi was not leaving the apartment to go anywhere, yet, he too felt an excitement of the approaching unknown, for he would be alone for the first time since he had come into the new world. Natan pulled him aside and forcibly handed him a credit card and a wad of shekels. Avi did not want to take it, but Natan pointed out that Avi would not be starting work until the next week, and, as such, would have no means to purchase food or anything else he may need. "Consider it a loan?" Natan suggested. "And whatever you don't use, you can always give back to me." Avi yielded. He put the money and credit card carefully into the black leather men's wallet Tzippy had bought him the week, and tucked it into his pocket.

Max, since he had to be at school for eight o'clock, was ready by seven. Avi had yet to visit the Old City, and as Max's yeshiva was contained therein, Avi asked if he could tag along and then spend the day exploring the place on his own. The others found this to be an inspired idea, and Tzippy handed Avi the map of Jerusalem she had bought earlier when she and Avi had been gallivanting around the city on their own. By five past seven, the two boys were set to embark. Natan and Tzippy were still in the middle of organizing themselves for their trip back to Tel Aviv, but they walked Max and Avi to the bus stop. Once outside, Natan shook both his friends' hands formally and wished them luck. Avi grinned and pulled Natan into a hug. "Thank you for everything, Natan," he said croakily. "I will take good care of your Saba's apartment."

"No crazy parties while I'm away, beseder?"

Tzippy hugged Avi tightly and promised to call him later that day from Tel Aviv. "And if you need me to come back, or if you want to come to Tel Aviv, just tell me, ok?" She pressed a pre-paid cellphone into his hand, then pulled away and looked Avi in the eyes. "I know it's silly, and I know I'm going to see you real soon, but I'm really going to miss you, Gramps." Avi smiled weakly at her. He had developed the strongest relationship with Tzippy and he would really miss her. He squeezed her hand in response.

The bus pulled up at that point, and with one last wave goodbye, Avi followed Max inside. They found a seat at the back and both sat down. Avi propped his chin on his hand and looked enthralled at the passing scenery on the short ten-minute ride down to the busy intersection at the David Citadel Hotel, the stop they needed to disembark at. Max thumbed through his siddur and pretended to focus on the words contained therein, but his mind was buzzing with thoughts.

The visit of Rabbi Eliezer had confused Max. After he had walked the rabbi outside the night before,

Max had realized that the man he had held in such a high regard was, in fact, as his friends had pointed out in their very impolite way, not a terribly endearing human being. However, at the same time, Max was still aware of the fact that the old man was one of the greatest living *poskim*, despite his overbearing attitude, and thus deserved a high measure of respect. But truth be told, Max was not particularly fond of Rabbi Eliezer after having met him. In fact, had the old man been anyone other than the esteemed Rabbi Eliezer Goldenberg, Max would have probably written him off as quickly as his friends had. Max felt conflicted—and he wasn't sure if this current conflict raging inside had anything to do with the internal struggle he thought he had conquered between his secular past and the tzaddik he aspired to be. Was his inability to like the venerable Rabbi Eliezer Goldenberg indicative of a relapse to being a hiloni? Had he stayed away from the yeshiva too long? Had he spent too much time in the company of the non-religious? Added to this confusion, Max was anxious about the meeting he had scheduled with the venerable rabbi. The rabbi had not said exactly why it was he wanted to talk to Max on an intimate level, but the reference to Max's speech gave Max a rough idea of what the rabbi wanted to discuss. Unfortunately, Max wasn't sure if he felt the same way he'd felt when he'd given the speech which had so impressed Rabbi Eliezer. True, much of what he'd said in his speech—even at the moment of giving the speech—hadn't been things Max had truly believed, but now that a few weeks had passed, and now that he had met Avraham Aveinu, Max felt even less convicted about the content of his speech.

Max's troubled thoughts swirled around in his head.

When the bus stopped before the busy intersection of Shlomzion haMalcha, Yitzchak Kariv and Gershon Agron, Max urged Avi up and they quickly jumped off the bus. It was early in the morning, but the streets were busy with pedestrians, bustling to work. Max cautioned Avi to stay close, and with Max in the lead, they hurriedly crossed the street and went up into the Alrov Mamilla mall complex. Avi was charmed by the Old City feel of the structure, and as he sped through the promenade and spotted the charming outdoor restaurants, he decided it would be nice to pass through on his way home and lunch there. He was glad of the money Natan had given him and he patted his wallet in his back pocket. They came to the end of the mall, and quickly made their way up the steps which led to the magnificent Jaffa Gate at the top. Max stopped and suggested to Avi that they part ways here.

"You have the map," Max said, "and I want you to enjoy the view of Jerusalem from here. I've got to rush to get to yeshiva on time, but once you've got the map, you are free to wander as you please."

Avi nodded agreeably.

"Keep your wallet in your pocket; don't stop to talk to vendors; and if you see anything—*anything*—odd going on, leave immediately."

Avi grinned. "Ok, dad."

Max looked at Avi. "You are sure you're going to be ok on your own?"

Avi smiled. "I should be."

Max wavered. "I could just skip class today and stay with you. I could be your guide."

Avi shook his head. "Go to school. I'll be fine. I'm a big boy."

Max shook his head.

Avi put his hand on Max's arm. "You guys are going to have to cut the umbilical cord sometime—might as well do it now."

Max sighed. "I don't know why, but all of a sudden I don't feel right about this."

"I'm Avraham of old, chaver," he said. "I've got God above me and my angel at my side—I'm covered. Don't worry about me."

Max hesitated, then hugged Avi. "I'll try to come and see you sometime this week, ok?"

"Ok."

"I'll call you later. And you call me at the yeshiva if anything goes wrong and have them page me, ok?"

Avi grinned. "Yes, dad. Go to class."

Max smiled back and backed away. "I'm going, I'm going. Take care of yourself, Heeb."

"Shalom, Jew."

Max made his way across to the imposing edifice that was the Jaffa Gate. He stopped before the entrance and turned back, but Avi had turned his back and was watching the view of the new city. Max closed his eyes and whispered a quiet prayer. "Look over him, God. Protect him, guide him, and be with him." He turned around and continued on to his yeshiva.

✡

Pastor Yuvie had been born Yuvraj Teelucksingh to a humble Hindu household in Guyana. Not the brightest of boys, he had passed through his elementary and high school years without distinction. Despite his subdued intelligence quota, he struggled for recognition from and influence over his teenage peers. He believed he was special and was destined for great things, but the realization of this hope was never achieved in school and it would continue to be an unfulfilled longing which would painfully follow him into his adult life. He was diligent in his studies, but was never able to rise above the lowest percentiles of his year. He tried out for sports, but proved less than mediocre in his abilities. He attempted to befriend the more popular boys, but his odd looks, drab personality, and unintelligent persona made him undesirable among the students.

Unable to find success in the academic arena, he turned his attention to religion, and in the Hindu mandirs of his country, he found the acclaim he desperately craved. Pastor Yuvie was blessed with a beautiful singing voice—and this, coupled with his unusual prowess at playing the *dhantal*, earned Pastor Yuvie a resounding respect throughout the nation's Hindu community. By the time he was nineteen, Pastor Yuvie was a popular and much sought-after figure at *satsangs*, where his beautiful renditions of *bhajans* resonated with the people.

Despite his thrust into the religious world of Hinduism, Pastor Yuvie had no real understanding or knowledge of the ancient Vedic faith. His family's caste was unknown; lost through the annals of migration to the New World—perhaps, and most likely, a voluntary act on the part of his ancestors. Many East Indians who had ventured to the British colonies of the West had purposely chosen to acquire new identities by casting off the centuries old caste system which had beleaguered them. It was highly plausible to suggest that Pastor Yuvie's family was of this ilk; their limited acquaintance with the religion of their forefathers was indicative of their original status in the Hindu hierarchy prior to their migration to Guyana. Pastor Yuvie was aware of this, and he knew that his acceptance and respect in the Hindu community was hampered by his inability to provide a chastely background. He reveled in his fame, but he was shamed by his status.

When he was twenty, Pastor Yuvie's singing troupe was invited to play at the *pooja* of a prominent Guyanese Hindu family. Whilst there, Pastor Yuvie happened to come across a young girl, two years his junior, who was everything he wanted in a companion. Her name was Mary, and like him, she was also of Indian descent. She had long, flowing black hair, a small waist and was a wide smile. Pastor Yuvie was smitten. Unfortunately, Mary, though Indian, was not Hindu. Her family had converted to Presbyterianism two generations before. He met with Mary's mother, who told him in no uncertain terms: "Mary will only marry a Christian. Convert or have nothing more to do with my daughter." Despite his family's protests, Pastor Yuvie was much too in love to care about religion, and thus, he converted.

To Pastor Yuvie's welcome surprise, the stigma of being without caste did not follow him into the Presbyterian arena—for the bulk of the congregation was made up of persons of East Indian descent who were similarly faced with Pastor Yuvie's predicament of being former Hindus without caste. Pastor Yuvie reveled in the unequivocal acceptance and he threw himself into being an exemplary Christian. He followed the rest of his previously Hindu brethren in turning up his nose at the Hinduism they had collectively shunned; and with a newly-instilled sense of superiority, Pastor Yuvie finally felt he had found a place where his destiny could unravel without impediment. Within three years, he had married Mary, switched from Presbyterianism to
222

Pentecostalism, received the gift of the holy spirit at church one Sunday morning, enrolled at and graduated from a local seminary as a pastor, and seen his entire Hindu family follow him into the world of Christian evangelism.

Pastor Yuvie felt fulfilled.

After the nine-month course, which resulted in him being ordained as a pastor, Pastor Yuvie felt his destiny beckoning towards him. He was pulled in the direction of opening his own church. It was the platform from which he would be able to achieve his goal of true recognition and glory. He saved up his money and with the assistance of his wife, he rented space at the back of a small grocery store, and from there, he began his ministry. This was not a difficult process in and of itself, as the world of Pentecostalism had no authoritative structure, and thus allowed for any self-proclaimed evangelist, apostle or prophet who had the wherewithal to do so to command a following in establishing their own church.

Unfortunately, Pastor Yuvie was entering a field which was awash with competition. There were numerous, small evangelical churches in Guyana, and many more larger ones besides. Although Pastor Yuvie's holy spirit had not exactly directed him to open a church, it did not forbid it either—and thus, Pastor Yuvie felt certain that this venture would be successful.

He was wrong.

No matter how hard he tried, his regular congregation would never swell to numbers greater than fifty persons at any given time. He decided to diversify, and keeping his church operative, he simultaneously branched out into evangelical work; he pitched tents throughout Guyana and made alliances with equally small churches in other countries and travelled there as a missionizing pastor. Initially, people would be attracted to the services. Pastor Yuvie's excellent singing voice had transitioned nicely into the world of gospel music, and his renditions of classic Christian hymns would pull participants in. Then, when he had a sizeable audience, Pastor Yuvie would wheedle the holy spirit into entering his body and with its aid, Pastor Yuvie would perform miracles—small acts of wonder he was sure rivaled those of the greatest of the Hebrew prophets. Unfortunately, the numerous persons Pastor Yuvie claimed to heal went on to find out that they were not exactly cured of their diseases or that they experienced serious relapses. Pastor Yuvie, like many of his contemporaries, argued that the fault lay not with him or the holy spirit, but rather, with the sinners themselves who had not truly repented. The mindless masses fed into this excuse and they prayed more fervently, but none ever witnessed a true recovery from whatever ailment it was which plagued them.

Despite of all this, Pastor Yuvie built a reputation as a miracle worker for himself. His services were requested by many ailing people, yet, it never translated into great numbers at his own church. Truth be told, Pastor Yuvie was not a great preacher; he did not have the depth to anchor the spiritually hungry masses. He could initially draw crowds in with his parlor tricks, but there was nothing of substance which kept them attached to him. His sermons were lacking, and most people ascertained this in their minds and shied away from fully committing to Pastor Yuvie by joining his church.

As the years passed by without him triumphing in the fruition of his quest for success, Pastor Yuvie began to falter and waver. He wondered if he had read the signs wrong. Was he not meant for greatness? He spent a week in fast and prayer, hoping to find some proper direction. He was on the verge of closing his church and exiting the world of pastoral ministry when he came across a program on the local evangelical television station which would concurrently fortify his belief in his abilities as a pastor and also add a new dimension to his Pentecostal theology.

It was in this television program that Pastor Yuvie was introduced to the modern messianic Christian movement which incorporated Jewish tradition and rituals into their evangelic practice, and it was exactly the thing he needed to confirm that he was exactly where he was meant to be. This would be the edge he would use to propel himself into the stratosphere of evangelical fame.

Every week, Pastor Yuvie would plop himself in front of his television and eagerly look at new segments of the program. He would later go to church and regurgitate these concepts, much to the delight and enthrallment of his flock, which had tired of the mundane Jesus-loves-you, fire-and-brimstone and the-kingdom-of-God-is-at-hand sermons. As more time went by and Pastor Yuvie became more entrenched in the new theology, he began to realize that in this messianic movement, the caste system he had left behind in his Hindu past had now once again descended upon him. In the Presbyterian and mainstream evangelical philosophies he had just exited, Christians, while not anti-Semitic in any sense of the word, saw themselves as being the inheritors of Judaism, and Christianity as being the superseding religion to Judaism. In the messianic Christian teaching, it dangerously borrowed snippets from Jewish life and thus propelled Jews who embraced
225

Jesus as being superior to non-Jewish Christians. The Hebrew Bible was carefully studied in its badly mistranslated English, and the conclusions drawn from it were eons different from traditional Judaic teaching. The result was a sort of reverse antisemitism: Jews were exalted, and non-Jews were not. It was a caste system through and through, and for the majority of non-Jews who ascribed to this philosophy, there was a definite feeling of inferiority, and Pastor Yuvie felt the poignant sting of the past rear its ugly head once again. But then, a brilliant idea struck his head. He stood in front of his pulpit and with his hand on his Bible, Pastor Yuvie testified that he was a descendant of Jews: claiming his paternal grandfather had been Jewish. He gave a riveting tale of seeing this concocted grandfather praying with a tallit wrapped around his shoulders when he was a child, and with tears streaming down his face, Pastor Yuvie almost convinced himself that he was not lying.

The fifty-odd members of his congregation were collectively shocked and they looked at their revered pastor in a new light. He was a completed Jew and was even greater than they had thought. The congregants rushed to shake his hand at the end of his testimony and Pastor Yuvie had never felt more in touch with his destiny. He beamed and walked around the decaying church and allowed the people to fawn over him.

It was a great day in the life of Pastor Yuvie.

It was at this point that Pastor Yuvie curbed references to his full name, Yuvraj, and began terming himself 'Yuvie'. Yuvie was less Indian and could be misinterpreted for being a condensed version of the Hebraic 'Yuval'.

Unfortunately, Pastor Yuvie's subscription to the obscure messianic Christian doctrine was still not

226

enough to pull in crowds and while he did see an initial slight surge in numbers, his lack of real knowledge quickly led to a drop and a return to the regular congregation. Pastor Yuvie tired of the fad and returned to mainstream evangelical preaching, but he kept the sobriquet of Yuvie—the only remnant of his short wade into the streams of an obscure Christian theology. Even his claim of Jewish descent was slowly forgotten by his congregants, and life reverted to simple heaven-and-hell, Jesus-died-for-your-sins sermons.

✡

To Avi's ancient eyes, the Old City of Jerusalem was nothing like a city from his time. It wasn't even like Tel Aviv or the Jerusalem Avi had just exited. The streets were narrow and cramped and the stones upon which it was built were dirty and dangerously smooth. Even the sun shone differently inside of its walls; unable to truly pierce through the narrowness of the cobbled streets. It was as if the tiny alleyways were intent on shutting the sun out, almost as if they screamed, "This is holy ground and the joy of the sun must be barred from entering here!" Cities of Avi's time were less cramped and built mostly out of hardened mud—with wider alleyways and more green. The Old City of Jerusalem was nothing like that, with its constricted, bumpy streets of grimy stone, its noisy and sweaty population, its crowded alleyways and its pungent smells. But all the same, underneath the layers of physical imperfection, there was a holy mystery to the city. A sober somberness emanated from every pore of the city's stones. The ancient majesty of the woeful city hung in the air. And Avi felt it deep inside of himself.

For a few minutes, he scanned the map Tzippy had given him, but then shoved it into his pocket and wandered around on his own. The city was too small to get lost in and it was too busy to ignore by consulting maps. He walked slowly, but purposefully.

He passed by nooks and cracks which were filled with tiny, hampered stores—and it was these numerous, easily forgettable stores, more than anything else, which reminded him most forcefully of the city he had grown up in as a child. The smell of exotic spices which wafted from these confined stores took Avi straight back to his previous life and he inhaled deeply and smiled nostalgically to himself. He passed through different streets and observed the different layers of the city. He constantly ran into pilgrims with their fanny packs wrapped around their waists, their hands clasped in the global symbol of reverence, marching quietly and resolutely along different parts of the Via Dolorosa. He bought a packet of potato chips and a bottle of water from a vendor, and lingered around the outdoor cafes where old Arab men sat at rickety tables, their keffiyahs draped over their heads, and smoked flavored nargila. He listened to the various Christian Orthodox priests in their drab, black, yet different gowns with crosses hanging around them, arguing over mops and brooms outside of the Church of the Holy Sepulcher. He freely gave of the money Natan had given him to the grubby hands of Gypsy children who lived in the city; their lives unaffected by the greater religious tensions that encumbered the place they called home. He followed the Jewish Orthodox men in their ill-fitting black suits and fedoras, with sweat dripping down their faces, as they hurried around, and he ended up in the Jewish Section of the Old City.

It was more open here than in other sections. After all, much of the Jewish Section was newly reconstructed after it had been destroyed during the Jordanian occupation. He passed by the rebuilt Hurva Synagogue, and stopped to take in the marvelous architecture of the enormous domed structure—a testament to the enduring Jewish connection and legacy in the Old City. He visited the Old Yishuv Court Museum and wept at the story it told of Jewish history in the Old City; it was the story of his children, and it pained him to learn of their collective and constant tragedy concerning this, their holy city. When he regained his composure, he ventured down to the immense plaza of *haKotel haMa'aravi*—the holiest site in modern Judaism. He knew what stood at the top of the wall. It was the Temple Mount, the eternal site of the now destroyed Beit haMikdash. In his past life, he had journeyed to the top of that mountain, long before any religion or people had laid claim to it, and he had almost sacrificed his dear, only son, Isaac, upon it. It had been a harrowing episode of his former life—but he felt far removed from it. The physical landscape of the place had changed so much, he almost felt as if that penultimate story from his previous life was just that: a story. He was grateful that he was no longer plagued by the terror of that day; instead, he could be here as just an observer, removed from the crushing history of the city, and just absorb it all.

He stepped forward towards the wall hesitantly, and stopping to don a cardboard kipa, he approached the wall reverently and placed his hands on it. It was cool to the touch as the desert sun had yet to throw her vicious rays where he stood and the silent shade of the imposing wall gave him shelter. He closed his eyes, bowed his head, and with the recent memory of Jewish misfortune from the Old Yishuv Court Museum still emblazoned on his mind, he silently prayed to his God to bestow peace on his descendants and this city of Jerusalem, the city of peace. He then walked backwards, away from the Wall, and returned the borrowed kipa to the entrance of the men's section.

The plaza had filled up since he'd first entered. He walked to the steps which led away from the Kotel and exited the space and returned to the Jewish section of the Old City. His mind felt less troubled than it had when he'd left the Old Yishuv Court Museum. His prayer had settled him. He reminded himself that the era of the mashiach had begun and he pondered what positive changes this would bring about in the world at large. Avi thought of Natan and the job that lay before his gentlemanly Israeli friend. The conversation and the knowledge Saba had imparted to Avi trickled through his mind, and as he walked, he pondered the information, particularly the information pertaining to the mashiach. He had talked it over with Michael and both of them, man and angel, had agreed that Saba's talk on the night of his death had a particular meaning for Avi and within the speech had contained pertinent information which related to Avi's task of finding the mashiach. Avi felt he needed to inform Natan of what Saba had told him concerning Natan's job as mashiach, for he was sure Natan had no idea about the deeply philosophical and theological implications that were attached to his job as the mashiach.

As Avi walked, lost in his thoughts, he felt someone touch him and say softly, "Father Abraham."

✡

Avi was intrigued by the man who knew he was Avraham. With the exception of Natan's Saba, no one had inherently known he was Avraham of old. Unlike Natan's Saba, however, Avi didn't sense any particular spirituality around Pastor Yuvie's aura, and Michael confirmed this. In fact, Michael was anxious about Avi spending time with Pastor Yuvie.

"I don't know why," Michael had whispered in Avi's ear, "but I don't feel right about this. There is something not right about this man."

"There is a mystery here," Avi had said, "and I plan to solve it."

"Not all mysteries are meant to be solved, you stubborn mule," Michael had replied tersely. He hovered close to his human charge.

Added to Avi's intrigue that Pastor Yuvie knew who he was, the fact that Pastor Yuvie was clearly of Indian descent had also piqued Avi's interest. In his life as Avraham, Avi's mother, Amathlaah, was actually Indian, and Avi had always felt a special affinity with his mother's kin. Indeed, Avi had spent time in India with his relatives there, as India was only a few weeks journey by camel from the city of Cutha in which he had grown up.

Initially, Avi thought that Pastor Yuvie had been among the group of Christian-Korean tourists from the week before, and thus, knew he was Avraham because he'd heard Avi broadcast it loud and clear, but that theory quickly disintegrated when Pastor Yuvie mentioned he had only arrived in Israel two days before. Which naturally brought Avi to the question: "So, how did you know who I was?"

"God told me," Pastor Yuvie answered simply.

The answer piqued Avi's curiosity. There was definitely a mystery to be unraveled.

Avi, who was quite hungry from his day of exploring the Old City of Jerusalem, suggested they have lunch, to which the hyped-up-on-caffeine pastor readily agreed. They walked to the Mamilla Mall and sat across from each other in Café Rimmon. They both scoured the menu and ordered what they wanted (Avi: a salmon and cream cheese sandwich and a glass of orange juice, and Pastor Yuvie: a bottle of water and a glass of Coke) and then looked at each other awkwardly.

"I'm curious about you," Avi said eventually.

"Likewise," Pastor Yuvie replied.

"Are you from India?"

Pastor Yuvie spasmed. "No, not at all."

"You look Indian to me."

Pastor Yuvie laughed nervously and fidgeted conspicuously in his chair. "Some of my forefathers were Indian—but trust me, I do not adhere to their superstitious religion."

Avi raised an eyebrow. "Some of your ancestors, you say? What were the rest of your ancestors?"

Pastor Yuvie sat up proudly. "My grandfather was a Jew. I am your descendant."

Avi looked at Pastor Yuvie closely.

"He is lying," Michael whispered. "He is lying so well, he's even convinced himself that what he said is true."

"Indeed," Avi responded quietly, then, louder, to Pastor Yuvie, "you don't seem to be proud of your Indian heritage."

Pastor Yuvie waved his hand dismissively. "What is there to be proud of? They are polytheists—their religion commands them pray to snakes and
232

demons and gods who are capricious and fickle. I rather identify with my Jewish roots because our great Western religions are the true and right pathways to God, and because, as a Christian descended from your bloodline, I am a completed Jew."

"I don't understand what you mean when you say you are a 'completed Jew'."

"I am a Jew who believes in Jesus," Pastor Yuvie replied. "I am a Jew who has completed my religion by believing in Jesus."

"Oh." Avi didn't know how to respond.

"I have chosen the right path," Pastor Yuvie continued earnestly. "I was born and raised Hindu, but in my adult years, I was lucky to have found Jesus and found my Jewish roots and embraced them both, while rejecting the erroneous ways of my lesser ancestors." He paused. "I pray that Hindus the world around will come to see the truth as well."

"Isn't that a little sanctimonious?"

"What do you mean?"

"You're assuming yours is the right way."

"I know mine is the right way."

"No one knows anything for sure."

"I know mine is the right way," Pastor Yuvie replied firmly. "And the Indian race, as long as it continues to practice Hinduism, remains doomed."

Avi smiled wanly. "Careful, my friend, you are very close to insulting me."

"How so?"

"My mother was Indian and she was Hindu. My formative years were spent studying the religion of my father as well as my mother—and Hinduism, in my opinion, is a worthy pathway to the divine."

Pastor Yuvie was astounded. "Your mother was from India?"

"Yes."

"Then surely you know that it is a polytheistic religion."

"It is better to be ethical than a monotheist," Avi replied simply. "The people of India have always exhibited the mitzvah of loving-kindness. They took in my descendants, members of the lost tribes, and gave them shelter for thousands of years. The Hindus are great people; their religion is deep."

"I beg to differ. I mean you no disrespect, but you are not acquainted with them as I am. They are pagans—barbarians. They may have some ethical goodness, but, at the end of the day, they don't recognize the God of Israel. They are not of God."

"All souls are fashioned by the Creator in His image and likeness and all souls will return to Him. God prefers us behaving ethically and lovingly to each other rather than simply running around helter-skelter believing there is only one God."

Pastor Yuvie guffawed. "So, Hindus won't go to hell?"

"All souls come from God. All souls belong to God. All souls return to God."

"There is no hell?"

Avi considered his words carefully. "The modern concept of hell is not something which existed in my time. This is a modern invention—a remnant of the Zoroastrian faith that found itself embedded in modern consciousness. I cannot say for sure if there is a hell, but in my spiritual understanding, such a thing is not possible."

"Didn't you just return from heaven? Surely you must know whether or not there is a hell?"

"I don't remember heaven."

"How could that be?" Pastor Yuvie asked, incredulously.

Avi shrugged. "I don't know. I just don't. It's the way it is meant to be."

At that moment, the waitress returned with their orders. After she had moved away from the table, Avi spoke, "We have strayed from the issue. You say God told you who I was. How?"

"Father Abraham," Pastor Yuvie began.

"Avi," Avi said firmly.

"Abi?"

"Avi," Avi said, emphasizing the 'v' in his name.

"Avi," Pastor Yuvie said.

Avi nodded and smiled encouragingly.

Pastor Yuvie took a deep breath. "Avi, last night, the most miraculous thing happened to me. I was lying in bed in my hotel room when the holy spirit descended upon me and told me you were back on earth. He then directed me to go to the Old City and wait on you. I was sitting all day, desperately looking around for you—and then, all of a sudden, I felt the most powerful manifestation of the holy spirit that I have ever felt in my life. It overwhelmed me and, I suppose, it overwhelmed itself, but it recognized you as you walked past us, and it directed me to you."

Avi scratched his head. "The holy spirit?"

"God—the third part of the god-head."

"Oh." Avi paused. "You say it entered you?"

"Yes, I was slain in the spirit."

Avi coughed. "I just want to be clear, you're telling me that a spirit entered you?"

Pastor Yuvie shook his head forcefully. "No, not a spirit—the holy spirit."

"You say this spirit led you to me. Is it still with you?"

"No, it left me when I met you. The process of channeling the holy spirit is difficult for both myself and the holy spirit and I suppose, given the strength of its manifestation when it recognized you, it needs time to recoup before it can return."

Michael bristled and whispered anxiously into Avi's ear. "This man is a medium! It was not God who told him you were here. It was a dead spirit which he thinks is God."

Avi excused himself and went to the washroom so he could speak freely to his angel.

"He channels dead spirits?" Avi asked out loud, once he made sure the bathroom was empty of other people.

"Yes!" Michael answered forcefully.

"How can you be sure that's what he meant? He himself said that it was a holy spirit. *The* holy spirit, he said."

"Avi—do not be stupid. God does not enter people and He does not direct them in such ways."

"I'm not being stupid. I'm being rational. How could a ghost possibly know I was here when no one alive does until I tell them, Michael?"

"It is difficult to explain the goings on of the spiritual realm in mortal terminologies. The best way I could explain it to you is that your reappearance on earth, whilst unbeknown to living souls, has caused a ripple in the ether of the unseen world around you, and those who occupy that world are very aware that you have returned."

236

"Ok, but the spiritual realm is not populated by only dead spirits. You know that," Avi said. "The guardian angel of Natan's Saba told him who I was. What if Pastor Yuvie is terming his guardian angel 'holy spirit'? In many ways, an angel is like a holy spirit."

"Did I ever enter you, Avi? Did the guardian angel of Natan's Saba ever enter him?"

Avi didn't answer.

"Angels don't possess people. Dead spirits which haven't left the earthly plane do."

"Well, maybe it is God."

"You are being stubborn. You spoke with God in your last life. Did He ever possess you?"

"Well, no."

"Exactly. God does not infringe Himself upon anyone when He needs to communicate with mankind. This man is dangerous—that spirit is dangerous. You know this."

Avi sighed. "Ok, fine. You are right."

"You must leave. You must leave now."

"My food only just arrived! At least let me finish my meal and then I can leave."

"Avi, leave now."

"I am Avraham of old," Avi answered, cheekily. "I am known for being hospitable. I am not going to leave mid-way through a meal with someone." He turned and went to the bathroom door. "But I promise I will leave once I am done eating, ok?"

Michael groaned.

Avi returned to the table and sat down and apologized for leaving.

"That's ok," pastor Yuvie said, beaming.

Avi smiled cautiously, picked up his sandwich, and bit into it.

"Can I ask you something?"

Avi nodded while he chewed.

"Why are you back?"

Michael bristled. "Do not tell him the answer to that."

Avi ignored Michael. "I was sent to inform the messiah that he is the messiah."

Pastor Yuvie's eyes opened wide. "Jesus has returned?"

"Jesus?"

"Jesus—the messiah who came and died for our sins. He is back?"

Avi was intrigued. "Tell me about this Jesus."

"You don't know about him?" Pastor Yuvie looked surprised.

"I've read about him, but I'd rather hear about him from your perspective. He is the messiah of the Christians, not so?"

"He is the messiah of the world!" Pastor Yuvie exclaimed and threw his hands excitedly into the air. "He is god born into the status of a humble man who was crucified on a cross for the sins of all of mankind."

"He is god?"

"Yes, he is god; the second part of the holy Trinity. Two thousand years ago, he was born into a Jewish household, to a virgin named Mary. He lived until the age of thirty-three when he was put to death; he then descended into the bowels of hell for three days, and retrieved the keys of that torturous domain from Satan, and thus ushered in the period of grace which has lasted since then."

"What is the period of grace?"

"It is the period of history we live in—where all people, Jew and Gentile alike, could have access to God

238

without the need for sacrificial rituals in the Jewish Temple."

Avi scratched his head. "But people, Jew and non-Jew alike, always had access to God, with or without sacrificial rituals. I only did one sacrifice in my life, to be honest."

Pastor Yuvie shook his head vehemently. "You misunderstand me. Before Jesus, only Jews had access to God, and only through the sacrifice of animals. After Jesus, the entire world was given access to Him."

"How?"

"Jesus died for the sins of every man, woman, and child who has ever lived. In his death, with the shedding of his blood, man no longer needed to shed the blood of animals. All that is needed now is the symbolic remembrance of Jesus' death and the recognition and acceptance that his blood was the ultimate sacrifice."

"The sacrificial lamb?"

Pastor Yuvie beamed. "Exactly!"

Avi thought things over. "What I don't understand is how Jesus came to be viewed as the messiah. How did his unfortunate death become propelled into the basis of the theology you speak of? Why did he become a candidate for messiah?"

"He is the messiah."

"Ok, but how did people start to believe that he was?"

"The prophecies in the Old Testament were all fulfilled within the person of Jesus."

"What were the prophecies?"

"There were many prophecies. A virgin shall be with child and they shall call his name Emmanuel; the chapter of the Suffering servant in Isaiah 53 which speaks of the horrors our lord endured prior to and during his death which led to the pathway of redemption for the entire world; the prophecy that he shall be born in the city of his ancestor, King David, that is, Bethlehem, thus making him a legal claimant to the throne of Israel; the fact that, like the Israelite babies in Egypt, he was pursued by King Herod, who massacred numerous Jewish baby boys; his family fled to Egypt to escape this persecution, much like—well, you did when you went to Egypt to escape the famine in Canaan. The prophecies are endless and they all point to one man and one man only: Jesus."

Avi coughed. "The actual Hebrew word used in the chapter actually means young woman and not virgin, and, besides, Jesus' name was not Emmanuel—the way the verse is structured points to the fact that the child to be born would be known by the man the prophecy had been made to, King Ahaz of Judah, as a sign to him that the kings of Israel and Aram would not be successful in their campaign against Judah. My understanding of the chapter on the Suffering Servant in Isaiah refers not to Jesus, but rather, to the suffering of the Jewish nation as a whole, and through them, redemption of the world shall be ushered in. It is written in the Christian Gospels that the census in Jesus' time ordered people to return to their ancestral cities, and this was what caused Jesus to be born in Bethlehem, but history teaches that no such migratory census took place. As for Jesus' descent from David, that is perhaps true, but the Christian scriptures mention explicitly that Jesus was descended from David's son, Nathan, and not from the rightful heir of David's throne, King Solomon. Let us also not forget that, as the son of Mary, Jesus had matrilineal claim to Davidic descent—since it was his mother who descended from King David—but a claimant to the
240

throne must have patrilineal descent. As for Herod, he is portrayed in scholarly historic accounts as a despotic mad man, and accounts of his many heinous acts have been documented, yet, no historically verifiable mention is made of this supposed massacre of Jewish baby boys outside of the Christian bible."

Pastor Yuvie looked put out. "If you knew about the prophecies and how to refute them, why did you ask me about them?"

Avi shrugged. "I was curious to hear your specific viewpoint, because I thought you had evidence other than what I already know about."

"Ok, well forget about the prophecies. What about the miracles Jesus performed?" Pastor Yuvie persisted. "He accomplished many acts of wonder, including bringing the dead back to life."

"The Torah explicitly warns against judging people based on the merits of miracles. In my previous life, I performed no acts of wonder; neither did my son, Isaac; nor my grandson, Jacob; nor any of Jacob's twelve sons. Concurrently, neither did the majority of the Hebrew prophets perform miracles. Belief which stems from the performance of miracles and signs of wonders is dangerous because such things can be accomplished without the assistance of God, and this is why Jews have long shied away from conferring special status upon miracle-workers. The claim that miracles are a measure of holiness is groundless when one considers that unholy men can perform them. Besides, the books of the Christian bible were written decades after Jesus' death and it is debated by many scholars that the authors of these books had not, in fact, actually ever met Jesus, and, thus, that the stories contained therein are not factual, first-hand accounts of Jesus' life and actions—including the supposed miracles."

"Fine, forget that. But you cannot ignore that the message he brought was one which changed the course of history. Whether it was written by someone who met him or not, the report of Jesus' message, as reported in the New Testament, was something which had never been preached by any man prior to Jesus."

"True, Jesus preached a powerful message, and yes, you are right, his insistence on brotherly love and all these other things did change the course of history—but the fact remains that nothing Jesus said was new or original. Rabbis and sages who pre-dated him had already mouthed every sermon he preached, including the content of his famous Sermon on the Mount. His directive to love others as you would yourself is part of the mitzvoth contained in Torah and was forever famously encapsulated as the essence of Judaism two centuries before Jesus by the great Rabbi Hillel. The fact is, subsequent to Jesus' death, he had a master marketer in the person of his follower, Paul, who promoted Jesus' copied sayings wider than the sayings of the original speakers, and thus, Jesus received the acclaim for words which, I'm sorry to say, were not originally his. The discovery of the Dead Sea Scrolls and the words contained therein, are eerily similar to everything Jesus said, including the outline of his life as recorded in the Christian bible—but the Dead Sea Scrolls were written a couple centuries before Jesus lived, and, I'm sorry to say, they report on a man called the 'Teacher of Righteousness' who lived long before Jesus."

"You speak almost as if you don't believe he is the messiah."

"Let me put it to you this way. Democratic countries have constitutions which clearly outline how their governments and leaders are chosen. The constitutions outline the basis of eligibility for the various positions; as well as outline how leaders should be chosen. For instance, in the United States of America, a person who was not born in the country cannot ever attain the position of President. You with me so far?"

Yuvie nodded.

"Can a man or woman who was born in, say, Canada, stand up say willy-nilly, that he or she is the President of the United States of America and then be President?"

Yuvie shook his head.

"What if that person finds a following of thousands, if not millions and billions, of people who aren't American? What if the majority of the world ends up supporting this person? Does that make the person the President?"

"I suppose it does."

"Actually, it doesn't. It wouldn't make the person the President of the United States of America, because America has a written constitution which dictates who the candidates for this position can be and it states that the voting process by American citizens only is necessary to install someone into this position. It would be a coup d'état, and the self-stylized President, while he or she may control the support of the majority of the world, would be outside of the American Constitution and thus, not leader of the country in its incarnation as the United States of America. He or she would have to form an entirely new constitution and an entirely new country, and be the legal leader of that—he would never be the leader of the old country, as he

243

positioned himself outside of the constitution which governed it.

"In the same way, the positioning of Jesus as the messiah went outside of the Jewish constitution, that is to say, the Jewish Scriptures. Jesus as messiah was an idea embraced by non-Jews. Jesus was not embraced by Jews as their messiah because he didn't fulfill the requirements outlined in their constitution. Regardless of the non-Jewish belief in Jesus as the messiah, the fact remains that Jews reject this, and, therefore, he is not the Jewish messiah."

Pastor Yuvie folded his arms and stayed quiet for a few moments. "It's like you're trying to convince me to believe Jesus is not God."

Avi shrugged. "My opinion is unnecessary. I am merely pointing out the facts to you."

"If Jesus wasn't the messiah—then who was he?"

"I am not sure. Was he a misunderstood rabbi? Perhaps. The fact is, the factualness of the sources for his life are highly doubtful; and the movement which sprang up following Jesus' death was different from who, it is reasonable to assume, he was. As a Jew, I don't think Jesus would've been happy with the pathway that the movement based around him chose to take. However, at the end of the day, who Jesus was is not directly relevant to my mission here on earth."

Pastor Yuvie sighed. "This is not how I envisaged our meeting transpiring."

"How so?"

Pastor Yuvie looked put out. "I had hoped you would come with the conviction that Jesus is lord. I had hoped we could work together to spread his gospel to the world." He sniffed. "But it's clear you're not even saved, so I guess that's not going to happen."

"I'm not saved?" Avi was genuinely confused.

"You've not accepted that Jesus is the Christ and that he is lord of all. You aren't saved."

"Like the Hindus?"

"I suppose."

Avi didn't know what to say. He took another bite from his sandwich.

"If you say you have returned to inform the messiah that he is messiah," Pastor Yuvie continued, "and you say it's not Jesus, then who is the messiah?"

Avi looked at the face of the desperate man with sympathy. "My friend, I am not saying that Jesus is not your messiah. That he is your messiah is no contest, and it is a wonderful thing that you have someone wonderful to believe in. He is your messiah; believe in him and follow his teachings and love—above all, love—because that was the basis of Jesus' entire philosophy. Do not let the trivialities of religious theology cloud this basic request of his followers. Do not judge; was that also not Jesus' teaching? Do not judge the Hindus or the Jews or anyone else. Focus on your messiah and emulate his humbleness and his acts of loving-kindness."

"So, you're saying he's my messiah, but he's not the messiah you've returned for?"

Avi sighed. "The messiah I come for pertains to the Jewish people only."

"So, this messiah is racist and he is only coming for the good of the Jews?"

"Not at all!" Avi exclaimed. "He comes to assist the Jewish people, and this, in turn, will assist the world at large. He is not racist—but he comes specifically for his people."

"Is he alive now?"

Avi hesitated, then nodded.

"Have you met him?"

Avi nodded again.

"Can I meet him?"

Avi shook his head.

"Why not?"

"I don't think he is ready to be presented to the world as the messiah just yet."

Pastor Yuvie folded his arms and looked daggers at Avi. "You lie. You want to keep me from meeting him because I am not Jewish."

"That's not true. I'm sure, had he been ready, the messiah would have been more than happy to meet you."

Pastor Yuvie continued to look at Avi piercingly. "You don't have to tell him you told me he was the messiah."

Avi shook his head. "I am sorry, no."

"It's because you think I'm not Jewish, isn't it?"

"That's not it at all—"

"Well, I am Jewish! My grandfather was a Jew! I am a Jew!"

Avi was surprised at the sudden outburst. For a moment, he just stared, but eventually he answered. "I don't know who's Jewish or not." Avi shook his head. "I don't even know who I am."

"Well, I am a Jew!" Pastor Yuvie exclaimed. "I am a completed Jew who knows that Jesus is the messiah and I am saved, and what's more, I don't care to meet this impostor antichrist the devil has awoken you for!"

"What?"

"This messiah is not Jesus—therefore, this messiah is anti-Jesus. He is the anti-Christ. He is a fake. And you've been resurrected by Satan to confuse the world and confound them and make them think that this antichrist is the messiah. Just as Jesus resurrected Lazarus, so, too, did the devil resurrect you for his purpose—and to think you are Abraham! You're actually following the devil! Thank God I have sense to see through all of this and not fall for it. My faith is strong. I have been tested and I have passed."

Avi coughed.

Pastor Yuvie glared accusingly at Avi. Unsure of what to do, Avi reached for his sandwich and took an uncomfortable bite.

"I am Jewish," Pastor Yuvie said quietly, out of the blue. "And I know Jesus is lord."

Avi nodded slowly. "Ok," he said hesitantly, dropping the sandwich. "I think we should agree to disagree and part ways here."

"I am a completed Jew," Pastor Yuvie continued, oblivious to what Avi had said. Tears began to fall unexpectedly from the man's eyes. "You think I'm stupid, don't you? You think that I will let Satan sway me as he's swayed you. You think you're better because you have a caste and you know where you come from. You think you're better because you're Abraham. Well, you're not! You did foolishness in your life! You lied about Sarah being your wife! You had petty squabbles with your nephew, Lot! You didn't keep kosher! Oh, yes, I know about that—I know you mixed meat and milk! I know that now you've fallen for the lies of the enemy! I know that you aren't great or special!" Pastor Yuvie wiped his wet eyes. "I am special. I am great and I don't need you or anyone else to confirm this for me, because the holy spirit already did!"

Avi fell quiet and listened to the broken man sobbing before him. He knew that Pastor Yuvie's outburst was psychologically deep-seated and went back further than this meeting. There was something pathetic and intrinsically unhealed about this man, and Avi wanted to help him, but didn't know how. He tried to direct good thoughts to the man, and at the same time, he began praying, asking God to send the man peace and soundness of mind.

They sat there for about five minutes, with Pastor Yuvie sobbing and Avi praying silently. Suddenly, Pastor Yuvie began to spasm violently. Avi was about to reach over and grab him, when Michael yelled out, forcefully: "No, Avi! Don't! He has worked himself up emotionally and opened himself up to his dead spirit, which is clamoring to get into his body right now. This spirit will attempt to harm you when it fully possesses him—that is its purpose. Get out of here. Get out of here now!"

Avi didn't need a second warning. He dropped a hundred-shekel bill on the table, frantically hoping it would be enough to cover the bill, and then he ran out the door.

CHAPTER 12

*"And God said to Abraham, 'As for your wife
Sarai, you shall not call her Sarai, but her name shall be
Sarah. I will bless her; indeed, I will give you a son by
her. I will bless her so that she shall give rise to nations;
rulers of peoples shall issue from her."*
—Genesis 17:15-16

Max hurriedly made his way through the Armenian Section of the erratically divvied up Old City, and entered the Jewish Section, in which his yeshiva was located. Given that he had missed a week of studies, Max went straight to the administrative office to report his return. His duffel bag of clothes was still in his hand, but as classes were about to start for the day, he figured he would keep it with him and deposit it in his dorm room during the lunch break.

To his surprise, he was directed to immediately go to his room and deposit his bag there. "You will not be attending Torah study session in the beis midrash this morning," the administrator said to Max. "Put your bag in your room and tidy your appearance, then come back here." Max nervously complied, but he felt trouble brewing. He was worried that he would be told off—or worse, expelled—by the yeshiva for having missed classes, and his mind lingered troublingly on Avi wandering the streets alone. He washed his face, tidied his rumpled clothes as best he could, then rushed back to the administrative office. His heart sank when the administrator said, unsmilingly, "The Rosh Yeshiva will see you now." Max breathed in deeply, knocked on the door of the Rosh Yeshiva's office, and entered the room.

The office was large and spacious. A compendium of Jewish books lined two walls, while the wall directly opposite the doorway was full, with a large window that gave a sweeping view of the Old City. A sitting area of four chairs and a coffee table was cunningly arranged in front of this window, and it was on one of these chairs that the Rosh Yeshiva, Rabbi Rubenstein, was seated, sipping a cup of tea. He smiled at Max and gestured for him to sit down.

Max apprehensively made his way over, his heart pounding in his chest, and he sat down awkwardly.

"*Boker tov*, Feldman," Rabbi Rubenstein greeted him. Good morning.

"Boker tov, Rabbi Rubenstein."

"How do you do?"

"Baruch HaShem."

"You know why you are here, I presume?"

Max gulped and almost burst into tears. His worst fears were being realized. He was going to be expelled. He knew it. "It's because I missed school last week, isn't it?"

Rabbi Rubenstein laughed. "No, mein sohn. Rabbi Goldenberg has requested a meeting with you—he will be here shortly."

Max felt relief wash over him and he slumped in his chair, thankful that his place at yeshiva was secure. He whispered a silent thankful prayer under his breath and slowly felt the worry dissipate from his body. At the same time, Max was surprised that the meeting with Rabbi Eliezer was scheduled to take place so soon after the meeting only the night before. True, Rabbi Eliezer had said he wanted to speak with Max the next day, but Max assumed that it would take place after the end of the academic day and not cut into his classes, given that he had already missed so many. Clearly, whatever it was

Rabbi Eliezer wanted to talk about was pressing. Max's curiosity was piqued.

Rabbi Rubenstein cut into Max's thoughts. "I have not had a chance to speak with you before today on a one-on-one basis. Do you mind if we chat before Rabbi Goldenberg arrives?"

"Of course not, Rabbi."

"You are baal teshuva, I believe?"

Max nodded.

"How are you adjusting? Are you following your classes? Is there anything that troubles you here at yeshiva?"

Max thought. "I think I am adjusting well. Some of the classes are a bit challenging, I admit, but it is nothing that cannot be overcome through diligence and determination. I am happy with my decision to become religious."

Rabbi Rubenstein smiled. "I am glad to hear. However, if you ever feel overwhelmed and need to talk, my door is always open."

"Thank you."

"How was your holiday away from school?"

Max coughed. "I spent the holiday with my cousin and friend in Tel Aviv."

"They are religious?"

Max shook his head.

"Kol beseder," Rabbi Rubenstein replied. "It is good to keep the links with your secular friends and family; good to be an example to them and entice them into the paths of righteousness. Even if you don't persuade them to become religious, at least your presence will educate them about religious life. All Jews are precious, regardless of their religious practice, and worthy of the mitzvos. It is up to us to show them the beauty of the life of Orthodoxy, right?" Rabbi Rubenstein smiled and Max grinned as he felt more at ease.

"I agree, Rabbi Rubenstein."

"You know, Feldman, your speech a few weeks ago, it was interesting."

Max didn't speak. After Rabbi Eliezer's praise of his speech the night before, he was sure the Rosh Yeshiva was about to do so as well. The only thing was, Max no longer thought it was ok to have mouthed the words he had.

"Do you truly believe those things?"

Max shrugged. "I guess."

Rabbi Rubenstein shook his head disapprovingly. "Ah, Feldman—you've missed the mark."

"What do you mean, Rabbi?"

"I suppose it's my fault. I should be more attentive to what is being taught in my yeshiva." He paused. "Feldman, you do realize that the *rabbinut* has ruled that the Falasha are authentically Jewish?"

Max looked surprised. "Did they?"

"They did, indeed. In fact, at the time of the operation to rescue these long-forgotten brothers and sisters of Clal Yisroel from the persecution and hardships they faced in Ethiopia, none were more supportive of gathering them into Eretz Yisroel than the rabbinut—of which I am a part." Rabbi Rubenstein paused. "So, you see, your derogatory references to them with the crosses tattooed on their foreheads was quite painful for me to hear. Do you know why many of the Ethiopian Jewish women sport tattoos of crosses on their foreheads, Feldman?"

Max shook his head.

"They were forced to do so. It was one of two choices for them: take the cross or die. And now they live everyday with this reminder of their painful past etched solidly into their skin for everyone to see. Theirs is a sad history—much of our collective Jewish history is sad, and we must not only remember the sufferings that our direct communities underwent, we must also extend sympathy to other Jewish communities and the sufferings they faced before being reunited here in Eretz Yisroel."

"I am sorry, Rabbi Rubenstein."

"You also spoke of the Russian Jews and their staunch antipathy towards religion. Are you familiar with the history of Soviet Jewry?"

"Vaguely."

"When communism came into power two generations ago, they were determined to wipe out religiousness from the fabric of Russian life. This antagonism towards religion was directed also towards our people who sojourned in Russia. Much like the Seleucids of ancient past, the Russian authorities outlawed the study of Torah and Jewish practice. The result, as we can see today, is a unique segment of the Jewish people who have no understanding of their Jewish heritage.

"They've come home to Eretz Yisroel seeking refuge, and they've found the home and comfort they need in the hiloni world and in Zionism, but at the same time, they find themselves repellent of the religious authority here. Why should they not be? The rabbinut tries to forcibly impress Judaism on these people without reaching out to them properly with love, understanding and respect to explain the tenants of our religion to them. What is the result of this? A mass portion of our population clings to hiloni secularism and secular

253

Zionism because we have not extended the hand of friendship to them in the true way of Torah."

Max mumbled something under his breath.

Rabbi Rubenstein smiled. "Speak up, yelid. Do not be afraid to say what's on your mind."

"Why is the rabbinut so dogmatic? Why don't we reach out to the Russian Jews with more love?"

"Precisely, Feldman. 'We'—for the rabbinut is not the only dogmatic culprit here. Do you see the similarities between your speech and the actions of the rabbinut?"

Max blushed.

"The rabbinut has performed many acts of chesed, such as with its acceptance of the Falasha community. However, being an organization headed by men—fallible men—it sometimes errs on the side of safety. The rabbinut strives for the continuity and uniformity of Orthodox Judaism; there is a deep fear that runs through its ranks, which influences many of the decisions made at its highest levels. The fear that prevails is that Judaism will die out; and, as such, it applies the most stringent practices to ensure that we do not filter down Judaism and consequently lose this Judaism which has kept our people bound together over the millennia. Just as strongly as the rabbinut pushed for the return of the Ethiopian Jews to their homeland—so, too, did the rabbinut not recognize the Ethiopian brand of Judaism, and thus stripped them of their unique Judaic heritage, positioning Orthodox, western Judaism onto the Ethiopian Jews.

"In many ways, like man, there is both the *yetzer hatov*—the compulsion to do good—and the *yetzer harav*—the compulsion to act in fear, ignorance of anger—within the individual ranks of the rabbinut, and throughout the organization as a whole. The rabbinut expresses Rabbi Hillel's school of thought, but the words and arguments of Rabbi Shammi, which, it must be remembered, were carefully preserved throughout the ages, also plays a role in the thought-process of the modern rabbinut.

"As Torah-observant Jews, we must apply both schools of thought carefully to our lives as individuals and even more carefully when approaching issues which affect Am Yisroel as a whole, because both Rabbi Hillel and Rabbi Shammai had valid points. However, at the end of the day, we must realize that—to quote Virgil—love conquers all; and Rabbi Hillel is the school of thought which won out in the end.

"Consider your words before you speak. Always think to yourself: will what I am about to say merit others or will it be harmful to them? It is said that we are given a mouth for two reasons: one, to offer prayer to our God, and two, to speak good of each other."

Max nodded.

"You also spoke harshly of the hilonim, yet you say the cousin and friend you stayed with for the holiday are secular, nachon?"

Max looked down ashamed-faced. "Yes."

"Do they know the way you feel about them?"

Max looked up pleadingly. "Rabbi Rubenstein, I didn't really mean half the things I said in that speech—I didn't. I really didn't."

"Then why propagate such things from your mouth? Your strict stance would no doubt influence some of your fellow-talmidim and find root in their hearts and aid in spawning a generation of hate-mongers. You may not believe it, but others who listen to you may."

"I'm sorry. I am truly sorry."

"Words are a powerful thing. Always remember that. Always choose them carefully." He paused and looked at the boy kindly. "The hilonim are our people, Feldman. We cannot cut them out from our midst. They are part of the Jewish chain and it is up to us, those who learn Torah, to reach out to them—not to convert them; not to make them adopt our lifestyle— but to reach out with love and with hope, to embrace them as they are and recognize the divine neshama which is contained within them. We do not fight them or attempt to remove them from their rightful place among Am Yisroel. They are Jews. They are part of our family, and we must embrace each other and try to understand each other.

"Our God is not only *Elokim*, the God of justice, He is also HaShem, the God of mercy and chesed. How can we expect chesed from the *goyim* if we cannot practice chesed among ourselves? Chesed—always chesed, Feldman. There was a reason Rabbi Shammai's school did not triumph over Rabbi Hillel's. To Judaize Virgil's quote: chesed always wins out in the end. The Romans, the Greeks, the Assyrians, the Babylonians, the Medes, the Persians, the ancient Egyptians all subscribed to a similar school of thought as Rabbi Shammai: power, dominance, strictness—but they are all gone, lost in the pages of time, while us Jews are still here, ever-present, ever-kind. We adopted Rabbi Hillel's school of thought and it was this which preserved us as a people. It was not a push for power, or might, or strict interpretation of Torah; it was chesed. Chesed trumps all, Feldman, always remember that; always practice it."

Max nodded again.

"Enough of the sermon," Rabbi Rubenstein said with a tinkled laugh, and he cheerfully patted Max on his arm. "Tell me, why did you not return to yeshiva last week when classes began?"

Max cleared his throat. "The friend I was staying with—Natan—his Saba died the day before yeshiva began. Natan was not religious, but his Saba was, and Natan felt compelled to sit shiva for his Saba. Although Natan's Saba was a rabbi, Natan was not religious, so I stayed behind to guide him through the period of mourning."

Rabbi Rubenstein beamed. "You have given me faith in your abilities to perform chesed, Feldman. It is a great mitzvah—a great act of chesed—to care for the grieving. I am sorry to hear about your friend's loss, but at the same time, it brings me joy to know that one of my talmidim exhibits such care and concern for his fellow Jew."

Max blushed with the unexpected praise. "I only did what I thought was necessary."

"You did exceedingly, abundantly well, mein sohn. I commend you." Rabbi Rubenstein thumbed the armrest of his chair. "What was the name of your friend's Saba, zikhrono livrakha?"

"He was Rabbi Yehonatan Nasi, *zekher tzaddik livrakha*, a wonderful man from the little I knew of him."

Rabbi Rubenstein looked surprised. "Rabbi Yehonatan Nasi? His son, Yossi, owns the supermarket chain?"

Max nodded. "Yes, that's the one. Yossi is my friend Natan's father."

Rabbi Rubenstein smiled sadly. "Rabbi Nasi has passed away, and I did not even know it. He was a great tzaddik; a true man of chesed. He and I served on the rabbinut together, and we remained friends for some years, but then we lost touch. It is a sad day for Clal

257

Yisroel when such a man is removed from our midst." Rabbi Rubenstein looked down sadly. "Heaven has gained, and we have lost. I will pray for your friend that he may find solace in this period of sadness."

At that moment, the door of the office opened unannounced and Rabbi Eliezer marched in, his broad face red. Rabbi Rubenstein stood to greet him and the two men exchanged superficial pleasantries, until Rabbi Rubenstein volunteered to take his leave and give Rabbi Eliezer the privacy he wanted with Max. Before leaving, Rabbi Rubenstein looked across at Max and smiled. "Remember what I told you, Feldman. *B'hatzlacha*." Good luck. He shut the door quietly behind him.

Rabbi Eliezer sat wheezily on the chair Rabbi Rubenstein had just exited.

"*Mah nishmah*, Feldman?" How are you?

"Baruch HaShem. How are you, Rabbi Goldenberg?"

"Baruch HaShem." Rabbi Goldenberg smiled at Max and Max wondered if maybe he had been too quick to let his friends mar his view of the venerated rabbi.

Max smiled back shyly. "I didn't think we would be having our meeting this quickly after last night."

"I am a man of action, Feldman. I like to get things done and I like to get them done now." Rabbi Eliezer looked at Max bemusedly. "However, there are some instances where biding one's time can result in marvelous outcomes."

Max nodded slowly.

"As I mentioned to you last night, your speech resonated with me."

Max nodded again, his mind lingering on the words Rabbi Rubenstein had just mouthed.

"I believe as you do that we can no longer pussy-foot around the undesirable elements in our society. Steps must be taken to ensure the survival of the Jewish people. Our people are marrying outside of themselves and assimilating at an alarming rate. Traditional Judaism is battling elements within world Jewry which have even greater potential to destroy Am Yisroel than the external, anti-Semitic, non-Jewish forces which threaten us on a daily basis. I speak, of course, of the threats to authentic Judaism which emanate from the hilonim of secular Jewish society and from the Reform, Liberal, Masorti and Conservative self-styled Judaisms.

"Ultra-Orthodox Judaism is the only authentic Judaism. We exalt Torah and we are the ones who are growing in numbers while Jews who ascribe to the fake Judaisms are disappearing quickly among the goyim masses. It is up to us, the Charedim, to ensure the continuation of Am Yisroel in its authentic and God-mandated way." Rabbi Eliezer sighed and pulled out a large white handkerchief from the breast pocket of his suit and wiped his face. "Feldman, I have fought long and hard to maintain the future of Torah Judaism—but I am only one man, and an old man at that. I have done many great things—our people will remember me as one of the greatest, but despite my many accomplishments, there is much more that needs to be done. I can light the spark of revolution, but I need a disciple to carry on my work.

"I need you.

"For years, I have hoped for one who will succeed me and learn from me and continue the work I have begun. I have searched long and hard for one who can be my protégé, and let me tell you, Feldman, many have come close but fallen short of the glory of attaining

259

that position. But when I heard your voice cry out—like a prophet in the wilderness; when I heard you speak with the passion and the conviction that you did in your speech, I felt as if I was listening to myself as a young man, and I thanked the Holy One, blessed be He, for I realized that the disciple I had so longed for had finally arrived.

"You are the one I want to teach. You are the one I want to carry on my work. After having met you, I have never felt a greater conviction in my life. You are the one who shall be called the disciple of Rabbi Eliezer Teivel ben Moishe." Rabbi Eliezer looked at Max beseechingly. "Will you accept my plea, Feldman? Will you be my protégé?"

Max was dumbfounded. Two completely different Judaic viewpoints had been presented to him in the space of twenty minutes and he didn't know what to think. The months of not thinking for himself had made him indecisive, and internally, Max knew that this was dangerous. He was mostly dismissive of Rabbi Eliezer's impassioned words, but at the same time, he couldn't fully embrace Rabbi Rubenstein's lecture. Max was at a crossroad and he didn't know which avenue to continue on. He sat there, his mouth agape, for what seemed to Rabbi Eliezer to be a painfully long time, before he said, "I don't know what to say, Rabbi Goldenberg. That you think so highly of me—it's an honor, it's humbling. But I am no tzaddik who can ever aspire to fill your shoes—"

Rabbi Eliezer laughed. "I should think not, Feldman. But I am offering you the grand opportunity to be my right-hand man—and, when I should die, you will stand to be the rightful heir of my legacy. Do you not want that, Feldman?"

"It would be an honor, but I am no Torah scholar, Rabbi. I am a mere baal teshuvah who became religious only a few months ago. My Jewish learning is severely limited at present. I can't even join the *semicha l'rabbinut* program here because I'm not qualified enough."

"*Bupkes*, Feldman. I have spoken with your teachers and read your file. Your advancement here has been phenomenal. Two of your teachers have reported that they've never seen anything quite like it. You are a natural Torah scholar, Feldman. I appreciate your attempt at tznius, but there is no need to downplay your abilities. I am quite aware of them."

"Rabbi Goldenberg, yes I am eager to learn, but I'm telling you that I can't hold on my own against true yeshiva bocherim who've been doing this all their lives. I don't have enough knowledge, I struggle every day—"

"You know what this reminds me of, Feldman?" Rabbi Eliezer interjected.

"What?"

"When HaShem asked Moishe Rabbeinu to lead Israel out of Egypt, initially, Moishe Rabbeinu was hesitant; he made excuses—but it all boiled down to one thing: Moishe Rabbeinu lacked confidence. So it is with you, Feldman, I am calling you forth to fulfill your great destiny, but you hesitate because you lack confidence."

Max frowned. *Did Rabbi Eliezer just compare himself to HaShem?*

"We don't have time for that," Rabbi Eliezer continued on. "You have to overcome it however you have to. Greatness waits on no man, Feldman." Rabbi Goldenberg opened his briefcase which he had placed on the ground next to his chair and pulled out two copies of two different newspapers: the *Yated Ne'eman*

261

and *haModia*—two daily papers aimed respectively at the *Mitnagdim* and *Chassidic* segments of the Charedi community. He dropped the newspapers on the coffee table that sat between him and Max. "The masses are clamoring for a hero—even going so far as to fabricate the most asinine of stories. Step up to the plate and be that hero for them so they won't have to invent heroes for themselves."

Max picked up the papers from the table. "What stories are people making up?"

Rabbi Eliezer waved his hand dismissively. "There are two articles today in both of those newspapers which say that Avraham Aveinu is resurrected and in Eretz Yisroel. As I understand it, these articles are reprints of original stories which ran in a secular paper last week."

Max blanched.

Rabbi Goldenberg noted his potential protégé's reaction with satisfaction. "It is unbelievable, I know. It just goes to show how desperate the populace is in their yearning for change. You can help be that change for them, Feldman."

Max ignored the rabbi. He picked up one of the papers randomly and hastily began flipping through.

"It's on page seven in haModia," Rabbi Goldenberg said.

Max quickly found the page and read:

THE RESURRECTED PATRIARCH — FACT,
OR HAVE WE ALL GONE MAD?
By Jonathan Strauss

We are all used to the very many persons who scamper around our country, afflicted with the very tangible, but generally harmless, mind-addling psychosis known as Jerusalem Syndrome, which affects both Jewish and non-Jewish persons alike. These poor souls begin to imagine that they are either particular characters from the Bible brought back to life, or claimants to the mystical position of the messiah. Generally, sufferers of Jerusalem Syndrome are confined to the holier areas of our country, like Jerusalem, Hebron and Safed, and the less-insane residents of these cities have grown mostly accustomed to the phenomenon and tend to ignore those who suffer from the disease.

But what happens when Jerusalem Syndrome strikes the Tel Aviv municipality: the city which prides itself on not being religious, and the place most passionately disconnected from the holy capital, a few kilometers away? Furthermore, what happens when, in that bastion of secular values, Jerusalem Syndrome strikes not just one man, but rather, the entire city?

Tel Aviv, for the past week, has been ablaze with the fervor of a story, which, in the opinion of this reporter, is true.

The story is asinine and, the unbelieving reader must be warned, it is completely at odds with everything secular, but, if this reporter is to remain of repute in the world of journalism, he must report the facts as he sees it, and the facts all point to one truth:

Avraham Aveinu, the first cause of the Jewish people, has returned to earth.

No less than four hundred persons were present at the popular Billy Jean bar last Thursday night, where it is reported that Avraham Aveinu made his debut on the Tel Aviv social scene. It is alleged that he entered with an entourage comprising an Israeli couple and a rabbi who, according to the witnesses there, seemed to be his personal rebbe. Various eyewitnesses claim that Avraham Aveinu was seen drinking, dancing, and generally enjoying himself.

Dalit Pereira, a 23-year-old student at the Tel Aviv University, was present that night. She reported that although she didn't personally spend time with him, he was in the company of her cousin and her cousin's friends. "I saw him having shots with them," Pereira said. "They were having a really good time. The girls all enjoyed his company." When asked whether Avraham Aveinu's interactions with the girls were inappropriate, Pereira responded: "Eww, no. He was very respectful. Although he's what?—our extremely great grandfather?—everyone treated him like their kid brother. He was very endearing. He looked really young and vulnerable."

Another eyewitness who was at the club that night, a 29-year-old fashion designer from Hod haSharon, Eldad Baranes, describes Avraham Aveinu as being of medium height, with a slender frame, and with a slight stubble on his face. "[Avraham Aveinu] was definitely Mizrachi. He had black hair and a nice tanned complexion." When prompted for a description of his outfit, de Costa answered: "He was dressed quite nicely, actually. I'll even go as far as to say he looked cool. He wore fitted grey pants and a black V-neck t-shirt. He had no watch or jewelry on him, but he did have a brown leather bracelet on his wrist. He could probably pass for a rocker, when you think about it."

The impassive reader who had not been at Billy Jean that night can argue that some sort of hallucinogenic drug must have been passed around, and was it this which caused the party-goers to collectively think they'd partied with Avraham Aveinu?

"Definitely not," said the nighttime manager of Abraxsas, 32-year-old, Kim Ivgi. "We are a strictly drug-free establishment. The hardest thing we serve and allow to be served on our premises is alcohol." Well, perhaps there was a case of bad alcohol? She laughed. "Not everyone drinks the same thing. However, if we hypothesize that all the customers that night had indulged in the same drinks from a hypothesized batch of bad alcohol, and were hypothetically subsequently hallucinating, how can you account for the staff who were working that night?" The staff doesn't drink? She answered with a vehement, "No—not while they are on the job. And let's say some of them had indulged that night—you can't stop everyone. But what about me? I didn't drink." The question is posed to her: although you didn't drink, do you still believe that Avraham Aveinu frequented your bar on the night in question? Ivgi looked amused. "I don't believe Avraham Aveinu came into Billy Jean, Jonathan," she said, emphasizing the word 'believe'. "I don't believe that some fraudulent, Jerusalem Syndrome fellow who thought he was Avraham Aveinu came in here and convinced my customers that he was Avraham Aveinu." Then what exactly do you believe Ms. Ivgi? She put down her cigarette and looked this reporter dead in the eye. "I don't believe anything. I know Avraham Aveinu was here. I met him, I saw him, I touched him. I heard the words come out of his own mouth confirming this to me." She picked up her cigarette again. "You're looking for facts for your story, Jonathan. I've given you the facts. Avraham Aveinu, the chief patriarch of our people, has returned to earth, and he came to my bar and announced himself to me, to the customers, and to the rest of my staff." Did Avraham Aveinu go to each person in the bar and introduce himself? "No—that would have been insane. There were too many people here that night. He told a few of us—I was one of the few—and the news just sort of skyrocketed from there." You heard him speak? What did he say? "I can't quote verbatim, but I think he said something like 'I am Avraham of old, returned to life'." So, he was direct about who he was with only the 'few of you'? "That's right." Then how was it the entire club came to firmly believe in Avraham Aveinu's being on earth. "I don't know exactly," she replied matter-of-factly. Ivgi scratched her head. "I do remember telling my mother the next day and she believed me."

As this reporter hunted down the many various accounts (all of which, it must be reported, were almost entirely the same as the accounts submitted by Pereira, Baranes, and Ivgi as outlined previously), one thing became apparent: not all the club-goers had actually interacted with the character who was alleged to be our first patriarch, yet, all the club-goers that were there that night believe the man who was identified as Avraham Aveinu was, in fact, Avraham Aveinu.

If the uninvolved man on the street who had not been there that night hears this story, such as this reporter, his first thought would be (because this reporter's first thought most definitely was): "*Ma pitom!*" followed by: "This is a hoax. It has to be." However, in an interesting twist to this strange and developing story, it seems that, should anyone who believes that Avraham Aveinu has returned verbally pass this information onto another person, the new person would become an instant believer in Avraham Aveinu's return.

Such was the case with this reporter.

Though this reporter did not have the fortune of meeting Avraham Aveinu, he is of the firm belief that Avraham Aveinu has returned.

And, it must be reported that this reporter is not the only person who hadn't been present the night Avraham Aveinu announced his arrival at the Billy Jean bar who firmly believes that Avraham Aveinu has, indeed, returned. The current poll on ynet.co.il has thus far registered a total of two hundred thousand persons living in the greater Tel Aviv area who believe in the return of our first patriarch. These numbers seem to be steadily increasing within the Tel Aviv municipality, while simultaneously, the belief in the return of Avraham Aveinu seems to be rapidly spreading to other parts of the country. The story has gone viral and is spreading at an unprecedented rate.

Even tourists have seemingly come under the spell of this belief. This reporter happened upon a group of Korean Christians at Ben Gurion Airport two days ago who were getting ready to leave Israel. They were not anywhere near Billy Jean the night of Avraham Aveinu's appearance, but they allege to have met him in the Judean Desert when they'd been having a prayer service there.

Head of the tour group, Reverend Emily Beyoung Keun, testified the following events: "We had been in the desert, in fast and prayer, conducting a prayer service, when all of a sudden, we saw this silhouette of a man on the hill above us. Of course, we became afraid and quickly retreated to the tour bus, leaving the bus driver, the tour guide, and the security that were with us to deal with the man. The man came down the hill and he was interrogated in English, and we could hear what he was saying. After a few minutes, he identified himself and we all heard him. We all knew he spoke the truth, that he was indeed Father Abraham of old, returned to life."

Reverend Beyoung Keun was asked if she could remember what it was he said. "I can't tell you verbatim, but he basically said he was Father Abraham of old who had returned to earth."

The similarities between Reverend Beyoung Keun's account of Avraham Aveinu's words and the account given by Ivgi, manager of the Billy Jean bar, are too close for comfort. Both ladies—neither of whom ever met the other—claims to have heard words emanating from the mouth of the Jewish first patriarch; words which said, basically, that he was Avraham Aveinu of old, returned to earth. Despite the obstruction of their different languages, and the glaring fact that their paths had never crossed, both women independently reported the same thing.

And similar to the Billy Jean bar story, Keun's account also testifies to three mysterious strangers who accompanied the first patriarch. "When we all realized who he was, we mobbed him— all of the Korean tour group and the Israelis in charge of the tour alike," she said. "I suppose we must have scared him, because he rushed off around the hill where there was a group of people waiting on him." When prompted to describe this 'group of people', Keun answered: "There was a man and a woman who were both very beautiful. There was also a rabbi."

Were these three people, as described by Keun, the same as the three people who reportedly accompanied Avraham Aveinu to the Billy Jean bar? The similarities between Keun's beautiful man, woman, and rabbi, and the accounts from Abraxsas which tell of an Israeli couple and a personal rebbe to Avraham Aveinu, are eerie, to put it mildly.

Many troublesome questions arise as a result of this belief in the return of the patriarch. Why has he returned? Who sent him? And who was his mysterious entourage of the Israeli couple and rabbi? An account of Avraham Aveinu's life in the Torah tells of three mysterious strangers who visited him after he had circumcised himself at the age of ninety-nine. It was speculated by many of the sages of our ancient past that the three mysterious strangers were actually angels. Has our returned Aba come with a contingency of angels to guard him? And, if so, why did he have to come with the protection of angels? Is the reason for his being here connected with some sort of dangerous mission?

Avraham Aveinu is here—this is something this reporter believes unequivocally. The question that remains is: Why?

Max closed the paper and looked at Rabbi Eliezer who had been quiet the entire time. "When was this written?"

Rabbi Eliezer shrugged. "Sometime last week, I suppose. HaModia and Yated Ne'eman picked up the story from the hiloni paper only today."

Max trembled.

"Yes, Feldman—to think that such folly is being believed. I heard that there was a follow-up report a few days later in the hiloni newspaper which carried photos of this charlatan who pretends to be our forefather."

"Photos? How?"

"Apparently the idiot posed with people in the disco and those people later posted the pictures on those so-called social networking sites: Headnovel and Chirper—"

"Facebook and Twitter."

"Exactly. The photos were posted there and the reporter managed to get access and publish them in his follow-up report. And not just photos of the fraud, but also of his so-called rebbe and the two hilonim disciples of his. I tell you, Feldman, when people have no faith in HaShem, this is the nonsense that happens."

Max gulped. "Did you see the photos?"

"Of course not. I am not going to waste my time any further on this ridiculousness. Reading the first article was enough."

Max shook his head woefully. "I had no idea any of this was going on."

"Of course you wouldn't," Rabbi Goldenberg said soothingly, and then he scowled. "Neither would anyone in our community—but it seems the editors of our religious papers are not doing their jobs of shielding the tzaddikim of the Charedi population from the nonsense which occurs in the hiloni world. I imagine the editors probably even believe this nonsense, which is why they picked up the story and republished it. I intend to have a firm word with both editors about this, I can guarantee you that."

Max stood up then sat back down.

"What's wrong with you, Feldman?" Rabbi Eliezer asked, perturbed. "Surely you don't believe this *narishkeit?*"

Max didn't know how to answer. He looked at Rabbi Eliezer helplessly.

"Feldman? What is the matter?"

Max considered the situation carefully. Avi had not restricted him, Tzippy, or Natan from telling anyone else who he really was, but there had been an unspoken agreement among the group to not tell anyone— particularly since Natan had cajoled Avi into outing himself at Billy Jean. Who knew that that one act of indiscretion would explode into the ruckus it had? It made no sense keeping the truth from Rabbi Eliezer, Max thought to himself. Sooner or later, Rabbi Eliezer was bound to hear that Avi was Avraham Aveinu. Max swallowed and spoke.

"Rabbi, the story is true," he whispered finally, his voice cracking.

"*Schmegegge.*"

"Two hundred thousand people in Tel Aviv believe it's true."

"And even more people believe in evolution—so what? Numerical statistics are no measure for truth."

Max sighed. "The story is true, Rabbi Goldenberg. My friend, Avi, the one you met last night is the one the article speaks of."

Rabbi Eliezer looked at Max for a second, then laughed. "You are a tease, Feldman. You expect me to believe that little Sephardi upstart is our patriarch, returned to life?"

"I am not teasing," Max insisted. "Avraham Aveinu has returned, and he is my friend, Avi."

The words fell on the old man like the roar of thunder. He sagged in his seat as the truth of the statement pierced his stony heart. He gripped the handles of the chair. He knew Max was speaking the truth, but he had to be sure. "You mean to tell me that the boy I met—the one I judged to be a hiloni—you are telling me, he is Avraham Aveinu returned in the flesh?"

Max nodded.

The rabbi shook his head and then slapped his forehead. "He is back and I met him—and I didn't like him," he moaned.

Max thought back to his own priggishness when he had first met Avi. He smiled at the rabbi. "He is very forgiving. First impressions don't count with him. I'm sure he will forgive you."

"You must tell me everything—how did he return? How did you meet him? How long has he been on earth? And most importantly, why is he back?"

Max sighed. "Let me start at the beginning—which, I guess, was about two weeks ago."

Rabbi Eliezer leaned forward and for the first time in years, he listened closely without speaking.

✡

Avi ran out of the café and kept running. He didn't stop to see if Pastor Yuvie was behind him—he just ran. He ran out of the Mamilla mall and ran pell-mell across the street to Rechov David haMelekh. He passed the bus stop he should have stopped at to return to Arnona and continued running. He ran all the way to the end of the street and still ran. He ran past Gan haPa'Amon and down Rechov David haRemez, past the Khan Theatre and past the Old Train Station, and continued onto Derech Hevron and kept running. He ran past the Dan Boutique Hotel, and ran up Rechov Hanoch Albek and took a right at the roundabout onto Rechov Shmuel Lupo and kept running. He ran straight past Saba's apartment building complex and kept running. He ran and he ran and he ran until he had run straight through the whole of the Tayelet, through the Scherover Promenade and the Goldman Promenade and reached the end, where there was nowhere left to run. He collapsed on the ground and with sweat dripping down his face, he began to sob. No tears poured from his eyes, and no sound emanated from his mouth. He was tired out from the running; almost on the verge of total exhaustion; thirsty beyond belief—but no physical distress could eclipse the enormity of the emotions which ravaged him. He cried and cried, a soundless heaving of sorrow, which tore at his guardian angel who tried desperately to comfort him.

Finally, as the sobbing subsided and the emotions receded, Avi began to feel the desperate pangs for water. He pulled himself up off the ground and made his way to the water fountain and drank hungrily for five minutes. Then, as he stepped away from the water fountain, his stomach recoiled and Avi doubled over as the contents of his lunch and all the water erupted from inside of him onto the floor. He made his way back to the water fountain and he drank again—less hungrily than before, with more purpose in his drinking than to quell the ignoble, instinctual thirst. He drank slowly, savoring the cool flow of the water, and when he was satiated, he splashed his face and rinsed his mouth. He felt steadier now, but his head pounded fiercely. He carried himself over to a bench under the shade of the large gazebo and he sat silently with his eyes closed, his body facing the wide undulating Judean hills.

There was no one else around. Avi almost felt as if it were him alone in the world. He opened his eyes and all he could see was the desert wasteland stretched out before him. With civilization placed securely behind him and only the desert in front, it was like a time capsule to the ancient era from which he'd come. Nothing reminded him more poignantly of his previous life at the desert, and in this moment of emotional turbulence, nothing made him yearn for his past life and his still-deceased wife, Sarah, more. He felt like crying again, but he stifled his tears. He sat quietly, and slowly, his exaggerated emotions regulated and he returned to a feeling of normalcy.

Michael, who had been sending out positive energy to his charge and had kept quiet the entire time, finally spoke gently, "Is everything alright, Avi?"

Avi nodded. "I feel much better now."

"What happened to you?"

"I don't know," Avi whispered. "It was like everything had come together all at once—all the emotions of the past few weeks came together and terrified me."

"I don't understand. The spirit scared you?"

"Yes, but it wasn't just that." Avi sighed. "It was everything that happened today: leaving the others and truly being on my own for the first time; traversing the streets of the Old City by myself; visiting the Old Yishuv Court Museum by myself; visiting the Kotel by myself; then that awful meeting with Pastor Yuvie where I was accused of being in league with the devil. How could I have allowed myself to fall into the trap of lunching with that man and putting myself in an arm's length of such obvious danger? When you told me to run, I ran purely to escape that man and his familiar spirit—but as I ran, it hit me. I was alone. I am alone. I am back on earth, but I am truly alone."

"But I thought you looked forward to being on your own?"

"I'm not talking about being on my own—I'm talking about being alone."

"Is there a distinction between the two? They seem the same thing to me."

"I want to be on my own in terms of being independent. I am thankful for the hospitality and generosity offered to me so kindly by my new friends, but I want to be able to support myself: to be my own man. It is who I was in my last life; it is who I am in this life. I have a fiercely independent spirit, Michael. I yearn for self-sufficiency. I want to be able to offer hospitality—not take it.

"But man is not an island unto himself. He needs companionship, he needs love. When I say I am alone, there is a difference: I feel like I have no one."

"What about me? What about Natan and Tzippy and Max? You still have us."

Avi smiled sadly. "I do—and I am grateful for all of you. But it's not the same thing."

"What do you mean?"

A tear dropped from Avi's eye and slowly made its way down his cheek. "I miss my wife, Michael."

The angel did not know how to respond.

"In my last life, every journey I made, every adventure I had, every joy in my life was shared with her. We were two parts of a composite whole. Everything I did and everything I became was because of her. The story of Avraham and Sarah was a story of us both, not just me. Our child, Isaac, merited the spiritual inheritance we had earned because of the both of us and what we'd built together as a couple.

"She was my companion, my best friend, my *bashert*. She was everything to me. I was never alone when she was alive, and now that I'm back, I realize that I am just that. Alone."

"You are never alone, Avi," Michael answered quietly. "The Lord watches over you and He hears the innermost yearnings of your heart. He speaks to me now. He will send comfort to you."

Avi wiped his face. "How?"

"Lift up your eyes to the hills, from whence comes your help; your help comes from the Lord."

"Which hill?"

Michael sighed. "Just turn around, Avi."

Avi turned his head around and, there, coming towards him, was a tall man wrapped in the traditional, billowing garb of a Bedouin traveller. The man's head and face were covered with a white veil, with only his eyes peeking though, as was prudent of the desert folk who did this to protect themselves from the glare of the sun and the dust of the desert, and not as a means to conform to any man-made attempt at superficial modesty. The man made his way leisurely down the hill toward Avi atop a camel. He looked as if he'd sprung directly from the dust of the desert which Avi had been looking at so nostalgically only a few moments before. Avi perceived no hostility from the man, in fact, though the man was some distance away, there was a definite aura of authority and wisdom which clung to him. Avi didn't know how he knew, but somehow, he did know that the man was older than his appearance suggested. The man dismounted the camel and came towards him. Avi was surprised that he wasn't more worried about the man's sudden appearance—particularly in light of his earlier disastrous encounter with Pastor Yuvie—but Michael said that God had sent Avi this stranger to give him comfort, and Avi felt his sadness disappear, replaced instead by a warm feeling of hope. As the man drew closer, Avi perceived a strong Jewish neshama in his aura, which was surprising, for the man was dressed as a Muslim.

The man reached Avi, he bowed low and, surprisingly, with a female voice said: "*Asalaam alaikum, Abouna Ibrahaim, Khalil-ullah.*" Peace be unto you, Our Father Abraham, Friend of God.

The stranger was no man. It was a woman. She unwrapped the cloth covering her face, and Avi found himself looking into the face of his former wife, Sarah.

CHAPTER 13

"The LORD took note of Sarah as He had promised, and the LORD did for Sarah as He had spoken. Sarah conceived and bore a son to Abraham in his old age, at the set time of which God had spoken."
—Genesis 21:1-2

Tzippy had always had a fascination with Disney movies. The magical stories of girls finding their princes and living happily ever after had left a deep impression on her psyche. Granted, as she grew older, she consciously shelved her childhood fantasies for more adult, pragmatic dreams of marriage, and yes, since coming to Israel, her love for the land of her forefathers had overshadowed everything else she'd ever desired— but the subconscious desire for a Cinderella-type, whirlwind romance where happily ever after seemed the inevitable conclusion continued to lurk quietly, just below the surface of who she was. She still privately indulged in her love for those princess-type movies: sometimes, she'd open her laptop and pop her *Aladdin* DVD or *Beauty and the Beast* DVD into the slot, and spend the next hour and a half lying on her bed, watching the familiar movies with hope shining from her eyes, and whenever a romantic comedy was released in theatres, she'd go quietly by herself to the cinema, to watch the movie with rapt attention, sighing ever so quietly throughout the length of the film. She'd always feel the familiar pangs of longing—but whenever the movies were over, she would berate herself for getting so caught up in what was clearly a fairy-tale. "Those things never happen in real life," she always convinced herself sensibly, and would shake herself and go have a pedicure.

It sometimes takes the loss of the possibility of a dream—no matter how childish and how unattainable we may think it to be—to make us realize how much we really wanted it. And this is what Tzippy felt as she stood in her tiny bathroom, watching herself in the mirror with the positive pregnancy test in her hand.

✡

Rabbi Eliezer sat in his office in Har Nof and carefully thought over the story Max had relayed to him. It was, by all means, a seemingly bogus tale—but somehow or the other, Rabbi Eliezer knew what he had been told was, in fact, true. Max had told him everything in blinding detail: his initial meeting with Avi in the desert, the shopping trip at the Namal, the return to the desert where Avi had inadvertently exposed himself to the Korean Christian tour group, the club excursion which led to the current public knowledge that Avraham Aveinu had returned, the frantic bolt to Jerusalem, the death of Natan's Saba, the week of mourning—all the events, directly tied to Avi's essential reason for being back on earth: Natan was the designated mashiach.

Rabbi Eliezer knew in the deepest recesses of his heart that Avi was indeed Avraham Aveinu resurrected to life, but he was troubled by the glaring fact that his first meeting with the patriarch had played out the way it did. He did not stop to consider his initial dismissive attitude towards Avi; rather, he pondered the effects of that initial meeting and wondered how to remedy it. He considered Natan being named the mashiach—and it was an appointment he did not wholeheartedly support. Why did God direct Avi to choose Natan? It made no sense. Not only was Natan not religious, he was also Sephardi.

In Rabbi Eliezer's mind, the ascent of a Sephardi mashiach would ultimately lead to a worldwide Jewish adoption of Sephardi minhag and a shunting to the side of Ashkenazi minhag, as world Jewry would clearly follow the lead of the mashiach and adopt his preferred custom. It was a troubling thought for Rabbi Eliezer.

He thought for hours.

By lunchtime, Rabbi Eliezer had formulated a plan of action. With the story of Avi's re-emergence to life quickly becoming common knowledge throughout the length and breadth of Israel, he realized it was only a matter of time before the actual identity of Avraham Aveinu—in the modern person of Avi—would be discovered by the country at large, and the reason for his return would quickly follow suit. The fact was, Rabbi Eliezer was part of a very select group of only four persons—himself, Natan, Tzippy, and Max—which knew exactly where Avraham Aveinu was and why he was back, and he planned to use this knowledge to his advantage and secure his place in the scheme.

Within an hour, Rabbi Eliezer had transferred himself from his dark office in Har Nof to the bright and airy living room of the Prime Minister's residence in Rehavia. It had not been difficult to arrange the meeting. Given that Rabbi Eliezer was the spiritual rebbe of the extreme right-wing religious political party, *Koach Shel Yisroel*—Strength of Israel— which formed a major part of the prime minister's government coalition, he was assured immediate access to the prime minister's ear whenever he deemed it necessary.

The prime minister had read about the story of Avraham Aveinu's return the week before in *Yehidot Ahronot*, but he had yet to have someone verbally confirm the story for him and thus coalesce his belief in it. Rabbi Eliezer was thrilled that he would be the one to instill the truth of Avraham Aveinu's return in the prime minister and he reveled in the moment when he pompously mouthed the words: "Avraham Aveinu has returned to life. And I know where he is and why he has returned."

The prime minister's belief in the resurrection was immediate. He wanted to immediately capitalize on Rabbi Eliezer's knowledge of the whereabouts of the patriarch and dispatch security to Avraham Aveinu to ensure the resurrected patriarch's safety. Although Rabbi Eliezer could ascertain the merit in the prime minister's argument that it was imperative that Avi have security, he was not ready to lay down his trump card.

"With the divisions inside of Judaism today, it is of the utmost importance that Avraham Aveinu be associated with Torah-observant Judaism before he is introduced to the Jewish public. If you were to send a security detail to him, it would only be a matter of time before who he is would be made public by the media, and he could be bombarded by unobservant Jews and this would ultimately cast an unfavorable light on the patriarch. No, it is more fortuitous that I meet with him and immediately take him under my wing, after which, we can introduce him to the world—under the dual auspices of Rabbi Eliezer Goldenberg, the leading posek alive today, and the Israeli prime minister."

The prime minister reluctantly agreed with the suggested plan of action—not because he sympathized with Rabbi Eliezer's quest for Orthodoxy to be endorsed by Avraham Aveinu (the prime minister was actually Masorti and, like most Israelis, was not entirely supportive of the rabbinut), but because he had dealt with Rabbi Eliezer before and he knew how intractable the man was. He attempted to press Rabbi Eliezer to divulge his sources and give him the reason for Avraham Aveinu's return, but the rabbi refused and pulled the information close to his heart. Rabbi Eliezer knew how to play the game of diplomacy: a man is only as important as what he could contribute, and Rabbi Eliezer intended to stay important in the whirlwind that would be the event of Avraham Aveinu's return, so he said nothing more to the prime minister.

With nothing left to say, Rabbi Eliezer stood and thanked the prime minister for meeting with him. The prime minister reminded Rabbi Eliezer that a security contingent was essential for Avraham Aveinu and asked that Rabbi Goldenberg please update him on the situation. Rabbi Eliezer ignored the man and walked out the door and made his way to his car, which was waiting on him outside.

"Back to Har Nof, Rabbi Goldenberg?" the driver asked.

Rabbi Eliezer shook his head. "To Tel Aviv. And step on it." He looked out the window and whispered quietly to himself, "I have a date with destiny."

✡

"Sarah," Avi whispered shakily—but ever so quietly that only he and Michael heard the word spring from his lips.

The woman bowed low before Avi could stop her, but she quickly straightened herself up. "My name is Zahira bint Yahya, of the tribe of Durani, of the Pashtun people of Afghanistan. It is an honor and a privilege to meet you."

Avi shook himself, and he looked closer. Though Zahira did bear a hugely remarkable resemblance to his still-deceased wife, Sarah, Avi realized it was not Sarah. Zahira was taller and more robust, whereas Sarah had been much more petite. Zahira's complexion was lighter, her nose slightly longer, her hair wispier, her neck less regal, and her eyes a less dramatic hue of brown. She was beautiful, it was true, and her face was eerily similar to Sarah's, but she was not Sarah, resurrected or otherwise.

A strong sense of disappointment rippled through Avi. Though he had only thought the mysterious stranger was his resurrected wife for all of twenty seconds, it had been a powerful belief, and the loss of it hit him hard. He swallowed and tried to smile at the woman, but instead, for the second time in the space of an hour, he buried his face into his hands and broke down into tears.

Zahira sat next to him and put her arms around his shoulders. What she thought of him crying there in the glare of the setting sun, he didn't know, but Michael had said that God had sent him this stranger to comfort him, and Avi was indeed comforted in the arms of this woman—who, with her powerful neshama, was clearly his descendant, and whose physical presence reminded him so much of his former love.

As his tears subsided, Avi felt a profound shame that he'd let himself fall apart so completely in front of a stranger. He gently pulled away from Zahira's embrace. "Today has been a very emotional day for me," he said croakily. "I am sorry you had to see me like this."

Zahira shrugged. "It happens to the best of us, *ab Ibrahim*—Father Abraham. You are only human."

Avi looked curiously at Zahira. He guessed she was in her late fifties but her face was remarkably smooth and her skin, supple. Her eyes were a somber brown, devoid of humor, but full of kindness, knowledge, and wisdom.

"Thank you."

"Do you feel better now?"

Avi nodded.

They sat in companionable silence and enjoyed the view of the desert in the fading light of the setting sun.

Eventually, Avi spoke. "You know who I am."

"Yes."

Avi took it in.

"I'm not sure who you are, though."

"I am Zahira bint—"

Avi laughed softly. "Yes, I got that the first time around. But what I meant was, who are you to me?"

Zahira looked confused. "I do not understand."

"Are you my descendant? You dress the dress of a Muslim; you speak the language of the Arab; you ride through the desert like a Bedouin—yet, when I close my eyes and feel your presence next to me, my soul knows that you are of Sarah's and my line."

"I am your descendant."

Avi trembled. "You know that you are descended from me? You know this for a fact?"

Zahira nodded firmly. "My people have always known we were descended from your line, ab Ibrahim."

Avi looked at the woman again. "I would've known you were my child just from looking at you."

"How?"

Avi smiled sadly. "You look a whole lot like my wife, Sarah."

Zahira faltered. "I do?"

"There are differences, yes, but at the same time, you could almost pass for her—if she'd had a sister. This was why I was so affected when I saw you. You remind me so much of her."

"I am sorry if my presence is painful for you."

"Not at all. It actually warms my heart to know that you look like her. It means she lives through her children and the beauty that was Sarah is still alive in some form on the earth."

"You flatter me. I am an old woman and no longer beautiful."

Avi patted Zahira's hand. "You are a daughter of Sarah. You are beautiful."

Zahira looked down at her hands. "To hear such words from you, ab Ibrahim, it is an honor. You are truly as kind and as gracious as I imagined you would be."

Avi laughed. "You've imagined meeting me?"

"Ever since I was a little girl."

Avi was surprised at her words. "You imagined meeting me as a child? But why?"

"I knew this day would come. I always knew that I would be the one chosen to meet with you."

Avi gulped. "You knew I would come since you were a child?"

"My people have known you would return for thousands of years."

Avi digested this bit of knowledge. "And your people are from Afghanistan, you said?"

"Yes."

"How did you manage to get into Israel? Surely you didn't board a plane and enter through conventional methods." Avi gestured to Zahira's camel.

She laughed for the first time, a deep, throaty chuckle, which was very unlike Sarah's soft, tinkled laugh. "It was not hard to enter the Zionist homeland; in fact, it was the easiest leg of my journey. I travelled, disguised as a Bedouin, on the back of my camel, Al-Hawa. People seek no truck with the Bedouin—even the great Israeli war machine didn't deny my entrance, and after searching me for weapons and seeing I had none, they let me pass through." Zahira smiled wryly. "The Bedouin are people of no land, and the city dwellers: *Yahudin*, *Masiheyin*, and *Muslimun*—Jews, Christians, and Muslims—alike, all understand that and give them leeway not accorded to others. It was the most logical disguise to adopt in order to reach you."

"How long did it take you to get here?"

Zahira considered. "Many months. I travelled through the mountains of Afghanistan and Persia; across the rivers of Iraq; through open plains of the Arabian desert—I journeyed until I entered the land of my forefathers two days ago, and have waited patiently since for your arrival."

For the first time, Avi noticed that Zahira's face was dusty and her lips were parched. His sense of hospitality erupted forcefully from within. He stood and put out his hand.

"Come—I am staying in an apartment not far from here. You can wash up and have something to eat and spend the night."

Zahira shook her hands and head. "I have not journeyed all this way to leech off of Abouna Ibrahim. I will tell you what I must and then I will take my leave."

He shook his head. "You will not 'leech' off of me."

"I am not worthy to accept the offer. Were I a better person, perhaps—"

"Zahira," Avi cut her off and shook his head more forcefully at her. "I am inviting you because you are a stranger in this land and it is only right that I offer you hospitality. I am not evaluating your worth. Please, come with me."

Zahira shook her head again. "I am sorry. I must decline. I have come for one reason and one reason only: to tell you what I came to tell you."

Avi was intrigued by the mention that Zahira had something specific to tell him, and his natural curiosity was keen to find out what that was, but his concern for her well-being was more pressing on him. "Whatever you need to tell me can wait until you've at least washed up and eaten. Please, accept my hospitality—I beg of you. You are my grandchild."

Zahira hesitated and then put her hands into the extended hand in front of her. She stood. "Very well—it would be nice to be clean for a change." She smiled widely. "*Shukran jazleean, jaad-di.*" Thank you very much, my grandfather.

✡

Natan quietly held Tzippy's hands as she sobbed. She had shown up at his apartment unannounced, her hair askew, her face uncharacteristically looking alarmed and her eyes full of fear. When she'd walked in, she had only one thing to say, "I'm pregnant," after which she collapsed into sobs.

Instinctively knowing that there was nothing he could say, Natan held her hand and led her to the sofa where she told him that she'd just come from the doctor who'd confirmed the pregnancy for her after she'd taken "like ten home pregnancy tests". She began to babble somewhat incoherently about her suspecting that she was pregnant after she'd missed her period for two months straight, about her parents and how they'd react, about the circumstances of her own conception and birth and how it led to her mother's total dependence of her father, about her future and what seemed like zero options open to her now, about the possibility of an abortion, about being too old to be thought of as "a cute teen mom from MTV", and about what was she to do now.

Natan felt partly responsible for the unraveled state of his friend. But at the same time, he knew there was nothing he could possibly say under the sun to comfort or bring relief to the young girl falling apart in front of him. He was supposed to go to the bank for a very important meeting, but with a quick whip into his pocket and a deft scurrying of his fingers, he texted the bank manager and told her that he was sorry but something had turned up and he wouldn't be able to make it that day.

He turned his attention back to Tzippy who continued to prattle, but had stopped sobbing.

"What do you think I should do?" she asked eventually.

Natan considered carefully. "I think it's your call. A woman has a right to choose."

Tzippy nodded slowly.

"I'll support you whatever you decide to do."

She remained quiet for a few moments, holding onto Natan's hands and then spoke. "My parents will be devastated, but I am not going to have an abortion." She looked straight into his eyes. "But you have to marry me."

✡

States and governments are naturally inclined to have methods of information-collection which can sometimes cross the boundaries of appropriateness and enter into the realm of the downright unlawful. However, given the security, economic, and political advantages that such spying affords them, it is oftentimes a necessity for governments to dabble in the covert world of espionage.

This was how Rabbi Eliezer viewed his own underhanded channels of information: as a necessary means to retain a competitive advantage. His lifetime had produced many sources which provided him with a constant flow of information and Rabbi Eliezer had always kept these sources well-paid and happy, in order to keep the information coming in: fresh, relevant and, sometimes, most advantageously, scandalous. There had never been any particular desire on Rabbi Eliezer's part to gather knowledge about private citizens—his interests had lain in the world of Orthodoxy, the other branches of Judaism, high-ranking public officials, and businesses and their owners that impacted him directly. For the first time in his life, Rabbi Eliezer had need to learn about a private citizen—and for the first time, he had to sit back patiently and wait for that information to be gathered. He had expected to have the information he needed at his fingertips by the time he reached Tel Aviv, but, when he arrived forty minutes after leaving Jerusalem, he was in the same position he'd been in when he'd left: completely clueless. He ranted and raved over his cellphone, but nothing could speed up the process. He eventually sighed and gave in to the inevitable and sat in the backseat of the darkly tinted town car and pulled out his siddur, while the driver drummed his fingers on the steering wheel, bored.

Finally, after a painful four hours, Rabbi Eliezer's cell phone rang with the information he needed and then some. It was startling news which he had not expected in his wildest dreams, and it threw everything into disarray. He snapped the phone shut and sat back, uncharacteristically quiet, his face betraying his shock. His driver looked at him through the rearview mirror. "Kol beseder, rabbi?"

Rabbi Eliezer shook himself out of his stupor and nodded slowly. "Take me to Rechov HaYarkon," he said. It would take them about fifteen minutes to get there from the spot they were parked in on the side of the road. Rabbi Eliezer hoped that he would be able to come up with a plan by the time he arrived at his destination.

✡

Zahira was delighted with the ability to shower—and while she did, she threw her Bedouin kaftan into the washing machine. She wrapped a long shirt Avi had loaned her around her torso and pulled on a pair of brand new men's pajama bottoms Avi had yet to wear. She knotted her wet hair into a towel turban on her head and joined Avi in the dining room where they had a simple supper of bread, cheese, avocados, and a peppery mango chutney sauce.

Avi felt a strong kinship with this descendant of his, who looked so similar to his wife, Sarah, but at the same time, he was in awe of Zahira. Unlike Natan,

291

Tzippy, and Max, Zahira was older, and thus exuded a mature persona. She was very regal in her mannerisms and seemed to not possess a sense of humor, for her speaking was very direct, and this was miles away from the person who Avi was, in both his lifetimes. But the ultimate reason for Avi's awe was the profound confidence and wisdom which saturated Zahira's being. There was more to Zahira than what met the eye, and though she spoke freely and openly of her life in Afghanistan and her journey to the holy land, Avi felt shy around her and slightly nervous to ask the questions which swirled vociferously in his mind.

When they had finished eating, Avi—the sweetmeat connoisseur that he was—suggested they have tea and dessert on the mirpeset. Zahira agreed amiably and helped him cut slices of cheesecake and pour the hot water over the bags of green tea and fresh mint leaves. They each balanced their own plate and cup and stepped onto the mirpeset. There was a slight awkwardness as a lull in the conversation enveloped them both. They ate silently and then sipped their tea. Zahira was the one to break the ice when she asked, "Is there anything you wish to ask of me?"

Avi couldn't suppress the curiosity inside of himself. This was the avenue he'd been waiting for. "How did you know where to find me? And how did you know I was here, Zahira?" he asked with a rush of words.

He blushed madly, embarrassed that he had asked the question, and braced himself for the answer. He didn't expect her to say a malevolent spirit had told her—after all, Michael had told him God had sent her—but at the same time, there was a slight twinge of fear in Avi that she would give him an answer which would not bode well with his spiritual and moral convictions.

Zahira turned his head and looked out over the railings of the mirpeset. "It was foretold that you would return."

Avi nodded. "You said your people have known I would come."

"There were prophetic signals."

"You mean the prophecy of the old bones?"

Zahira did not know what Avi referred to and he related the vague biblical prophecy to her quickly. She shook her head.

"I have not heard of any other prophecies relating to my return."

"The prophecy I speak of," Zahira said, "is much more direct."

Avi looked surprised.

"There are many prophecies regarding your resurrection."

"Told by whom?"

"Do you know my people, the Pashtun?"

"No, I'm afraid not."

"We are descendants of your sacred lineage, ab Ibrahim, through your grandson, Jacob, and his wives, Rachel and Leah. Our people are a remnant of the lost tribes who left in the Great Exile from this, the land of our forefathers, twenty-seven centuries ago. We wait there in exile until the *masih* returns and calls us back to our homeland to be reunited with our brothers, the Jews.

"My particular tribe, the Durani, is charged with the keeping of an ancient and hallowed knowledge. We are descended from the first King of Israel: Saul, of the tribe of Benjamin. When his throne was given to King David, Saul's descendants kept the secret knowledge close to themselves for fear that public knowledge of it would cause great harm to mankind as a whole. After the

Great Exile, my people took with us this particular, secret knowledge and wisdom which has been lost to the other tribes—knowledge and wisdom which was passed from one generation to another, until it was finally passed to me: the last of my line."

"What knowledge is this?"

"The knowledge which I speak of contains many prophecies, many hidden truths, many esoteric teachings, which have sustained my people throughout the long, hard years of exile."

"This is how you knew I returned?"

"Yes. There are numerous prophecies in our tradition which hint at your return. But there are three in particular which address this event directly."

"What are the three prophecies?"

"The first prophecy was spoken by the prophetess, Sarah—your wife in your last incarnation on earth."

The mention of Sarah caused Avi to do a double take. "Sarah made a prophecy concerning my return? But how can that be? Who recorded this prophecy? How did I hear nothing of this?"

"The prophetess Sarah was a powerful woman and highly favored by Allah." Zahira shrugged. "I do not know how her prophecy was remembered and recorded, but the fact is, it was, and furthermore, it spoke of your return."

"What does it say?"

"'Thus says the Lord of the heavens and the earth to the prophetess Sarah: 'The day shall come when your issue shall be ripped at the seams, and the miracle of your progeny shall be scattered across the face of the earth. For one hundred generations, the children of Sarah shall weep and wail, separated from each other and kept
294

from the land that the Lord promised to their mother. Then, in the final hour, the Lord will call forth the consort of the prophetess; he shall rise in flesh from the grave, erect, alive, with the angel of the Lord at his side. The first father shall return to bring anointing and hope to the house of Judah. He shall bring peace and shall crown Israel. The shofar shall sound and with a lion's roar, the exiled tribes shall answer the call: from every corner of the earth, the children of Sarah will heed the call of Judah and they shall return home and Israel will be one again."

Avi sat quietly and digested the words of the prophecy. "Break it down for me. How did you know that this prophecy pertains to my return and how did you know it means now?"

"The first part of the prophecy clearly relates to the Great Exile. It speaks of Israel being 'ripped at the seams', 'scattered across the face of the earth' and 'separated from each other' as they 'weep and wail'.

"With regards to you, the prophecy speaks of the Lord calling 'forth the consort of the prophetess'—since the prophecy was given to Sarah, *alayhas salaam*, the consort the prophecy alludes to must be hers, ergo, it is you. As for your resurrection, the prophecy says quite clearly that the 'consort of the prophetess' will 'rise in flesh from the grave, erect, alive'—which clearly means bodily resurrection and not merely reincarnation. The prophecy then speaks of this person as 'the first father'. Who else is the first father but you, the first cause of our people?

"As to how we know the prophecy was to be fulfilled now: twenty-seven hundred years have passed since the time of the Great Exile. In our tradition, a generation spans twenty-seven years." Zahira looked at

Avi intently. "I am the hundredth generation since the Great Exile. It was known that you would come in my lifetime."

Avi was awed. Zahira clearly had no dealings with dead spirits and her knowledge of Avi's return had come, not just from any prophet of God, but had emanated from the love of Avi's previous life, his wife, Sarah. The last vestiges of Avi's circumspection disappeared. As he looked at Zahira, he could see Sarah in an even more pronounced way. "This is amazing. So, it was explicitly foretold." He didn't say anything to Zahira, but he was even more impressed that the prophecy had mentioned "the angel of the Lord at his side"—a clear reference to Michael.

Zahira nodded thoughtfully. "The final portion of the prophecy, of course, speaks of the return of the tribes living in the Great Exile back home to the land of our forefathers. It is deceptively vague, but the scholars and sages of my people have deciphered that it means the *masih* will sound the symbolic shofar and call us home."

Avi was about to tell Zahira that the mashiach she referred to as the masih had been found and named, and that it would only be a matter of time before the masih would sound the call for the lost tribes to leave the exile, but something inside of him gnawed at him and stopped him from doing so. He didn't know what it was that was keeping him from telling her—but the fact was, every sinew of his body was screaming at him to keep silent. With much difficulty, he swallowed the words he wanted to scream out and instead asked, "What were the other prophecies?"

"The second prophecy was revealed to the prophet Joseph, son of Jacob, *alayhis salaam*. It says,

'Thus says the Lord of Avraham, Isaac and Jacob: Abouna Ibrahim will be resurrected from the dead in the days before the coming of the masih, and he shall expose his legs.'"

Avi giggled and Zahira looked at him strangely. "Why do you laugh?"

"Well, that one was pretty direct. You don't even have to go through the trouble of deciphering it, it was so direct. It even mentioned my cargo shorts!" He gestured to the shorts which he wore that showed his legs off.

Zahira shrugged. "Sometimes prophecies can be very ambiguous, sometimes they can be very direct. But while they both speak of your return, one overtly, and the other somewhat inconspicuously, they contain different truths."

"Such as that I would be showing off my chicken legs?"

Zahira stared at Avi blankly. Her lack of humor was never more evident.

Avi coughed. "So, um, what was the third prophecy?"

"The final prophecy is the most interesting and it is what led me directly to you here today—it was the prophecy which spoke of your actual location."

Avi guffawed. "What was it? Did it tell my underwear size and GPS location?"

The humor was lost on Zahira. "No. The teller of this final prophecy is unknown, but we have remembered it and passed it through the ages. It says: 'When the kingdom of the West twice transcends the hate of color but then falls again into the hands of hatred, when the union is slain because the green isle has left it, when the evil ones rise from the desert in

Mesopotamia and Padan-Aram to proclaim a wicked and cursed kingdom under the flag of black, *Storay* Ibrahim will ascend the sky for twelve moons. At the place of My people's *qibla*, where the city which calls My Name fades and the desert blooms, on the street of the gold man, *Storay* Ibrahim will descend to seek comfort from *Storay* Bilyamin.'"

"Wait, what? Kingdom of the West? Hate of color? New age foretold by the ancient ones of the west? *Storay* Ibrahim? *Storay* Bilyamin? Street of the gold man? The city which calls My Name fades and where the desert blooms? This is unbelievably ambiguous! What's next? A walk through Unicorn Garden and a frolic over the rainbow?"

Zahira adjusted the towel on her head. "The prophecy does not mention unicorns or rainbows."

"Never mind. Explain the prophecy to me, please."

Zahira brightened. "Certainly." She excused herself and ran into the bathroom and returned with a big bag from which she pulled out a wad of Internet pages, printed out on paper. "It took a lot of time to figure this one out. In fact, it was not until the past few years that we were able to understand what this prophecy meant as the events which it alludes to only fell into place recently.

"The kingdom of the West and its twice transcendence of the hate of color refer to America and its racial divisions, which were seemingly overcome with the election and subsequent re-election of Barack Obama. The reference to falling again into the hand of hatred signals the election of Donald Trump. When these two milestone events occurred, it was then that the meaning of this prophecy began to unravel." Zahira pulled out a page of paper from the wad in her hands and handed it to Avi. It was a well-read piece of paper, like all the pages in Zahira's hands, and it outlined Obama's and Trump's respective ascendancies to power.

"The reference to 'the union being slain because the green isle has left it', refers clearly to the British exit from the European Union." She handed Avi a sheath of pages which detailed the event.

"The reference to 'when the evil ones rise from the desert in Mesopotamia and Padan-Aram to proclaim a wicked and cursed kingdom under the flag of black' – this clearly refers to the rise of the Islamic State in Iraq and Syria.

"The 'qibla' of His people referred to in the prophecy was the only bit of the prophecy we'd figured out on our own. For centuries, although our people have adopted Islam, given our Israelite roots, the qibla we prayed towards was always Jerusalem and not Mecca. The allusion to the 'city which calls His Name' further strengthened our belief that it meant Jerusalem as we know—from our understanding of the Torah—that the only place referred to in Scripture, either Jewish or Islamic, that meets this description is, in fact, Jerusalem." She gave Avi another page, this one outlining Jewish mysticism.

"My people have always been astute astrologers and the unexpected appearance of an unknown, brilliant star exactly one year ago, which shone directly over Jerusalem in this, the hundredth generation since the Great Exile, confirmed our conviction that it was the Star of Avraham—Storay Ibrahim—as mentioned in the prophecy." She handed Avi a page from an astronomy site, which detailed the sudden and unexpected appearance of a comet the year before, and also a copy of a map of Jerusalem.

"It was only when I arrived here a few weeks ago and saw the topography of the area that I realized that what the spot referred to as the 'street of the gold man' actually was—as you can see on the map—the place in which we met, which is called the Goldman Promenade." Zahira pointed to the promenade. "Where else does the city fade and the desert bloom but here? To the west is civilization; to the east is the desert. The Goldman Promenade sits on the seam of them both." Zahira shrugged. "Besides, Storay Ibrahim shone directly over the Goldman Promenade, and it's twelve-moon cycle came to an end last night. The prophecy speaks of Storay Ibrahim descending to this spot, so I knew I would find you here today. I saw when you ran down the promenade and I knew it had to be you, for in the whole day I kept watch over the spot, no one else had happened by."

Avi nodded slowly. Zahira's logic in deciphering the tricky prophecy made sense.

Zahira blushed. "There is just one hitch."

"What's that?"

"I'm not egotistical, but it says that 'Storay Ibrahim'—presumably you—'will descend to seek comfort from Storay Bilyamin'—the Star of Benjamin—presumably, me? As a descendant of Saul, and a member of the tribe of Benjamin, perhaps it means me." Zahira blushed a deeper red. "But I don't want to be presumptuous."

"Zahira means 'shining', doesn't it?"

Zahira nodded.

"It is you," Avi said decisively. "I've not yet met someone else who can so decisively trace his or her roots to the tribe of Benjamin. It has to be you. And, the fact that the timing of the prophecy coincides with the reality which you and I are currently experiencing leads to one logical conclusion: that you are Storay Bilyamin, that goes without saying." He paused. "And let's hope to God that I am Storay Ibrahim and you really weren't supposed to give comfort to an actual star or comet." Avi grinned and Zahira slowly smiled. Avi was excited to be part of the deciphering process. It made him feel like a detective almost. "But how does Storay Bilyamin offer comfort to Storay Ibrahim?"

"At first I wasn't sure. Even up until the hour before I met you I wasn't sure. But when I met you, I knew. You were so shaken up when you met me—and my appearance reminded you so much of the prophetess Sarah, that I couldn't help but wonder if, perhaps, maybe, you weren't, possibly, missing... her... Sarah, that is."

Avi looked at the ground. Zahira was perceptive. "That was it exactly. I was missing her. I was missing her so much, Zahira, it hurt. When you showed up, out of the blue, it was like God Himself had sent you." Avi looked up and into Zahira's eyes. "Your mere presence makes me feel better. This is how you comfort me."

Zahira fumbled with the bag she'd brought out of the bathroom. "Perhaps there's more I can do to make you feel even more comforted."

"Like what?"

She pulled out a necklace from the bag and dangled it from her fingers. "I believe this was Sarah's?"

Avi gasped. "That was the wedding necklace I gave to Sarah to seal our betrothal!"

Zahira smiled and extended the necklace to Avi. He put out his hand and she dropped it into his open palm.

Avi felt the familiar coolness of the ancient jewelry. It was a mix of semi-precious stones, somewhat gaudy, but it had been all he could afford on his own in his youthful days while he lived in Cutha and had wanted to marry Sarah. It was a silly trinket, really, but it was the one material thing which most powerfully signified the love which had existed him and his wife, and the touch of it propelled him back across the millennia to the first time he had seen the face of his soul mate. He clasped his hands around the necklace and looked up at Zahira. "How did you find this? When Sarah died, I gave it to our daughter-in-law as part of her inheritance. I didn't think she valued it, because she packed it away and wore the terribly expensive wedding necklace my son had bought her instead."

Zahira shook her head. "You underestimate the wisdom of Rebecca, ab Ibrahim. She knew what this necklace meant to you and Sarah—she knew what it would mean to the family as a whole. When she had her own daughter-in-law—the favorite wife of her son Jacob, the prophetess, Rachel—Rebecca passed it on to her, who, in turn, passed it on to her son, Benjamin and his family, and thus the necklace passed through the ages until it came to be mine." Zahira smiled. "The story of the necklace has passed through the ages with it, and its story spins the fantastic tale of the powerful love which existed between you and our grandmother, Sarah. This necklace is the symbol of the most passionate love story and it is said among my people that the love shared between you and Sarah is what brought the presence of Allah down upon the earth to choose you both to be the founders of our great nation." Zahira paused and looked at the necklace fondly. "This necklace brought hope to many generations of your descendants."

Avi choked. "It brings hope to me; it brings comfort, more than I can explain to you." He stood and hugged Zahira tightly. "Thank you for returning this to me, blessed woman."

Zahira nodded and answered huskily, "Thank you for loving our grandmother so much that even Allah wanted to be a part of it."

Zahira stood, put her hands on Avi's shoulders, and turned him around. "Hand me the necklace," she commanded. He dropped it behind, into her hand. She reached over the much-shorter Avi with the necklace and fastened it around his neck. "The clasp is new. It was replaced in my father's time. It will not come undone."

Avi touched the beads at his neck and turned around and smiled widely. "Thank you for this."

He was about to hug Zahira again, but at that moment, there was a sharp knock at the front door.

✡

"Marry you?" Natan asked incredulously. He let go of Tzippy's hand and looked at her, flabbergasted. "Marry you?"

Tzippy's eyes widened. "No. Not marry. Just say we're going to get married so my parents won't be as disappointed in me."

Natan shook his head. "But the baby isn't mine."

"I know, I know," Tzippy said. "But you're so successful and good-looking and everything. If we pretend you're the father, at least for my parents' sake, then it wouldn't be so hard of a blow for them to hear that I'm knocked up. We can pretend the baby is yours and then we can have some big dramatic fight or something and call off the wedding."

"Tzippy, if I pretend to be the baby's father, that can't be called off. That's a commitment for life."

Tzippy sniffed. "No, I won't ask you for anything. I just need for my parents to think you're the father."

"What about the real father? Have you thought of asking him to stand in as... the father?"

"I can't."

"Why not?"

Tzippy looked at Natan miserably. "I don't know who he is."

"You don't know who he is?"

"It was a random hook-up with some guy I met when I was drunk. We never exchanged numbers or names or anything."

Natan frowned. "Or condoms, obviously."

"We did use condoms!" Tzippy exclaimed. "I guess they just didn't work."

Natan sighed. "So basically, you're telling me you've got a fatherless child growing inside of you."

"Yes." Tzippy looked at Natan desperately. "You see why I need someone to pretend to be the father? I won't name you as the baby's father on the birth certificate and I won't ever ask you for anything. My family has money. My baby will never lack for anything. This is just a favor I need done for the benefit of my parents."

"Tzippy," Natan started, then he stopped.

"You're the only one I can ask," Tzippy said quietly, "not just because you're successful and
304

everything—but because, well, you're good at pretending."

Natan looked at her.

"You know what I'm talking about. I won't hold it against you if you won't do it. I know it's asking a lot of you—and this isn't your problem. But as my friend, if you can be a little empathetic and help me out here, considering your own situation..." Tzippy's voice trailed off.

Natan coughed. "You know?"

Tzippy nodded sadly. "I figured it out a while ago."

"How?" Natan asked cautiously.

"Woman's intuition? It was many different little things. The night you disappeared on us after we'd taken Avi shopping; your keen sense of style; the clothes that Avi found in the tent when he came of out the cave that clearly weren't yours and your reaction to us asking whose clothes they were was the real tip-off. Whose clothes were they anyway?"

Natan coughed. "This guy."

"Boyfriend?"

"Not exactly."

"Random hook-up?"

"Not exactly."

Tzippy shrugged. "Ok, if you don't want to say."

Natan blushed. "Please don't tell Max. Or anyone else."

"Of course not. Natan, I don't want you to think I'm holding this over your head as blackmail, you know! Cause I'm not. I won't tell anyone regardless of what your decision is concerning my... situation, because clearly, it's not something you're comfortable with yet, otherwise you wouldn't have hidden in it. Although, in my opinion, it's nothing to be ashamed of."

Natan opened his mouth to speak, but before he could, the buzzer to his apartment rang.

CHAPTER 14

"Abraham came forward and said: 'Will You sweep away the innocent along with the guilty? What if there should be fifty innocent within the city; will You then wipe out the place and not forgive it for the sake of the innocent fifty who are in it? Far be it for You to do such a thing, to bring death upon the innocent as well as the guilty, so that innocent and guilty fare alike. Far be it from You! Shall not the Judge of all the earth deal justly?' And the LORD answered, 'If I find within the city of Sodom fifty innocent ones, I will forgive the whole place for their sake.' Abraham spoke up, saying, 'Here I venture to speak to my Lord, I who am but dust and ashes: What if the fifty innocent should lack five? Will You destroy the whole city for want of the five?' And He answered, 'I will not destroy if I find forty-five there.' But he spoke to Him again, and said, 'What if forty should be found there?' And He answered, 'I will not do it, for the sake of the forty.' And he said, 'Let not my Lord be angry if I go on: What if thirty should be found there?' And He answered, 'I will not do it if I find thirty there.' And he said, 'I venture again to speak to my Lord: What if twenty should be found there?' And He answered, 'I will not destroy, for the sake of the twenty.' And he said, 'Let not my Lord be angry if I speak but this last time: What if ten should be found there?' And He answered, 'I will not destroy for the sake of the ten.' When the LORD had finished speaking to Abraham, He departed, and Abraham returned to his place."
—Genesis 18:23-33

Rabbi Eliezer was a man who liked order and routine. He did not, under any circumstances, enjoy surprises. As far as he was concerned, surprises were unnecessary and not a bit distasteful. Rabbi Eliezer preferred—*much* preferred—to always be in the know, to be sure and steady, and to have things go according to plan.

Generally speaking, his go-to emotion in situations where things were out of his control or where things did not unravel in the way most fortuitous to his circumstances was to either get angry or get very angry. Although the events of the past day did not go according to his expectations, they were so unbelievably unexpected that Rabbi Eliezer couldn't bring himself to experience the familiar feelings that would have normally erupted inside of himself when things don't pan out the way he wanted them to. Instead, Rabbi Eliezer couldn't help but feel overwhelmed and not a bit awed at the surprises which the day had presented to him.

The first surprise had been the revelation that the little Sephardi pipsqueak he had met the night before was none other than the great Avraham Aveinu of biblical fame, returned to life on a peculiar mission to meet and greet the mashiach. It had been the single most astounding piece of news he had heard in his entire life and it had initially floored him, but Rabbi Eliezer was a shrewd man and overwhelming though the news was, it had to benefit him in some way.

His first stop after visiting the Israeli prime minister was to go directly to the reason of Avraham Aveinu's return: to the mashiach, Natan Nasi, in Tel Aviv. The naming of Natan as the mashiach had been the second surprise Rabbi Eliezer had experienced that day—but unlike the first surprise, this second surprise had the potential to lead to a disintegration of Ashkenazi power: something Rabbi Eliezer was firmly set against as he considered his minhag far superior to what he considered to be the more watered-down Sephardi version of Orthodox Judaism. Quick on the draw as ever, Rabbi Eliezer realized what he needed to do in order to properly ingratiate himself into the maelstrom which would inevitably come in the future with the public learning about Natan: he needed to get in good with Natan. He realized that, like Avi, Natan probably was not too keen on him given the way things had transpired the night before, but Rabbi Eliezer knew he could be charming when it suited him, and he was eager to apologize to both the patriarch and mashiach and start over anew with both of them. Unfortunately, as a private citizen, it had been somewhat difficult to gather information about Natan, but Rabbi Eliezer's channels of information were—though not particularly expedient today—efficient, and they had found Natan's address, his school records, and (the third big surprise of the day) the most startling bit of information about the named mashiach: that he, allegedly, was an in-the-closet homosexual man. Such a thing was outrageous and not at all salubrious for world Jewry.

How could God have chosen such a character to be the mashiach? Rabbi Eliezer wondered to himself as his driver sped off to Rechov HaYarkon. *A homosexual mashiach?*

It was an abomination of extraordinary proportions and Rabbi Eliezer couldn't fathom it. His sources were always generally on the mark—and he wondered whether, perhaps, at least this time, they were wrong. When he pulled up outside of Natan's apartment, he decided he would confront Natan immediately and not waste time. In Rabbi Eliezer's experience, homosexuals—particularly hiloni ones—were eerily proud of their unnatural tastes, and he was sure that

309

Natan would be too. However, he knew he had to go about his questioning in as tactful a way as possible so as to keep himself likeable, regardless of what he thought about the matter.

Like everything else that day, the meeting with Natan did not go down according to plan. Firstly, the frekha from the night before was present, and while her previous presence had made Rabbi Eliezer turn up his nose at Avi and Natan for erroneously thinking she was sleeping with them both—her present appearance in the home of the mashiach was quite welcome, for it suggested the possibility of a carnal relationship between the two youngsters, which, of course, would lay the homosexual rumor to rest. Rabbi Eliezer was welcomed into Natan's apartment with a somewhat hesitant stance, but the mashiach was less antagonistic than the night before. Unwilling to betray the fact that he knew Natan was the mashiach, Rabbi Eliezer presented his visit in the context of an apology for his behavior from the night before. Tzippy, the frekha, continued right off from where she left off the night before: rude and obnoxious as ever. Unsure of the relationship between her and the mashiach, Rabbi Eliezer was forced to keep his cool and put up with her outright hostility. "You're a man who wouldn't just come down here to apologize," Tzippy had said bluntly. "You're here for a reason. What is it?" Rabbi Eliezer painted the most hurt look on his face and replied calmly that Tzippy was right. Surprised at his candor, Tzippy asked, "Well, go on then. Tell us why you're really here." Rabbi Eliezer sighed and launched into a quiet, yet emotional plea that he was concerned for Natan's welfare, for he had heard a vicious rumor that Natan was a homosexual—and he wanted nothing more than to help Natan overcome this illness through prayer and counseling in memory of Natan's Saba, who Rabbi Eliezer was sure would not want to have grandson live the life of a sinner.

Natan's and Tzippy's simultaneous shocked reaction was immediate, and it registered in Rabbi Eliezer that his sources were right. Tzippy, after a moment, regained her ferociousness, and she jumped up quickly and yelled that it was a lie and that she and Natan were a couple. Natan smiled weakly at the frekha and he shushed her. Unlike the frekha, Natan seemed to have been swayed by Rabbi Eliezer's politeness. He looked wearily at the rabbi and informed him that the rumor was true. He was indeed gay. Rabbi Eliezer's heart plummeted to the ground. Natan went on to speak of his sexuality and his troubled relationship with his father and hence the reason he was not ready to come out. "But I don't believe that being gay is an illness," he said, summarily. "I have come to terms with who I am. I have accepted myself for who I am. However, I am not ready to publicize this yet, and with the passing of my grandfather, I know my openness as a gay man would sully his memory in the Orthodox world, so I am just not ready."

Rabbi Eliezer nodded silently, thoughtfully, but he was raging inside at the thought of the mashiach being unwilling to admit to the gross sinfulness of his ways and being uncompromising in his approach to the sin. But Rabbi Eliezer could mouth none of these things without isolating himself further from Natan's good graces. He appealed to the young man to please allow him entrance into his confidences. "I want nothing more than to be here for you. I'm sure you are still coming to terms with the loss of your esteemed Saba, but please know, I am here for you if you need me." Rabbi Eliezer left his card on Natan's coffee table and Natan walked him to the door. Before the door had closed, however, Rabbi Eliezer heard the frekha say quite loudly, "That old geezer is up to something. There is no way he is that selfless and giving." Rabbi Eliezer swallowed his anger and continued out of the building and into his car and directed his driver to return to Jerusalem.

✡

Max didn't know what to do. After he had regaled Rabbi Eliezer with the entire story of Avi's return to earth, Rabbi Eliezer had abruptly dismissed Max from the office and cautioned him to say nothing of Avi to anyone else and to also not tell Avi, Natan, or Tzippy that he had confided in Rabbi Eliezer. "I suggest you attend the remainder of your classes for the day and stay at the yeshiva."

Max opened his mouth to protest, but Rabbi Eliezer cut him off brusquely. "That will be all, Feldman."

Max shuffled out of the room.

He had not been able to concentrate in any of his classes, and the morning classes he had sat through after leaving Rabbi Eliezer had been pure hell. He kept thinking about what he had done, and he wondered whether he had made a mistake in telling Rabbi Eliezer about Avi being Avraham and about Natan being the mashiach. What was worse, now that he had been ordered to stay at the yeshiva and told to not talk to his friends, he wasn't able to warn them that the Avi story had exploded in Israel. He didn't know if his friends had yet heard about it, but he was desperate to be with them. He felt stifled and cut off. He shuffled around the
312

corridors listlessly during lunch, and as he passed the pay phone that stood in the hallway, to his surprise, he'd found that the receiver had been ripped off by the cord. Max didn't own a cell phone, and the loss of the pay phone hit him hard. It left him feeling isolated and stranded. The compunction to be with his friends overwhelmed him. He needed to talk to them—any one of them. By the time lunch was over, although he felt compelled to obey Rabbi Eliezer's directives, Max knew what he needed to do. He rushed to his dorm room and stuffed the few hundred shekels he had into his pocket and made his way to the gate of the yeshiva compound. He was just about to stride through when two tall Charedi men who worked in the maintenance department of the school stopped him. "I am sorry, Feldman," the taller man said. "You cannot leave. Rabbi Goldenberg has requested that you remain here today."

"I must leave," Max shrilled. "It's a matter of life and death."

The men shook their heads menacingly.

"Can I at least make a phone call? I have money. I'll pay for it. The pay phone is broken."

"Rabbi Goldenberg has requested you have no contact with outside for the day."

Max threw his hands in the air, frustrated. "What is this? A monastery? What next? You're going to give me penance and ask me to take a vow of silence?"

Max turned on his heel, and marched back inside.

✡

When he was back in his car, the profoundness of the mashiach's announcement that he was a homosexual fully hit Rabbi Eliezer. Homosexuality was expressly forbidden in Orthodox Judaism. It was as clear as day, written in the Torah: 'Man shall not lay with mankind as with womankind'. There was no need to extrapolate further. It was *wrong*.

Rabbi Eliezer couldn't understand it. He tried to, but he couldn't. While some Orthodox rabbis believed that a person who practiced a homosexual lifestyle could be rehabilitated into a heterosexual stance, Rabbi Eliezer didn't support this view. He had seen too many men go through various programs, only to return to their life of sin.

Why did God choose a homosexual man to be the mashiach?

Rabbi Eliezer pondered the situation carefully.

He rewound the story Max had related to him that morning in Rabbi Rubenstein's office and a particular portion from Max's story came back to him: "Avi—that's what we call him, Avraham Aveinu, I mean—walked up to Natan and told him he was the mashiach. Of course, we all laughed and thought he was crazy, but then he told us he was Avraham Aveinu, returned to earth to do HaShem's bidding and immediately we all knew that this was no joke. Avi then repeated that Natan was the mashiach and, for a second, I thought I saw hesitance flash across Avi's face, almost as if he wasn't sure he'd made the right choice in choosing Natan. He kind of narrowed his eyes and squinted at Natan after announcing him as the mashiach. It was almost as if Avi was sizing Natan up because he wasn't one hundred percent sure he'd made the right choice. Oh, don't get me wrong—I don't think Avi erred in his decision, but it just seemed as if he was a tad bit unsure. Anyway, that was all cleared up within a few minutes, because it came out that the tent Avi had been staying in for the three days prior to meeting us was actually Natan's. So, that sort of legitimized the whole thing, you know?"

Avraham Aveinu hadn't been sure. *He hadn't been sure?* Then wait just one minute—if he hadn't been sure, was it possible...?

Like a light bulb going on above his head, the idea hit Rabbi Eliezer so suddenly, it almost caused him to pass out with giddy glee.

What if Avraham Aveinu hadn't made the correct choice? What if the mashiach was not Natan, but rather... Max?

Rabbi Eliezer felt a thrill pulsate through his entire body. He'd solved the mystery. The mashiach *wasn't* a Sephardi homosexual because the mashiach wasn't Natan! It was no wonder Rabbi Eliezer had felt compelled to visit Natan first, and saved meeting Avraham Aveinu for last. Sheer human ingenuity (of which Rabbi Eliezer knew he possessed in copious amounts) had sent him to Natan to determine that Avraham Aveinu had made the wrong choice—and now God was compelling him to relay that information to Avraham Aveinu.

The only sticking point was that he wasn't in Avraham Aveinu's good graces, and he doubted Avraham would immediately begin to confide in him, and more than anything, Rabbi Eliezer needed exactly that—Avraham Aveinu's unmitigated trust—to convince Avraham Aveinu that he had made the wrong choice. He needed Avraham to relate to him—word for word—the exact directive God had issued to him. Unless Rabbi Eliezer could make Avraham Aveinu trust him, there was no way he could get to the bottom of the story and convince him that a gross mistake had been made.

The future of Judaism depended on this meeting and Rabbi Eliezer felt the weight of the meeting's importance bear down upon himself. He flirted with the idea of calling Natan's Saba's apartment where Avraham Aveinu was residing from his cell phone and announcing his impending arrival, but he eventually decided against that plan of action. It had always served Rabbi Eliezer well to show up unexpectedly, and he was much too comfortable with his ways to change now. He dismissed the idea immediately. He would return to Jerusalem, go to shul and say *minchah*, return home to have dinner with his wife and refresh himself, and then go to meet Avraham Aveinu. Now that he had a plan, Rabbi Eliezer felt much better.

"Can't you drive any faster, man?" he barked at his driver. "What is this? A who can go the slowest contest?"

Yes, Rabbi Eliezer felt better—much better.

✡

Max needed to get out of the yeshiva—even if only for a few minutes, just to call Tzippy or Natan or Avi to tell them that Avi's reappearance on earth had been documented by the press and was being believed by all and sundry. Knowing his friends and their lack of interest in current affairs, he doubted any of them had yet heard about the breaking news sweeping the country. Unfortunately, Rabbi Eliezer's dictates to the yeshiva administration left him marooned in the school which he once loved but now looked upon as a prison.

He paced his room, trying to think of his options. Perhaps he could climb over a wall? No, that would be crazy; he would have no way of getting up the fifteen-feet walls which surrounded the school, much less for climbing down the other side of it without being hurt. Perhaps he could make a mad dash out the gates? A quick look out the window of his dorm room showed that the gates to the school were uncharacteristically shut—no doubt on Rabbi Eliezer's orders. Definitely no mad dash happening there. Perhaps he could call someone and say he was being held against his will? That would require the use of a phone, and with the pay phone in disrepair and the administration working on Rabbi Eliezer's orders, he knew he wouldn't be allowed a call from the office. He considered his options: there were none. He slumped unto his bed.

There was a rap at his door.

"Come in," he said.

A boy from his class walked in. "Shalom."

"Shalom, Schwartz." Schwartz was Max's *chavrusah* during the study period after minchah.

Schwartz stood nervously by the door and wrung his hands. "Are you coming down to the beis midrash? You've been gone for a week and I have not been assigned another chavrusah."

Max shook his head. "I can't come down—I've got a lot of things going on."

Schwartz hopped on his foot. "But we are both way back in our study—I thought that now you've returned we can try to catch up with everyone. We have a lot of reading to go through."

"I'm sorry, Schwartz. There are more pressing issues at hand right now."

"Rabbi Rubenstein is going to be upset if he knows you are missing class for no good reason."

Suddenly, it dawned on Max. He had one possible ally in this school—one person whose outlook on life differed markedly from Rabbi Eliezer's and probably wouldn't agree with Rabbi Eliezer's holding Max hostage while Rabbi Eliezer traipsed around the outside world doing God alone knows what.

Without another word, Max dashed out of his room, past a bewildered Schwartz.

✡

The fourth surprise of Rabbi Eliezer's day came when he pulled up outside of the apartment complex in Arnona he had visited the night before and found a camel covered with a thick blanket tethered to the hedge of flowers which bordered the pavement. Rabbi Eliezer had been accused by detractors of being unable to realize that he lived in the Middle East and not sixteenth century Europe and, though it was an insult, Rabbi Eliezer never responded to the accusation because it was, simply put, true. As far as he was concerned, Moishe Rabbeinu had worn a black suit—quite similar to one which covered Rabbi Eliezer's rotund body, Sampson had yelled "oy vey!" when he learnt of Delilah's treachery, King David had the most beautiful lily-white skin, and the patriarchs had all dined on bland, fatty central European food.

Notwithstanding this, Rabbi Eliezer approached the animal with an open palm. The camel chewed the flowers in its mouth and watched the fat rabbi approach him with apprehension. When Rabbi Eliezer was close enough to touch it, the camel let out a screeching noise and splattered him with gooey spit.

"Stupid creature," Rabbi Eliezer murmured, and he pulled a pristinely white handkerchief from his pocket and wiped his face.

The entrance to the apartment complex was, expectedly locked, but almost as if it were a sign of good fortune, before Rabbi Eliezer could press the buzzer, someone exited the building and allowed the spittle-soaked rabbi in. Rabbi Eliezer went up the elevator and made his way to the door of the apartment in which he knew the great resurrected Avraham Aveinu was currently using as his earthly abode.

He rapped at the door and waited patiently until he heard a voice call out. "Who is it?"

"It's Rabbi Eliezer Goldenberg," he said softly, struggling to announce himself humbly.

The door opened, and there before him, clad in cargo shorts and with a lady's necklace wrapped around his neck, was the great Avraham Aveinu, Rabbi Eliezer's very great grandfather.

Avi seemed shocked to see Rabbi Eliezer when he opened the door, but he politely invited the rabbi into the apartment. This led to Rabbi Eliezer's fifth surprise of the day: for Avi—Avraham Aveinu—was entertaining a guest. Not just any guest, but a clearly Arab, older woman guest. Rabbi Eliezer did not know what to make of it. Despite the fact that the mixing of unmarried sexes was something which went against everything Rabbi Eliezer stood for, he said nothing. He forced himself to smile at the woman and he whispered a greeting and gave a curtailed introduction of himself. The woman looked at him, bewildered, and then looked to Avi who translated everything Rabbi Eliezer had said to her in

319

rapid Pashto, which surprised Rabbi Eliezer even further to know that the patriarch had such an advanced command of another language. The woman listened closely to Avi's translation and she smiled welcomingly at Rabbi Eliezer and in the global gesture of welcome, she touched her chest and extended her hand out to him. Rabbi Eliezer was too astounded to do anything other than to stare at the oddly dressed woman with his mouth open. He turned to the patriarch, hoping to get some explanation, but all Avi said was that the woman, Zahira, was not from Israel and was, in fact, from Afghanistan and this was the reason why she didn't speak Hebrew.

"B-but why is she here?" Rabbi Eliezer stuttered uneasily.

"She came to see me," Avi answered simply and evenly, clearly aware that Zahira's presence unsettled the old rabbi.

Sensing that Avi had closed the topic of the mysterious Zahira, Rabbi Eliezer sat again in the chair he had sat in only a day before. He looked at Avi nervously, who had gone back to talking to his visitor in her native tongue. Zahira nodded and then with a wave of her hand, retreated to a bedroom.

Avi sat on the sofa across from Rabbi Eliezer. "Why are you here?" Avi asked him, pointedly.

Rabbi Eliezer took a deep breath. He didn't expect to have to get into the meat of the matter so quickly. "I came for two reasons: first to apologize. I am sorry—truly sorry— for the way I behaved last night towards you and your friends."

"And what's the second reason?"

Rabbi Eliezer raised an eyebrow. "It's not often that I give an apology—"

"The second reason," Avi said, firmly.

Rabbi Eliezer swallowed. "The second reason is that I know who you are."

"Who I am? Who do you think I am?"

"You are Avraham Aveinu, returned to earth."

Avi's eyes grew wide. "How do you know this?"

"Feldman relayed the information to me this morning," he replied and he went on to recap everything he'd been told. Avi sighed as he listened to the rabbi's tale, but he visibly relaxed when he heard the source of Rabbi Eliezer's information.

"So," the rabbi said summarily, "I went to visit with the mashiach."

"Natan? Did you tell him you knew he was the mashiach?"

Rabbi Eliezer hesitated. "No. I did not think it was prudent to convey that I knew who he was just yet. I merely apologized and that was it."

"So, you went under false pretenses."

"No. I went to apologize."

"But you didn't tell him you knew he was the mashiach. Clearly you went to scope him out."

Rabbi Eliezer experienced an odd sensation of déjà vu. He almost felt as if it was Tzippy in front of him. If he squinted just right, he could almost see the frekha in the patriarch. The resemblance unnerved the rabbi. He cleared his throat. "Yes, I did go to 'scope him out' as you say, but I had my reasons."

"Pray tell, what were your reasons?"

"To determine whether or not he was a homosexual."

Avi didn't react at first, but then burst out laughing. "Are you even kidding me?"

"At first, my wanting to meet him was purely on the level of curiosity. But then, it came to my attention

321

that he was a homosexual and this made me want to meet him even more. I did meet him, and he did confirm his homosexual status to me."

Avi did a double take. "Natan is gay?"

Rabbi Eliezer nodded. This was exactly what he wanted—for Avraham Aveinu to be appalled and then reconsider his choice. "So, you see, Avraham Aveinu—"

"Avi."

"I don't feel comfortable referring to you in such informal terms."

"Suit yourself."

"You see the predicament this puts us all in?"

"No."

"A homosexual mashiach? It's preposterous!"

"How so?"

"The mashiach must be married and have children."

Avi shrugged. "And what's stopping Natan from committing to a life partner and having kids with that man? Modern science affords him that right."

"You don't have a problem with him being a homosexual?"

"It's his life. Does it matter if the person he chooses to love is male or female? Love is love—and children should always be raised in homes of love."

"But, Avraham Aveinu, what about Sodom and Gomorrah? HaShem destroyed the two cities for their wanton homosexuality."

Avi shook his head. "You are a Torah scholar—you know that is not true. God allowed for the destruction of those cities because of their wanton inhospitality and penchant for rape. There are no similarities between the culture espoused in the cities of

Sodom and Gomorrah and the life of an ethical homosexual man."

Rabbi Eliezer was floored. "So, you are fine with the mashiach being a homosexual?"

"God sent me to tell Natan he was the mashiach. If God is fine with it—who I am to argue?"

Rabbi Eliezer raised an eyebrow. "Did HaShem send you to tell Natan he was the mashiach?"

"Yes, God did."

"HaShem sent you to tell Natan—Natan specifically—that he was the mashiach?"

Avi shifted uncomfortably in his seat.

"Well? Was it Natan, specifically, to whom HaShem sent you?"

"No, but the signs all point to him."

"Do they now? What are the signs?"

"I don't know," Avi said, frustrated. "It's him. I've thought it through. It has to be him."

Rabbi Eliezer didn't answer immediately. "Feldman seemed to think that you were initially unsure whether HaShem sent you to Natan."

Avi didn't answer.

"To whom did HaShem send you?"

"He sent me to the mashiach," Avi whispered.

"What did HaShem tell you exactly regarding the identity of the mashiach?"

Avi sighed. "He said that the first mortal soul I encountered was to be the mashiach."

"Was that first mortal soul Natan? Or, perhaps, it was someone else."

Avi looked at the rabbi desperately. "I don't know who it was!"

"What do you mean?"

323

"When I first saw Natan, Max, and Tzippy, it was from the top of a hill. They all came into my view at the same time." Avi paused. "I didn't know which was the first one I saw, so I chose Natan."

"Why?"

"Because he was tall and good-looking and older than the other two. He fit the bill. Plus, when I left the cave, it was Natan's tent that I happened upon. Surely that was a sign?"

"Perhaps, but what if you misread the sign? What if the sign was to lead to you to someone connected to Natan and not Natan himself?"

Avi considered. "Maybe," he admitted.

"Think about it, Avraham Aveinu. Natan is not religious—and what's worse, he's a homosexual."

"He's a good person."

Rabbi Eliezer waved his hand dismissively. "There are greater things in life than simply being 'a good person'."

"You want me to say that the mashiach is Max, don't you?"

"I want you to open yourself up to the possibility that you've erred. Tell me, has Natan embraced his calling since you've told him he was the mashiach?"

Avi didn't want to answer, but he knew he had to. "No," he said miserably.

"Precisely."

Avi looked at his toes and didn't answer.

"I am not asking you to change your original casting. I am merely asking you to consider that you, perhaps, chose erroneously."

"All this because Natan is gay?"

"Homosexuality is a sin, Avraham Aveinu. It is written in the Torah as clear as day."

324

"Love is never a sin," Avi whispered softly. "I will not judge my friend."

"Misdirected love is a sin. When a man loves death and straps a bomb around himself and sets it off, killing himself and others—is that not a sin? When a woman plunges a knife into the heart of her newborn baby because she loves a heathen god who directs her to do so—is that not a sin? Love can be misdirected and skewed. You've lived through the era of unethical religions where people committed heinous acts all for the love of their heathen gods. You know what I say is true."

"Let me make my position on this issue clear: I have no problem with a person being gay. Besides, Natan never told me he was gay."

Rabbi Eliezer coughed. "Despite your liberal viewpoint, a homosexual mashiach is, definitely, wrong. It is explicitly laid out in the Torah. As a private citizen, Natan would be entitled to do whatever he wished with his life. But as the man who has been, assumedly, chosen by HaShem to be the mashiach, to lead Yisroel to redemption, he cannot himself be a sinner."

"All men sin, Rabbi Goldenberg. It is through sin that we are able to repent, and it is through repentance that we find God."

"Bupkes. Public sin is sin—there is no romanticizing it. Homosexuality flies in the face of halacha."

Avi sighed.

"I have given you much to think about, I know, so I will take my leave now. However, there is just that small matter of my apology."

"What about it?"

"I would like if you could forgive me for my behavior last night."

Avi looked at the rabbi. "No. I can't."

"Why not?"

"Let me put it you this way: had you not found out who I really was, would you have come here to apologize tonight? Be honest."

"I suppose not, no."

"The man you slighted last night was the nobody you perceived him to be. It wasn't me. You thought he was of no consequence and thus, you treated him accordingly. He is the man who has the power to forgive you, rabbi. Not me."

Rabbi Eliezer clenched his fists. "So, you will not forgive me?"

"It's not up to me to do so."

"Very well." He stood. "I beg for no one's forgiveness."

Avi shrugged.

"Please consider my suggestion regarding the mashiach. Lila tov, Avraham Aveinu."

Avi stood and walked the rabbi to the door. "Lila tov."

It had been quite a day.

CHAPTER 15

"When the sun set and it was very dark, there appeared a smoking oven, and a flaming torch which passed between those pieces."
—Genesis 15:17

Natan closed the door behind Rabbi Eliezer and looked at Tzippy. "Do you really think he had an ulterior motive in coming here?"

"Unequivocally," Tzippy answered forcefully.

"But what possible reason could it be?"

"I think he doesn't want his precious talmid to be sullied by us—so he came to check up on us. He knows you're gay, Natan! The man must have some serious clout and connections to have found that out, because you are so far back in the closet it's not even funny. It's only a matter of time before he finds out that I am pregnant and not married and that will make the old geezer even more determined to remove us from Max's life."

Natan frowned. "He seemed so sincere."

"He's been in this business for a long time. He knows how to play the game."

"His interest in Max is intense though—if we suppose that was his real reason for coming here today."

"Intense? It's downright odd! He came to see Max last night and only God knows why. Have you ever heard of a former chief rabbi running around the place checking up on students who are playing hooky?"

Natan shook his head.

"The man is clearly in love with my cousin—the only thing is: I don't want my cousin being in love with *him*. Did you notice how quiet Max was this morning before he and Avi left? It makes me wonder what Goldenberg talked to Max about outside on the mirpeset last night. I guarantee you, everything Goldenberg is doing is part of his scheme to brainwash my cousin."

"But why Max?"

"I don't know." Tzippy paused thoughtfully. "I have my own problems to deal with—and maybe that's what's making me so testy—but something isn't right. I feel it in my bones. I want to go to Jerusalem and check up on Max."

"We can't just march into his yeshiva, Tzippy. I think you're a little emotional right now and not thinking logically."

"I'm telling you that something is wrong. Call it woman's intuition; call it instinct; call it whatever. Just trust me on this. Something isn't right."

"So, you want to go do what exactly in Jerusalem?"

"I don't know. Maybe all I need is to see Max and make sure he's ok. You don't understand, Natan, he's my cousin—I love him. And I know that the further he goes into this whole black hat lifestyle, the further he is going to be brainwashed into their way of thinking. I just want to go see him." She looked up at Natan obstinately.

Natan sighed. "Fine. I'll drive you."

"Thank you. And we can stop by Avi later and check in to see if he's ok."

"Do you want to call him?"

Tzippy checked her watch. "It's only one thirty. He's probably still in the Old City. Let's not disturb him. I'll call him after we've seen Max."

"Beseder."

✡

Major General Shoshana Arbela, the fifty-nine-year-old head of the Aman division of the Israeli Intelligence Community, stepped lightly into the car which was parked outside of her home. Dressed casually in a blue pant suit, with her sunglasses on her face, she carried a manila folder under arm.

She positioned herself in the backseat of the car and turned to face the man who sat next to her.

"Rosh haMemshala," she murmured quietly. "I didn't realize you would be coming in person."

The Prime Minister smiled dryly. "The matter is much too sensitive to be delegated to anyone else." He looked to the front of the car, which was empty. "Have you found anything for me?"

Arbela opened the manila folder. "Operation Aleph Yehud is underway with full force. You didn't give me much time, but my people have been working non-stop on this." She pulled some photographs and handed them to the Prime Minister. "These are the photos of the three persons who accompanied Aleph Yehud to the Billy Jean bar which we found on the Facebook profiles of persons who had been there on the night in question. The three persons have been positively identified. The male and the female you see here," she pointed to images of Natan and Tzippy, "are Israeli citizens. The male is Natan Nasi, son of the supermarket magnate, Yossi Nasi, and the female is Tzipporah Feldman, an American *olah* who made *aliyah* two years ago. Both reside in Tel Aviv." Shoshana pulled out another photograph, this time of Max, who was embracing Avi. "The Charedi male has also been identified. He is an American on a student visa and has been in Israel for a

329

year now. His name is Max Feldman and he learns at haMerkaz shel Emet in the Old City and lives at the dormitory there. He and the female Feldman are first cousins and it appears that it was the male Feldman who initially befriended Nasi."

The Prime Minister nodded gravely and looked at the pictures closely. "Good work. What about Aleph Yehud? Has he been found? Has his reason for coming here been determined?"

Arbela shook her head. "*Ani mitzta'eret,* but we cannot seem to identify or locate Aleph Yehud. It's almost as if he doesn't exist."

"I see."

"However, we did determine that for the past week, Nasi and the Feldman's were staying in Arnona, in the apartment of Nasi's Saba, Rabbi Yehonatan Nasi, who passed away last week. Since then, all three have returned to their regular lives: Nasi and the female Feldman returned to Tel Aviv this morning and it has been confirmed that the male Feldman is back at his yeshiva as well. Although..."

"Yes?"

"The female Feldman visited Nasi at his apartment in Tel Aviv this afternoon and a few minutes later they had a rather interesting visitor."

The Prime Minister raised a curious eyebrow. "Who?"

"Eliezer Goldenberg," Arbela said grimly.

"That is indeed extremely interesting. How long did Goldenberg stay there?"

"Not long, only about fifteen minutes."

The Prime Minister didn't answer.

"Also, my agents have indicated that soon after Goldenberg left, Nasi and the female Feldman went into

Nasi's vehicle and it appears that they are, as we speak, making their way to Jerusalem."

"I see." The Prime Minister piled the photographs together and handed them back to Arbela.

"Would you like us to bring the three identified suspects into custody? I have agents tailing Nasi and the female Feldman and agents are monitoring the yeshiva in which the male Feldman is at. Say the word and you can have them in front of you within the hour."

The Prime Minister considered. "No. Keep the agents on them. Perhaps they will lead us to Aleph Yehud. Also, I want someone to follow Goldenberg."

Arbela's eyes grew wide. "Mr. Prime Minister, you know if Goldenberg finds out he will be angry."

"This is bigger than Goldenberg now. Just do it."

"Very well." Arbela pulled her phone out of her pant pocket. "When do you need an update?"

"I'll give you an hour."

Arbela nodded and exited from the car. Before she closed the door, she looked back in at the Prime Minister and spoke hesitantly. "Rosh haMemshala?"

"Yes?"

"Surely you don't believe Aleph Yehud is really and truly—you know—Avraham Aveinu."

The Prime Minister looked the seasoned military officer straight in her eye. "Avraham Aveinu has returned to life, Shoshana, and he is Aleph Yehud."

Arbela froze for a second, and then she fainted to the ground.

✡

Max rushed down to the administrative office, and, bypassing the startled looks of the men working there, he ran up to Rabbi Rubenstein's office door and knocked loudly. Without waiting to be audibly admitted, he opened the door and barged in. "Rabbi Rubenstein!" he exclaimed breathlessly. "I have to talk to you urgently!"

Rabbi Rubenstein looked startled. "What is it, Feldman?"

Max began speaking in such a rush of words that was difficult for the older man to comprehend.

"Stop. Please, sit down. Catch your breath."

Max collapsed into the chair and gratefully accepted the bottle of water Rabbi Rubenstein handed to him. He drank heavily and then, with a deep breath, launched into his tale. Max realized he had made an enormous error in confiding in Rabbi Eliezer earlier, but something inside of him was urging him to rectify the mistake in telling Rabbi Rubenstein. For far too long Max had ignored his instincts; the past six months had been an unnatural suppression of his emotions, and now, as he related the same tale for the second time, he felt himself listen to his heart and, once again, felt the connection reestablish itself among his mind, heart and soul. And it felt good.

Rabbi Rubenstein listened to Max's relation of the story as quietly as Rabbi Eliezer had done. When Max had exhausted himself of his tale, Rabbi Rubenstein nodded at the boy. "I know Avraham Aveinu is back. It was confirmed to me a few days ago by a hiloni friend of mine and I believed the truth of the message as soon as I heard it. I knew that many in our community have no connections with the outside world, and I did not want them to suffer for it, so I pushed the religious papers to reprint the article."

"You did that?"

Rabbi Rubenstein nodded.

"Did it work? Did people who read the story believe that Avi—Avraham Aveinu—has returned?"

"No. It seems that belief in the story is only realized when a person hears it directly from another person and not through reading."

"Oh." Max coughed. "I'm sorry Rabbi, but if we can get back to my being here now?"

"Of course, of course. I apologize, Feldman. What do you wish of me? I will do anything to assist you."

"I'm not asking you to go against Rabbi Goldenberg and let me leave. I just need you to let me call my friends and tell them what's going on—particularly Avi. He's in the Old City walking around without a care in the world. If someone recognizes him, it's going be pandemonium. I need to warn him."

Rabbi Rubenstein nodded and passed the telephone to Max. "He has a cellular phone with him?"

"Yes," Max replied, already punching in the number. "And thank you, Rabbi."

Rabbi Rubenstein smiled.

Max put the telephone down. "It's just ringing. There isn't any answer."

"Try again in a few minutes. There is nothing else you can do."

Max sighed.

"I didn't know why Rabbi Goldenberg requested you remain cloistered in the yeshiva today. But he asked me to keep you here, which I did." Rabbi Rubenstein shook his head. "I didn't realize such great things were at stake."

Max grimaced.

"So, Avraham Aveinu has returned to inform Natan Nasi that he is the mashiach?"

Max nodded.

"It is a wise choice. His Saba was a marvelous man."

Max nodded again.

"Your mind is elsewhere. Call your Avi again."

Max smiled gratefully and tried calling again, only to have the same result.

"What about your cousin and Natan Nasi? You should try to reach them."

Max nodded and dialed his cousin's number.

Tzippy answered on the first ring. "Shalom?"

"Tzippy!"

"Max!" Then, as an aside, Max heard her yell to whoever she was with, "It's Max!"

"Put it on speakerphone," came Natan's voice over the phone.

"Max, you're on speaker. I'm here with Natan. We are on our way to Jerusalem."

Max blanched. "Why? Has something happened to Avi?"

"Avi?" Tzippy asked. "No, we're coming to see you."

"Me? Why?"

"Rabbi Eliezer came to see Natan today," came Tzippy's grim reply.

"What?"

"Yes," Natan responded.

Tzippy filled Max in quickly on what had transpired. "So, we think he came to scope us out to get ammunition to come back to you and make you stop talking to us."

"What ammunition could he possibly get on you guys that would make me want to stop talking to you?"

There was no response from the other end.

"Hello?"

"Yes, we're here."

"He didn't come to see you because of me. He came because he knows Natan is the mashiach."

"How does he know that?"

"I told him."

"Are you out of your mind?" Tzippy yelled.

"It was out of my control. I had to tell him. People know Avi is back. There was an article in the papers about it. Do you remember Avi telling us about the domino effect? If he tells someone and they tell someone then each person who hears about it, provided the original source is Avi, will believe the person who tells them."

"I've no idea what you're talking about."

"Look, it doesn't matter. Rabbi Goldenberg knows. By now, half of Israel probably knows!"

"They know Avi chose Natan to be the mashiach?"

"No! They know Avi is back. There are photos! Forget Natan, forget the mashiach! This is about Avi! Have either of you talked to him today?"

"No"

"Where are you now?"

"About twenty minutes from Jerusalem."

"Try reaching Avi on his cell. And come pick me up. I'll be outside waiting."

Max hung up the phone. "Rabbi Rubenstein—"

The rabbi cut him off. "Go. Go with your friends. Find the patriarch. His safety is of paramount importance."

"I hope this doesn't get you into trouble with Rabbi Goldenberg."

Rabi Rubenstein waved his hand. "I'll deal with him. I'm going to call the men at the gates and tell them to let you through. Go with HaShem."

"Thank you, Rabbi."

✡

Max made his way through the gate without any hassle. It was, as Rabbi Rubenstein had promised, opened and no one tried to stop him from exiting. Unsure of where his cousin and friend were, Max decided it would be more prudent to wait right outside of the yeshiva so they could come collect him, as the portion of the Old City in which Max's yeshiva was located did not allow for vehicular traffic.

Half an hour later, he spotted his cousin with Natan close at her heels, flying through the thick crowds. The sun had just set and, in the glistening light of the streetlamps, he had never seen his cousin look more beautiful. She ran straight into him and hugged him with all her might.

"You saw me only this morning," he said, blushing, slightly embarrassed at Tzippy's uncharacteristic show of affection, but he hugged her back without any care that he was violating Orthodox protocol.

Tzippy pulled away and Natan clapped Max comradely on the shoulder.

"Fill me in," Natan said, and Max hurriedly rushed through his adventures since they had parted ways that morning, as the three of them made their way back to Natan's jeep.

"Now, you tell me what's going on," Max said. They'd reached Natan's jeep. "You guys were hanging out?" Max looked genuinely confused.

Tzippy and Natan looked significantly at each other.

"Please tell me what's going on!"

Natan nodded, and Tzippy quickly answered her cousin. "Natan is gay and I am pregnant. And we know where Rabbi Eliezer is headed next. He's going to look for Avi."

Max did a double take. "What?" He looked at Natan. "You're gay?" He looked at Tzippy. "You're pregnant?"

Tzippy nodded exasperatedly. "Yes! But we don't have time for all of this. Avi needs to get out of the public arena. You were right—we have to find Avi. If someone who knows who he is spots him—"

The three of them exchanged dark looks and bundled themselves into the vehicle.

"Tzippy and I have been trying to call him since we've left Tel Aviv," Natan said, buckling his seat belt, "but there's been no answer."

"What were his plans for today?" Tzippy piped up from the backseat.

"He said he was going to bum around the Old City. That's all I know," Max replied anxiously.

"So, he could still be in here somewhere!" Tzippy cried.

Natan raised his hand. "The smartest thing for us to do is to go to my Saba's apartment and see if Avi is there. If he's not, we can just wait there until he shows up."

"But what if he's recognized?" Tzippy asked. "He won't be able to just show up at the apartment! He'll be mobbed like at the club!"

Max shushed his cousin. "Natan is right. We would never find Avi traipsing around the Old City. He could be anywhere. The best place for us to be is at the apartment." He looked over at Natan, who sat next to him in the driver's seat. "*Yalla*, let's go."

Natan put the Jeep into drive and they headed out of the Old City.

✡

"Shalom, Rosh haMemshala," came Arbela's voice across the secure telephone line.

"It's not been an hour," the Prime Minister said, surprised to hear Arbela so soon. "Has something happened? Have you found Aleph Yehud?"

"I'm sorry, no, we haven't. But there's been an interesting development."

"What's that?"

"Nasi and the female Feldman have just met the male Feldman outside of his yeshiva and they are currently in a vehicle on their way to, it appears, Arnona."

The Prime Minister sat up excitedly. "To the apartment of Nasi's Saba?"

"It would be safe to assume so, but let's not jump to conclusions."

"Would it be safe to assume that they will lead us to Aleph Yehud?"

"I don't know, Prime Minister." Arbela paused. "If I may offer my professional opinion?"

"Of course."

"I think we should immediately take the three suspects into protective custody for questioning."

"But we cannot be sure they would tell us where Aleph Yehud is."

"I agree, but it's the most pragmatic move to make at this point in time. These characters are young. For all we know they are probably going to get dressed and go to a club. We are wasting valuable time scoping them out when we should, instead, be questioning them. The longer we wait, the harder it will be for us to find Aleph Yehud."

The Prime Minister considered. "I have a gut feeling that they are going to the apartment in Arnona—and I am strongly convinced that Aleph Yehud is there. If they go to the apartment in Arnona, I authorize you to storm the apartment and search it for any sign of Aleph Yehud. Whether Aleph Yehud is there or not, bring everyone in that apartment in for questioning immediately."

"Very well," Arbela responded. "Just one more thing."

"Yes?"

"Goldenberg. Since he left Nasi's apartment in Tel Aviv, he's returned to his home in Har Nof. I doubt he is going to leave again for the evening. I don't think we should tail him anymore."

"Do you think that's wise?"

"I do. It's been a waste of our effort following for the past five hours. He's done nothing out of the ordinary and we have informants inside his home who have gone on record testifying that there is no one inside of the home even remotely resembling the images of Aleph Yehud in there."

"Very well. You can stop following Goldenberg."

"What should we do if we don't find Aleph Yehud in the Arnona apartment?"

"Then, bring the three suspects to Beit Aghion. I will question them directly."

"Very well, Prime Minister."

"And Arbela?"

"Yes?"

"Try not to frighten the youngsters. They are not terrorists."

"I'll try my best, sir."

✡

Had Natan, Tzippy, and Max known when they pulled up at the apartment in Arnona, that the ancestor they were so desperately searching for was actually right down the street on the Goldman Promenade, conversing with a distant cousin of theirs from Afghanistan, perhaps things may have turned out quite differently. As it stood, the cellular phone Tzippy had given to Avi that morning had, inadvertently, been placed on a silent ring tone, and, as such, all the frantic phone calls which were being placed by the three friends were unfortunately not being registered by Avi as he couldn't hear it.

The three friends rushed up the elevator to the apartment. They called out Avi's name and looked everywhere but the elusive Avi remained just that.

"So, we wait?" Natan asked.

The drive to the apartment had been awkward. Max turned to the others every few minutes and looked like he was about to say something, or ask a question, but he would just close his gaping mouth and turn back

340

to watching the road while the wheels in his brain were clearly turning.

Natan was ready to answer any and all questions Max had about either himself of Tzippy, but the questions hadn't come in the car ride. Now that they were all alone, and sitting around the kitchen island with naught to do except wait for Avi to hopefully show up, they all knew that the inevitable had come: Natan's sexuality and Tzippy's unplanned pregnancy were up for discussion.

Max looked at the others sheepishly and opened his mouth, when all of a sudden, there was a pounding at the door.

A voice boomed out at them. "This is the Shin Bet! Open up!"

The three friends looked at each other, terrified, and then, slowly, Natan rose from his chair and opened the front door to find the corridor full of Shin Bet personnel.

A man dressed in all black leveled a gun at him. "Natan Nasi?"

Natan nodded.

"Please come with me."

"I don't understand. Am I being arrested?"

A woman with a blond chignon walked up to him. "No. You are not being arrested. You are being taken into protective custody."

"I don't understand."

Natan moved to the side as other men moved into the apartment with guns leveled at Tzippy and Max. Two of the men stopped next to the cousins; Natan could hear the Shin Bet officers telling them the same things the blond woman had just told him. He could hear other Shin Bet officers running through the apartment.

"What are they looking for?" Natan asked the blond woman.

"I am afraid I cannot discuss that with you here."

"What do you want from us?"

"I'm afraid I cannot discuss that with you here."

"This is a free, democratic society. We've done nothing wrong and we don't have to come with you unless you arrest us."

The woman smiled wryly. "I can have all of you in handcuffs if that's how you want to play the game." She tapped Natan lightly on his hand and peeked over his shoulder at Tzippy and Max. "Please, this is not an arrest, but it is an order. You've been summoned."

"Summoned by whom?"

The woman looked at Natan. "The Rosh haMemshala."

"The Prime Minister wants Natan?" Tzippy asked from inside.

"He wants all of you. Natan Nasi, Tzipporah Feldman, and Max Feldman."

One of the Shin Bet officers came up to the blond woman. "No one else is in the apartment," he said.

The woman nodded and signaled the men who stood around the room. The men nudged the three friends forward with their guns. "Sorry that we have to be so... forceful. But your protection is necessary." She looked back at one of the men. "Turn the lights off and lock the door behind you. I want no trace of our presence here."

They began walking down the corridor and were bundled into the elevator.

"Why do we need protection?" Natan asked the woman. "And why are we being shuffled around like criminals?"

The woman kept walking. "I'm just following orders. The Rosh haMemshala wants all of you. You are a top priority."

The friends looked at each other and a sinking thought filtered through their minds at the same time: The Prime Minister had found Avi.

The woman smiled at them and ushered them out of the elevator and outside of the building. There, parked alongside the curb, were ten black vehicles of different shapes and sizes, with darkly tinted windows. The woman led them into a generic SUV. They looked at her expectantly, but she ignored them and continued to hold the door open. A prod by the gun of one of the men urged them in. The woman beamed at them.

"Enjoy your ride. The Rosh haMemshala is eagerly looking forward to meeting all of you."

She shut the door and jumped into another vehicle. "Let's go," she said, and within ten seconds, the vehicles had ripped away from the curb and were roaring into the center of town.

Two minutes later, a boy, a tall woman, and a camel made their way up the street.

✡

In the backseat of the SUV into which they had all been bundled, Natan, Tzippy, and Max sat quietly at first, afraid to talk while there was a driver up front who could hear them. They looked at each other nervously, and watched the scenery passed them by until they pulled up in front of a house which was familiar to them all: Beit Aghion—the Prime Minister's residence.

The door was opened by a man in a crisp black suit who bade them to follow him, which they did since they had no other choice.

They went into the house and up the stairs and were shown into a tiny sitting room. They were asked to wait and were told that the Prime Minister would see them soon, and the man in the crisp black suit closed the door, leaving the three friends alone in the room. At once, Tzippy and Max opened their mouths to speak, but they were quickly shot down by Natan. "Shut up, shut up, shut up!" he hissed. "They are probably listening to what we say. Do not talk about You Know Who."

Max scratched his head. "But if they've found— You Know Who, then whatever we say makes no difference."

Natan shook his head. "We don't know what they've found or what they know."

"Max and I are nothing maybe," Tzippy said quietly. "But not you. If they've found Avi, I'm pretty sure they know who you are, Natan."

Natan sat. "We don't know anything. So anything involving You Know Who should just be kept quiet."

Max folded his arms and leaned against the wall. "So, what do we talk about?"

Natan looked up at Max. "We don't have to speak."

"Oh, but I want to."
Natan sighed. "I figured."
"So, you are gay?"
Natan nodded.

"Why didn't you tell me?"

"I didn't see it as a big deal. It's not the sum total of who I am."

"But it's a huge part of you! And I thought we were friends." Max looked hurt. "You told Tzippy. Why not me?"

"He didn't tell me," Tzippy interjected. "I figured it out."

"You still should have told me. You owed it to me," Max insisted.

"No! I don't owe it to you or anyone to tell them about this!" Natan exploded and pounded the armrest. "I haven't told anyone I'm close to that I'm gay—none of my family know, none of my friends know. No one! And you expected me to tell you? A Charedi man whose first thought would be, 'Oh, a gay Jew? Well, I condemn you and all your sinful brethren.' Why do you possibly think I'd put myself in that position by telling you, Max? Why?"

Max looked shocked. "Is that what you think of me? That I'm a close-minded ultra-Orthodox who can't think for himself?"

"Well, you haven't given us much else to go on, have you?"

"My best friend back home in America is gay, Natan," Max said quietly. "He's gay and he is who he is and I love him. I don't love him regardless of him being gay, I love him because he is who he is and that includes him being gay. He's my best friend—and if that's how God made him, then I love him. And if I call myself your friend, then I would love you, respect you, and support you equally." Max turned to Tzippy. "And I guess you didn't tell me you were pregnant because you thought the same thing about me?"

"Not exactly. I only found out I was pregnant this morning. But yes, I suppose I was hesitant about telling you because I was afraid of your reaction."

"I see."

"And there you go—judging me."

"I'm not judging you." Max shrugged. "These things happen. Nothing happens outside the will of God. A child is always a blessing."

"You don't judge me?"

Max shook his head. "How far along are you?"

"Ten weeks." She peered at Max. "Are you sure you don't judge me?"

"No."

"Even if I were to have an abortion?"

Max snorted. "We're Jewish, Tzippy. We're not the Christian right. A woman is entitled to her choice. Besides, the soul only enters the fetus at the end of the first trimester. Everyone knows that."

Tzippy laughed. "Right—*everyone* knows that." She sighed. "I'm not going to have an abortion."

"You're going to have it?"

"Yes."

"Are you ready to raise a child?"

"I don't know. I haven't had time to properly process everything. I only found out I was pregnant this morning, and well—today hasn't been the easiest day, has it?"

"Whatever you decide to do, Tzippy, I support you."

Tzippy moved across and held her cousin's hand. "So, we're ok?"

"We were never not ok."

"And us?" Natan said quietly from the chair.

"We were never not ok either," Max repeated.

The three friends smiled at each other.

At that moment, the door opened. The Prime Minister, Shoshana Arbela, and the head of the Shin Bet entered the room.

"How are things?" the Prime Minister said, with a smile. "It's a pleasure to meet all of you. You are Natan Nasi, Tzipporah Feldman, and Max Feldman, I presume?"

The three friends looked at him stonily.

The Prime Minister sat down and crossed his leg. "I agree—no need for chitchat. Let's get right into it then, shall we? Tell me, where is Avraham Aveinu?"

✡

Avi awoke the next morning with the lazy, happy contentment that only a good night's rest can bring. The previous day had been taxing on his emotions, and though it was still very early in the morning—the sun was just rising in the east—he felt refreshed and recharged, ready to face whatever the new day had in store for him.

He lay quietly on the bed for a few minutes, enjoying the satisfaction of stretching, when suddenly, he remembered he had a guest. He bolted from his bed and tapped on her door ever so quietly. There was no answer. She was probably still asleep.

He backed away from the door and stretched again, but he noticed that Zahira's bag, which she'd left in the hallway, was gone. He put his hand on the doorknob of the bedroom and slowly turned it open and peeked in.

The bed was made and there was no one in the room.

"Zahira!" he called out.

There was no response.

He ran from room to room, calling out her name, but she was nowhere.

On the dining table, he found a note written in Pashto with beautiful penmanship. He fingered the necklace, which still hung around his neck, as he read it.

"Ab Ibrahim," the note said, "thank you for your kind hospitality. I must return to my people now as I have fulfilled my portion of the prophecy by bringing you the comfort you needed. I do not know why you've returned or when you will leave earth, but I wish the remainder of your time here full of joy, happiness, success, and peace. My people and I wait for the coming of the masih when the shofar shall be sounded and we shall be called back to the land of our forefathers and we can be rejoined with the congregation of Israel. I leave you with wishes of peace. Thank you for everything. Zahira."

Avi put down the note and felt regretful that he had not told Zahira that the mashiach had indeed returned and would soon sound the shofar to bring Zahira and her people home to the land of Israel—at the same time, he remembered that he had felt compelled to not tell Zahira about the mashiach. Why had he felt that way? What had stopped him from telling her that tidbit of news which would give her and her people the sustenance and comfort to know that their sojourn in the exile was nearing its end? Why hadn't he told her when he had so quickly and openly told Pastor Yuvie and Natan's Saba before that?

Avi put the note down and sat down, troubled. Something had stopped him from telling Zahira, and his mind flickered over Rabbi Eliezer's point from the night before. He couldn't help but wonder if the intractable old man had a point. Had he made the wrong decision in choosing Natan as the mashiach? Avi had no qualms about Natan being gay—his ancient sensibilities were not disturbed by the modern religious aversion to homosexuality. But at the same time, Rabbi Eliezer had asked a very poignant question: "Has Natan embraced his calling since you've told him he was the mashiach?"—the answer to which was a very resounding no.

Did Rabbi Eliezer have a point? Was Natan the wrong choice? Did Avi not mention to Zahira that he'd found the mashiach because—instinctually—he knew he hadn't and he didn't want to lie to her?

Avi didn't have much time to contemplate his musings—or even to brush teeth. A knock at the door brought him to alertness.

"This is the Shin Bet!" a voice said from outside the door. "Please open the door."

CHAPTER 16

"At that time Abimelech and Phicol, chief of his troops, said to Abraham, 'God is with you in everything that you do. Therefore, swear to me here by God that you will not deal falsely with me or with my kith and kin, but will deal with me and with the land in which you have sojourned as loyally as I have dealt with you. And Abraham said, 'I swear it'."
—Genesis 21:22-24

Two and a half months had passed since the announcement to the world by the Israeli government that Avraham Aveinu/Abraham our Father/Abouna Ibrahim had been resurrected to life by the grace of the Almighty God. The Abrahamic legacy had spread throughout the length and breadth of the planet, and no less than four billion persons revered him as their spiritual father. The knowledge that Avraham had returned spread like wildfire, and billions of souls across the world were struck with religious fervor. The Israel Airports Authority was seeing an increase in tourism like never before. From every corner of the planet, dignitaries, religious leaders, businessmen, tourists, paparazzi, and curious gawkers descended upon the Ben Gurion Airport to meet the man whom three world religions claimed as their own especial founder.

Pictures were snapped of the slightly built, spritely, surprisingly young, dark-haired patriarch with the mischievous smile (who insisted that everyone refer to him simply as 'Avi') having lunch with the pope; a video on TMZ showed him and the Dalai Lama exiting a vegetarian restaurant in Jerusalem, with a contingent of bodyguards helping them both through the crowd; newspapers were abuzz with the historic headlines that the Saudi Arabian King and his family were making an official visit to the State of Israel to meet the man they regarded to be the first Muslim; Time Magazine named him the Man of the Decade and a candid photo of a smiling Avi, wearing a simple shirt and cargo pants shone out at the world from the cover of the magazine; the Ayatollahs of Iran issued a statement welcoming Abouna Ibrahim back to life and they invited him, along with the President and Prime Minister of Israel, to visit their country and re-establish ties between the two governments; the Japanese Emperor had tea with Avi on the rooftop of the Mamilla Hotel and the Queen of England knighted him in absentia; a joint press conference between Avi, the Israeli Prime Minister, and the President of the Palestinian Authority announced the official end to the Israeli-Palestinian conflict, and the immediate establishment of a demilitarized, democratic Palestinian State in Gaza and parts of the West Bank and the Galilee—a state which fully recognized the Jewish character of Israel and its capital, Jerusalem, and laid no claims to either; an amateur video uploaded to YouTube showed Avi running through Gan haPa'Amon with a dozen children and collapsing in giggles on the ground as the children swarmed over him playfully; MTV broadcasted a reality show which documented the visit by Leonard Cohen, Bob Dylan, and Adam Levine— who'd come to Israel to meet their distant ancestor— which culminated in a night-long jam session with the four of them; volunteers at the Ichlu Reim soup kitchen delighted reporters with accounts of Avi standing alongside them and serving people food each Shabbat for the past month; the hash tag "Avi" was the top trending hash tag on Instagram and Twitter for the past two weeks, with hundreds of thousands of candid photos of the young resurrected Avi being shared.

The media outlets dubbed it 'Avi Fever' and the world was ablaze with the fire that it brought.

Interestingly, the return of the patriarch caused an even more excited stir in the scientific community. Atheist and religious scientists alike carefully interviewed the only man in all of mankind's long history who was documented to have been resurrected from the dead; all of them eagerly searching for the scientific explanation which could be attributed to Avi's miraculous resurrection. Various theories were put forth and scientists were lining up by the thousands to determine the logistics behind the resurrection. The fact that Avi had not only returned to life, but had returned with youth and vigor, made many believe that he carried with him the secret to immortality. Anthropologists, sociologists, and historians were delighted that, through Avi, they had a veritable time machine with which to travel back in time and better understand the ancient world. A carefully selected panel of experts from the Hebrew University of Jerusalem was chosen to question him and to construct a report detailing the information Avi disseminated to them. Archaeologists, likewise, were in a flurry of activities, as they readjusted their understanding of ancient life. Particularly troubling to them was the fact that the Cave of Machpelah—which had always been reasonably assumed to be the one identified for the past few thousand years—was, in fact, not the actual Cave. They set out into the Judean desert with their brushes and pickaxes, determined to find the true Cave, despite Avi's caution that it was a vain quest as God had purposely hidden the Cave's location. Geneticists humbly requested a sample of Avi's blood to analyze his DNA; a request Avi happily granted. Though they still had much work to do, it was abundantly clear that the DNA contained in Avi could only be the DNA of a person from a bygone era, as Avi's Y-chromosome contained a specific marker which identified him, unequivocally, as the progenitor of all the branches of the Judaic family tree—and a few branches of other Middle Eastern Semitic peoples.

The living presence of Avi on earth was rippling change through every area of study, religion and human thought, and scientists, theologians, historians, anthropologists, sociologists, and all other professional persons alive were rethinking their specific fields of study and seeing greater and greater possibilities. It was a period of remarkable harmony and progress, and everyone knew whom they had to thank for ushering it into the world.

While the world had been uniting under the banner of Avi's miraculous resurrection to life, within the ranks of religious Judaism, however, a highly covert war was raging. The leaderships of the different factions of the Jewish religion were fiercely sparring amongst themselves—each trying to assert itself by claiming Avi as their especial patron, and thus emerge as the winner. Orthodoxy maligned the Reform movement; the Conservative movement attacked the Orthodoxy; the Reform movement roared against the Conservative movement—and all of them railed against the secular, non-affiliated members of their tribe.

As chaotic as the fighting was, those involved in it realized that the *balagan* hinged on one very important question: who exactly was the mashiach Avi had been sent to locate?

✡

The Israeli Prime Minister had turned out to be quite a lovely man whose primary concern was Avi's welfare. He apologized to Natan, Tzippy, and Max for forcibly bringing them to Beit Aghion, but, he told them it had been necessary to do so, as they seemed to be the only persons other than Rabbi Eliezer who would possibly know where Avi was. The Prime Minister assured the friends of his sincerity, but after having been betrayed so overtly by Rabbi Eliezer, none of the friends were willing to divulge any information. The Prime Minister insisted that all he wanted was to issue Avi the security that was desperately needed, given the unique situation that had arisen with Avi's resurrection.

Obstinately, the three friends crossed their arms and refused to say anything—not before Tzippy had dramatically cried, "Torture us if you want! You won't get anything out of us!" The head of Aman and the head of the Shin Bet bristled at Tzippy's outburst, but the Prime Minister sighed and assured them that he would resort to no such means, as torture was illegal according to Israeli law, but asked if they would kindly give him the information that he needed. None of them answered. By midnight, it was clear that no information would be forthcoming from the three friends. They were taken from the sitting room in which they'd underwent the attempted interrogation and shown to three connecting bedrooms. The friends were surprised at the generous accommodations, and when they had been left alone, they held a hurriedly whispered conference and decided to not trust the Prime Minister despite what was clearly an effort on his part to win them over. They showered and went to bed, each of them dreading the next
354

morning when they were sure the attempted interrogation would continue where it had dismally left off.

While the three friends slept, the Prime Minister and his team continued their search for the elusive patriarch. Security dispatches were sent to Max's yeshiva to search the compound there, while others were sent to Rabbi Eliezer's house to search his premises. The Prime Minister wouldn't put it past Rabbi Eliezer to have Aleph Yehud tied up and stashed in a closet somewhere in his home. When both dispatches reported back empty-handed, the Prime Minister broadened his search and authorized a search of Natan's apartment in Tel Aviv and the premises of his business; a contingent was also sent to Tzippy's apartment. An hour later, when the sun had begun to rise, the Prime Minister was given the news that there was still no sign of Aleph Yehud.

He sighed and sat back in his office chair—his brain thinking furiously.

"Arbela," he said thoughtfully to the trusty head of Aman. "Was the apartment in Arnona searched?"

"Yes—it was thoroughly searched when we brought in the Feldman's and Nasi."

"Has it been searched since?"

Arbela's eyes lit up and she quickly issued the command for the security forces to move in and search Natan's Saba's apartment again.

To the delight of the Prime Minister and his security forces, the one they had so earnestly searched for, Aleph Yehud, had been found and apprehended.

When Aleph Yehud was brought in to Beit Aghion, the Prime Minister was waiting at the front door, excitedly fidgeting. He shook Avi's hand firmly and beamed at him. Avi cocked his head to the side for a moment, and, almost as if he were listening to someone, nodded, and then straightened up and smiled widely at the Prime Minister.

They chatted amiably, the Prime Minister inquiring about Avi's health and his experiences thus far being back on earth. Avi spoke enthusiastically about everything he'd seen, and a half hour later, to his delight, his three friends were shown into the room. Avi sprung from his chair, and together, the four of them embraced in a group hug. The Prime Minister almost thought he heard Avi whisper, "My guardian angel says to trust him", but he decided that must've been a mistake. Angels would be stretching the limits of his belief a bit too far.

For the rest of the day, they all sat in the Prime Minister's office and filled him in on the saga which was Avi's resurrection on earth; Natan, Tzippy, and Max now showing real warmth to the man they had decided only a few hours ago to not trust. They each contributed to the conversation and, by the time they were finished, the Prime Minister had built up a composite sketch of everything Avi had been through since his return and it was late afternoon. They were served lunch in the office and then it was the Prime Minister's turn to speak. He candidly discussed his feelings on Avi's return. While miraculous, he said, it was reasonably fair to assume that the resurrection of Avi could become a divisive issue within world Jewry. He told of his meeting with Rabbi Eliezer—the meeting which had coalesced his belief in Avi's return—and he quoted the rabbi's line which demonstrated how desperately the rabbi wanted Avi to endorse ultra-Orthodox Judaism. "This return is going to cause quite a bit of competition among the various branches, as they would each struggle in the attempt to have Avi cast the light of legitimacy upon themselves," he said wisely. "My advice would be to not endorse any and stay neutral." Natan pensively interjected and asked whether the Prime Minister wanted to reveal Avi's identity to the world. "I'm afraid we must. The story has captivated the attention of the entire country and everyone believes it's true. It's only a matter of time before Avi becomes known. Better for him to do it on his terms, rather than someone else's. Whether you like it or not, Avi, you are a public figure." Avi nodded at the sage advice. Thus, it was decided.

Two days later, mere hours before Avi's public revealing to the world, the Prime Minister held a private conference with leaders of the various sects of Judaism, including as many representatives as he could from the major streams of Jewish thought. He gave a brief introduction and allowed Avi to take the podium and introduce himself, for the benefit of those who had yet to believe in him. Most of the rabbis there already believed that Avraham Aveinu had returned and they were eager to fire off questions at him. Avi answered all their questions with ease and wit, and charmed the congregation which sat before him. As time slipped by, Avi requested one final question. At that point, Rabbi Eliezer, who had been sitting quietly all along, lost and fuming in the crowd, stood and asked Avi pointedly: "You haven't told us why you've returned."

Avi narrowed his eyes at the calculating old man, but he answered the question truthfully. "I have come to locate the mashiach and inform him that he is mashiach."

The pandemonium in the room was instant, but as the press conference announcing Avi's return to the outside world and general public was scheduled to take place in the next few minutes, Avi was forced to exit, with the answer left hanging in the air.

Rabbi Eliezer stood and made his way to the vacuum at the podium. "Gentlemen—and ladies," he said with a slight sneer directed at the Conservative and Reform female rabbis, "our esteemed Avraham Aveinu has indeed returned to fulfill the purpose of finding the mashiach."

"How do you know this?" came a shout from the crowd.

"Because Avraham Aveinu told me this himself—he came to locate the mashiach, except, he's not sure who it is."

There was a hushed silence, and, as one, the congregation leaned forward and listened to Rabbi Eliezer speak.

✡

Within days, the story of Avi's purpose for returning and his subsequent confusion on top of the hill when he'd spotted Natan, Tzippy, and Max became common knowledge in the Jewish world and Avi's three friends were immediately shunted into the spotlight. Although Rabbi Eliezer had no desire to associate with the other branches of Judaism, he had thought that in telling them his view that Avi had erred in choosing the mashiach would lead to a natural yielding to his position by the Conservative and Reform movements. Unfortunately for Rabbi Eliezer—as was turning out to be the norm with him these days—he had miscalculated the reactions of others, and the leadership of the other two movements took a surprisingly different path. While they agreed with Rabbi Eliezer's assessment that Avi had chosen Natan wantonly, they didn't believe that the automatic choice for mashiach was Max—and, as such, a competition of sorts, which further alienated the different Judaic branches from each other, began in earnest.

When Rabbi Eliezer had made it clear that his support was in favor of Max's candidacy as mashiach, the rest of the ultra-Orthodox world naturally followed suit and unanimously threw their support behind Max.

The Masorti Olami, however, speaking as the official voice of the Conservative movement, argued against this and continued to support Natan, since he was Avi's original choice. Their stance on Natan's now-public homosexuality was that the movement accepted, embraced, and celebrated diversity and, therefore, it had no issue with Natan's sexuality.

The Union for Reform Judaism, after a week of careful consideration and debate, issued a statement which rallied behind Tzippy as their choice for mashiach, for they felt that, as a half-Ashkenazi, half-Ethiopian Jewess, she was the one who best represented modern Judaism—and, as far as the Reform movement was concerned, to say that the mashiach had to be male was chauvinistic and parochial; not at all in keeping with the tenets of progressive Judaism.

Traditional Sephardi Jews were equally divided between supporting Natan, and not supporting him—based on individual liberalness and comfort with homosexuality.

Unaffiliated, secular Jews either ignored the whole controversy or aligned themselves with the Masorti or Reform position.

It was a confusing time for Jews as a whole.

Only the modern Orthodox movement, represented by the Orthodox Union and Rabbinical Councils of the World, remained neutral and withheld from casting support for anyone, stating that they needed to meet with Avi first and hear the story from his mouth to ascertain whether or not a mistake had been made, and whether Avi had chosen correctly.

The squabbling intensified as the days went by, and the movements involved in the conflict persevered to meet with Avi, who staunchly refused them all. They complained to the Prime Minister that Avi was openly meeting with non-Jewish religious leaders and unreligious Jews, but he was purposely refraining from meeting with any of them. As it was the Prime Minister who had initially suggested that Avi steer clear of the infighting exploding in the Jewish world, he shrugged and did nothing to address their complaints. Immediately, the cry went up from the religious movements, and they unprecedentedly joined forces. Screams of "conspiracy!" and "brainwash!" echoed outside of the Knesset as their members came out in the thousands to protest what they termed *The Government's Hidden Agenda To Keep The Patriarch Away From His People*. The protests achieved their aim, and the Prime Minister eventually arranged a symposium titled *The Avrahamic Answer to the Issue of the Mashiach*, between the different factions and Avi. Still unwilling to meet with any single faction individually, Avi agreed to meet with all of them at the same time. Although Avi was apparently avoiding meeting with the various Jewish leaderships as a matter of principle, the truth was, he was dreading the interrogation he was sure to receive regarding the issue of the mashiach.

Avi didn't know who the mashiach was supposed to be.

Rabbi Eliezer's taunt that Avi had made a mistake in his choice of mashiach had struck a chord in Avi because there was substance in the statement: Avi hadn't known—and still didn't know—which of the three friends he had spotted in the valley below was the actual mashiach. He made Michael repeat the command God had given to him and he had re-played the command in his mind in every conceivable way, but he couldn't discern anything hidden in the command. The first person he saw when he exited the cave was supposed to be the mashiach. Avi thought carefully, back to those first few days spent in Natan's tent with Michael. Did he catch a glimpse of himself in some mirror-like surface? Was Avi the mashiach? No—it couldn't be. The prophecies spoke of the mashiach being a descendant of King David, which Avi clearly was not—and furthermore, Avi hadn't seen himself in any reflection prior to meeting Natan, Tzippy, and Max.

So, it had to be one the three friends, but which one was it?

Which of them was the first mortal soul Avi encountered?

Avi clenched his eyes together and relived the moment when he had seen the friends in the valley below: which had he seen first?

He couldn't remember.

And so, with the ultra-Orthodox clamoring for Max, the Conservative movement rallying around Natan, and the Reform lobbying for Tzippy, Avi simply didn't know what to do.

He swallowed his apprehension and, like a lamb being led to the slaughter, he went to the *The Avrahamic*

361

Answer to the Issue of the Mashiach meeting with the leaders of all the Jewish factions and also representatives from the World Jewish Congress, the World Zionist Organization, the virulently anti-Zionist Neturei Karta, and members of the Israeli Knesset—but the only thing was, Avi didn't know the answer. The meeting was as intense and as disastrous as Avi had feared it would be: the religious factions pummeled him for information; they interrogated him until he felt like a sponge wrung free of every drop of water; they challenged his memory and questioned the command he had been given. And with each answer he gave, he knew they were less and less pleased about what he could offer to them in terms of the mashiach. Nothing they could ask could change the fact that Avi simply didn't know. He felt the palms of his hands break out in sweat, and he almost felt like screaming with frustration. Eventually, everyone forgot about Avi and began arguing amongst themselves. Avi looked down the table and smiled wearily at Natan, Tzippy, and Max who were also present, and were sitting with the respective delegations which had nominated them each.

Finally, a lone voice was heard in the midst of all the noise: it was the president of the Orthodox Union—the representatives of the modern Orthodox movement—and the only group which had not yet cast its support for any of the mashiach candidates. "This arguing is irrelevant," he said. "We will never come to a conclusion this way. Our scriptures teach that the mashiach's authority and legitimacy would be conferred upon him, or her," he said, politely, looking at the president of the URJ, "by the vote of the Sanhedrin. Perhaps this was why God set up the scenario so Avi would come across three mortal souls instead of just one. Not to confuse him or us, but to give us a choice—each candidate has his or her own strengths and weakness. They are three remarkable individuals with remarkably different personalities. Let the Sanhedrin be reconvened and let the democracy of Clal Yisrael make the choice."

The contingent from Neturei Karta immediately began to hiss. "The Sanhedrin can only be reconvened by the moshiach!"

"And the mashiach can only be conferred with official authority by the Sanhedrin," the president of the Orthodox Union said calmly.

"The Sanhedrin can only be housed adjacent to the Beis haMikdash—without the Beis haMikdash, there can be no Sanhedrin!" was the Neturei Karta reply.

The President of the Orthodox Union shrugged. "You also need the Sanhedrin to demarcate the boundaries of the Beit haMikdash. It is a chicken and egg situation; a juxtaposition of the highest order. Which comes first? The Beit haMikdash or the Sanhedrin? The mashiach or the Sanhedrin? The Beit haMikdash or the mashiach? In all cases, at least from the perspective of necessity, we need the Sanhedrin to come first, because clearly, as we stand, we cannot come to a decision on the matter of the mashiach. We need the Sanhedrin to conclusively determine this for us. This is my suggestion."

Avi clapped. This was the smartest and most logical suggestion he had heard—and what was more, it offered a reasonable explanation for why he'd seen the three friends all at once. Hadn't Natan's Saba told him that God yearned for mankind to be involved in the process of creation? What better way for God to partner with man than to give him three choices and allow mankind to make the ultimate decision?

Avi stood up and clapped harder, and slowly, everyone else in the room stood and followed suit. The clapping grew until the thunderous applause was replaced by the chanting of one phrase: "Reconvene the Sanhedrin! Reconvene the Sanhedrin!"

CHAPTER 17

"As he was about to enter Egypt, he said to his wife Sarai, 'I know what a beautiful woman you are. If the Egyptians see you, and think, 'She is his wife,' they will kill me and let you live. Please say that you are my sister, that it may go well with me because of you, and that I may remain alive thanks to you.'"—Genesis 12:11-13

<u>Four weeks earlier</u>

The Reform movement approached Tzippy the day after the Israeli Prime Minister had introduced Avi to the world with their idea that she was the mashiach. Tzippy's first thought at their asinine suggestion was: *Are you sure it's me or the baby growing in my tummy? Hail Tzippy, the new virgin Mary.* She giggled inwardly. She was still in the first trimester, and her body had yet to betray the changes it was experiencing. She was tempted to tell them that she was pregnant, but with the rapid speeches of the rabbis in front of her, Tzippy was unable to get a word in and the issue of her pregnancy remained unknown.

She thought it was preposterous that God could have chosen her to be the mashiach. Unlike Natan and Max, she had absolutely no idea about halacha; secondly, she couldn't envisage a female mashiach. Feminist though she was, and irreligious though her life may have always been—Tzippy's very limited exposure to Judaism had been through Orthodox lenses, and, as such, she was unable to view the religion outside of its gender-specific roles. She had only a passing acquaintance with the Conservative and Reform movements, and she was aware of the highly progressive

365

stances they took on everything from the ordination of female rabbis and the mixing of sexes in their synagogues, to their acceptance of gay Jews and their marriage ceremonies for persons of the same sex, but, Tzippy's personal experience with Judaism had not been as liberal and, though she loathed the thought which entered her mind, she couldn't help but think that the Judaism presented to her by these movements were, a bit, watered down.

Tzippy noted the enthusiasm in the eyes of the rabbis who sat before her and though she didn't exactly agree with their synopsis, she figured it would afford her some excitement in her life before motherhood came to claim her in six months. Besides, the rabbis were right. Nominating Tzippy as the mashiach would be a step in pushing the issue of female equality forward.

She nodded at them, and they broke out in smiles.

It would be a fun story to tell her kid when he, or she, was born.

She would pretend to be the Reform movement's mashiach.

✡

Natan breathed a sigh of relief when he read the headlines in Yehidot Ahronot which carried the report of Avi's announcement to the congregation of rabbis that he had returned to earth to locate and inform the mashiach that he was the mashiach. The article mentioned Rabbi Eliezer's conviction that the said mashiach was Max Feldman.

There was no mention of Natan.

Natan put down the paper and drank his cup of coffee. A few minutes later, the door to his bedroom cracked open.

"Boker tov," Natan said.

"Boker or," the visitor said, and he walked up to Natan and kissed him on the lips.

Natan pulled out a bag from beneath the table. "It's your clothes," he said to his visitor. "The clothes we'd left behind in the tent that day."

"The ones Avraham Aveinu wore?"

Natan nodded.

"Did they fit him?"

"He's a lot smaller than you."

"Are you saying I'm fat?"

They grinned at each other and ate and then both hurriedly got dressed. Natan was due to the bank to sort out his affairs, which he had sorely neglected throughout the entire saga that had been Avi's return.

They walked down the stairs together, and to Natan's surprise, there was a crowd of people waiting there for him.

"Natan Nasi!" came the cry when they spotted him.

Natan backed off, surprised.

There were people waving rainbow flags, and others carrying signs with his name on it and the word mashiach below.

What was going on?

Three women and two men dislodged themselves from the mass and went up to Natan. They shook his hand and introduced themselves as rabbis from the Conservative movement. Would Natan spare them a moment?

Overwhelmed at all the people outside of his building milling around on the street, Natan nodded and led the five rabbis up the stairs to his apartment. He poured them cups of tea and immediately, the rabbis launched into their reasons for being there.

After careful consideration, the Masorti Olami did not believe that Avraham Aveinu had erred in his original choice of mashiach. To say that he had would be to undermine the infallibility of God. "If God had sent Avraham Aveinu with the dictate that the first person he saw was to be the mashiach and Avraham Aveinu chose you—it is our opinion that you were God's original choice. God makes no mistakes and He endowed Avraham Aveinu with the authority to choose the mashiach, and Avraham Aveinu chose you." The Conservative movement unanimously threw their support behind Natan, and it was clear, given the crowd gathered outside Natan's house, that the gay community did as well.

Natan shook his head. "How did you—and they," he nodded outside, gesturing to the crowd, "know about me? There was no mention of me in the papers."

"Your name was thrown about in a private meeting the government had arranged between Avraham Aveinu and rabbis, prior to his public introduction to the world. Word of mouth goes a long way in the Jewish world, particularly in Israel. You know that."

The rabbis explained that they did not agree with Rabbi Eliezer's position, and they were, at present, unsure of what the Reform position was—but their support was unequivocally behind Natan. Besides, think of how much a gay mashiach could do in terms of the issue of equality?

"But I am not out of the closet," Natan protested weakly.

"Maybe you weren't yesterday, and we are sorry that this balagan has erupted, but now you are."

Natan considered carefully. He had already been thinking he would have to be the mashiach for the past few weeks since Avi's return, and though, to be honest, he did agree with Rabbi Eliezer's conclusion that Max was a far better choice than he, Natan ascertained the merit in the Conservative rabbi's points. He did not want to be the mashiach, and, indeed, if the situation culminated in such a scenario, he would resign promptly. But in the meantime, while the struggle for just who the mashiach was carried on, he could do much to assist minorities like the Sephardim and the gay community.

"Beseder," Natan replied.

He would pretend to be the Conservative movement's mashiach.

✡

Max sat quietly in a corner of the beis midrash and thumbed through the book which lay on the table before him, but he couldn't concentrate. He was acutely aware of the stares and the hushed whispers emanating from the other boys, and he detested it. He felt embarrassed and angry all at once, but he knew there was nothing he could do to stop anyone from talking about him, even if the whispered talk was nothing more than curiosity on the part of the onlookers and bore him no malice.

While Max had soured towards Rabbi Eliezer following the rabbi's betrayal the day Max confided in him, Max found it difficult to completely lose his awe of accomplished posek and tell him off. And thus, when Rabbi Eliezer came to Max the day before and explained that he believed Max was the mashiach, Max couldn't bring himself to tell the man where to stick it. Instead, Max listened to the Rabbi's argument, and though he didn't agree with the conclusions the man had drawn, Max quietly allowed the rabbi to take control and he meekly succumbed to the man's wishes.

He had been sequestered in his yeshiva for the past couple days, unable to see Avi, or his cousin, or Natan. Rabbi Eliezer didn't want his mashiach candidate seen fraternizing with the competition and had banned Max from seeing them, but Max had learnt his lesson; he surreptitiously slipped out of his yeshiva and bought a pre-paid cellphone which he immediately put on silent mode and would use to call his friends at night when no one was around. But during the day, it was impossible to maintain any contact with Avi, Natan, or Tzippy, so here Max was, stuck in the beis midrash with no one to talk to at the moment; only the gawkers who whispered openly in front of his face. Though it had been only a day, he had already been made to receive the nobility of the Charedi world; men who fawned over Max and tried to plump his mind with flattery, compliments and grand gestures, hoping that, if Max should be the one to win the mashiach bid, he would remember them and grant them favors. Max hated the insincerity of it all but he smiled benignly whenever these unwanted guests were granted an audience with him and he inwardly sighed at how uncomfortable it all made him.

Max had never expected anything like this to happen: to be named mashiach? He had never aspired to or coveted such a position; he had never wanted a life which put him in the spotlight. When Avi had chosen Natan, Max had harbored no ill will or jealousy toward his friend. Power, recognition, and fame were not the goals of Max's life, and these would be the inevitable accompaniments of being the mashiach.

Am I the mashiach?

Max didn't think so.

But Rabbi Eliezer and the whole host of Charedi rabbis seemed to think so—and though they impressed upon Max the precariousness of the situation, he simply couldn't wrap his mind around the role. This was no misplaced modesty on Max's part; he knew his capabilities and this was something he was simply not capable of doing. He was a struggling baal teshuva who shied away from being made the center of attention— how could he possibly be the one to bring about the redemption of Israel and the world?

"You are running from your calling," Rabbi Eliezer had told him sternly that morning when Max had offered a mild protest, "just like you tried to do when I asked you to be my understudy. Do you remember what I told you about Moishe Rabbeinu? Even he felt unworthy, Feldman, but you must put aside your modesty and do the job which HaShem calls you to perform. I knew you were special from the moment I heard your speech; I just didn't realize how very special you are. You will be the mashiach, Feldman. You are the mashiach. Any alternative will lead to the immediate destruction of Torah-observant Jewry. Can you imagine a homosexual mashiach? Or a woman leading our holy nation and the world? No, I tell you, I will not have it. HaShem is testing us with this current confusion over who the mashiach is. He tested Avraham Aveinu and now He tests Am Yisroel as a whole. Do we choose the

371

correct candidate: you, a man of such humble virtue, that you can be likened to Moishe Rabbeinu himself? Or do we choose unlettered, near-heathen candidates who will destroy the holiness of our people? We must struggle and fight to maintain our traditions and beliefs. And you, as the mashiach, will ensure this for us and bring the whole of Clal Yisroel back to proper observance. Yes, Feldman, embrace your calling."

Max nodded speechlessly. He was expected to be the champion of the minority Charedi world; it was a prodigious responsibility and though he did not look forward to it, he had to try. Too many people were counting on him and supporting him for him to do otherwise. Max turned a page and pretended to read.

He would pretend to be the Charedim's mashiach.

CHAPTER 18

"Then the King of Sodom said to Abram, 'Give me the persons, and take the possessions for yourself.' But Abram said to the King of Sodom, 'I swear to the LORD, God Most High, Creator of heaven and earth: I will not take so much as a thread or a sandal strap of what is yours; you shall not say, 'It is I who made Abram rich.' For me, nothing but what my servants have used up...'"
—Genesis 14:21-24

The reconvening of the Sanhedrin was a historical milestone in the book of the Jewish people and should have been the foremost story of the day. Unfortunately, it coincided with an abysmal breakdown of relations between Israel and her neighbors, and all the progress that had been achieved since the announcement of Avi's return had reverted, and things were even worse off than before.

The reason for all of this negativity was directly due to a hard-hitting interview of Avi conducted by Anderson Cooper. The interview was progressing smoothly until Cooper brought up the issue of the Abrahamic religions. He asked Avi which of the religions he most identified with, to which Avi replied, simply, firmly, and truthfully: "Judaism. The Jews are my legitimate spiritual heirs. They are my direct descendants—as has been proven by genetic science—and they have followed the tradition I begun and built upon it in the most ethical and moral way. They are the only ones who call upon the God I knew. While there are indeed vestiges of my teaching and spiritual movement in Christianity and Islam, these two religions have veered sharply in different ways from my original teaching. Christianity ignores the monotheism which I believe in, and the Wahhabi, Ash'arite and Shiite Islam of today ignores the reason and logic of the ethics and morality which I taught, and both these religions seek to stamp out opposition and position themselves as the only true pathways to the Creator. This has never been something I adhered to. God speaks to all men through different religions; the notion of a 'one true religion' runs counter to who I am and to the spiritual pathway I earnestly attest to. Of course, I am generalizing here, and I recognize that there are Christians and Muslims who have internalized the religion of Abraham and I, thus, recognize them as my kin. But my practice of rational, ethical monotheism has only been embraced by my spiritual and direct descendants: the Jews. These are my children."

The outcry was instantaneous.

Immediately, Protestant and Catholic denominations claimed that the Israeli authorities were brainwashing the patriarch. Sunni and Shia sects roared that Abouna Ibrahim was being held hostage by the Zionist entity and being forced to capitulate to their demands by mouthing these heretic words.

The friction grew worse when news of the mashiach hit world headlines, and when asked for an official statement from the BBC, Avi said that, while he was unsure who the exact mashiach was, there were three very worthy candidates for the position. Zeinab Badawi, who conducted the interview, expressed her surprise at this revelation. "What about Jesus as messiah? Has he returned?" Avi shook his head and said, categorically, that the mashiach had not been the person of Jesus, and that the mashiach he had come to locate was definitely not Jesus returned—a direct contradiction of both Christian and Islamic belief.

The Holy See recalled its ambassador to Israel in protest at Avi's statements; the Saudi King cancelled his planned trip to Jerusalem; the Iranian Ayatollahs rescinded their invitation to the Israeli Prime Minister and President; Egypt and Jordan recalled their ambassadors from Jerusalem; Turkey, whose ties with Israel were already strained, accidentally-on-purpose bombed an Israeli cargo ship, killing fifteen Israeli citizens on board; the newly formed Palestinian State announced that any peace treaty it had signed with Israel was *hudna* and it immediately began launching rockets into Israel; joint Hezbollah-Hamas forces raided northern Israel and the Negev; UC, Berkeley spear-headed a North American effort for the American and Canadian governments to expel Israeli diplomats, and they received over forty million signatures on their petition; the European Union declared Avi persona non grata; the UN voted Avi's statements as divisive and accused him of positioning the world for a religious war; the International Court of Justice charged Avi with war crimes based on the biblical accounts of his life and angrily called for him to be extradited to Hague; PETA followed suit and declared Avi a murderer of animals since in the Bible he had asked Sarah to prepare meat for visitors and had sacrificed a goat, and billboards with Hitler's famous moustache was superimposed upon a Photoshopped image of a leering Avi holding a knife over a cartoon goat; the Venezuelan president gave an impassioned speech claiming to have historical proof that Jesus was not a Jew and thus, Avi had no bearing on Christianity; John Galliano held a press conference asking for redemption for his previous anti-Semitic

375

comments, stating that, "If their founder holds such racist and bigoted views, is it any wonder Jews are equally as arrogant and pig-headed?"; all Evangelical tour groups to Israel were summarily cancelled and they held vigil and prayers that Jews convert to Christianity immediately and accept the truth that Jesus was the messiah or face the dire consequences of death and hell.

The era of mashiach had never seemed more out of reach.

Within Jewry, the reconvening of the Sanhedrin caused internal friction as the different Jewish religious movements clamored for a place in the soon-to-be reestablished body. The matter was taken to the courts and quickly reached the Israeli Supreme Court, which ruled that any reconvened Great Sanhedrin must have equal representation from each recognized branch of Judaism. At first, the ultra-Orthodox Charedim refused to acquiesce to the ruling; adamant that they would not sit on any Sanhedrin which allowed for non-Charedi Judaism to be given equal status to them, but, when it became clear that world Jewry would only recognize a mashiach voted in by this body, they quickly capitulated and scrambled for the few remaining seats.

The position of Nasi, or head of the court, was given to the Israeli president, who, as a secular Jew knowledgeable about halacha, could be counted upon to remain unbiased. Due to the Charedim's initial refusal to join the Sanhedrin, the twenty-three seats allotted to Orthodoxy had been populated overwhelmingly by representatives from the modern Orthodox movement. Three Charedi rabbis quickly filled the remaining vacant seats, but they bristled at their inferior position and they demanded more prominence in the council. As a result, the station of Av Bet Din, the second-in-command to the

376

Nasi, was offered to the Charedim, and Rabbi Eliezer enthusiastically grabbed the position.

The elements for the reconstitution of the Sanhedrin were finalized and the first meeting, to discuss the issue of the mashiach, was about to begin.

✡

With the world determinedly against him, Avi had never felt more alone or more pressured. His phone rang off the hook, until he pulled it out of its plug and threw it out the window. He dismissed the staff who had been assigned to him and sat alone in the house which had been offered to him by the Israeli government and he begged the Prime Minister to take back the security guards who guarded his premises, a wish the Prime Minister could not grant, but he did caution the guards to not enter Avi's house and to remain vigilant on the outside. Finally alone, Avi fell into a dismal depression. With everything going on in their own lives, he had heard not a peep from Natan, Tzippy, or Max in the past few days.

Avi fingered Sarah's necklace, which hung around his neck, drew the curtains, and sat in the dark.

✡

The site for the setting of the Sanhedrin was the cause of almost as much debate as the membership of the Sanhedrin had been. Some rabbis suggested that a building be built to permanently house the council, either on the Temple Mount, next to the Dome of the Rock mosque, or in the Kotel Plaza. Others suggested it be held in the Great Synagogue on Rechov King George, and others even suggested it be convened in town of Tiberius, the site of the last Sanhedrin meeting. Eventually, it was decided that, as the Sanhedrin served as the highest authoritative Jewish-religious court, it was equal in stature to the Israeli Supreme Court, and thus, the site for the first reconvening of the Sanhedrin was to take place on the premises of the Supreme Court; two bodies, diametrically opposed to each other—one secular, and the other religious—but sharing the same values of democracy, openness, accountability, and fairness and serving as the highest courts of appeals for their respective jurisdictions.

Although the Jewish world was facing painful anti-Semitic discrimination from the outside world, and Israel was facing an undue number of attacks on all its borders—the majority of the Israeli Knesset had shown up to view the proceedings of the newly convened Sanhedrin's first meeting. The issue of the mashiach carried hope for every person present: a hope that with the determination of the mashiach, peace would somehow finally visit the shores of the Jewish narrative.

Natan, Tzippy, and Max were also present, almost like living pieces of evidence. They sat quietly on the sidelines, having no official role to play in the meeting, and from time to time, people would look at them, just to reassure themselves that the possibility of the messianic era was on the verge of beginning. Avi was notably absent, but to the majority of people there, it was a welcomed absence. Avi's words in the Anderson Cooper interview and his subsequent comments to Zeinab Badawi—which culminated in the excruciating backlash Israel was now receiving—was viewed by most people as a signal that the patriarch was a living fossil who had served his purpose and was no longer needed.

Avi had provided the candidates for the mashiach position, and as far as everyone was concerned, it was time he faded away into the history from which he had come.

The members of the Sanhedrin sat in their seats and they all stood as the Nasi and Av Bet Din walked in. After a particularly moving rendition of *haTikvah*, the Israeli national anthem, the Nasi called the meeting to order and offered the Av Bet Din the opportunity to present the issue for discussion. To the surprise of all persons present, Rabbi Eliezer stood and said in his loud voice, "The issue for discussion: is Avraham Aveinu a Jew?"

✡

When Avi's unfortunate words to Cooper and Badawi caused the backlash that it had, Avi found himself isolated and reviled by the majority of the world. It was a few days before the Sanhedrin met, and he was desperately trying to clarify his statements to the New York Times over the telephone when Rabbi Eliezer showed up in his usual unannounced way.

Avi ended the conversation and invited the rabbi in, who did not waste time in getting to the reason for his visit. Avi, Rabbi Eliezer pointed out, in his current incarnation, was the most hated person on the planet at present. Christians, Muslims, and Jews alike were disliking his statements: the Christians and Muslims were severely offended at his words which debased and invalidated their religious beliefs, and Jews hated Avi as the physical consequences of his words were being directed at them and the Jewish state. Avi had put himself in this position and there was only one way he could regain the trust of the Jewish world.

"What way is that?" Avi asked wearily.

"Confer your endorsement on Max Feldman as the mashiach. This is the only way. The Charedim would rally behind you, and slowly, you would find the rest of Am Yisroel will follow suit. You are alone now. Not even the Rosh haMemshala or any of your former friends want anything to do with you—tainted and reviled as you are."

Avi was amazed at the old man's gall. Vilified and alone though he felt, Avi was not going to do what Rabbi Eliezer suggested. Firstly, Avi was not going to endorse Max as the mashiach, because he didn't know if Max was the mashiach. Secondly, there was no way in hell Avi would give in to anyone just to make friends and be universally liked. Avi had experienced the bitter taste of being cast out in his previous life—and he had survived, persevered, and come out on top. This was the camel that broke the proverbial back when it came to Avi's tumultuous relationship with Rabbi Eliezer.

"Get out of my house," Avi said forcefully. "You are an evil man with an evil agenda. That you are a descendant of mine is a curse upon my wife's memory. Be gone, spawn of evil. Be gone."

The old man walked to the door and looked at Avi with a sneer. "You will regret this."

Avi slammed the door. "Funny, but I really don't think I will."

✡

Rabbi Eliezer was a vengeful man. He had cultivated himself to a position of such great authority that being belittled was not something he had been used to, and ever since he had first met Avi, Rabbi Eliezer had received nothing but a constant flow of rudeness and insubordination.

He had had enough.

Despite the importance of having the mashiach question answered punitively, he concentrated his energies on fueling the fires of hate which fanned throughout the Jewish world towards their patriarch. He commissioned the Facebook pictures of Avi cavorting in dance clubs and various other pictures of him from the media canoodling with non-Jewish religious leaders, to be compressed into one article in the Charedim newspapers, accompanied by a report which asked, basically, if this was the example Charedi mothers and fathers wanted for their children. The article was well-received by the Charedi community, and they voted decisively to bar all contact with Avi, and Rabbi Eliezer felt the sweet satisfaction of securing a minor victory in his campaign to malign Avi.

However, Rabbi Eliezer knew that for him to win the war, he needed to expand his strategies to the much larger non-Charedi Jewish world. Unfortunately, given his repute in the non-Charedi sphere, it wasn't as easy for Rabbi Eliezer to discredit Avi there as he'd done on his own stomping ground. Besides, the strategies that would work on unsuspecting Charedim would not cause even a murmur among the hiloni population. Eventually, Rabbi Eliezer was seized with an idea, which did cause a stir of discussion amongst the hilonim. He commissioned an article, written by a popular Russian-Israeli gossip columnist, which discussed the character of Avi and contrasted it with the Avraham Aveinu as documented in the Bible.

"We all know that they are the same person," the article concluded, "but we must ask ourselves the disturbing question: does Avi of today possess the same upstanding character as the Avraham Aveinu of yesteryear? When one considers the steadfast humbleness of Avraham Aveinu and contrasts this with the man called Avi that we all know today, could there be two persons who were more opposing? Avi dines with royalty and is chauffeured and protected like a king; our patriarch ate the simple meals of a nomad in his tent with his wife and tended sheep. Are they the same character? The Avraham Aveinu who has returned is a boy who is clearly in his early twenties. Midrashic sources confirm that Avraham discovered his God when he was at least fifty years of age. Would it be safe for us to conclude that the man who struts about our country and openly lives off of the bounty of the nation is, in fact, the corresponding pre-God Avraham: that is to say, Avram?"

The article did fuel debate, but it wasn't enough to totally discredit Avi. Eventually, however, when Rabbi Eliezer was given the post of Av Bet Din at the Sanhedrin, it struck him as obvious what he should do: use that forum to properly evaluate Avi in the context of the biblical accounts of Avraham Aveinu, and in so doing, invalidate Avi's authority and leave the road free and clear for Max to win the mashiach position.

Rabbi Eliezer grinned and counted down the days, the hours, and then the minutes when he could pull the proverbial cat out of the bag and cause the Jewish maelstrom of the century—even bigger than Avi's return, even bigger than the mashiach.

He was going to question Avi's very soul.

✡

"This is not on the agenda for discussion," the Nasi hissed at Rabbi Eliezer.

Rabbi Eliezer looked up at the great assembly which sat across from him. "Honorable Nasi, distinguished members of the great Sanhedrin, reconvened for the first time in nearly seventeen hundred years, you may think that my question is capricious, but I assure you, it's not. It is directly co-related to the issue which brings us all here today: the issue of the mashiach. The great Avraham Aveinu, who has been resurrected to life and whose rebirth has touched us all in a most profound way, has identified the three persons who are in the running for this position.

"But who is this man? We know he is Avraham Aveinu—none of us doubt that or question it, but in regards to the Judaism which exists today, how does he fit into our equation?"

"He was the first Jew, Rabbi Goldenberg," came a shout from the Sanhedrin.

"He was the first convert!" came another shout.

"He was?" Rabbi Eliezer asked, imbuing his voice with the tone of surprise. "Indeed, we are all taught from an early age that he was the first of our nation—and there is no disputing that. But that was over three thousand years ago and it was before the giving of the Torah and the establishment of universal Judaic principles regarding the issue of converts. In the context of today, the man is not a Jew. Did he study Jewish law? Was he a part of an *ulpan giyur*? Did he stand before a bet din and have the stamp of Jewishness conferred upon him? Did he dip in a *mikvah* to emerge reborn as a Jew? Who was the *moyel* who circumcised him? Does he keep kosher? Does he observe the Shabbos or any of the Yamim Tovim? Has he been observant of the mitzvos in any way, shape, or form? Or is all of that unnecessary because he was born of a Jewish mother?

"No, distinguished members of the Sanhedrin, the Avraham Aveinu of today went through none of these things. He did not convert according to the standards of any Jewish movement and he was not born of a Jewish mother."

The crowd murmured uncomfortably.

"Let us also not forget, fellow talmidim, that the actions of this one man in the past few weeks has jeopardized world Jewry in ways we cannot even begin to comprehend. As a direct result of his gaffed words, we have seen the breakdown of international relations with the Jewish state on an unprecedented scale, as even our closest allies have pulled away from us. Millions, if not billions, of Christians and Muslims are offended, and rightfully so, by his unsavory comments. Even as I speak, a barrage of rockets and attacks are accosting Eretz Yisroel from every corner. This man—who didn't even think it necessary to be present here today, although he was invited—this man will be the cause of the destruction of our people. He is our first cause, but may also be the cause which ends us as a people, as a country, as a nation."

"How does this tie in with the issue of the mashiach?" the Nasi asked.

"The mashiach will be heralded by the dual resurrections of Moishe and Eliyahu," Rabbi Eliezer replied. "That is basic Jewish teaching and even the Christians know this. This is approved prophecy and we all look to it as a signal of the coming of the mashiach. Nowhere is there any indication that the body of

Avraham Aveinu should arise and partake in the process of redemption that shall occur when the mashiach comes. Prophetic sources speak only of Moishe and Eliyahu being resurrected to announce to the world the coming of the mashiach: two men who are indisputably Jewish, both having been born of Jewish mothers. The question of the Jewish mashiach can only be answered by a person who is Jewish. Avraham Aveinu has returned, and, from his own mouth, he says he was sent to identify and locate the mashiach. But if he is not Jewish, does his opinion have any bearing on this final answer of Jewish redemption? Not only was his return not mentioned by any of the prophets, but also, his status among us is questionable. Yes, members of the great Sanhedrin, I ask you today, is Avraham Aveinu a Jew? Yes, the Avraham Aveinu of yesterday was the first of us, the one who first found HaShem and who started it all. But the Avi of today? I am of the opinion that he, unquestionably, is not."

There was a hush across the Sanhedrin.

✡

Rabbi Eliezer argued strongly against Avi's Jewish status. He brought out newspaper clippings which documented Avi's meetings with non-Jewish religious leaders, reminding the Sanhedrin that Avi had been reluctant to meet with any of them. He displayed the Facebook photos of Avi, drunk at the Billy Jean bar, asking if this was appropriate behavior for the patriarch of the Jewish people. He showed the TMZ video of Avi leaving the vegetarian restaurant with the Dalai Lama, noting that the restaurant was not kosher, as it operated on Shabbat. He detailed the accounts of Avi helping out at the soup kitchen on previous Shabbats, a direct violation of Shabbat law.

And then, he brought out the most damning piece of evidence of them all: Zahira's visit to the apartment where Avi stayed at before the public had known who he was. "He spoke with this woman in her native tongue," Rabbi Eliezer said, "and he spoke fluently. I heard it with my own ears; I saw this woman with my own eyes. Who was this woman? A woman from Afghanistan, he told me. Afghanistan? A country which we regard as an enemy state? A country which refuses to recognize us and has repeatedly called for the destruction of Israel? A country that spawned the hateful Taliban? Is this who Avraham Aveinu associates himself with? And what's worse—what's *incredibly* worse—is that our patriarch was not only being friendly to this woman, he allowed her to spend the night at his abode! What was he up to? What was this person, Avi, doing spending all that time with an enemy of the Jewish state?"

There were some rabbis who had argued against Rabbi Eliezer's opening arguments—some of them disagreed with his dissertation, and some simply disagreed with him as a person, but this final revelation silenced everyone. No one knew how to respond.

The Nasi finally spoke, "Avraham Aveinu is hereby summoned to the Sanhedrin to answer the charges levied against him by Rabbi Goldenberg. His status as a member of the Jewish nation will be decided after he gives his defense in two days."

The Sanhedrin was dismissed for the day.

✡

"That scheming, horrible old fart!" Tzippy muttered quietly through gritted teeth as she meandered her way through the building to the elevators. "He's making it seem like Zahira was a spy! Or worse, that Avi had something sexual with Zahira! When it comes out who Zahira really was, boy is he going to look stupid."

Natan sighed. "If Avi hadn't told us about Zahira's visit, we'd probably be on Goldenberg's side."

"How could you say that?"

"Goldenberg would have made a great prosecutor. Unless Avi comes to answer the charges, no one is going to know who Zahira was besides me, you, and Max. Otherwise, everyone will continue to willfully misconstrue the relationship."

"It's disturbing how easily Goldenberg's mind slips into passing everything off as sexual. Who does he think he is? Freud?"

"What's more disturbing to me is what he's building this all up to: the questioning of Avi's Jewishness."

They'd reached the elevator. Natan pushed the button.

"Why is he attacking Avi like this?" Tzippy asked.

The elevator opened and they went in. "One, I think he's just an evil, vindictive old man and this is just his way of being nasty to Avi. Secondly, it stems from his own struggle for power and control. If Avi is judged to not be Jewish, he would have no part to play in the naming of the mashiach. That is what Goldenberg wants most. With Avi out of the way, he would have full control over the naming of the mashiach."

"But the majority of the Sanhedrin isn't even Charedi, and most of them dislike Goldenberg anyway.

Besides, Avi wasn't even here today. He told us he wants no part in this vote."

"Yes, but despite the hate being leveled at Avi by the media, he still does have influence. As the patriarch of our people—albeit, a presently much reviled patriarch—Avi's words carry weight which pose a challenge to Goldenberg's authority. Do you really think Goldenberg thinks Max is the best choice for mashiach in the Charedi world? I'm sure Goldenberg thinks there are better candidates to be found in from the Charedi ranks—heck, I'm sure Goldenberg thinks he is the best candidate; but the fact of the matter is, Avi has offered only three options, and Max is the best of those options as far as Goldenberg is concerned." Natan smiled wryly. "Yes, Goldenberg wants to discredit Avi as thoroughly as possible to make sure that he is silenced. There are no other strong personalities in the Sanhedrin to stand up to Goldenberg. His only possible opposition is Avi."

The elevator doors opened to the parking level, and to their surprise, Max stood outside.

Tzippy rushed to her cousin and threw her arms around his neck. "Max! I am so glad to see you!"

Max hugged her back and then bear-hugged Natan.

"Managed to get away from your keepers, huh?" Natan asked with a grin.

"I am not going back there. I want nothing to do with that evil Koresh. How could he possibly start a case against Avi? To question Avi's Jewishness is to question the Jewishness of us all! This is pure madness."

Natan nodded and told him his theory as the three of them made their way to Natan's jeep.

"So, you think he's afraid of Avi opposing him?" Max asked, buckling himself into the passenger seat.

"That, and I think he's afraid of Avi presenting an alternative to Max as mashiach." Natan started the car.

"You or Tzippy?"

Natan looked at her grimly. "No, the three of us together."

Comprehension dawned on Max's and Tzippy's faces.

"Think about it. Avi doesn't know who he saw first. I don't feel like a mashiach—"

"I don't either," Tzippy interjected from the backseat. "I'm just doing this to humor the Reform movement."

"And I don't either," Max said. "I was pressured by Goldenberg to accept the nomination because he said it would be good for the Charedim to have someone to rally around."

"Exactly. None of us feel like we are the mashiach. The three of us appeal to different factions of the Jewish world for different reasons. I don't know all the theoretical philosophies which are behind this whole mashiach balagan—what I do know is that singularly, all three of us are awful candidates for the mashiach position, but together, we represent a diverse cross-section of what modern Judaism represents and maybe, just maybe, this is what Avi was intended to locate when he was sent to find the mashiach."

Tzippy nodded thoughtfully. "What better way to consolidate all Jewish movements and make everyone happy other than compromise and inclusiveness? Unity—all for one and one for all."

"Precisely."

"Goldenberg would have thought about that as well. He's been in this business of politics for a long

389

time. So, his plan is to shut Avi down before Avi could make the suggestion and cut the two of you out of the equation," Max said.

"Do you guys really think Avi thinks this?" Tzippy asked. "What if we're just projecting here? What if what we feel is true: that none of us are the mashiach."

"Maybe none of us are the mashiach, individually or collectively, but the fact is, the collective option is the most logical one that will ensure every aspect of Jewry today is represented," Natan said.

"And, let's not forget," Max replied, "that the mashiach has to have the full support of the entire Jewish population—that's a basic component of who the mashiach will be. Anyone rejected by the congregation of Israel becomes immediately disqualified."

"What are the components of the mashiach?" Tzippy asked.

Max shook his head. "To be honest, I think that's irrelevant. The way things have unraveled in the past few months, I've come to realize that you really shouldn't put a whole lot of faith in prophecies and projections, because they really don't ever play out the way we envisage they will."

The others nodded at Max's sage words.

"When last did either of you speak with Avi?" Natan asked.

"A couple days ago."

"I haven't spoken to him since last week."

"I've been trying to reach him on his home phone line and his cell phone, but I haven't gotten through to him on either," Natan said.

"I hope he doesn't think we've gotten caught up in this mashiach business and have abandoned him."

"I hope he's not taking on everything everyone's saying about him."

"I hope he hasn't been taken back up to heaven."

They looked at each other meaningfully.

"Should we go visit him?" Natan asked.

"We should've done that days ago."

✡

When he had been announced as Avraham Aveinu returned, Avi had been moved from the apartment in Arnona to a house right down the street from the President's residence in the Talbiya neighborhood of Jerusalem. In terms of security, the location was much more feasible—and, with a full staff of assistants, housekeepers, and cooks at his disposal, the spacious house was much more convenient.

Avi hadn't wanted to move and he definitely didn't think it necessary to employ full-time staff, but the Prime Minister had thought it befitting of Avi's stature, and within hours of Avi's public introduction to the world, his new abode had been set up. Avi was given a chauffeured car for his convenience and had been issued an Israeli diplomatic passport. Avi, however, who had never been keen on grand displays of wealth, had bought himself a used ten-speed bicycle with the stipend he had been given by the Hebrew University of Jerusalem for his work with the anthropology department there, and was often seen pedaling mischievously around town with his security team hot on the chase. Despite the all-expenses-paid-for invitations extended to him by the various governments of the world, he had tucked his glossy passport into a Kenneth Cole messenger bag Natan had bought him and put the bag in his closet.

Tzippy had visited Avi at his new house regularly. Natan had been there only once. Max had been stuck at his yeshiva. When they arrived, they were surprised that the grounds were empty, except for a lone security guard who snoozed under a tree. They tiptoed past the unconscious man, and rang the bell, but no one answered.

"Do you really think he's gone back to heaven?" Max asked anxiously.

They went around the back, but the door was locked.

Tzippy picked up a pebble and threw it at the side of the house. It bounced off the wall and fell noiselessly to the ground.

"That's not how you do it," Max said. He picked up a sizeable stone and pelted it. It broke through an upstairs window, causing a shower of glass to rain down on them.

Tzippy groaned. "Real good, Max. The security is going to wake up and kick us off the property for trespassing."

Tzippy's prediction proved inaccurate, and within a minute, a familiar face popped out from the window above and widened into a smile when it spotted them.

"I'm coming down!" Avi yelled.

They heard his footsteps pound down the stairs and then, the door was flung open and a thoroughly excited Avi threw himself pathetically into their arms.

He led them inside into the kitchen where they poured themselves drinks and sat around the kitchen table.

"So, why have you been so MIA recently?" Natan asked.

Avi shrugged. "I've been in a funk, I guess."

"Why?"

"It's not easy being the most hated man alive."

Tzippy rolled her eyes. "You're not the most hated—"

"Maybe in the top ten—" Max said.

"Most disliked. Definitely not most hated," Natan finished.

They all burst out laughing.

Avi held his chest and panted. "I needed that laugh."

"How do you feel now?" Tzippy asked.

"I feel better—much better. I've spent the past couple days by myself," Avi gestured around, "as you can see, I dismissed everyone, and I've been here by myself just—thinking and praying."

"About what?"

"About you guys. About the mashiach. About the things I said that caused so much controversy. About everything."

Natan looked at Avi closely. "And what conclusions have you come to?"

"Absolutely none. I've gone over everything with my guardian angel. We've talked it out as much as we could and we both have come to the ultimate conclusion that we have no idea about anything." Avi beamed.

"You look awfully chipper for someone who has no idea about anything," Max observed.

"It is what it is. I have beat myself up long enough about it and I'm over it." He paused. "Tell me about the Sanhedrin meeting."

They hesitated, but eventually, the details of the day were relayed to Avi.

"So, I'm the hot potato, huh?" Avi said when they were finished.

"You're Jewish. There is no way the Sanhedrin could rule otherwise."

"But that's the thing. I'm *not* Jewish."

"Yes, you are!"

"I'm not."

"You're just talking semantics here, Avi," Max said pointedly. "You are the first Jew; the first Hebrew; the first Israelite; the first of our people. It's like I told you on the beach that day when Tzippy fell asleep, Hebrew, Jewish, whatever you want to refer to it, it's your neshama, and it is the same neshama which sparks me and every Jew alive today—to deny that in you is to deny it in ourselves."

Avi smiled. "Thank you for your vote of confidence, chaver, but I'm not going to win that case. I appreciate your support nonetheless."

"Spoken like a true politician," Natan remarked.

Avi sighed. "I'm not going to answer the summons. I'm not going to debate who I am."

"Scared?"

"Weary. I'm tired of all of this. I messed up in identifying the mashiach—no offense, Natan—I don't know which of you it is. Had I just gotten it right from the beginning, none of this would have happened and I'd have been back in heaven, sipping tea with God, or whatever it is people do in heaven."

Natan, Tzippy, and Max looked at each other.

"What?" Avi asked.

Natan coughed. "I thought you'd have figured it out by now."

394

"Figured what out?"

"Figured out who the mashiach is."

Avi smiled grimly. "Well, I haven't."

"I think I know who the mashiach is."

"Who?"

"I think it's all of us. All three of us."

Avi looked like he was about to laugh, but then his eyes furrowed. "That makes sense." He jumped up. "That's it! That's it exactly!" He clapped his hands. "I couldn't figure out who I saw *first* because I didn't see any of you *first*. I saw all of you *at once*! You were all the first souls I encountered after I left the cave. You are all the mashiach!"

Tzippy frowned. "Avi, it's just a theory—"

"But it's a theory which makes the most sense!"

He went off to a corner. "Michael!"

"Yes?"

"You heard what Natan said?"

"Indeed, I did."

"And?"

"And what?"

Avi moaned. "Michael!"

"Wasn't it my initial suggestion that the mashiach was all three of them? Didn't I tell you that when you first saw them?"

"So, it's them? All of them?"

"It's certainly plausible."

"Give me a concrete answer."

"For the seven-hundredth-and-ninety-second time, I know nothing more than you do." Michael paused. "But it does seem highly likely. You should tell them they're the mashiach—all three of them—and maybe, if it's true, just maybe, they'd believe you because it's the truth."

Avi nodded. "Thank you, dear angel."

"Anytime."

He turned around and walked back to the table. His friends had gotten used to his impromptu conversations with his guardian angel, and they'd entertained themselves by playing rock, paper, scissors while he'd been occupied thus.

Avi sat and looked at them seriously. "When I was coming down the hillside towards you, I was trying to figure out which of you was the mashiach. That was when my guardian angel said to me, 'What if it's all three of them?' I pooh-poohed his idea, but it fits. It's the only idea that makes sense and which accounts for me still being here." He looked around the table. "Natan Nasi, Tzipporah Feldman, Max Feldman—I am Avraham of old, resurrected by the grace of the one true God of Israel, here on earth once again to do His bidding. I have been sent by He Who will be what He will be, to say unto you: you are, all of you, the mashiach."

Avi looked at them expectantly.

"Well?"

"Well, what?" they asked back.

"Do you see the truth in my words? That you are all the mashiach?"

The three friends shifted uncomfortably.

"Not really, Avi," Max said softly.

Avi sighed. "I don't know what else to do!" He threw his head back and looked up at the ceiling. "Give me direction, Lord! Nothing has gone according to plan! I need help! Why won't you answer me?"

"Ok, Avi, let's not get dramatic here." Max stood and walked to the sink. "We can figure this out. Don't blame God. Here's what we do: we separate each problem and deal with them individually.

"First problem, the mashiach business: none of us can figure it out. The three of us—Natan, Tzippy, and I—have discussed it and none of us feel like we're the mashiach, at least not singularly. I know you think that by telling us we are the mashiach collectively, it's going to work like some sort of magical incantation and make us believe it, but it didn't work that way. We've all tried to figure it out, and none more than you, Avi, but none of us have been able to. For now, let's put this mashiach business on the backburner and give our brains a rest from it. Agreed?"

Everyone nodded.

"Moving along, this whole mess with everyone being against Avi. I'm no public relations person, but I'm certain that this will all blow over. Avi, you're being vilified today, but today's headlines are tomorrow's garbage. Someone else will grab the attention and this will seem like a dream. There is nothing any one of us can do but wait it out. You can issue statements but it's not going to make a difference. Just let it be.

"Next item in need of attention: the summons from the Sanhedrin. Avi, are you going to answer the charges?"

Avi shook his head firmly.

"Personally, I think you should go. I think you should go and present your case and shut Goldenberg up once and for all, but if you are sure you don't want to go, then that's your choice. If you don't want to go to the Sanhedrin, then, I have a suggestion. Avi, you have a passport?"

"Yes."

"Good. I have my passport as well. I always have it with me." Max patted his pant pocket. "Tzippy, Natan, we're going to go get yours and then we are all going for a little vacation so all of us can have a break from all of this."

The others looked at Max.

"Are you crazy?" Tzippy asked incredulously

"We can't just pick up and leave," Natan said.

"Yes, we can," Max said firmly. "Enough is enough. I am not going back to yeshiva as long as Goldenberg's tentacles can reach me in there. I'm tired of being the champion of the Charedi world; that's not who I am. I have had enough of the limelight and politics to last me a lifetime and I need a break. Avi, do you need a break?"

"I wouldn't mind a break."

"Great. Tzippy and Natan—if you guys don't want to come with us, that's your call, but Avi and I are leaving."

"And where will you go? If you buy tickets, word of your leaving will get out and the media will mob you the moment you get to the airport."

"Not if we buy our tickets at the airport," Max said and winked. "It'll be too late for them to catch up with us."

"Tickets to where exactly?" Natan asked.

"Who cares? Just tickets out of Israel—anywhere but Israel right now. On the first flight that's leaving, we're going. Whether it's Timbuktu or Kathmandu, we are going."

"I don't think El Al flies to Timbuktu," Natan murmured.

The others laughed.

"What about your stuff? Do you want to stop at your yeshiva?"

Max shook his head. "No. I can always get new stuff. Let's go."

"Now?" Natan asked, surprised.

"Yes, now."

"You should let Avi at least pack some stuff—" Tzippy started to say.

Avi shook his head. "No. I can always get new stuff, too. I agree with Max. The sooner we leave, the better."

Tzippy sighed. "How are you guys going to pay for all of this?"

Avi grinned and pulled out a black credit card from his wallet. "Courtesy of the kind people at Amex who sent me their most exclusive credit card and told me anything I buy is on them. I haven't had a chance to use it until now." He slipped the card back into his wallet. "Natan, Tzippy, I can't force you guys to come. I don't expect you to just drop everything and come with us, but if you can—"

Natan's jawline hardened. "I'm coming. You clowns wouldn't manage a day without me."

Avi smiled.

Tzippy sighed. "Of course, I'm coming, too. But I am not going to Timbuktu!"

"Well, I think we can get a connecting flight to Kathmandu," Avi said with a grin.

✡

For the first time in days, Avi felt happy and light. Though he and Max were ready to go, Tzippy and Natan, "being the divas that they are," Max said, needed to stop in Tel Aviv to sort out a few issues before they could leave. As they didn't have airplane tickets yet, and therefore, had no pressing time constraints, Avi and Max agreeably consented for an early evening drive to Tel Aviv.

They waited outside of Tzippy's apartment, and as she rushed in to quickly stuff a bag with clothes, look around, and make sure everything was switched off, the three boys listened to the radio station carrying a news story of what happened at the Sanhedrin meeting and the three of them giggled. Tzippy soon returned with a duffel bag in tow, and they then proceeded to Natan's apartment. There were a number of fans camped outside of the entrance to Natan's place, so Tzippy took the wheel, dropped Natan off, and then circled the block a few times and picked him up at the curb where he was just about to get molested by the crowd of fans had Tzippy not returned at that most opportune moment.

They were all excited for the spontaneous trip, but none more than Avi, who had never travelled on an airplane and looked forward to the trip with an undue amount of excitement. He had been so lost in his depression for the past few days that just being in the presence of his friends was enough to cheer him up a million-fold. A number of times, the cell phones of the three nominated mashiach's rang, but they ignored the calls as they were all from their respective sponsoring organizations. To Avi, nothing was more indicative of the strength of the friendships he had established with these three individuals: that they would turn their backs so firmly on fame and fortune spoke to him more than any words could. They all felt a bit naughty about what they were doing, but it was so thrilling and so unbelievably exciting to think of leaving the chaos behind them, that they didn't care one bit.

Before they left Tel Aviv, Natan wanted to stop and buy a pack of cigarettes. Tzippy, who was still driving, pulled up outside of a makholet and Natan jumped out of the jeep. "*Sonya!*" One second! he called and he ran inside. Tzippy hopped across to the passenger seat and left the vehicle running. She turned around and smiled at Max and Avi in the backseat with her characteristically beautiful smile.

Out of nowhere, hands flew into the jeep, grabbing and pulling at the three of them. It happened so suddenly and so unexpectedly that there wasn't time to think, only to react. In the front seat, Avi could just make out Tzippy spitting and biting and yelling, and he could hear Max grunting next to him, as the subtle sound of clothes being ripped belied it all. The last thing Avi remembered was seeing, out from the corner of his eye, a metal bar speeding towards his face; then everything turned blissfully black.

When Natan came out of the makholet a few minutes later with his cigarettes in his pocket and a grocery bag full of snacks for his friends, his jeep was nowhere to be found and his friends had disappeared.

CHAPTER 19

*"Behold, you are with child and shall bear a son;
you shall call him Ishmael, for the LORD has paid heed
to your suffering. He shall be a wild ass of a man; his
hand against everyone, and everyone's hand against
him."*
—Genesis 16:11-12

Avi came to with a pounding in his head. The sticky feel of dried blood caked the side of his face. He tried to move, but he couldn't. He was tied up, gagged, and blindfolded. His body had been dumped on the ground and he could feel the hardness of it below. He had no idea where he was or who was with him. He tried to adjust himself into a more comfortable position, but he couldn't move.

He panicked.

He had never been good with enclosed spaces; claustrophobia had always been a problem he'd experienced. He broke out in a cold sweat and he felt his heart palpitate in the curiously anxious way it always did whenever he felt constrained.

He felt a body nuzzle him, and he initially recoiled, but he relented when he realized that the body was trying to help him get free. It was a pathetic attempt at help, but it was help nonetheless.

Suddenly, through the thickness of his blindfold, he realized an artificial light had been switched on. The body which had been pressing against him and trying to help him froze. He heard footsteps stride towards him and a violent squelching sound reached his ear.

Whoever had switched on the light had kicked the body trying to help him.

He heard an instantaneous, painful, muffled groan. The footsteps had been clad in boots, maybe they were heavy shoes? Whatever footwear it was that clad the foot which aimed the kick, it was definite that steel-tipped prefixed the noun, for the kicking sound was much too violent to be levied by anything other than steel.

Avi felt a rough hand grope his face and rip the blindfold away. He closed his eyes as the brilliant light of the single light bulb at the center of the room momentarily blinded him, but slowly, his eyes adjusted and he swiveled his pupils around, trying to make sense of the situation.

To his left, he saw Max, doubled over in pain; it was he who had been futilely trying to help Avi and it was he who had been brutally kicked as a result. Avi couldn't see his face, but if Max's ripped clothes were any indication of anything, he was in bad shape. Tzippy lay propped against a wall, caked blood covering the lower portion of her face. Her head hung listlessly and there were deep cuts and bruises all over her person. The unmistakably violent color of purple-blue tinged both of her swollen eyes. Avi moaned involuntarily. The brutality of the scene was overwhelming.

His eyes fluttered around the room. They were in an underground bunker or tunnel of some sort. Coarse mud walls made up the boundaries of the room and the heat and stink of the underground room was unbearable.

He looked up at their captor.

It was a man, dressed entirely in black, with a checkered black and white keffiyah ominously wrapped around his face. The man's eyes were the only part of his face visible, and they were evil and yellow, and they peered out from a soulless body and looked straight down at Avi.

"Ab Ibrahim," the man said softly, reverently, and then he bent over Avi with a glistening knife.

✡

Natan hadn't heard the loud scramble which had taken place outside of the makholet, so when he came outside and found his jeep and friends missing, he was understandably confused.

He scratched his head and saw a gaggle of people conversing excitedly on the street. He moved closer to them and heard snatches of their conversation, which caused his heart to plummet.

"Four masked men—"

"They pulled up alongside the jeep—"

"There was a girl in the front seat—"

"It happened so quickly—"

"A minute or two, tops—"

"I didn't have time to react—"

"I could swear Avi Aveinu was in the backseat—"

"They beat them—"

"They were clearly Arabs—"

"They jumped into the jeep and drove it away—"

"The girl got her face bashed in—"

"I saw them beat the people with big metal bars—"

"It was a kidnapping. It was definitely a kidnapping—"

Natan dropped his bag in horror, walked away from the crowd, pulled his cell phone from his pocket and anxiously dialed the number to the police.

✡

The yellow-eyed man stooped over Avi and placed the knife at Avi's throat.

Terrified, Avi moaned, the sound muffled by the gag which covered his mouth.

The yellow-eyed man picked up Sarah's necklace which hung around Avi's neck with the knife. "What is this, ab Ibrahim? Are you wearing women's jewelry?"

"Michael!" Avi yelled inaudibly through the thickness of his gag.

Michael answered promptly. "Avi, I am here."

"Help us," Avi tried to say, his eyes fixed on the knife in the yellow-eyed man's hand, but through the gag, his words came across muffled.

"I don't know what you're saying," Michael said, distressed. "I am trying to help you, but there is only so much I can do. I am praying for deliverance. Do you hear me? Nod if you understand."

Avi nodded.

The yellow-eyed man dropped the necklace and he looked at Avi closely. "Who are you calling for, ab?" he asked softly. "Who are you nodding to?" He straightened up, strode across the room to the doorway and called out: "Abdullah! Hakim! Ahmed! Khalel!"

Four men ran into the room. Avi recognized them as the ones who had accosted them outside of the makholet.

"Did you search the captives thoroughly?"

The four men nodded.

"Search them again. In my presence."

The men patted down all three captives and stuck their fingers roughly into every bodily crevice which could have concealed anything like a communication device or otherwise.

"There is nothing."

The yellow-eyed man nodded. "Place them all against the wall and undo their gags. It's time to talk."

The men complied. They propped their three captives next to each other against the dirt wall and pulled out their gags.

"Good, good," the yellow-eyed man said.

The four men moved behind the yellow-eyed man, who was clearly the leader and sat on a chair and played with the knife in his hand.

"Do you know why you are here?" he asked softly.

Tzippy and Max looked confused. Avi stayed silent, unwilling to betray that he understood.

The yellow-eyed man nodded knowingly. "I forgot you Jews refuse to learn the language of the great Arab nation." He switched to Hebrew. "Do you know why you are here?"

Tzippy spat on the dirt ground, her spit a reddish-hue. "Because you are a sick *ben zona* with nothing better to do other than kidnap innocent people?"

The yellow-eyed man laughed. "I suppose from your perspective that seems true. But no, my dear girl, you are anything but innocent." His yellow eyes held Tzippy's. "You and your religious friend are infidels and thus are guilty of being outside of Allah's divine protection."

"You're guilty of being completely psycho," Tzippy muttered.

The man's yellow eyes flashed with red anger, but within seconds, they had cooled. "Don't test my patience, little girl. Your people have held ab Ibrahim hostage and forced him to say things he didn't mean. You have made him lie and speak out against the one true faith." The yellow-eyed man looked at Avi expectantly.

Avi coughed. "Anything I said, I meant it."

The yellow-eyed man remained silent for a few moments. "The Zionist war machine has brainwashed you. You are the first Muslim—such statements against the religion of Allah will never be uttered by a prophet of your stature."

Avi laughed throatily. "No one has brainwashed me. You're just proving what I said by kidnapping us and beating us and tying us up. You lack ethics and morals. Sure, you run around screaming monotheism—but monotheism without ethics, morals, and the respect for the sanctity of life is nothing more than evil."

The man's yellow eyes glistened.

"Are you truly ab Ibrahim?"

"I am Avraham Aveinu."

"You are not ab Ibrahim?"

Avi sighed. "I am Avraham, husband of Sarah, son of Terah, father of Isaac and Ishmael, grandfather of Jacob, who was later called Israel, and was my only spiritual heir. Whether one calls me Avi, Avraham Aveinu, Father Abraham, or Ab Ibrahim, it doesn't matter—provided one recognizes the essence of who I am and what I stand for."

"I know who you are what you stand for. You are ab Ibrahim: the first Muslim."

Avi shook his head warily. "I am Avi, the resurrected, the father of the Jewish people."

"I do not contest that. You are the father of the Jews but also of the Muslim people."

"I am sorry, but I am not."

"How can you say such a thing?"

"Spiritually and physically, the Jews are my descendants and none other. Ishmael was my son whom I loved, but he was not chosen to be my spiritual heir."

"But you were the first Muslim! The *Ummah* is yours! How can you deny such an army? Over one billion adherents! You are our spiritual father. You are the first who submitted to Allah. You are the first Muslim."

"No. I am—" Avi stopped speaking and closed his eyes tightly. It was remarkable that it took this terrifying situation to put things into perspective for him. Finally, Avi knew where he fit in this crazy, mixed-up, contemporary world. He breathed in deeply and then, as he exhaled, he opened his eyes and stared the yellow-eyed man directly into his soulless eyes. "I am the first Jew. It is the faith of Israel and the God of Israel whom I recognize and it is the children of Israel who are the inheritors of the Abrahamic legacy. Their numbers may be small, but is to them that I belong. I am theirs and they are mine; I am the first Jew."

The yellow-eyed man was taken aback. "You say this," he said quietly, "with all the conviction in the world."

"I say it because it is true."

"You have been brainwashed. The Zionists have done this to you."

"Believe what you wish. I have told you the truth."

"You are the first Muslim. Avraham Aveinu or ab Ibrahim, it matters not. You are the first Muslim and you must join the Islamic world and show that Islam is superior to every other religion in every way. You must let go of the fallacies injected into your head by the Zionists and give us the legitimacy that only you can bestow."

"Why must you validate yourself and your religion by invalidating someone else's?"

"We have superseded Christianity and Judaism. It is not a matter of invalidating anyone else. Ours is the true religion; theirs and all others are false."

Avi sighed, but didn't answer.

"Why did Allah send you back if not to join the armies of Islam?"

"I came to locate the mashiach."

The yellow-eyed man nodded. "Yes, I read in the Israeli newspapers you said that was the reason for your return. But you also said that the masih was not Jesus, alayhi s-salaam?"

"No, he is not."

"Ab Ibrahim, you are mistaken."

Avi shook his head. "I assure you I am not."

"The Qu'ran explicitly says the masih who came before and who shall return is the prophet Jesus, alayhi s-salaam."

"Well, I am sorry to say this, but you are mistaken."

"I see." The yellow-eyed man nodded at Tzippy and Max. "You've identified the masih as one of these two, not so?"

Avi answered carefully. "I am not sure."

"The Zionists seem to think that they, and one other, are candidates for this position."

Avi sighed.

"Ab Ibrahim, you sadden me."

"You sadden me."

"Why is that?"

"This unnecessary violence and hate."

"The Zionists have started it."

"How?"

"They dare rise above their inferior status and challenge the supremacy of Islam by establishing a state on Islamic *Waqf*, ab Ibrahim! The land they live on was given to us by Allah. If they wish to live here, they must do so under *dhimmi* status."

Avi shook his head. "This land is their ancestral homeland. Let's ignore the religious connotations and arguments—"

"You cannot ignore the religiousness of this conflict, ab Ibrahim. It is the raison d'etre of our hate and disdain for the Zionists."

Avi sighed. "You shouldn't hate anyone. It's not the way of God. Love your neighbor; love the stranger. Love, love, love. Love as God is love. This was my teaching."

"The Qu'ran does not speak of this."

"The Torah does."

The yellow-eyed man stared at Avi. "You are not the warrior for Allah I imagined you to be; a man who would strike fear and terror in the hearts of the infidels. I did not expect you to be a weakling and to side with the Zionists."

Avi shook his head. "God can fight His own wars. He doesn't need minions. He is all-powerful."

"He has commanded us to expand *dar al-Islam*, ab Ibrahim, through any means necessary. Or have you forgotten the words of Allah to you when you first traversed the earth?"

"God never commanded me to expand anything." Avi sighed. "Your accounts from my life are incredibly flawed and misconstrued."

"The Zionists have swayed you from the true path, ab Ibrahim. You have forgotten the words of Allah."

"My God will never sanction what you have done here today: kidnapping innocent people; beating them; torturing them. It goes against the very nature of God; it goes against the very nature of who I am."

"None can fathom the nature of God. He has given us the direction and laws to live a perfect life. If Allah commands us to kill the infidels, we do it."

"But that isn't humane."

The yellow eyed-man shrugged. "Our rationale is not Allah's rationale."

"Allah doesn't sound like he values justice very much."

"We cannot discern Allah's thoughts. If Allah decrees something, then, by default, it is justice."

"But surely you can think for yourself and see that some of these decrees violate your own internal conscience? Your heart tells you what is right and what is wrong. You can't do what you've done today and think that God commands you to do this."

"Human nature must be transcended," the yellow-eyed man said patiently. "Our base instinct is to be self-serving, but Allah has given us the pathway to ascend above this and become the great creature which he wishes us to be. Instead of spending days doing whatever we want, we are taught discipline by praying five times a day. By nature, man is selfish, but Allah has commanded we rise above this and give alms to the poor. Man instinctively feels pity for fellow human beings when they suffer, but Allah has taught us that we must inflict justice upon others when they reject him and our prophet. Man inherently shuns death, but Allah teaches us that death is the greatest gift he has bestowed upon us, as it is the portal through which we enter paradise for eternity. The nature of man is base, ab Ibrahim—it is only through Islam that we submit to the will of Allah and transcend our animalistic urges." The yellow-eyed man looked at Max and Tzippy. "Tell me, Zionists, do you agree with me?"

The cousins didn't answer. The yellow-eyed man noticed Tzippy tremble and he zeroed in on her. "Girl—Tzipporah. Do you agree with me?"

She looked at him through her swollen eyes. "No."

"Why not?"

"It's wrong to torture other people and to take vigilante justice in one's own hands."

"It is wrong to violate the true religion."

"How have I violated your religion?"

"You refuse to recognize its superiority and join it, thus, you violate it."

"Because I ignore your religion, I violate it?"

"Yes."

"I have nothing to do with your warped sense of thinking, you evil man. I violate nothing. I respect your right to your religion. Why can't you respect me as I am?"

"What are you? A Jew?"

"I'm Tzipporah Feldman—a girl who loves life and wants to live."

The yellow-eyed man laughed softly. "This life is but a passing illusion when compared with the bounties of heaven that us Muslims will enjoy for eternity. It is the next life that we yearn for. Death is a gift from Allah."

Max looked at the yellow-eyed man defiantly and spoke for the first time. "Our lives are gifts from God."

"Your deaths will be a gift to the one true God," the yellow-eyed man said, his voice sharp as steel. "You Zionists crave life, but we, the *muhajideen*, crave death where we can be in the presence of Allah. It has always been your greatest error—this illogical emphasis on this world when there is a better world to come."

"No one knows what's on the other side of death," Avi interjected softly.

"Did you not return from Paradise?"

"I don't know where I came from. I just know that I was reborn into life a few months ago. That's all I know."

"Allah knew you would succumb and join the Zionists, so, he has made you forget the wonders of Paradise."

"God made me forget the wonders of the World to Come because it is not the concern of this world. This is the life which we live; this is the life which is important."

"And I agree. This life is important as a transition to the next."

"No. You don't understand—"

"No, *you* don't understand," the yellow-eyed man hissed. "None of you understand. You will never understand my actions, my thoughts, my world-view. You will never understand any of my people because you erroneously think that we think like you do." He

413

closed his eyes and then re-opened them with fresh hate coating his yellowed-eyes. "Enough of this foolish debate. I have wasted enough time on this."

The yellow-eyed man signaled his minions. They roughly picked up Tzippy and Max and made them stand, then dragged Avi by the collar to the other side of the room. They brought in a video camera on a tripod and placed it directly across from the cousins.

"What are you doing?" Avi asked.

Tzippy and Max, though their hands were bound, managed to hold fingers and they looked each other in the eye.

"What are you doing?" Avi asked again, more querulously.

The yellow-eyed man knelt next to Avi. "Do you know what the *dajjal* is?" he asked quietly in Arabic.

"It's the Islamic antichrist."

"Yes, do you know who the dajjal shall be?"

Comprehension dawned on Avi's face. "Please, no," he begged.

The yellow-eyed man nodded. "The Jewish masih will stand opposing the true masih: the prophet Jesus, alayhi s-salaam, when he returns. The Jews will call on their false masih—the dajjal—to wage war upon the Ummah and to spill the blood of Muslims. These two are the dajjal. They must die before they inflict their terror upon my people."

"No, no, no," Avi moaned. "You have it all wrong. They've never done anything to you; they've never done anything to any Muslims; they have no thoughts of war or killing in their heads; they don't even think they're the masih! Please, I beg of you. Don't do this."

414

The yellow-eyed man put out his hand and brushed the side of Avi's face gently. "It is a blessing, really. They will be given the option to say the *Shahada* and repent from their ways before they are freed from this life—it is up to them to say it and enter Allah's heavenly abode or face an eternity in the fires of *jahannam*. It is their choice."

"Please no, I beg of you," Avi mumbled and tears slipped down his face. "This is wrong. They aren't the masih; they never claimed to be. They aren't your dajjal. You are making a mistake—a grave mistake!"

"Perhaps they are not the dajjal. But they are Israeli; they are Yahudi—their deaths will bring glory to Allah's name."

The yellow-eyed man pushed a piece of cloth into Avi's mouth and quickly tied another gag around his face. "I prefer silence from you from now, ab Ibrahim." He kissed Avi gently on both cheeks, then turned to face Max and Tzippy.

✡

Within minutes of Natan's call, personnel from the Shin Bet had picked him up outside of the makholet where the incident had occurred and a nation-wide search was underway. The news of the kidnapping of Avi and the ultra-Orthodox and Reform candidates for the mashiach spread like wildfire. News vans screeched up and down the country's roads, following leads, following tips, following the IDF wherever it went. The situation became increasingly menacing as no terrorists group stepped forward to claim responsibility for the kidnapping, and it became even more terrifying that no ransom had been made for the hostages. No one wanted to admit it out loud, but the thought lingered at the back of everyone's minds: they kidnappers did not call for a ransom, because the kidnappers did not intend to let the hostages go.

Despite the spate of rockets assaulting Israel for the past week, the government had not retaliated. But with this act, the Israeli Prime Minister had had enough. The kidnapping of three persons who meant so much to the Jewish people as a whole was not something he or his cabinet was going to take lying down. Already, all ports of entry and exit into and from the country were closed, and now he authorized the ground entry of Israeli troops into the West Bank and Gaza. The Israeli Air Force dropped leaflets into the invaded areas, outlining to the Palestinian citizens that this was not war and that the Israeli forces were entering only for the purpose of locating its kidnapped people.

Never before had so much effort been put into a search, and within two hours, the Shin Bet had secured the information as to where Avi, Tzippy, and Max had been taken: they were being held in an underground tunnel near the Rafah Crossing between the Gaza Strip and Egypt by an unknown Islamist terrorist organization. Despite the breakdown of relations between Israel and Egypt due to Avi's controversial statements, the Egyptian authorities collaborated willingly with their Israeli counterpart. Avi was equally as important to them as he was to the Israelis, and they were anxious for his safe and speedy recovery.

The IDF forces that had entered the West Bank were instructed to immediately withdraw back into Israel, and the strength of the Israeli military was focused in on Gaza: where the hostages were being held. An enormous Israeli battalion was poised and ready to go further into the Gaza Strip from the north, while the Egyptian army was coordinately ready to enter from the south.

It was projected that the patriarch and his two friends would be rescued within the hour.

✡

"Avi, be still. I am here," Michael said softly. "I am with you."

Avi wanted desperately to scream; to yell at the men to not do this; to beg them to free Tzippy and Max and kill him instead; to beg Michael to intervene, perform an angelic miracle and rescue Tzippy and Max, but with his mouth stuffed and gagged, he had no means to communicate with the men, with Tzippy and Max, or with his angel.

Tears cascaded down Avi's face and he projected his thoughts upwards—to the only Being Who could hear him in his time of need. He prayed to his God, with all the hope and yearning he could muster in himself, for deliverance.

✡

The yellow-eyed man loaded a gun with bullets and then nodded to one of his henchmen, who stepped forward, went behind the camera, focused it on Tzippy and Max, and switched it on. Another of the men went to the cousins and pulled their gags off of their mouths. The other two men pulled guns out of their robes and held them in their hands ominously. The yellow-eyed man positioned himself next to the camera, staying out of the shot.

"*Alhamduillah*," he said in Arabic. Tzippy and Max continued to hold fingers as best they could, but they turned their attention to the yellow-eyed man. "My men and I have been blessed by Allah, the all-knowing, all merciful, who has delivered to us the two dajjals of the Zionist regime. As Allah was merciful, so, too, am I merciful, and before I execute these infidels for their crimes against the Muslim Ummah, I offer them the gift of repentance." He switched to Hebrew, "Son and daughter of pigs and apes, I grant you the boon of redemption from your sins. I give you the option to say the Shahada before you die: to say that there is no god but Allah and Muhammad was his final messenger—to submit and accept Islam unto yourselves. Say this and you shall be forgiven of all sins and when you die, your souls will ascend to heaven."

Tzippy and Max turned to look at each other, their bound hands intertwined. Neither of them answered the yellow-eyed man.

"Do you understand what I said?"

They didn't answer.

"It is your choice."

"We are Jews," Tzippy said quietly in English. "And if we have to do die, we will die Jews."

The yellow-eyed man laughed. "I should have known. As the Qur'an says of you Jews: 'We cursed them and made their hearts hard', and your own Torah says you are a stiff-necked and stubborn people. I shouldn't have expected anything from my generosity. You refuse to submit to Allah—that is your choice." He shrugged and then went in front of the camera, his face still hidden by the keffiyah. He switched to Arabic again. "'The punishment of those who wage war against Allah and his apostle and strive to make mischief in the land is only this: that they should be murdered or crucified or their hands and their feet should be cut off on opposite sides or they should be imprisoned; this shall be as a disgrace for them in this world, and in the hereafter, they shall have a grievous chastisement.'" He turned from the camera and leveled his gun at the cousins. "O dajjals of the Zionist war machine, you have warred against the Muslim Ummah, against our prophet, and against Allah. The judgment is death in accordance with Sharia law."

✡

Natan breathed a sigh of relief when he heard that the location where Avi, Tzippy, and Max were being held had been uncovered. He was sitting in the office of the Prime Minister, slightly to the side and out of the way of all the bustling people, but he listened intently to the rapid unraveling of events.

He was desperate and anxious that his friends would be home soon. Though he had not known them for very long, they had become the biggest part of his life. People don't go through the adventures and mishaps that they four did without establishing a truly deep, familial bond—and that was exactly how Natan viewed his three friends: as family. Yes, there was a direct linkage between him and Avi, but the fact was, Avi represented the unmistakable truth that Tzippy and Max were also family: they were all part of one nation—one nation which had sprung from the loins of one man.

They were family.

He couldn't help but feel responsible for the kidnapping. He should have never stopped for cigarettes; he should have been aware that there had been people stalking them. There was no way that this was an impromptu kidnapping. He was only thankful now that his friends had been found.

He sat quietly on the side and for the first time in many years, Natan closed his eyes and whispered, "Baruch HaShem." He then turned to his boyfriend and kissed him, full on the lips.

Everyone in the room applauded.

✡

Tzippy and Max held on desperately to each other's fingers, despite the cords which bound their wrists. They turned their attention from the yellow-eyed man and looked at each other.

"So, this is it?" Max asked.

Tzippy smiled. "Not unless the Mossad storms here in the next, oh, say, sixty seconds."

"Any regrets?"

"Only that my child wouldn't have the chance to be born." A tear slipped down her face.

Max smiled sadly. He looked across the room. He could hear the yellow-eyed man speaking in Arabic to the camera. He didn't know what was being said, but he knew that his and Tzippy's death sentences were being passed. He looked across the room at Avi, where he lay, bound and gagged, his eyes closed tight. At that moment, Avi opened his eyes in frantic terror.

Max smiled at him.

The yellow-eyed man had stopped talking. Together with the other two men who held guns, they lifted their arms and aimed at Tzippy and Max.

"Thanks for being part of my life, cousin," Tzippy said, her voice struggling to stay steady.

Max swallowed deeply and looked back into his cousin's eyes. "I love you, cousin."

"*Am Yisrael chai.*" The people of Israel live. Tzippy's voice cracked.

"*Shema Yisrael Adonai Elokenu Adonai echad,*" Max sang softly. "*Baruch Shem k'vod malkhuto—*" Hear, Israel, the Lord our God, the Lord is one. Blessed be the Name of his kingdom—.

The men fired their guns.

CHAPTER 20

"'Fear not, Abram, I am a shield to you'."
—Genesis 15:1

Avi closed his eyes. The guns kept firing, over and over and over again—and in the small space, the terrifying scream of the guns, as they emitted their bullets and cut through the air, blotted out all other sounds. Avi felt the reverberating thud of the falling bodies. Blood splattered over him. He screamed from behind his gag, but he knew that no one could hear him.

He felt the neshama of his descendants exit the world.

He could not look.

Gagged as he was, he could not speak, but he felt the presence of his angel wrapped around his body—and at the same time, he felt the terror arise sharply from inside of himself.

No tears emanated from his eyes, but the sadness was overwhelming. Unable to speak, he continued to direct his thoughts to his Maker.

"My God, my God—why have You forsaken me?" he screamed inside his head.

The still, cool Voice of Avi's God answered him inside his head. "I have not forsaken you, Avraham. I am always with you. I am the Lord, your God."

✡

Avi clenched his eyes tightly, still aware that he was in that horrifying room under the ground somewhere, but in shutting his eyes, he hoped to contain the Presence of his God which has descended and spoke to him in the impenetrable, innermost thoughts of his mind. Unable to speak, Avi frantically answered through his thoughts. "You have come!"

"I am always with you."

"Why didn't you save them, Lord? Why did you let this happen?"

"It was their time, My child."

"It didn't have to happen. You could have stepped in. You could've struck those terrorists down. You didn't have to let them die, Lord. You didn't."

"Who made the choice to kill them? I have given man Free Will: the ultimate choice resides in the hearts of men. Each man, woman, and child is the master of his or her own destiny. Those men made the choice to end the lives of Tzipporah and Max. I had no part to play in this atrocity. I allow evil to happen, but it is not My will."

"It's not fair, Lord."

"It was Tzippy's and Max's time. They accepted that."

"Why? Why was it their time?"

"The reasons behind the how, why, and when all born and all die is not for man to know in this reality. Accept that it just is."

"I've been through this before. I've lost people close to me—and it doesn't get any easier."

"Death is never an easy thing."

"You still could've saved them. They were so young. And Tzippy was pregnant."

"It was their time."

"You brought me back to suffer."

"I brought you back to live."

"And suffer."

"It is a part of living. It builds character; it propels growth."

"These are just words. They do nothing to ease the ache inside of me."

"Would you feel comforted to know that Tzippy and Max are with Me now?"

"They died a horrible death. Nothing can take that away."

"They lived full lives. They fulfilled their purpose."

"Why have You come to me now?"

"I am always with you."

"I've prayed to you numerous times since I returned. I begged You to give me clearer directions regarding the mashiach and You didn't answer."

"I always answer."

"I didn't hear any answer."

"I exist in stillness and perfect calm."

"I am anything but still and calm now, thank You very much. And yet, You've showed up."

"It is only now that you truly listen to hear My Voice; I am not a God of force or imposition. I am always with you; always there for you; always speaking—but it is up to every man to hear My Voice. You shut out everything else, despite the horrors of this room and you hear Me. The choice was always yours as to when you'd listen."

"You are here to take me back to heaven, aren't You?"

"I cannot answer that. Life is meant to be lived. For you, the future remains unscripted."

"But You know the outcome."

"Yes."

"Then just tell me."

"That I cannot tell you. It is up to the men who are the architects of this scene."

"But You know everything. You hear the thoughts of my mind when not even my guardian angel can."

"Not everything is meant to be known."

"It would be nice to know, though."

"I suppose."

"They are going to kill me, aren't they?"

"It is their intention, yes."

"Would they succeed?"

"We will have to wait and see."

"I haven't accomplished what You asked of me. I've failed."

"You have never failed Me, Avraham, My friend. You did what I asked you to do."

"No, Lord. You asked me to find the mashiach, Lord, and I couldn't do it. It remains an unsolved mystery. I don't know who it is. Will You tell me who it is, now that we are on speaking terms; now that I'm so near the end? It's Natan, isn't it? Tzippy and Max died because they were never meant to be the mashiach. It was Natan all along. Right?"

"What was my directive to you in the cave concerning your mission?"

"You said, 'The era of mashiach is here. I need you to make known to mashiach that I have called and it is time to answer.'"

"Exactly. Michael conveyed exactly what I said to you."

"I don't understand, Lord."

"How did I tell you to identify the mashiach?"

"You said that the neshama I encounter upon exiting the cave will be mashiach; I will know I have found mashiach and mashiach will answer me."

"Precisely."

"You are being willfully ambiguous. Is Natan the mashiach?"

"Did you know you'd found mashiach when you identified him as such? Or what about when you hypothesized that mashiach were all three of your friends? Did you know you'd found mashiach? Or were you still unsure? Did Natan answer your call? Avraham, I never used the definite article of 'the'—I told you that your mission concerns mashiach. I never said 'the mashiach'. Nor did I tell you that the mashiach was the first neshama you encountered after venturing into the world. I merely said 'neshama'."

"I don't understand, Lord."

"There is no "the mashiach'. There is only mashiach."

"I still don't understand."

"It is a riddle which you must solve, Avraham. I have given you the tools, but I can only direct you. Use the tools I have equipped you with; use the intelligence I have blessed you with; follow your heart. I've sent you advisors who've given you huge clues as to who and what mashiach truly is: Natan's Saba, Pastor Yuvie, Zahira, even this yellow-eyed man here—they altogether compositely point you to mashiach. Ponder my directives; ponder my instructions, and you will discern the answer in yourself. When you have found the truth, call mashiach and mashiach shall answer."

"What's the sense? I am about to die anyway."

"Only I know when the time of a person's death shall be."

"You just said they intend to kill me and that You aren't going to save me. I think it's pretty safe to project that my death will happen anywhere within the next few minutes."

426

"Man not only has the capacity for bad Avraham; he also has the capacity for good. Where some choose to maim, torture, and kill, others choose to uplift, rescue, and help. I am with you. I am always with you. I will never leave you. Even at your darkest moments, I am there. Feel my presence surround you and fear no man. You are the friend of God; you are Avraham of old, resurrected by My grace, to do My bidding. I am with you, My friend. Keep still. Stay at peace. Now open your eyes."

Avraham blinked his eyes open and saw the figure of the yellow-eyed man stoop over him.

✡

The yellow-eyed man smiled benevolently and stroked the side of Avi's face gently. "Ab Ibrahim, we have succeeded. We have defeated the dajjal. Allah has been most gracious to us."

Still gagged, Avi could only look at the man's yellow eyes.

"Aren't you happy?"

Avi shook his head.

"But we have defeated the dajjal, ab Ibrahim. We have won."

Avi shook his head again.

"You are displeased with our success?"

Avi nodded.

The yellow-eyed man sighed. "You persist in disowning Islam, despite the obvious triumph that Islam has secured before your very eyes over the infidels. I do not understand it." He hesitated and then reached down and pulled the gag off of Avi's face. Avi spat out the piece of cloth which had been stuffed into his mouth and coughed.

"I am sorry we had to be so rough with you."

Avi didn't answer.

"Please, Ab Ibrahim. Speak."

"And say what?" Avi asked, his voice devoid of emotion.

"I wish to hear your thoughts."

"I am uncomfortable, bound as I am."

"I am sorry, but it is preferable that we keep you tied up."

"Why? It's five of you against me."

"You will stay bound."

"Suit yourself. If you're scared of me, that's your business."

"I am not afraid of anyone."

"Ok."

The yellow-eyed man stood. His face was covered with the blood of his victims. "You are as infuriating as the girl—Tzipporah."

"Well, she is my descendant—was my descendant." Avi stopped himself from looking over at Tzippy's mangled body.

"As am I."

"You are not."

The yellow-eyed man furrowed his eyebrows. "Yes I am. My family can trace descent through Muhammad, *sal-Allahu alayhi wa-salaam*, and he was descended from you."

"I've never met Muhammad to tell if he was descended from me, but I can assure you: *you* are not. You do not have the special spiritual spark within you that identifies who is and who isn't one of my descendants."

428

The man's yellow eyes flashed with anger. "You've insulted me."

"I am only being truthful."

"When you were brought to me, I imagined you shouting for joy at being rescued from the Zionist pigs. I imagined you helping me kill the dajjal. I imagined announcing you to the Islamic world and having the first Muslim come home to his true religion. I imagined you embracing me as your child. None of these things have happened."

"You didn't rescue me, you kidnapped me. You didn't kill any dajjal, you murdered my friends. I am not the first Muslim, so you couldn't announce me to the Muslim world in that regard. I cannot embrace you as my child, as you are not of my family."

"And I suppose you will stand by what you said: that Allah is not your God?"

"The Allah whom you worship isn't my God. The way you conceive him to be—he cannot be my God."

"What are you saying exactly?"

"Every man has a different concept of who God is—we all imagine Him in a different way, and thus, exalt Him in a different way. Despite that, there are certain infallible truths about His Essence and Existence which are standard throughout our varying understandings of Who He is. Supreme, Just, Merciful, and the Giver of life are some of His attributes. He compels us to choose life, to understand the sanctity of it and to preserve it at all costs. The one you worship, who calls on you to murder innocents, who has no innate sense of justice and mercy, is not the God of Avraham; it is not the God of a pious and earnest Muslim. The Allah you call upon has none of the attributes of my God or the Allah of a good Muslim."

"How can you say such a thing? The Allah I worship is the supreme creator of all things. His essence and existence cannot be understood—his reasoning is above our understanding. If he commands us to kill the infidel, then, we do it. His reason is not our reason, he is above petty human attempts at reasoning."

"God has blessed us all with the ability to reason—we are created in His image, and as the ultimate Reason, we are mirrors of that attribute of His."

"Blasphemy, Ab Ibrahim. We are not created in his image for Allah has no image; he is formless."

"I am speaking about our intellect, of course. Not about our physical exteriors."

"It is a dire sin to even metaphorically attribute human characteristics on him. Allah is the supreme will, and if he reasons something to be good that goes against our inferior intellect, then, it is good."

"Even if it contradicts our consciences—our intelligence?"

"He is supreme and unfathomable."

Avi sighed. "It amazes me that you think like this. Such hate towards human reasoning."

"But a love for Allah—who is pure will and therefore, pure reason."

"This Allah of yours sounds capricious and petty, and he uses supremacy to explain away his illogical nature."

The yellow-eyed man looked at Avi sadly. "We are taught that the prophets were all perfect, and you, as ab Ibrahim, were one of them. You were supposed to be a man perfect in stature and countenance, doing everything pleasing to Allah. Yet you violate him by casting such aspersions on his character."

"Perfection is subjective. Everyone's perception of the ideal state of 'perfection' is different. What one views as perfect, another man may view as imperfect. You cannot expect the entire world to follow one creed. We are all created differently—with different strengths, weaknesses, backgrounds, cultures, personalities, and nationalities. We must embrace the diversity of each other and celebrate it; not try to stamp our image of perfection on other people and judge them when they fall short of our standards."

"The Qu'ran has given us the instructions on how to live a perfect life. It tells us what is perfect and what is not. There is no middle ground to this. No man will ever be as perfect as the prophets were, but we must try."

Avi shook his head vehemently. "You want to know what the prophets did? How they thought? You have one right here in front of you—and I'm telling you, there is no such thing as perfection in any man. There is only the struggle to be good and to do good. That is what we must all strive for, using our own gifts, abilities, and talents to do so. Do not emulate another person. His or her situation was different from yours. Each man and woman is created uniquely; each man and woman must find their own way to reach goodness."

"We emulate the prophet, for he was perfect and everything about him was good."

"He was who he was. You are who you are. It's never too late. Be the best that you can be. Don't try to be someone else."

"The Qu'ran—"

"Stop! Please! Stop! And for once, just use your own head! Not every bit of knowledge comes from the Qu'ran!"

"The Qu'ran is the perfect book. It contains all knowledge."

Avi sighed. "You are missing what I am saying."

"And you are denying the authenticity of the good book, in addition to having denied Allah, through whose mercy you were resurrected."

"I am trying to make you think for yourself and stop aiming for ridiculous measures of 'perfection'!" Avi shunted his chin out towards the bodies of his slain friends. "This is what perfection is? Us, stuck here in this stifled, confined room under the ground somewhere like weasels, while the blood of two innocent children whom you murdered soaks the dirt floor? This is what you call 'perfection'?"

The yellow-eyed man stared at Avi. "The perfect book was given to us by our perfect prophet who followed our perfect Allah. Our book tells us to be perfect and it tells us how to aim for perfection. And that includes the directives on how to deal with those who hinder our attempts to perfect ourselves in emulation of all the prophets who set the example for us." The man nodded at his henchman who grabbed Avi up into a standing position. "I am sorry, Ab Ibrahim, but in this life, you are not the prophet you were in your previous life. 'See how they forge the lie against Allah, and this is sufficient as a manifest sin'."

"Sura 4, verse 50."

"Yes. That's what you're doing; that's what you've done."

"I've forged lies against Allah?"

"Yes."

"So, I guess I'm going to get the same verdict as my friends? Guilty and thus given the death penalty?"

"It is the only way. The ab Ibrahim of yesterday was a man of untold virtue and strength—the greatest Muslim of his time; the Avi of today is an infidel."

"Do what you must."

Avi bowed his head and closed his eyes, prepared to die a second time. He had known it was coming to this. Surprisingly, he felt at peace. He may not have figured out who the mashiach was, but his God was with him. This he knew. He prayed only that his death would come quickly and he wouldn't suffer much pain.

He heard the sounds of the guns being loaded. He heard the men debate whether they were doing the right thing. He heard them yell *"Allahu ackbar!"* and he waited for the bullets to cut through the air and splice into his flesh as they'd done only a few moments before to his two friends.

He waited and listened, but the guns were not shot.

He could hear the sound of footsteps trampling the earth above him. He opened his eyes and saw his captors looking up. He looked up as well, and then, suddenly, the ceiling above him caved in and a troupe of IDF and Egyptian soldiers deftly descended into the hole. His captors screamed and fired their guns at the surprise visitors, who shot back with ease. The smoke cleared, and, lying next to the badly mangled bodies of Avi's two friends, were the equally dead bodies of three of his captors. The yellow-eyed man and one other man lay on the ground, bleeding, but not dead. Soldiers clamped handcuffs on them and paramedics rushed to tend to them. They would stand trial for their heinous crimes in an Israeli court of justice and would spend the rest of their lives in prison.

Avi lifted his eyes up to the night sky which glowed through the newly created opening above and thanked his God for sending him help.

"You're welcome," God replied.

CHAPTER 21

*"As for Ishmael, I have heeded you. I hereby
bless him. I will make him fertile and exceedingly
numerous. He shall be the father of twelve chieftains,
and I will make of him a great nation. But My covenant I
will maintain with Isaac, whom Sarah shall bear to you."*
—Genesis 17:20

Avi lay quietly in the back of the ambulance
which drove him across the rough desert terrain. He
could hear the sound of sirens wailing alongside his
vehicle, and the helicopters chopping away above.
Through the darkly tinted window, he could just make
out the flashing lights. An intense retinue of security
surrounded his ambulance.

Avi sighed and wrapped his arms around his
chest.

The paramedic, a mid-twenty-year-old Egyptian
man, smiled down at him.

"Well, you seem to be relatively ok, despite the
superficial injuries which should be healed within the
next week." The paramedic handed Avi a cup of water.
"You were rescued in the nick of time."

Avi didn't respond. He drank his water slowly,
then tried to sit up.

The paramedic stalled him. "Whoa, there. You
can sit up when we get to Egypt. For now, just rest."

Avi nodded and closed his eyes. Now that he
was out of immediate danger, he could reflect upon the
true horror of what he had just been through: finally,
what had transpired in that hellish room under the
ground sunk in. Images of Tzippy and Max in their final
moments, clasping fingers, floated through his head. An
involuntary tear slipped out of his eye.

"Are you alright?" the paramedic asked, anxiously. "Are we driving too fast? Are you feeling pain, ab Ibrahim?"

"My name is Avi." He kept his eyes shut. Another tear dribbled out of his eye.

"Avi," the paramedic said cautiously, "is everything ok?"

Avi clenched his mouth shut. He nodded.

"Were they very awful to you?"

Avi swallowed and nodded again.

"The two Israelis they murdered—they were your friends?"

Avi nodded.

"I am sorry."

The Israeli soldier who sat next to the driver turned around. "Let him rest," he barked at the paramedic. "Stop badgering him."

Avi opened his eyes and turned his head to the soldier. "He's not badgering me. He's just making conversation."

Mollified, the soldier whipped back around.

The paramedic brightened. "Thank you."

"You weren't badgering me. I'm just not in a talkative mood."

The paramedic nodded. "You should rest. You've been through a lot."

Avi closed his eyes and tried to still his mind. He desperately wanted to talk to his God, but he couldn't hear the Voice. His thoughts were encumbered with the memory of his late friends.

The ambulance slowed down and came to a stop.

"Why are we stopping?" Avi asked.

"We are at the border crossing."

"What does that mean?"

"We are going to enter Egypt, and you'll be flown into Israel from there."

Avi gulped. He didn't know how he felt about going back to Israel. For one, only a few hours ago, he had been trying to escape Israel, and secondly, everything about Israel now reminded him painfully of his two recently murdered friends who had been the center of his world since his resurrection. A look of apprehension crossed his face.

"What's wrong?" the paramedic asked.

Avi looked at the man. "I was running away from Israel before those—those terrorists kidnapped us."

"Running away to go where?"

"I don't know. Anywhere but Israel."

"How come?"

"Too many people were angry with me there."

"Why were they angry?"

"I put my foot in my mouth too many times."

"You must be quite flexible."

Avi stared at him blankly. "What?"

"Sorry. Humor is my go-to strategy. It helps me cope."

"With what?"

"With everything—with life."

"Surely you can't have been through anything as terrible as the horrors that I experienced tonight?"

The paramedic looked down. "I've lost my entire family to terrorists. I know what it is to suffer."

Avi looked at the man sympathetically. "And you cope with humor?"

"I cope with laughter. Smile and the world smiles with you—frown and you frown alone. It is an age-old truth."

Avi considered. "Yes, I suppose you're right."

"Try it."

Avi hesitated.

"Just smile, Avi."

Avi forced himself to smile.

The paramedic smiled back at him. "See? That wasn't so hard."

Avi smiled wider.

"Even better."

"I do feel less sad."

"Keep smiling—you'll see. It will help you cope. You look so different when you smile."

"How?"

"Easy, happy—just like the photo that Time magazine had of you."

Avi flushed. "You saw that?"

"I'm a bit of a fan."

"Oh."

"Not that I want your autograph or anything," the paramedic said hastily, "you just seem so real and normal. You seem like you'd be a great friend."

Avi didn't know how to answer.

The ambulance started and drove off.

The paramedic pulled the blinds apart and peered outside. "We've crossed the border. You are in Egypt."

"I guess there are a lot of people in Egypt who are angry with me as well."

The paramedic shrugged. "People will always be annoyed with public figures one way or the other. You can't please everyone."

Avi nodded.

"We don't have long before we reach to where the helicopter is waiting to take you to Israel. You can rest if you want."

Avi shook his head. "I can't rest. My thoughts are churning too much inside my head."

"Better out than in—that's what my mother always said."

Avi hesitated.

"There's always Someone there to listen." The paramedic pointed upwards. "Or you can talk to someone who is tangibly right in front of you, if you want." He grinned and pointed to himself. "I'm no psychiatrist, but I've got a pair of ears that work just fine."

Avi laughed. He breathed in, and in the next fifteen minutes, managed to tell the paramedic everything he'd been through in the past few days, which culminated in the double murder of his two friends. "I don't know how to go back to Israel now," he said, summarily. "Too many memories. Too much to deal with."

"So, what do you want to do?"

"I still kind of wouldn't mind being someplace other than Israel right now and return when all of this balagan dies down."

"Problems always catch up with us, no matter how far or how fast we run."

"That's true, but—"

"No buts. It's true. Full-stop."

"What I was going to say was that I wasn't really running away, per se. I just wanted to get away from them temporarily."

"*Hookah, nargila.* Same thing."

Avi laughed and nodded again.

"Sort your problems. Face your fears. Make your wrongs right. You can lead the camel to the water, but you can't make it drink. Walk a mile in my shoes. There's a pot of gold at the end of every rainbow. I'll never let go, Jack, I'll never let go." The paramedic made a face.

"You're right."

The paramedic nodded knowingly. "It's a feather in my turban." He patted his bare head and smiled.

The ambulance pulled into smooth ground and then halted.

"I think we're here," the paramedic said.

Avi smiled falteringly. "Thank you for all your help. With my body and with my mind."

The paramedic blushed. "Anytime." He pulled a business card out from his pocket. "If you decide you want to leave Israel after you've sorted your problems and you want to come back to Egypt, look me up," he said shyly, placing the card in Avi's hand.

Avi looked at the card and then looked at the paramedic and broke out in a genuine smile. He had no idea who this kind Egyptian stranger was—whether he prayed to Allah or Jesus or Jehovah or even the moon that shone above. This man practiced the religion of loving-kindness, and thus, he was Avi's kin, through and through. "You're an angel," Avi said softly, and he sat up and hugged the paramedic. "That's what I'll do. I'll go back to Israel and sort my problems. And I will definitely come back to Egypt and visit you. You can count on that."

"Insha'Allah."

CHAPTER 22

"Sarah said, 'God has brought me laughter; everyone who hears will laugh with me.' And she added, 'Who would have said to Abraham that Sarah would suckle children! Yet I have borne a son in his old age'."
—Genesis 21:6-7

The helicopter flew Avi across the Sinai, directly to Eilat. He boarded an airplane at the Eilat Airport, which took him to Ben Gurion Airport, where he spent an hour being thoroughly debriefed by IDF officials. He was then driven directly to Jerusalem. It had been a bittersweet experience for Avi to be on a plane without his friends. Had things gone according to plan, he would have been up in the air somewhere, with his three friends at his side, happily flying towards some exotic destination. But that was not how things had panned out—and more than anyone else, Avi knew from his cumulative experiences that life always had a way of throwing a curve ball into things, just for the heck of it.

It was a subdued Israel that Avi returned to. The populace was overjoyed that their patriarch had been found, rescued, and returned to them in relatively one piece—all remembrance of his gaffed statements thrown to the wind—but the news of Tzippy's and Max's murders had tempered what should have been, otherwise, tenacious joy. Israel had lost too many soldiers; too many of her people had been sadistically lost throughout the millennia. As a people, they were bound by the tragedy of all the deaths that they had suffered—and this was an even more poignant loss, for the two victims in their candidacy roles had become enormously celebrated figures in the past few weeks, and there was nary an Israeli or Jew worldwide who hadn't heard the names of Tzipporah and Max Feldman. The violent execution of two such well-known personalities profoundly affected the whole nation, regardless of where individual religious loyalties (or lack thereof) lay.

Israel was united in its grief.

Questions lingered at the back of every mind. Would antisemitism end now that there was only one surviving candidate position for the mashiach position? Was Natan going to usher in the messianic age which would finally put an end to the thousands of years of Jewish suffering?

Who exactly was the mashiach that Avi had been resurrected to locate?

No one knew.

Once back in Jerusalem, Avi was taken directly to the Hadassah Hospital on Mt. Scopus to be properly evaluated. The Prime Minister, the King and Queen of Jordan and their adorable young children, the Chief Rabbis, the Greek Orthodox Patriarch, the Israeli President, the Grand Mufti of Jerusalem, the Shaykh al-Aql, Natan and his now public boyfriend, members of the Knesset, and other various dignitaries, anxiously awaiting news from the doctors. Like the general public, they too—all of them—put to rest their discontent with Avi's previous statements and relished in the fact that Avi had returned safe, if not sound.

When the doctors declared that Avi was indeed healthy, with only superficial injuries, Avi consented to meet with everyone who had come to wish him well. He could not spend any considerable amount of time with any one visitor, but he graciously accepted them all and gratefully received their well-wishes, although he was a bit cautious when Rabbi Eliezer walked into his room to enquire after his health. The Israeli President—who served as the Nasi in the Sanhedrin—suggested that the Sanhedrin meeting be pushed back to the next week. Avi demurred vociferously.

"But the meeting is tomorrow!" the Israeli President exclaimed. "Everyone will understand. We can postpone it."

Avi shook his head. "I am leaving the hospital today, Your Excellency," he said firmly.

"But why?"

"I have to be there for Tzippy's and Max's funeral which is this afternoon. I have to go there to pay my respects to my friends."

The President nodded sympathetically. "If your doctors give you the green light—"

"I am going regardless of what the doctors say."

"Avi—"

"I am going."

The President folded his arms and pursed his lips.

Natan had waited while everyone else went in to visit with Avi, and when the last visitor tiptoed out of Avi's room, Natan knocked on the door softly and walked in. Avi looked up from the bed, his eyes bloodshot, weary, and saggy. For the first time since he had returned to Israeli soil from his captivity in Gaza, Avi began to sob. Natan, who had not cried since he was a little boy, walked over to his friend, hugged him, and allowed the sorrow to flow out of himself as well. No one else alive could understand the true loss that had occurred with the deaths of Tzippy and Max other than these two surviving members of the group which had been spontaneously and erratically formed when they had first met in the Judean wilderness; Avi and Natan had shared their lives with their two friends for the past few months—a sharing which had created a most unique and powerful bond. The two men wept, embracing each other, and in so doing, allowed themselves to feel the magnitude of the loss that had been inflicted on their lives with the murders of their two friends. They comforted each other, and in so doing, they took the first step of recovery by accepting the tragedy which had befell them. It would be months before either of them would truly come to terms with what had happened, and years before either of them would be able to live a day without thinking of the Feldman cousins, but in that moment, they—the ancestor and the descendant—hugged each other and began the arduous process of healing.

Avi spoke openly about what had transpired after he, Tzippy, and Max had been kidnapped by the terrorists outside of the makholet. His voice broke as he spoke about the execution-style murder of his friends, but there was reverence in his words as he spoke of how nobly they had faced the inevitable death. He told Natan about the yellow-eyed man, whose evil eyes were devoid of all humanity. He spoke of the Presence of God descending upon him in the final moments of limbo, where he was sure he would face the same end as Tzippy and Max, and he spoke of the serendipitous, altogether opportune arrival of the Israeli and Egyptian soldiers who had saved him.

Natan wept silent tears throughout Avi's recollection. He took pride in Tzippy's and Max's quiet defiance at their end, but he couldn't help but think of Tzippy's unborn child—the third casualty of the crime, whose murder would never be known as Tzippy had managed to keep her pregnancy under wraps from the general public. As Avi wound down his tale, Natan began to speak, and he told Avi of how he'd prayed they'd be rescued; despite being unsure of God's existence—he had prayed earnestly, and he had thanked that God when he'd heard that the location of his friends had been determined. He spoke of the guilt he felt for having stopped to get the cigarettes and of the bag of goodies he had bought to surprise them, including the four packs of Bamba, which was Tzippy's chief delight and biggest craving, now that she'd entered her second trimester. He spoke of the intense despair he'd felt when news of Tzippy's and Max's murders had reached his ear. He spoke of the comfort he'd found in the arms of his lover; a lover he had secreted away for far too long, and only now, with the passing of his friends, did he realize he loved and no longer wanted to keep hidden like a shameful secret.

Eventually, the issue of the mashiach came up and Natan asked nervously whether he was to be officially cast in the role, now that he was the sole candidate for the position.

Avi hesitated in responding. Even though Natan was the only person he counted as a friend in the whole wide world, Avi was apprehensive about telling Natan about the conversation he'd had with his God in the underground room. In the time he'd spent travelling back to Jerusalem, Avi had given the issue much thought—but he needed more time; more time to pray and to think, to truly unravel the mystery that was the penultimate reason for his current existence on earth.

Avi answered with the only honest answer he could give: "I'm not sure who the mashiach is. I'm working on it."

✡

The doctors were reluctant to discharge Avi, but he was determined to leave. This was no false act of bravado on his part. He was in pain and needed time to recuperate, it was true, but he wasn't going to miss the funeral of his two friends. He also knew that he needed to go to the Sanhedrin trial the next day. The doctors suggested that he continue as an in-patient overnight and just discharge himself the next day so he wouldn't miss the trial. Avi gave them a solid no and pointedly got out of the bed and sat himself on a wheelchair.

Having barely enough time to return to his home in Talbiya to wash and dress himself, Avi was thankful that the chauffeured car had once again been made available for his use. A cadre of security followed his car—the Israeli government had no intention of putting their patriarch at risk again, and Avi had no intention of doing so either. He looked wistfully at his bicycle as he walked out of his house, but he quickly shrugged the whimsy away as the practicality of being driven in a car was never more apparent than when he sat in the backseat and his aching body delighted in the simple pleasure of being able to sit and rest. He had not slept in almost forty-eight hours, but he knew he wouldn't be able to rest until Tzippy's and Max's bodies had been securely returned to the earth.

Avi arrived just as the funeral was about to begin. He wished he could be inconspicuous, but with the entourage of security which surrounded him, it was an impossible wish. He stood at the back and ignored the stares and excited whispers which had accompanied his arrival. His eyes scanned the crowd, and at the front, he spotted the parents of his two slain friends. Natan had said that they'd flown immediately to Israel when they'd
446

been informed of the deaths of their respective children, and that they'd come straight to the cemetery from the airport. It was clear that they were grief-stricken. Both mothers were collapsed in the arms of their husbands, and both fathers were sobbing. It was heart-wrenching to witness. Avi debated whether or not he should introduce himself to them, but then decided against it. He had been with their children in their final moments; his presence would not bring them any relief.

News vans from local, regional and international news agencies lined the entrance to the cemetery. The story of the kidnapping of the Jewish patriarch and two of the persons he had identified to possibly be the mashiach had caused an instant worldwide media frenzy. Avi had issued no public statement, and when he arrived, the cameras instantly zeroed in on him. His security team pushed them away and kept them at bay. Undeterred, from the peripheries of the cemetery, the journalists reported on the event, their cameras gliding smoothly from shots of the holes in the ground, to images of the weeping, broken parents, and back to Avi, who stood wordlessly at the back.

The funeral was over as quickly as it had begun. Jewish funerals never lasted long. The two bodies, wrapped in simple white shrouds, were lowered into their resting places and the onerous work of filling the graves began. The crowds petered out. Natan passed by, holding his boyfriend's hand and stopped to hug Avi. The Prime Minister and President nodded to Avi as they exited the cemetery. Even the grieving parents were guided away from the gravesite. But Avi stayed behind, watching the dirt slowly cover the once giggling, happy, alive bodies of two of the most important people in the world to him.

Eventually, all that was left was Avi and his security team. Avi had held himself with dignity throughout the ceremony, maintaining his composure. Reporters would comment on his behavior; some regaling him for his dignified stance, others projecting that he was in shock. Avi was neither of these things.

Inside, he was devastated.

While those closest to Tzippy and Max had found comfort in their better halves, Avi had no such person to rely on to give him comfort. His security team was—as was to be expected—more intent on securing the area around Avi than asking after his well-being; not that Avi was looking for comfort from nameless faces he had no personal relationship with. Michael hovered close to Avi, offering him words of comfort, but it did little to ease the ache in Avi's heart. He wanted to collapse into someone's arms and feel the tangible hold of solace. But he continued to stand, seemingly indifferent to the scene—just standing there: looking, watching, observing.

The limp bodies had been interred in their underground dwellings, and within an hour, the graves had been filled in. The aura of sadness hung over the cemetery like a dismal curtain. The sun had begun to set over the Jerusalem hills to the west. Still, Avi stood—almost as if he was keeping watch—or waiting.

His security team was discreet. They asked no questions. They propped their sunglasses onto their head and spoke quietly into the little walkie-talkies which were attached to the shoulders of their shirts. They continued to remain vigilant, securing the area, and would be ready to move whenever Avi was.

But Avi gave no indications of wanting to leave.

A rustle in the trees behind them finally broke the hypnotic lock Avi's eyes seemed to have on the gravesites. Immediately alarmed, Avi whipped around, feeling the terror of the day before engulfing him once again. The image of the yellow-eyed man popped into his head and an irrational fear arose inside of him that the man would step out from behind the trees. Half of the security team jostled to block Avi from the possibility of a threat, and the other half quickly aimed their guns at the trees. Avi was frozen in his fear and could not move. His hand went instinctively to the necklace which he wore around his neck.

With the security team blocking him from the threat, Avi couldn't see what was going on. He heard the security yell out for the person to come out from behind the trees. A crackle of noise and then silence indicated that the person had followed the order.

"Identify yourself!" one of the security men yelled.

A familiar, sweet, clear feminine voice reached Avi's ear. "I am Sarah of old, resurrected by the grace of the one true God of Israel, here on earth to do His bidding. I am looking for my husband."

CHAPTER 23

*"Now the LORD had said, 'Shall I hide from
Abraham what I am about to do, since Abraham is to
become a great and populous nation and all the nations
of the earth are to bless themselves by him? For I have
singled him out, that he may instruct his children and his
posterity to keep the way of the LORD by doing what is
just and right, in order that the LORD may bring about
for Abraham what He has promised him."*
—Genesis 18:17-19

Thousands of years may have passed by since they last beheld each other, but the recognition was instantaneous. Her eyes were the same, her face, her hair, her body, her neck, and her hands were all the same. She was exactly as he had remembered her from her late teenage years: beautiful, petite, regal, with that unmistakably mischievous gilt in her rich, deeply brown eyes—the matriarch of Israel, Sarah.

The security team fell to their knees when they beheld their mother in the form of this spritely girl. Like Avi, it seemed that Sarah had been blessed with the boon to have people believe her when she told them who she was.

"Sarah?" Avi called out, afraid that the vision of the girl that stood before him was nothing more than a mirage projected out from his grief-addled mind.

"It's me, Avi," the girl responded. "I've returned." She smiled hesitantly.

It *was* she. This was no apparition. He felt his heart expand inside his chest as the joy exploded forcefully within.

Avi pushed his way through the kneeling security and ran directly to her, a smile wide with unexpected happiness plastered on his face. He crashed into her—this beautiful woman, the love of his life, his wife.

She snuggled her head into his neck and they both breathed in the recognizable scents of each other. They pulled apart and Avi held her face in his hands, absorbing every detail which sprung at him. Sarah stroked his face lovingly and brushed the bangs from his eyes, her eyes lingering on the bruises on his cheekbones and the dark circles which framed his eyes.

"You really do get yourself into a mess when I'm not around, huh?"

Avi smiled even wider, and before he knew what he was doing, his mouth was pressed onto hers.

They pulled apart, both their faces flushed with the delight of the physical feeling. Avi grabbed her hand and eagerly pulled her towards his chauffeured car. The security detail jerked out of their stupor and quickly followed their excited patriarch and matriarch.

✡

Sarah's story of her return—as she related it to Avi in their drive back to his home—was remarkably similar to his. She had found herself outside of the Cave of Machpelah only two days before, with a designated guardian angel at her side; resurrected to do her God's bidding.

"What bidding is that?" Avi asked quietly.

"To find you and be your partner again—you needed me."

Avi absorbed what she said.

Sarah had found no ready-made, fully-stocked tent awaiting her outside of the cave, but there had been

451

a parked jeep with no owner in sight. She peeked into the vehicle and spied the keys dangling from the ignition and a freshly-laundered suit of clothing, neatly folded and waiting on the passenger seat. Expecting her luck to be too good to be true, Sarah was exuberant when the door to the jeep opened effortlessly. After she'd dressed herself, Sarah spent the day acclimatizing herself to the new world she had stepped into, using the fully charged iPad she'd found in the glove compartment. When the iPad's charge ran out, she decided it was time to move on, and, with a little contentious advice from her guardian angel, she managed to drive the jeep all the way to Jerusalem. Whether it was fate or God guiding her hand, Sarah had driven directly to the King David Hotel on Rechov David haMelekh, where the jeep promptly ran out of gas. Glad that she had found civilization, she went into the establishment, only to run into the owner of the jeep: an eccentric Arab-Israeli millionaire, who, overcome with thanks that Sarah had brought his jeep back to him ("although I can't quite figure out how it is you knew I was staying at this hotel," he'd said), had magnanimously booked her into a suite for the week until she got on her feet since she'd told him she had nowhere to go and was unacquainted with the city. He pressed a map of Jerusalem into her hand and handed her one of his very many credit cards and told her to do with it as she pleased—he was grateful to her for returning his jeep. A cursory scan of the Internet had vaguely informed her that Avi was living in the Talbiya neighborhood. She decided to wash up, load herself into a taxi, and go there immediately to find Avi, but breaking news on Channel 10 informed her that Avi, along with two of his modern friends had been kidnapped.

"I was terrified, Avi," she said, squeezing his hand tight. "What did it mean? Were these fiends going to kill you?" She sighed and touched his face gently. "But I knew you would be alright. God wouldn't have brought me back to life to go to you, only to take you back unto Himself."

She'd spent all night awake—closely following the rapid unraveling of events on the television. When it was announced that Avi had been found and was on route to the Hadassah Hospital, Sarah fell to the ground and prostrated herself and gave thanks to God for the speedy recovery of her husband.

"I wanted to go to you there and then, but my guardian angel counseled me that it would be more prudent to see you when you were discharged. I agreed that made more sense, because we figured the security around you would be heightened, and I knew you'd need rest after your ordeal." Sarah laughed. "But some things never change. You are still the man of action that you were all those thousands of years ago. I napped for maybe two hours and when I awoke and checked the news: it reported that you had discharged yourself. I knew you would go to the funerals of your fallen companions, may they rest in peace. I knew it was where I had to go to find you."

Once back at Avi's house, they found themselves to be ravenous. Avi explained to Sarah that they didn't have to cook in order to satisfy their hunger; such was the miracle of the modern age in which they'd found themselves—and within half an hour, there was a large cheese pizza in front of them. Avi grinned at Sarah, excited that she would be having her first taste of tomato sauce. As she bit into the slice of pizza, Avi looked at her expectantly. She smiled. "I love it," she said. Avi beamed and tucked into his own slice.

They ate in the kitchen, holding hands and giggling—relishing the thought that they were both alive and together again. As the slices of pizza disappeared into their mouths, they shyly cast surreptitious glances at each other. Theirs was a powerful attraction, and the passage of time had done nothing to damper the feelings they had for each other.

When they were finished eating, Avi took Sarah around the house and showed her the place he'd come to call home. It was a marvelous, two-story Arab-style mansion. He took her through the downstairs—showing her the official sitting room that had been designed for him to host dignitaries ("but which I never use otherwise"), the comfortable, informal living room with its plush sectional and large screen TV and Wii, the formal dining room which he'd never eaten in, and the old-fashioned study which housed his computer and growing collection of books—and then led her up the stairs and culminated the tour in his masculine bedroom with its palette of whites and varying shades of gray. She took it all in, but more than the house, she took him in. She fingered the necklace which peeked through the nape of the white shirt he wore. "What is this?" she asked, an electric thrill running through Avi when her hand made contact with the skin on his neck.

He pulled the necklace out from inside of his shirt. "Do you remember this?"

Sarah cried out with excitement. "That's mine!"

Avi nodded and began to undo the clasp.

"But how? Where did you find it?"

Avi put a finger to her mouth. "Before I tell you, will you let me hang it around your neck again? Will you
454

be consecrated to me in this incarnation as you were in the last?"

Sarah put her hands up to meet Avi's, where it waited, poised to fasten the necklace around her. "It's a new world we're living in today. Egalitarianism rules— girl power, you know? I'll be consecrated to you, if you promise to be consecrated to me." Her eyes twinkled.

Avi laughed. "There has never been and there will never be any love of my life other than you, sweet Sarah. I am consecrated to you for all eternity."

"And there has never been and there will never be any love of my life other than you, amazing Avi. Now consecrate us to each other, baby, and let's christen that bed of yours."

Avi grinned. He fastened the clasp securely around his wife's neck and they fell onto the bed together.

✡

Avi and Sarah fell into a deep sleep, wrapped lovingly in each other's arms. They had both been through much in the past two days, and the sleep, when it hit them, took hold of them firmly. They slept soundly, until at around five in the morning, Avi awoke. His first thought was of Sarah—had it been just a dream? He looked down. Her head was resting securely on his chest and her arm was cuddling him. She was very much there; it had been no dream. He smiled happily, feeling rested and contented, but his thoughts were quickly clouded over by the memory of his two fallen friends, and the pressing issue of the mashiach, which he still hadn't quite figured out yet.

He eased himself out of the bed, and with Sarah still asleep, he moved into the bathroom and stepped into the shower. The warm water relaxed him, soothing the physical aches of his bruised body, and offered a temporary reprieve from the stresses which had entered his mind. He stayed in the stall for half an hour, and then dried himself off and dressed. He opened the bathroom door cautiously, and to his delight, Sarah was awake.

"Boker tov," she said shyly.

"Good morning," he responded and he jumped on the bed. "Did you sleep well?" He cuddled next to her.

Sarah giggled. "You're tickling me." She playfully jostled with him and then collapsed into his arms. "I slept wonderfully. Did you sleep well?"

Avi nodded.

Sarah put her hand on his chest. "Your heart beats quickly."

"You do that to me."

"You teaser," she said playfully, and propped herself on her elbow. She looked at his face. "Ok, what's going on?"

"What do you mean?"

"Come on, Avi, what's wrong?"

Avi smiled at her. He didn't want to worry her. "Nothing, my love. Everything is fine."

Sarah pulled away from him. "Avi, I know you. I've known you for a lifetime. Something is up—I can see it on your face as plain as day. Something is bothering you.

Avi opened his mouth to protest.

Sarah put up a silencing hand. "This is why I was sent back—to share your burdens, to be your partner. Last night we talked about me—today, we talk about you. Start at the beginning."

Avi didn't speak.

"Avi," Sarah said, her voice hardening. "You have to tell me."

"I want to protect you. There is horror in my story."

"Protect me from what? In our last incarnation, you shared everything with me. It wasn't the Avi show. It was the two of us, together, against the world. I am not some idiotic, bumbling girl—I have tasted the bitter pill of horror, and I have come out stronger because of it. Or have you forgotten who I am?"

Avi stared at her. "You're right."

"Misery shared is misery halved. Tell me what's going on. Tell me what the problem is. Maybe we can figure it out together."

Avi nodded and began to speak. He started at the very beginning and shared with her all the particulars of his return—in blinding detail. This was his way of bridging the gap of the past few months that he had existed without her. When she had died in his last life, he had been devastated; it was a pain the likes of which he had not felt since, not in his past incarnation, or in this present one. Having her back, physically, right there next to him—her body pressed against his, her eyes focused into his, her hand holding his—was heaven. He wanted her to know, to understand, to share his story, to be part of who he was. He wanted her to fully join with him and share his life, and this was the only way he knew how. He had felt the acute ache of loneliness without her since he'd returned, and now, God, blessed be He, saw it fit to return his betrothed to him, and Avi was not going to miss this opportunity. Sarah had been

457

everything to him; she was going to be everything to him now—but the only way to ensure the true union of their souls was to open his vulnerability before her and share his life. And this he did in blinding detail.

She listened attentively; not fidgeting, not interjecting, not commenting—just listening. For hours, Avi spoke, and for hours, Sarah listened. She was his soul mate, in every sense of the phrase. They were, together, the formidable duo. Without one, there could not be the other; the greatness of Avi was Sarah. It was their union which begat the Jewish nation. It was them together—and as Sarah listened, she felt her soul intertwine with her husbands', and once more they were united as one: two parts of one composite whole; the two persons God had resurrected to call mashiach forth.

Avi was exhausted by the time he had wound up his tale; but Sarah was invigorated with inspiration. She kissed him on his lips and he kissed her back, his mouth salty from the tears.

"We have to figure this out. This mashiach business is the reason we're both here."

"I've thought about it so much since I was rescued from that hellhole in the ground. I feel like I'm almost there—the answer is right there, lurking right beyond the horizon. So close, yet, so far. I feel it, Sarah, but something's still missing."

"We have to approach this logically. We have to go over God's directives to you in the cave. There were three different ways He told you what your mission was, and there was one way He told you how to identify the mashiach. We need to separate them and attack them individually."

Avi couldn't help but smile.

"What?"

"That's just how Max would've approached this."

"It sounds like he'd inherited a full dose of the Sarah neurosis."

Avi laughed. "He was really very similar to you, now that I think about it."

"Well, he was one of my descendants. May he rest in peace, may Tzippy rest in peace, may all our children who have gone on from this world rest in peace."

"Amein."

Avi told her about the theories he had started to grapple with regarding the mashiach for the past day—each theory more asinine than the next, but still, each of them plausible. Sarah nodded at his analyses and methodically applied them to the context of the mission and the means of identifying the mashiach. They went over the conversation Avi had had with God when he had been kidnapped, carefully dissecting each word God had uttered, as they tried to make sense of it all.

"There is no 'the mashiach'. There is only mashiach," He'd said.

They pondered His directives, meticulously going over each word. They expanded their discussion to the lecture Avi had received from Natan's Saba, trying to integrate it all. Avi recounted Zahira's prophecies, and Sarah perked at the mention of her own prophecy. They mused over the Christian and Islamic approaches to the concept, and wondered if there was anything within those traditions to point them to the answer. They picked up the Tanakh from Avi's bedside table and went over the stories of the first Jewish kings: Saul, David, and then Solomon. There must be a clue in there, somehow—those kings were the forerunners of the ultimate mashiach. They pored over the Bible, pulled out commentaries from Avi's library, and dichotomized the more direct and concise Talmudic extrapolations from the vague and subtle references given in the Written Scriptures. Then, adding a curveball, Sarah questioned the prophecies themselves and the general understanding of those prophecies, asking Avi, "Do they mean what they seem to mean or are they pointing to something hidden and subtle?"

For another hour, the couple sat on their bed, dissecting, analyzing, debating, and studiously pondering the issue which had been the cause for both of their resurrections, and suddenly, like a light bulb going on above their heads, they realized that they both knew the answer to their conundrum: that the answer was now so glaringly obvious, that it was any wonder that they'd not figured it out before.

They looked at each other, ultimate comprehension shining from both their faces.

"Could it be—?"

"Do you think—?"

They hesitated.

"You tell me what your theory is," they both said in unison and then they giggled.

"I'll tell you in your ear what I think and you nod if it's what you're thinking, ok?"

Avi nodded agreeably.

Sarah leaned over and whispered into his ear, then drew back apprehensively. "Well?" she asked.

Avi nodded and then smiled widely.

Sarah pounced on him with excitement and he fell onto his back in fits of laughter. He felt lighter than he'd felt in months. They'd solved the riddle! They knew who the mashiach was!

"Let's pray about it," Avi said, when he'd managed to subdue his laughter.

Together, they crawled to the floor and prostrated themselves. With their eyes closed and their hands touching, Avi led the prayer. "Blessed are You, O Lord our God," he whispered quietly, "Creator of all things, and by Whose grace Sarah and I were resurrected to undertake the mission of locating the mashiach. We kneel before You in reverence and in thanks, gracious and compassionate Father, and we thank You for this life that You have once again bestowed upon us. I thank You for the privilege of letting me experience this life once again with my partner and soul mate, my beautiful wife, Sarah. Thank You for returning this woman to me, without whom my abilities have been hampered and severely restricted. I thank You for trusting us to fulfill this most important mission of locating mashiach as You have directed us to do. Although I have fallen short, I believe that You have always been guiding me and leading me forth, and this mission has always had Your especial favor. There were times when I felt like I had failed you; there were times when I doubted Your wisdom in choosing me—but Your wisdom passes all understanding, and I know that You have helped us to crack the riddle. When I first prayed to You, I asked that You guide me to mashiach, and You did. You sent me three wonderful friends, two of whom You have seen fit to take back unto Yourself—but without those three, I would have never been able to understand the true purpose of my mission and Your true intention in returning me to this life. I understand now, Gracious Father, why You have allowed me to live these past few months, for it is in this moment that I can truly appreciate Your mercy and love which You have

461

showered on me with such abundance. My Great Friend, I can only hope that I have truly figured out the mystery that is mashiach, and I ask that You continue to guide Sarah and me, and bestow Your blessings upon us and upon mashiach. I lay prostrate before You once again, Lord, like I did when I first entered this world, but this time, with a metaphorical hill between myself and the completion of Your mission. I ask only that You guide my words as I mount this daunting hill that will be the Sanhedrin. I ask that You continue to show me favor and give me strength to do what is right and pleasing before You. I thank you, Gracious and Compassionate Father, for all the wonders You have given to me and all the wonders You will continue to give to me as I cross the final hurdle. May the thoughts of my heart and the expressions of my mouth find favor before You, O God, my Rock and my Redeemer."

They rose from the ground slowly.

"Do you think He'd answer?" Avi asked.

"Maybe He is answering. Let's listen harder."

They both strained.

"Do you hear anything?"

"No. Do you?"

"No."

They both turned to their guardian angels and asked, "Do you hear anything?"

They both shook their heads to indicate their angel's answers.

"Do you think we were wrong in our synopsis?" Sarah asked, waveringly.

"It just feels so right. I feel so much lighter and freer than I've felt since I've been back. It is the right answer. It has to be."

Sarah looked up to the ceiling. "A sign would be nice, God! Please?"

A knock at the bedroom door made them both jump.

"Yes?" Avi called out nervously. He half expected the door to blow open and God, in the pillar of light disguise He favored whenever He traversed the earth, to whirlwind into the room.

One of Avi's security answered from behind the door. "I am sorry to disturb you, but you have a very insistent visitor downstairs. I could ask him to leave if you'd like."

Avi looked confused. He had specifically told his security that he wanted no visitors, except for Natan. Who could possibly be so important that his security would let them in? "Who is it?"

"Rabbi Eliezer Goldenberg."

✡

Rabbi Eliezer sat quietly, nervously. Avi had never seen the man look so worried—and, curiously, so humbled. Holding Sarah's hand, Avi entered the formal sitting room.

Rabbi Eliezer stood, and if he was surprised to see Sarah, he gave no indication of it.

"Thank you for seeing me," he said, his voice uncharacteristically soft.

Avi and Sarah sat on the loveseat.

"This isn't a very good time," Avi answered, but he gestured for the man to sit. Rabbi Eliezer nodded and sat.

"I know. You have only a few hours before you must go before the Sanhedrin, but that is why I came. If you can spare me just a few minutes to explain, I would be most obliged."

Avi raised an eyebrow. "Have you come to push your agenda again?"

"I deserve that." Rabbi Eliezer threw his hands up in surrender. "I was wrong, Avraham. I was wrong every step of the way. I was wrong the last time I came, and I was wrong from the first night I met you. And I've come to tell you how sorry I am."

Avi didn't know what to say.

"I can understand your skepticism—I have a history of arrogance which isn't going to be washed away with one apology—"

"To be fair, you've apologized to me before. And it isn't something you usually do, as you pointed out."

Rabbi Eliezer blushed. "My last apology was not sincere. It was manipulative. I have much to be sorry for and many people to apologize to. I have to make things right. I have done so many foolish things in my life, all because of my own prejudices and arrogance."

"It's never too late to make amends for your wrongs," Sarah interjected softly. She felt pity for the clearly contrite man.

"I hope so," Rabbi Eliezer. Then, to Avi's surprise, he looked at her and smiled. Sarah smiled back warmly.

Avi coughed. "What has happened to bring you to this—to this conclusion?"

Rabbi Eliezer looked down at his hands. "All my life I thought I was being directed by HaShem for greatness. I thought He needed me to fight for Torah-observant Judaism and to push for the supremacy of

Ashkenazi minhag. All my life I believed I was destined for greatness. All my life I was wrong.

"When I met Feldman—Max—I had thought he would be my protégé who could carry on my legacy. I had discerned something special in him, but for all the wrong reasons. Then, when I heard about your return, and his connection to it, I began to vie for him to be positioned as the moshiach. I became so obsessed with his ascendancy to this auspicious role—and since I'm being honest here, I must tell you, I felt that with Max as moshiach, it would mean my legacy would be officially enshrined into the Judaic story.

"But it didn't happen. When I heard that he had died, something inside of me changed. I had always been accused by the secular media of being hard-hearted—sometimes the charge was even that I had no heart—and they weren't far from the mark. I was hard inside; I was cold. The beauty and wonderment of my religion were eclipsed by my own fears and my own press for power. But with the passing of this astounding young man, I realized how much I had wronged him. His was an earnest quest for HaShem; an earnest press for truth and for understanding his religion, while mine had been the fight for tradition and the keeping of the law. I realized that the Judaism I had practiced all my life and the one practiced by Max Feldman were two completely different religions, though, to outward appearances, we were part of the same team. His quest was sincerely spiritual, mine was political. I had removed HaShem from my equation, and instead, I idolized halacha. Halacha was given to assist in our quest to serve HaShem; it was not given to enslave us or politicize us.

"Avraham, I am old man and a sinner. I have done so many wrongs and isolated so many people—perhaps there will not be enough time for me to say sorry, but I feel I must start somewhere, and I start with you.

"I have tried to malign you in the public. I have hated you in the recesses of my heart for being different from my brand of Judaism. I have tried to discredit you and disown you—but in so doing, I have discredited myself and the entire Judaic civilization, of which, my brand of Judaism, I now see, is only a very minute part. To question your authority; to question your very Jewishness, is to question us, collectively, as a people. We have merited our blessing because of you. You are our first—and to challenge you was the height of idiocy. You've been resurrected by HaShem: a modern-day miracle! Your rebirth is a direct sign of HaShem's favor to His people; a modern manifestation of the direct Hand of HaShem in the Jewish narrative. How marvelous is your return!—but it has been overshadowed by the politics and bickering and divisiveness, of which, I am sad to say, I am a main contributor of.

"HaShem has sent you, Avraham Aveinu, and you have returned upon His authority and you speak on His behalf. You are His prophet, and who am I—a pathetic, power-hungry old man—to challenge you and question you? You came and you identified the moshiach you had been sent to locate—but like the evil Korach, I have planted seeds of doubt in the hearts of the people and I have led them astray. That the earth has not yet opened its mouth and swallowed me whole is telling of the merciful nature of HaShem, Who sees into the hearts of men and recognizes the regret which exists in mine for all my rabid actions and behaviors. Perhaps one day the earth will open up and I will sink into the ground—for such a punishment is deserving for the modern-day Korach that I have become, but until that punishment comes nigh, I will make amends for my wrongs. I will say I am sorry—and to you, I give my heartfelt apology.

"I have wronged you by not only challenging you, but by also causing you to think you had to flee. Had I never questioned your Jewishness and called you to defend yourself; had I never made you feel as if all the world was against you, you and the Feldman cousins would never have thought of running away, and, thus, would never have been kidnapped. Max Feldman and his cousin would still be alive today, and the blood of those two innocents would not be upon my head. I can only praise the holy Name of HaShem that murder did not come to your door and you had been spared. Nothing I say can ever make up for the deaths of those two children, whose last moments, I am told you were forced to witness.

"There is nothing I can do but say sorry. I do not expect forgiveness—I just want you to know that I am sorry, Avraham. From the bottom of my recently thawed heart, I am sorry.

"And this is why I urge you to not attend the Sanhedrin meeting. Do not go there and meet my silly charge with a defense. You have nothing to answer for, You have no man to answer to. I have tendered my resignation to the Nasi and have withdrawn from the Sanhedrin. I tried to rescind the case I brought against you, but, alas, it cannot be undone. I cannot take it back, but it will be counter-productive for you to go. You were right all along. You had correctly identified the moshiach, but I had made you doubt yourself. HaShem works in mysterious ways, they say—and perhaps, just perhaps, if I had not been such an arrogant dolt, He would not have had cause to unleash the angel of death upon the Feldman cousins. But because of my meddlesome, interfering ways, HaShem has removed the other candidates for the moshiach position and left the one whom you had originally chosen as He had wanted you to. Natan Nasi was left because Natan Nasi is he whom you came to anoint. No man can fathom the Mind of HaShem, and if He chose a man whose lifestyle contradicts general Torah-observant Jewry, then it is His Will and His Will is always good. HaShem chose the Moabitess, Ruth to be the great grandmother of his servant, David haMelekh. HaShem knows what He does, and what He does is always for the best."

Avi wasn't sure what to make of Rabbi Eliezer's speech. A part of him was skeptical, wondering if this was a ploy of the man's, but a bigger part of him had heard the sincerity in the man's voice. "Rabbi Eliezer, before anything else is said, I have to say sorry as well. I have also played a wrongful hand in our relationship. I was rude and obnoxious to you—"

"Yes, but only after I exhibited such behavior to you in the first place."

"No matter. It is never right to respond to negativity with negativity. I am older than you—eons older. I should have known better. I accept your apology, for you seem sincere, but I must also ask that you accept mine."

"You have nothing to be sorry for."

"Thank you all the same, but I do, and I am."

Rabbi Eliezer nodded in response. "We are both sorry. We have both behaved badly."

"Indeed." Avi moved over to the old man and knelt next to him. "It is not your fault that Max and Tzippy died. The men who chose to kill them had decided the fates of our friends. It was not you."

"But had I not questioned your original choice of Natan Nasi—"

"Then what? They would have just kidnapped Natan and myself and now Natan would be dead?"

Rabbi Eliezer looked at Avi.

Avi touched the old man gently on his hand. "You cannot blame yourself for the deaths of Max and Tzippy. I assure you, it was not your fault."

Avi was surprised to see a tear slip out from under the old man's glasses.

"You said it yourself, none can fathom the way God works. Everything He allows to happen is for a deeper reason. I was unsure of who the mashiach was—but that was not without reason. You had a role to play in this whole mashiach business, in that you brought me up to be tried as a Jew—and that was not without reason either. Had you not done that, I would never have realized who I really am and, thus, just a few minutes ago, discover the answer to the mashiach question—the two issues are interrelated."

Rabbi Eliezer nodded. "You're right. You need to answer both questions definitively."

Avi stood and smiled at the old man. "I may be Avraham Aveinu, but I am no posek when it comes to halacha. You've resigned as Av Bet Din, but you are still one of the foremost halachic authorities in the world. Temper your knowledge with chesed and hospitality and you will be one of the most prolific sages in Jewish history. Do it for love, not for power, and accompany me as my personal rebbe at the Sanhedrin meeting later."

"Politically, it will be suicide for you to show up at the Sanhedrin with me at your side."

"I don't care. I want you there with me."

Rabbi Eliezer hesitated and then put his hand into his pocket and pulled out a curious device, which looked like a cross between an iPod and an old-time telephone.

"What's that?"

"Many moons ago, I was privy to some special, dangerous technology which the Israeli government had discovered. This technology was harnessed by Israel and the result was this." Rabbi Eliezer handed the piece of equipment to Avi. "Only twenty of these had been made—nineteen of which remain in the government's possession. This last one I managed to secure for myself through my... powers of persuasion." Rabbi Eliezer smiled wryly.

Avi turned the instrument around in his hands. "But what is it?"

"It's a *Mechona Yehudi*—Jew machine. It determines whether a person is Jewish or not."

Avi did a double take. "A machine to determine someone's Jewishness? You mean it could tell if the person is genetically Jewish?"

Rabbi Eliezer shook his head. "It has nothing to do with genetics." He paused. "It can measure their neshama."

"But that's not possible!" Avi cried out. "A material device to find something as intangible as the soul?"

"I assure you, it's very real."

"Does it really work?"

Rabbi Eliezer nodded slowly. "I've never known it to fail."

"Have you used it on yourself?"

Rabbi Eliezer beamed. "Yes. The results were one hundred percent Jewish neshama."

Avi looked at the Mechona Yehudi. "How does it work?"

"You just put it to your mouth and blow."

"That's it?"

"That's it."

Avi looked at Sarah, who shrugged and nodded. He put it to his mouth and blew firmly on the device. It glowed a brilliant blue.

Rabbi Eliezer cracked a smile. "I've lost my case."

"What do you mean?"

"You're one hundred percent Jewish. It glows blue for the breath of one who has a neshama within. I've never seen it blow quite that brilliantly, though."

"Well, he is the first of our people, resurrected by the grace of God," Sarah said, speaking for the first time.

Rabbi Eliezer nodded and gazed at Avi with awe. "Indeed, he is."

Avi stretched out the Mechona Yehudi to Sarah. "Would you like to try?"

Sarah giggled and took the device and blew on it. It shone blue as brilliantly as it had done for Avi. A look of disconcertion passed over Rabbi Eliezer's face, but it faded as quickly as it had come.

Avi spoke. "This Mechona Yehudi is quite an instrument."

"Isn't it? I thought if I couldn't convince you to stay away from the Sanhedrin today, I might as well give this to you to use on yourself and conclusively prove your Jewishness, thus dismissing the whole case against you."

Avi fumbled with the machine. He didn't know what to do. The device was tempting: an easy way out of this mess. But while it would prove conclusively that he had a neshama, it would be dangerous and potentially divisive to show the machine to the public. While it was a truly remarkable instrument, he knew the test of a man's soul should never be left to such cut and dry means. Life was never about black and white (or in this case, brilliant blue, apparently), but rather, most definitely about varying shades of grey—each person choosing his or her own color, rather than having it decided for them. The instrument reminded Avi of that dark period of Jewish history when there was no escaping one's ancestry; when Jews who had even the smallest amount of Jewish blood were rounded up like cattle and sent off to be gassed. Avi had no idea where the technology for the Mechona Yehudi came from, but he felt instantly revolted by the thing.

He quickly handed the machine back to Rabbi Eliezer. "This is a dangerous weapon," he said. "I don't want it."

Rabbi Eliezer didn't answer.

"I think it can be used to propagate much evil."

"I have used it for the wrong purposes at times. Selfish purposes."

"I think you need to destroy it and all the rest of these instruments. Harness their technology for something more worthwhile."

"For something good," Rabbi Eliezer whispered.

Avi couldn't believe this man had been his archenemy just a few hours ago—and now, here Rabbi

Eliezer was, amending his opinion to Avi's. Avi warmed towards the old man.

"So, the Sanhedrin meeting?" Avi asked as Rabbi Eliezer placed the Mechona Yehudi back into his pocket.

"If you need my support, you have it fully—publicly and privately. Whoever you name as the moshiach will have my unreserved support. The mission was given to you, and only you can bestow official authority upon the moshiach."

"Then you'll accompany me?"

"Yes." Rabbi Eliezer nodded firmly.

Sarah, who had been quiet all along, interjected from the love seat. "And I would love it if you were there as well."

Rabbi Eliezer looked over at her, looking directly into her eyes. "I am sorry. The last time we met, I did not introduce myself. Forgive me for being rude." He stood and went over to her. He hesitated and then stuck out his hand. "I am Rabbi Eliezer. Your name is Zahira, if I am not mistaken?"

Sarah shook the man's hand, but looked over at Avi, confused.

"This is not Zahira, Eliezer. There is a strong resemblance between the two of them, which is why you'll naturally be confused." Avi bade Sarah to stand. "This woman," he said, his hand pressed gently against her back, "is my wife. This is your great-great-great grandmother, many times removed. Eliezer, meet Sarah."

Rabbi Eliezer did a double-take. *"Sarah Immenu?"*

Sarah smiled.

"But how? When?" The old man's mouth was agape.

Avi laughed. "I'll tell you in the car on the way to the Sanhedrin. Right now, you'll have to excuse us to get ready."

"Of course, of course." Rabbi Eliezer backed into the chair he had just vacated and crumpled into it. Before Avi and Sarah could exit, however, he spoke again. "Just one thing?"

The couple stopped and turned around expectantly.

"In my last meeting with Avraham—which, I must admit, was a little heated since I was particularly priggish that day—he said to me that being his descendant was a curse upon your memory, Sarah Immenu." Rabbi Eliezer gulped. "While the man I was yesterday indeed deserved such a statement—"

Sarah ran across to the old man and threw her arms around his neck. "The man you are today is a blessing upon me. To know that a child of mine exists in such a man is the greatest blessing I can ever hope for."

Rabbi Eliezer blushed and with a burst of spontaneous inspiration, put his arms around Sarah. "Thank you, sweet lady. You have redeemed me."

CHAPTER 24

"I will make of you a great nation and I will bless you. I will make your name great, and you shall be a blessing. I will bless those who bless you and curse him who curses you; and all the families of the earth shall bless themselves by you".
— Genesis 12:2-3

Avi stood at the podium and looked out at the crowd. He had given public speeches before, but this was the penultimate speech he would ever have to make and he knew it. Every fiber of his body was awake with that peculiar rush of adrenaline that came with speaking publicly. His palms were sweaty, his eyes wavered, and his heart pummeled speedily in his chest.

This was it.

Although it was time for Avi to speak, there were still many voices murmuring throughout the Sanhedrin. So many intrigues had happened in such a short space of time, that it was difficult to make sense of it all. Rumors, embellishments, exaggerations, and insinuations were rampant throughout the room, throughout the country, and throughout the world at large. Avi's kidnapping and subsequent rescue had not been met with any official statement from him. The public did not know what to make of it; all they had were snippets of information released from the Israeli government, which were too vague and too impersonal to provide any real information. Media coverage of the debacle that was Avi's rescued return to Israel and his subsequent appearance at the funerals of Tzipporah and Max Feldman had been met with no response from Avi, as he had been shielded from the media glare by his competent security staff. The local and international media had turned out en masse to the Sanhedrin meeting, for the story of the disgraceful questioning of Avi's Jewishness had gripped the world. Christian authorities from all the various denominations forcefully concluded that as Jesus had been rejected by his own people, so, too, would Avi suffer the same fate. Islamic authorities condemned the kidnapping and murders of the Feldman cousins, but in the same breath, seethed at the seeming Jewish apathy toward their patriarch. They issued public statements saying that though Avi may be shunned by the children of his second child, the children of Ishmael welcomed him home with open arms, regardless of his previous, diminishing remarks about Islam. Israelis condemned the Sanhedrin for putting Avi on trial—and polls showed that ninety-five percent of them were of the opinion that Avi was Jewish ("He is the first Jew!" they bellowed from outside of the Sanhedrin and in blogs and in editorials and on television programs) and ninety-nine percent of them thought that Avi did not have to answer to Rabbi Eliezer's charge.

Avi had gone, in one swoop, from being the most disliked man in Israel, to being the one the common man most identified with. His popularity had never been higher.

Added to the complexities of the situation and the intrigue in general was the fact that Avi had arrived at the Sanhedrin that day in Rabbi Eliezer's car, with a beautiful stranger on his arm and Rabbi Eliezer at his side—the same Rabbi Eliezer who had initiated the case against Avi's Jewishness. The people were stunned.

Eventually, the murmurs subsided, as the Nasi pounded his gavel for order. Silence hung in the room and all eyes were fixed on Avi, who stood at the front of the room.

Avi gazed across the crowd, his eyes passing over the faces which amalgamated the story of his return. There was Natan, there was the Prime Minister, there was the President, there was Major General Arbel, there was Rabbi Eliezer. And there, in a white sundress, was his beautiful wife, Sarah. All of them there. All of them looking at him, expectantly, waiting. Avi couldn't help but think of the two faces which weren't in the crowd— two faces which should've been there as well. He felt his eyes grow damp, but he flitted the tears back.

He lowered his gaze and silently prayed for strength, for resolve, for truth. He didn't hear any answer, but he knew his God was with him. He knew he'd discovered the answer to the mystery of his mission. He raised his eyes confidently and spoke clearly.

"I am Avi of these times, resurrected by the grace of the one true God of Israel, here on earth once again to do His bidding. This council, the Sanhedrin, has questioned my Jewishness, and I am here to answer that question definitively and to fulfill my mission, to call mashiach forth. These two questions: 'am I Jewish?' and, 'who is the mashiach?' are inextricably linked."

The crowd murmured excitedly.

"The God of Avraham resurrected me to this world to find the mashiach, but to find the mashiach, I had to first find myself and where I fit into the equation that is today's society. The Avraham of yesterday had found his place in the ancient world, but I had to meander this life and find my place in this world.

"To be questioned by the Sanhedrin regarding my Jewishness is not a frivolous charge. I have endorsed the Jewish people as my spiritual heirs, but I have spent much of my time here wondering how I fit into their world. Am I a Jew? Or am I still Avraham the Ivri—the

477

Hebrew—the other? Who am I in today's modern, religious landscape?

"A wise man I was lucky to meet in this incarnation, told me: 'The Hebrew of yesteryear is the same as the Israelite which he spawned, and the same as the Jew of today and the Israeli of tomorrow', and my dear friend, Max Feldman, may he rest in peace, reminded me that the labels didn't matter, that, at the end of the day, the thing which defines Jewishness is the neshama—the Jewish soul—that spark of 'otherness' which shines from every Hebrew, every Israelite, every Jew, and every Israeli who ever lived and who ever will live. That neshama is what sets us apart from other nations and makes us uniquely who we are: the covenantal partners of a most gracious and loving God. The neshama signals a deep-seated longing for the accomplishment of tikkun olam through the conduit of our constitution, the Torah, and tempered with the most honorable virtue of chesed.

"The neshama is the essence of all the words we, as a people, use to define ourselves. Without that special neshama inside of us, there is no such thing as Israel, or Hebrew, or Jew. The neshama is our enduring connection to each other and to our God. The neshama defines who I am; it defines who every Jew is. Orthodox, dati leumi, Charedi, Reform, Conservative, Masorti, Sephardi, Ashkenazi, Mizrachi, Israelite, Bene Israel, Hebrew, or Jew—all of these words inextricably linked and given meaning because we share the same Jewish soul. The philosophical differences we diverge upon are nothing compared to the neshama which unites us as one people.

"Hear O Israel, you are one; we are one.

"A few days ago, I was kidnapped, along with my friends, Max and Tzipporah Feldman. As all of you know, my friends were murdered by the terrorists who had kidnapped us. What happened to us was evil of the highest order—but the God Who unites us uses all things for His divine purpose. It took this act of evil to make me realize who I am in today's world. When I was kidnapped, terrorized under the ground, I was asked that very question: 'Who are you? To which people do you belong?', and in that terrifying moment—with death and evil all around me—the answer came to me with clarity. All my months of wondering where I fit in and who I am in this modern world finally came to a head. When I was holed up in that bunker under the ground, when I'd seen my friends' bodies ripped apart by the roar of those bullets, their blood splattering everything around me, it was in that moment that I realized the truth: I am the eternal Hebrew, the immortal Israelite, the enduring Jew, the Israeli of the future. My neshama binds me to these descriptive words of my faith, my spirituality, my people, my religion, and my God; my neshama is what linked my fate to those of my friends, Max and Tzipporah Feldman. It is what links me with each and every one of you. I have cast my lot with you; you are my people. I look to all of you, some of you descended from the lineage of Avraham and Sarah, Isaac and Rebecca, Jacob and Leah and Rachel; others who follow in my footsteps and converted to the religion of Avraham. We are all one. You are my children, and I am your father. No matter what they call us—we are the eternal nation of the neshama, and we will forever struggle for what's right, struggle against oppression, struggle for good, and in that struggle, we will have to face the darkness of evil which ever so constantly rises to challenge our collective mission here on earth.

"In this moment, as I stand before you, the esteemed members of the Sanhedrin, I formally declare this to the Jewish people: 'For wherever you go, I will go; wherever you lodge, I will lodge; your people shall be my people, and your God is my God.' I am Avraham. I am Avi. I am a Jew."

The crowd burst into thunderous applause, cutting into Avi's impassioned speech. He was warmed by their response—as all factions of Judaism stood together and welcomed him formally into their midst. For once, Israel was united—no one denomination vying for prominence, as they recognized their patriarch more fully than they'd ever done before. They clapped on and on and on, until Avi put his hand up and they settled to hear him speak again.

"When the Lord resurrected me from death and returned me to this life, He tasked me with a mission: the mission to find mashiach. To quote God verbatim: 'The era of mashiach is here. I need you to make known to mashiach that I have called and it is time to answer.' These were His exact words to me, and, as a fallible human, I did not listen properly and it was only earlier today that I realized who mashiach really was.

"As I told you before, I needed to find who Avi was in this world before I could come to the full realization that I am a Jew. Likewise, I needed to fully comprehend the enormity of this issue that is mashiach, before I could properly identify who mashiach really is. For the past few months, I'd been wondering to myself: 'Is it Natan? Is it Max? Is it Tzipporah?', and the more Elijah and Moses tarried to announce mashiach to the world, the more I worried that I'd not fulfilled my part in
480

the mashiach story. Mashiach is a concept alien to Avraham of old, and, as Avi of today, I had to fully realize what it meant. And today, I did. With a little help, that is."

Avi grinned at Sarah. She grinned back at him. He was about to beckon her forward, but she shook her head slightly. She didn't want the limelight. Avi understood. He nodded slightly and then carried on.

"The journey is sometimes worth more than the final destination. It is in the journey that we experience, we yearn, and press forward, and in so doing, we learn the lessons we are meant to learn. The past few months I've spent traversing this earth have unraveled the mystery of mashiach to me, and the time has now come for me to share this joyous news of who mashiach is with you.

"Mashiach is not singularly Natan Nasi. Nor was it singularly Max or Tzippy Feldman. Nor was mashiach collectively all three.

"Mashiach, in the Jewish mindset, is the image of the ultimate hero. The one who will rise from the ranks of Israel and free her from oppression, from hatred—both internal and external, from spiritual subjugation, from political strife, from religious bickering, from cultural disagreements, from war, from famine, and from drought. Mashiach will unite and redeem the Jewish people and help them achieve their own mission that God has charged them with: to bring about tikkun olam—perfection of the world. Mashiach will be the force which will rebuild the sovereign nation in its ancestral homeland, rebuild Jerusalem, gather in the exiles, rebuild the Temple, reconvene the Sanhedrin, and restore the Davidic monarchy. Mashiach will bring about peace among the nations, and will bring hope to the saddest corners of the world. Mashiach will be all the Jewish heroes, rolled into one composite super-hero. He will be Moses and Avraham, and Jacob and Leah, and Joshua and Samuel, and Daniel and Ezra, and Devorah and Solomon, and Sampson and Ruth, and David and Judah the Maccabee, and Theodore Herzl and Golda Meir—mashiach will be all of these people, but so much more.

"Mashiach is you.

"Mashiach is every single one of you: every Jew who shines forth with the blazing neshama. Mashiach is the collective neshama of Israel. We are, all of us, mashiach—all of us tasked with the perfection of the world. We are each given particular strengths, particular facets of goodness which we must harness and use to contribute to the mashiach ideal. All of the heroes of yesteryear, their glory was that they took control of their own destinies. We are a people who have been given many stories of heroes, yet we miss the moral of those stories; we are blinded to the majesty of our heroes. Our heroes were great because they did what they had to do. Joshua did not emulate Moses. Devorah did not emulate Sarah. No—they found their own paths and fought for Israel. None of them waited for someone else to do it for them. They did it themselves. They were all mashiach for their own times. Can you imagine what can be accomplished if all these heroes lived in the same era? The answer to that is that the heroes are all alive inside of all of you. Every Jew is a hero, every Jew is mashiach.

"Mashiach is here.

"Mashiach is you.

"The Lord resurrected me with the instruction as plain as day: 'the era of mashiach is here.' It is here. It's here already. It is not in the future. It is not in the past.

The era of mashiach is in the here and now. It is in this moment. Has Israel not already fought bitterly for her independence in her ancestral homeland? Has Jerusalem not already been united under the banner of Israel? Are the exiles not being painstakingly searched for at this very moment and gathered home? Has the Sanhedrin not already been reconvened? Is the State of Israel not already contributing to tikkun olam—what with the many brilliant contributions her citizenry has made to the world in science, in the arts, in philosophy, in economics, and in literature? Is Israel not always first on the scene to assist in tragedies around the world—be it the earthquake in Haiti or the devastation of tsunamis in Eastern Asia? Is Israel not finding cures for cancer and unraveling mysteries of the human DNA? Have we not given the world our Einstein's, our Freud's, our Boas', our Herschel's, our Feynman's? Israel is fulfilling her own destiny—she is not waiting for some mythical knight in shining armor to deliver her. Her knight is her God, and He is with her in all that she does, and when Israel realizes that she is mashiach—that mashiach already exists inside of her—even more marvelous things will happen.

"Yes, there is much yet to be done—there are many in this world who still wish to see us disappear and extinguished. The fight still carries on. There are still things to be achieved. Our independence as a sovereign nation is not secure; we have not yet found peace. But we can find peace if we put our heads together and stop bickering among ourselves and putting up divisions among our ranks. Mashiach is here, but we push mashiach in ourselves into tarrying. We are our own worst enemies. Everything is within reach if we see that we can do it ourselves; united we stand, divided, we make mashiach tarry.

"There are some who will ask, but what about mashiach being a descendant of King David and his son, King Solomon? Ponder this: who among you today is sure that he is the first son, of the first son, of the first son, reaching back through the millennia, linking him directly to King Solomon primogeniturely, and, thus making him a legal claimant to that extinct throne? My wise friend I mentioned earlier, also imparted this bit of wisdom to me: 'we can only perceive the divine purpose of tragedy in hindsight'. The total obliteration of the Davidic throne and lineage was entirely destined and divinely purposed. God had never intended Israel to be a monarchy. In fact, He cautioned them against wanting such a thing. This warning fulfilled itself through King Saul's disastrous reign, and later, with King Solomon's foolish, bourgeois and arrogant reign, which unduly taxed the people and made them moan under the yoke of his oppression. No, I say to you: absolute power corrupts absolutely, and if we look at all the stories of the Israelite kings, it's here that we realize that this saying is never truer. There is no ruling elite in Judaism—there is no caste system. Before God, all men are equal; all Jews, too, are equal in stature, promise, and worth. We are the kingdom of priests and kings—and God has preserved us as a people, but eliminated the so-called nobles among us for this very reason: to keep us grounded in the remembrance that we are all kings before His eyes.

"I foresee a day when mashiach will accomplish all mashiach has been tasked to accomplish; when tikkun olam will be achieved because the Jewish people have joined together in unity and become mashiach. In those days, peace will have come to earth and the

Temple will be rebuilt, for it shall be built by men of peace and in a time of enduring peace. And when it is rebuilt, I see visions of all people: Jew and non-Jew alike, gathering there to give thanks for the peace which reigns on earth. I see Jew and non-Jew praying to the Almighty, and I see peace. Those days are within reach—it is up to all of us to make it a reality.

"I was asked to come here today to defend my Jewishness, but I am here, also in my capacity as your first patriarch, to fulfill my mission that I have been tasked with: to find mashiach. God, Most High, has sent me to call mashiach forth, and He has promised that mashiach will answer. I stand before you and say to you: Israel, you are mashiach and your God has called you forth."

Avi held his breath, and looked nervously at the crowd, hoping, earnestly praying, wishing beyond belief that he was right this time and that he'd found mashiach. As sweat dribbled down his forehead, and his throat tickled with soreness from speaking, his eyes darted around nervously.

There was silence in the room as the power of Avi's words sunk into the hearts of all who listened. Avi's speech had been broadcast live around the country and around the world, and all over, millions of Jews had heard Avi's call. For a painful few moments, there was no sound, until finally, from the room and from living rooms and cars and on freeways and all over the world, as one, the Jewish people loudly answered their first patriarch: *"Naaseh v'nishmah!"* We will hear and we will obey.

Avi closed his eyes and smiled, and then heard the soft Voice of his God whisper in his head: "Thank you for calling mashiach forth. Mashiach has answered."

CHAPTER 25

"This was the total span of Avraham's life: one hundred and seventy-five years. And Avraham breathed his last, dying at a good ripe age, old and contented; and he was gathered to his kin."
—Genesis 25:7-8

"People are going to wonder where you disappeared to," Natan remarked, amused.

Avi feigned horror. "Another scandal? How will I ever survive that?"

They laughed and Sarah giggled along, securely holding her husband's hand.

They stood at the end of the Goldman Promenade, where Avi had met Zahira all those weeks before. The sun was setting behind them to the west. In front of them was the open desert.

After Avi had announced mashiach to the world and mashiach had believed him and answered, there was pandemonium. The entire Sanhedrin had burst spontaneously into jubilant dancing; men and women, wrinkled and old, rapturously shuffling their legs and laughing as they hugged each other and exclaimed, "Mashiach no longer tarries! We are here!" All over Israel, Jews ran in the streets, hugging each other as they sang "I believe, I believe with complete faith that mashiach is here and we are all mashiach! Mashiach! Mashiach! Mashiach! Oy oy oy oy oy oy! We don't tarry, we have seen who we are; we are all mashiach!" People who hadn't even known they were Jewish felt the pull of their neshama inside of them, and they answered Avi's call with a loud roar. All over the world, Jews and non-Jews alike took to the streets and danced and sang in wild abandon. Christians and Muslims alike, unconcerned with how this revelation affected their theological, religious, and philosophical beliefs, joined in the celebrations, embracing their Jewish brothers wherever they could find them.

Avi, meanwhile, had slipped outside with Sarah in tow, and had joined Natan in his jeep. Together, the three of them made their way to their present, deserted location, far away from the messianic euphoria which had gripped the city.

"Are you sure this is what you want to do?" Natan asked, waveringly.

Avi smiled at his friend. "This is what we want." He looked at Sarah who nodded along.

"But you don't have any money or food or water."

Avi put his finger to his lips. "Have faith, my tall friend. God always provides."

Natan shook his head and then laughed. "I am mashiach. I should have more faith."

Avi looked at him piercingly. "You believe you are mashiach?"

"I know we are all mashiach," he answered slowly.

Avi beamed. "See? I wasn't entirely wrong when I first met you and identified you as mashiach."

Natan laughed. "You just had twenty million more to go and then you'd have gotten all the mashiach's."

Avi smiled. "Thank you for everything, my child—my friend. This was quite an adventure."

Natan swallowed. "It was indeed." He paused. "So, to Afghanistan?"

Avi squeezed Sarah's hand. "To Afghanistan, yes—Zahira and her people need to know that they are mashiach as well. Time for them to come home and for the other pockets of lost tribes to come home as well."

"I can't believe you've found another adventure. If I were you, I'd just want some rest and relaxation."

"I'm Avraham of old—rest and relaxation aren't part of my vocabulary." He looked out to the desert. "There are many of my children still exiled out there who don't have contact with the outside world. They don't know that mashiach has come. They haven't heard the shofar sounding. It's the little Sarah and I could do to contribute to this enterprise."

"You've done so much already."

"A person can always do more."

Natan shrugged, shook his head, and then roughly hugged Sarah and then Avi.

"You have my number, so call me if you need me, or if you decide to come back to Israel. My door is always open."

Avi sniffed. "Goodbye, Natan."

Natan smiled and waved. He couldn't bring himself to say goodbye. He watched as the patriarch and matriarch of his people walked down the hill and out into desert, fading away like a dream in the dusk—footnotes to be remembered only in stories: Abraham and Sarah, the first Jews.

EPILOGUE

*"In the days to come, the Mount of the LORD's
House shall stand firm above the mountains and tower
above the hills; and all the nations shall gaze on it with
joy.*

*And many peoples shall go and say: 'Come, let
us go up to the Mount of the LORD, to the House of the
God of Jacob; that He may instruct us in His ways, and
that we may walk in His paths.' For instruction shall
come forth from Zion, the word of the LORD from
Jerusalem. Thus He will judge among the nations and
arbitrate for the many peoples, and they shall beat their
swords into plowshares and their spears into pruning
hooks: nation shall not take up sword against nation;
they shall never again know war."*
—Isaiah 2:2-4

The red-haired man put his binoculars down
and poked the dark-haired man who sat on the ground
next to him.

"What?" The dark-haired man rubbed his arm.

"They've gone."

"Who?"

"Avraham and Sarah. They've gone out into the
desert."

"So, they've completed their mission?"

The red-haired man nodded. "It's time for us to
go down."

The dark-haired man shrugged. "I guess it is."

The two of them stood, and the dark-haired man
helped the red-haired man prop himself onto his walking
stick.

They ambled down the hill and onto the Goldman Promenade, where they spotted the tall fellow who had bid farewell to Avraham and Sarah.

"Greetings, mashiach!" they both said to the tall man.

The tall man drank in the particulars of the peculiar dress of the two strangers. They wore loose fitting tunics, and had long, bushy beards. The tall man felt an odd sense of déjà vu. "Shalom," said the tall man slowly. He wiped his eye. The dark-haired man wasn't sure, but he was fairly certain the tall man had been crying. "Can I help you?" the tall man asked.

They beamed.

"I am Elijah the Tishbite of old, resurrected by the grace of the one true God of Israel, here on earth once again to do His bidding," the red-haired man answered.

"I am Moses, your Rabbi, resurrected by the grace of the one true God of Israel, here on earth once again to do His bidding," the dark-haired man answered.

The tall man seemed stupefied. He stared at the men for a full minute and then looked up to the heavens. "Really, God? So soon? Really?"

The red-haired man and the dark-haired man did not know what to make of this. They continued to look at the tall man quizzically, who eventually slumped his shoulders and threw up his arms. "You guys better come with me," the tall man said. He beckoned to the two men and they followed him to his jeep.

THE END
--February 14th, 2013. 2:28am

ACKNOWLEDGEMENTS

I would like to express my gratitude to all those who supported and assisted me in the writing of this book. To all who read, critiqued, discussed, offered suggestions, gave helpful feedback, supported and encouraged me, I am forever thankful and indebted to you. This work was very important to me and couldn't be written without you.

To my wonderful best friend, Khara Persad: you have read everything I've ever written and believed in me with unwavering faith; and not just this, but also my never-ending emails! You pushed me in ways that no one else ever did; always selflessly taking the time out of your schedule to read, critique, encourage and delight in what I write, giving me the motivation to keep trudging along and keep writing. Your belief in me is a huge part of why I am where I am today: getting this book published! Thank you for printing my original draft of this in a hard copy all those yeara ago: it was so motivating to see it on my desk as a tangible motivating tool. Thank you for reading as I sent you updated chapters, giving your insight and input, and becoming attached to the characters and loving them and crying as you read about their journey. Thank you for always holding my hand; even when doors seemed closed, your quiet support made me look for different avenues, and made me determined to make this book see its culmination in publication. Thank you for listening to me cry, and never letting me give up. You are my number one cheerleader, and I would be nowhere without your support, encouragement and friendship.

To Kirk John-Williams: as I neared the end of each chapter, I eagerly sent each one to you and waited for your sage advice and input. I cannot thank you enough for challenging me and contesting my ideas, pushing me to look beyond and to make necessary changes. My doubts about the book were assailed when you gave me positive feedback on how informative it was and how much you learned. You were better than an editor and invaluable in this process. Thank you, from the bottom of my heart.

To my mother: thank you for giving me the tools, the foundation, and the wonderful literary childhood that you did, which propelled my imagination and love for the written word. Thank you for giving me the religious bedrock that you did, which encouraged me to love the Bible and all the characters therein. I wouldn't have been able to imagine a book along these lines without this (and your daily rule of reading the Bible every day!). Thank you for reading the manuscript, and for giving me all you have.

To my father: thank you for your support over the years and being my rock with all my weird undertakings; always consistently supporting me in all my endeavours. This book would never have happened without you (or the Mac you bought me!). Thank you, and I want you to read it now that it's in its published form!

To Aunty Annmarie: I did not share the manuscript with many people before I set about publishing it, but I shared it with you, because of your constant love and belief in me. Thank you for reading!

To Resa Gooding, Rabbi Marc Angel, Hans Stecher (z'l), and Serge Chriqui, having you read and give feedback meant more than you know. You were the first people I willingly sent my manuscript to in it's entirety, and your praise and encouragement bolstered me in ways I cannot even thank you enough for. Hans, though you were working on your own story when I was writing mine, and though your vision wasn't what it used to be, you took the time out of your schedule to read what I wrote and to send me words of encouragement. You will be forever missed. Rabbi Angel, thank you for understanding my vision and being supportive of it and your gentle, helpful and thoughtful suggestions. Resa, thank you for your encouraging review and praise which gave me so much confidence (comparing me to VS; let's hope the book sales and reviews reflect this!).

To all those who have helped shaped my worldview and my religious understanding over the years, which brought me to writing this story: to the teachers at Machon Pardes, who gave me my first proper understanding of Judaism in an academic setting; to the rabbis at the RCA Jerusalem Ulpan Giyur program, who allowed for such a beautiful and relaxed English-speaking environment that assisted in my first steps into wading into Judaism and expanded my theological understanding of the faith that I love and practice today; to Pastors Wilfred Samm, Snr., and my late uncle, Pastor Ravi Ramnath, who were my spiritual teachers and counsellors as I grew up and who were instrumental in helping shape me and instilling in me a consistent love and faith in God.

To my high school literature teacher, Mrs Sylvia Sawh, and my aunt, Noreen Hosein: my love for literature was nurtured by both of you, and without either of you, I would not have excelled the way I did at this subject in my formative, high school years! Aunty Sandra, thank you for teaching me how to dig into the written word – for teaching me how to decipher the symbols in Chaucer, and thus, be able to use symbolism in my own writing!

To those I cannot thank individually, as space does not permit, just know that you are cherished and I appreciate you!

Made in the USA
Middletown, DE
23 June 2018